Ripples in I

The Seri

Shadow Step

by

JS Powell

Copyright © 2019 JS Powell

ISBN: 978-0-244-51614-7

All rights reserved, including the right to reproduce this book, or portions thereof in any form. No part of this text may be reproduced, transmitted, downloaded, decompiled, reverse engineered, or stored, in any form or introduced into any information storage and retrieval system, in any form or by any means, whether electronic or mechanical without the express written permission of the author.

Acknowledgements

I would like to thank Mum and Dad for their continuing support and David for his encouragement and feedback. I would also like to thank Butser Ancient Farm for allowing us to film a short promotional video at their site.

Chapters

1. Benjamin Johnson and Sarah
2. Lars and Stefan
3. Xenis
4. Thomas and Raphael
5. Sarah
6. Lars
7. Thomas
8. Sarah and Cody
9. Xenis
10. Lars and Stefan
11. Glen and Cody
12. Thomas and Raphael
13. Sarah
14. Lars and Stefan
15. Thomas
16. Xenis and Valene
17. Cody
18. Lars
19. Adam and Ceola
20. Thomas
21. Glen, Sarah, and Cody
22. Karen
23. Lars and Stefan
24. Adam
25. Thomas
26. Karen
27. Lars
28. Adam and Faxon
29. Xenis and Valene
30. Cody
31. Adam
32. Karen
33. Adam
34. Lars and Stefan
35. Thomas
36. Adam

37. Glen and Cody
38. Karen
39. Lars
40. Adam and Ceola
41. Xenis
42. Thomas
43. Glen, Sarah, and Cody
44. Karen
45. Lars and Stefan
46. Adam
47. Xenis and Valene
48. Thomas
49. Cody
50. Karen and Xenis
51. Lars
52. Adam and Faxon
53. Thomas
54. Glen, Sarah, and Cody
55. Karen
56. Lars and Stefan
57. Adam
58. Thomas
59. Cody
60. Ellen and Brennan
61. Karen, Xenis, and Valene
62. Lars
63. Adam
64. Ellen and Brennan
65. Thomas
66. Glen and Cody
67. Xenis
68. Adam
69. Ellen
70. Cody
71. Thomas
72. Adam
73. Ellen and Brennan
74. Lars and Stefan

Glossary
Drow (Dark Elf) House Names and House Colours

Chapter 1

Benjamin Johnson and Sarah

Ben shivered as a cold sensation, trickled down his spine. It felt odd, almost like fear or a dawning dread that something had gone terribly wrong. His heart began to beat faster. Little puffs of mist formed with each rapid breath as he stared anxiously into the clear night air. His home should stand at the base of this rocky outcrop where the gentle slope ran down toward the undulating plain, but instead of a welcoming light, he saw nothing. Yet a house could not just up and vanish. Besides, he knew the Arizona desert. He'd lived here all his life, but tonight somehow, he felt like a stranger in an unfamiliar world.

"Rufus!" he called. "Rufus, where are you, boy?"

Ben shivered in the cold night air, pulled his jacket around his shoulders, and listened. No reply, no mad bark followed by an equally ecstatic greeting. He snorted, trying to dispel the feeling of unease as he ran his hands through his grey hair. After all, he needn't worry. Even if he stood on the wrong outcrop, he could walk downhill and meet the highway. He just needed to find his bearings.

The clear night sky winked above him, as he looked around, searching for the familiar constellations. He would begin with the Big Dipper and above it the Little Dipper, which led to the North Star. From there it should be simple, except Ben couldn't identify a single constellation. With growing panic, he desperately scanned the night sky. Nothing, not a single star, or pattern leapt out. His mind whirled in confusion. Where was he? A feeling of vertigo flooded his body, and Ben sank panting to the ground, his head cupped in his hands. He sat and waited. His breathing gradually slowed as an ache deep within his chest, reluctantly faded. The pain reminded him to make a physician's appointment. Something he intended to do now that he'd retired and sold the horses.

As he rested, a faint rustling sound caused him to turn, but when he scanned the scrub, he couldn't see any movement. Perhaps something hid deep within the shadows. From long experience, Ben knew that desert animals weren't much danger to humans. Even so, he climbed shakily to his feet, not wanting to make himself an easy target. Another sound echoed from his left, a strange noise, not animal but something else, something unsettling. It reminded him of trees blowing in the wind, not the rustling of leaves, but the way branches creaked and scraped together.

"Is anyone there?"

Ben felt stupid calling out into the night. No one would answer. Yet something did respond. It unfurled in the moonlight. Ben backed away, horrified by the sight, and fled downhill. He ran panting, stumbling, over the stony ground, pushing through the sagebrush where it grew thickly on the slope.

In minutes, he reached the plain below. Not able to continue he slumped onto a rock, wheezing from the panicked flight. Ben did not believe what he'd seen. Like something out of a horror film. First the house, then the stars and now the creature, what had happened? Somehow, he'd lost the home he knew, and loved. The familiar desert replaced by a phantom version.

Another sudden pain shot through his chest. It felt constricted as if someone had taken a leather belt and fastened it tightly around his torso. A sensation of weakness followed, leaving him feeling sick and dizzy. Ben sank to his knees and waited for the pain to subside. Thank God, not a heart attack. He still had enough time. Whatever he'd seen wouldn't catch up with him. After all, plants couldn't run, but then it occurred to him, plants couldn't move, and that one had.

Behind him, a small noise caught his attention. As he turned sharply to his left, he saw a subtle change in the shadows, but before he could rise, something leapt towards him. He yelled in fear as the creature landed on his back. Cord-like tendrils wrapped themselves around him, their barbed edges biting deeply into Ben's battered leather jacket. He screamed, trying to stand then twist free. One arm out of the sleeve, he overbalanced and fell to the ground. A sharp crack followed and then another sound like snapping twigs as he rolled over. Ben felt the tendrils loosen. He tumbled away and rose shakily to his knees. As he knelt, panting hard from the exertion, Ben stared down in disbelieving horror. Beneath the jacket, the creature twitched feebly, apparently broken by the fall. It looked such a strange thing, all tendrils, and barbs, but without a real body.

Without warning his moment of victory crumbled. Beyond him, in the moon-etched darkness, the sagebrush swayed. The creatures came from all directions, their spines rattling on the dirt as they leapt. Ben wanted to stand, wanted to run, but his limbs felt too weak. Not that it made any difference. Within seconds, the creatures covered him in a writhing mass trying to feed. They searched for the most succulent portions, and when their tendrils snaked into his open screaming mouth, he blacked out.

Ben woke face down in agony, exhausted and sweating with fear, expecting the worst. Yet as the pain inexplicably faded, nothing happened. Silence replaced the horrific creatures from the nightmare realm. Instead of dirt, cool wooden floorboards pressed against his cheek. In the dim light, he recognised his sitting room. The battered green sofa and two chairs arranged neatly in front of the hearth. Outside in the yard, a lonely dog barked.

"Rufus?" he whispered and noted that his voice sounded oddly quiet as if coming from far away.

The wolfhound heard his master's voice, scratched at the door, and whined. Ben tried to move, to reach for the door handle, but his limbs wouldn't respond. He felt so cold and tired. Somehow, he was at home, and those creatures now seemed a world away, like some dream, half-forgotten on waking. Had it really happened? He sighed, confused and deeply weary. Perhaps, if he rested, he would have enough strength to reach his beloved pet. As he closed his eyes, his breathing slowed, and the world gradually faded into darkness.

****

In the late afternoon sun, Sarah began to make her way back towards her truck. Thank goodness, she had one last camera to check, and then she could go home. Sarah longed to change out of her shirt and dusty dungarees.

Without much enthusiasm, she wound her way slowly through the sagebrush on the side of a hill towards the final site. Once there, Sarah unpacked her ecology notes and began to work. Head bent, her short brown plait tucked under a sun hat, she knelt to record the observations. A strange noise made her pause for a moment and listen. It sounded like a faint bark. No, she must be imagining things, but sure, after a few more minutes, there it came again. She could definitely hear a dog barking, not the frantic noise of an animal defending its territory, or the sound of greeting, but a short soft bark that tailed off into a miserable whine. It reminded Sarah of her Aunt Jane's dog, long dead now. How she hated to see him chained up and left alone. As a child, she could do nothing for the sad and sorry creature, but now she always checked on any animal.

After putting her notes away, Sarah hoisted her backpack over her shoulder and listened intently. The faint bark had carried on the wind, but she thought that it came from somewhere not far behind the hill. In the waning heat, Sarah trudged up the slope towards the rocky outcrop. As she walked, she looked around for any movement, but nothing showed its head above the sagebrush. The dog hadn't made another sound, so once she reached the top, she turned and walked parallel to the rocks trying to find the right location. Not long afterwards, a wooden house came into view. Sarah could see a large shaggy wolfhound sprawled on the ground, its head resting on its paws.

As she drew closer, it raised its nose and whined pathetically. Careful not to alarm the creature, Sarah crouched and tipped her head on one side.

"Are you alright boy?"

The dog whined again and tried to wag its tail, but without much success before it rested its head back on its paws.

"You're not ok, are you? Let's see if we can find your owner."

Sarah stood and began to walk towards the house. A whine caused her to turn, and she saw the old brown dog standing on wobbly legs. It trotted unsteadily towards her before slumping to the floor. It looked so pitiful that she bent down and awkwardly picked it up. Almost doubled under the weight, Sarah staggered to the side of the house, where she noticed a kennel and two bowls. One marked food, the other water, but both filled with only dust and dirt. Sarah felt a spark of anger as she put the dog down. What sort of person allowed a dog to starve or die of dehydration? They didn't deserve to own an animal! She picked up the bowl and began to look around for some water. Nearby, she found a tap hanging over a trough. Stiff with rust and grime it finally turned with a drawn-out squeak, followed by a nasty bang, a clank, and some rattling before the water appeared. As the liquid gushed into the trough, the panting dog brushed up against her leg, and she looked down into its hopeful eyes. Sarah smiled, filled up the bowl, and put it down. He emptied it in seconds.

"Wow, you're thirsty!"

She filled the bowl twice before the wolfhound just wagged its tail and didn't drink the entire contents. As she patted the dogs head, she noticed a flash of bronze beneath his long-matted fur. A collar and attached to it, a tag with some writing on the metal disk. It read Rufus, Mr B Johnson, at Outcrop House. This must be Outcrop House so where had Mr Johnson gone.

"Mr Johnson?" she called out, but only the wind replied.

Rufus slumped to the ground panting as Sarah began to explore. Past a battered beige truck and some bins, she saw a fenced corral that had seen better days. With no one around, Sarah turned to look at the house. Its poor state of repair matched its surroundings. Paint peeling, slates missing, and the windows clouded and dirty. Worn wooden steps led up to a covered veranda and beyond a tatty green door. A gust of wind whipped up the dust, and as she shielded her eyes, she noticed the undisturbed layer on the veranda. Despite the heat, her skin prickled with apprehension. The green door seemed to loom out of the shadows as if compelling her to approach. Sarah placed a reluctant foot on the first rickety step. Each board creaked as she mounted the stairs towards the sagging porch. When Sarah reached the top, she grasped the tarnished metal knocker that graced the age-flecked paint and rapped.

"Mr Johnson, are you there?"

No reply answered her call, so she reached gingerly for the handle. When it didn't turn, Sarah moved to the window, breathed on the grimy surface, and rubbed it with her sleeve. Nose pressed against the glass, she looked in and gasped. Her heart leapt. A man's body lay on the floor, his arm outstretched, his face turned towards the door.

"Mr Johnson?"

She tapped on the window, but he didn't respond. Dead or just unconscious she didn't know, but then in the low light, she noticed his torn and bloody clothes. Strange pockmarks peppered his face and arms, and his skin had a shrunken appearance. Sarah unslung her backpack and fumbled for her phone. She went to dial 911 but found it low on battery power and the signal bar empty. No help could come. In desperation, she rattled the door handle and then pushed hard against the old wood. Not that it mattered; it didn't budge. Instead, she just hurt her shoulder.

As Sarah looked around, she wracked her brains, trying to think of a way inside. The yard didn't contain anything useful to break down the door, and the tiny block windowpanes looked too small for her to get through, even if she managed to smash one. Her mind went blank as she bit her lip in defeat, wondering what to do when something brushed against her leg. Sarah yelped and jumped, her heart pounding, but it was only the dog. She sighed, feeling silly and patted Rufus on the head.

"You sure crept up on me."

He whined and lay down as if to say; it's all up to you now. After filling his water bowl, Sarah jogged back to her jeep and drove towards the town in search of help.

Chapter 2

Lars and Stefan

His mother stood, hands on hips and glared at her son. "I can't believe you are going to do this to me."

Lars didn't reply. He couldn't. Her blatantly selfish statement left him speechless, amazed, and incredulous.

Malena tapped an impatient foot. "Well, aren't you going to say something?"

Lars spluttered. He didn't know where to start. Out of the corner of his eye, he could see his young sister peeking through a crack in the door. Asta had run into the bedroom as soon as the argument had begun. He felt a stab of guilt. He would leave her again, although the first time had not been by choice.

Asta pouted then shrugged. Lars gave an involuntary smile. Thank goodness, she understood.

Malena didn't. "Oh, so you think this is funny, do you?"

"No."

This seemed to settle her down. She relaxed and brushed back her long dark hair. "Good, well, it's not. Now you should stop being silly and think of your family."

Lars knew she only thought of herself, not Asta. His temper flared, and he yelled, "That's all I've ever done. Have you?"

"What do you mean? I looked after you both even before your father passed away; I always put you first."

Lars sneered and said, "Really? You were quick enough to pack me off."

Malena rolled her eyes and paced, her full skirts swirling when she turned. "Everything is always about you."

"Well, in this case, yes, I was just eight."

"With your father dead, we needed the money."

"What did you do? Sell me to the highest bidder."

"Oh, don't be so dramatic."

"Mother, why didn't you try to get me an apprenticeship? I could have made something of myself."

Malena regarded her son. Sometimes she could hardly believe he was family. She despised his weak affable kindness. His short, wiry stature lacked nobility, and his untidy blond hair only accentuated that impression. She had wanted a son who stood out from the crowd, but he did nothing to impress her.

"No one wanted you. You weren't a gifted child."

Lars' heart lurched, stung by her opinion. "Oh, so it's my fault now, is it?"

"Of course not, don't be silly boy."

Lars lowered his voice. "I've spent the last ten years of my life indentured to the Overlord. I've been a dog's body. I can't read, I can't write, but I'm great at slopping out buckets and cleaning up shit."

"There's always a job for people who can do that."

"Is that my life? To be Lars of the shit, I want more. I'm capable of more."

"And you think this is the way to do it? You'll get yourself killed and then where will I be?"

Lars noticed she never mentioned Asta. His mother didn't seem to care about his pretty little sister except to tie up her child's long blond plait in an elaborate style. He suspected that even this had an ulterior motive. Asta was just another bargaining chip to further her mother's ambition.

"I don't care," he lied. "This is my one chance, and I'm going to take it."

"I forbid it!"

"You can't stop me."

"I can. I'll speak to the Overlord."

Lars froze. He couldn't believe she would betray him like that.

"It's for your own good. Scavengers only die."

He couldn't stand the look of triumph on her handsome face.

He turned. "I'm going out."

"Don't turn your back on me, my boy." She went to grab his arm but missed. He dodged, slammed the door, and ran down the hill towards the carpenter's shop.

When he arrived, Lars could hear yelling.
"That's it! You're finished! I'll make sure you never work around here again!"

Lars couldn't see anything over the crowd that barred his way, but he didn't like the situation. He pushed through the throng only to see Stefan holding Master Colborn the enormous carpenter, at arm's length, while the man swore and struggled. To one side, the master's lovely young wife stood wailing. Even from here, Lars could see that her eyes were red from weeping. Behind her, the carpenter's new apprentice merely watched, looking smug. Lars began to understand.

Tall, blond, and muscular, for some reason, women seemed to find his friend attractive even though his stature swamped them. Shy in their presence, Stefan only mumbled occasionally, but oddly, that never bothered them either. From what Lars could hear, the carpenter's wife had spent too much time sniffing around Stefan. Not a wise move, for the carpenter was a jealous man. Now the accusations flew.

"I've seen how she acts around you."
"Master Colborn, honestly, I didn't touch your wife."
"Liar, I can't believe I trusted you!"
"Please, Master, I never lied to you. I didn't touch your wife."
The carpenter ignored him and continued to rant, "You deceived me. I thought you were a good lad. I should never have taken you on."
"No, honestly, I didn't deceive you."
"This is your fault. The whole town is laughing at me behind my back. They think I'm too old to satisfy my wife and that she has to find her pleasures elsewhere."
"Master Colborn, please listen. I never touched your wife."
His protests angered the carpenter further. The older man suddenly lunged and pushed Stefan hard.
"You are scum, a treacherous piece of filth. You saw what you liked and took what you wanted."
Stefan held the man back and yelled, "I would never do that!"

Lars watched the scuffle. At less than half the size of either man, he wondered somewhat reluctantly, if he should intervene. Other people must have had the same idea because it took several villagers to pull them both apart. Stefan complied not wishing to hurt anyone, but this didn't stop the carpenter.

He just ignored them and kept struggling screaming threats, "You may have slept with my little slut of a wife, but I'll make sure you get what's coming to you. You've ruined my reputation, and now I'll ruin yours. Your family will starve in the ditch! Then I'll throw their rotting corpses to the wargs!"

"Leave my family out of this. They didn't do anything wrong. I haven't done anything wrong."

"Don't lie to me you piece of shit. I know what you did. He saw you!" The carpenter pointed to the young apprentice, who quickly erased his smug expression.

Stefan turned red in the face. "Master Colborn, I swear on my life he's lying to you."

Lars didn't doubt that for one second, but the new apprentice gave a look of mock indignation.

The carpenter laughed. "Why would he do that?"

Lars held his breath, guessing what would come next.

Stefan blurted out the truth, "So, that he could inherit your shop."

Stefan had become so skilled that he often completed his master's work. When the carpenter took on another apprentice, the new lad soon realised that he wouldn't inherit the business. Instead, everyone agreed it would go to Stefan, until today.

Master Colborn snarled confirming Lars' worst fear. "Better him than you!"

"But I served you well."

The master severed their contract. "Perhaps once but now you're no apprentice of mine!"

Stefan slumped in defeat. "Can I at least take my tools? I made them. I should keep them."

The carpenter shook off the villagers and stalked through the gathering crowd. He emerged from the shop with a significant number of tools and threw them on the floor.

"Keep them! I want nothing of yours in my shop!"

With that, he strode off, his tearful wife in tow as she tried to explain that nothing had happened. The new apprentice followed with one last smug glance over his shoulder and in that moment, Lars wanted to slit that boy's throat. Instead, he crushed that feeling and helped his friend pick up the tools lying in the mud.

"I've got to oil these before they rust," Stefan mumbled, then as he looked at his friend he asked, "What am I going to do now?"

Lars grinned and clapped Stefan on the shoulder. "Don't worry about that! I have a plan."

As they walked towards his home, Stefan ran through his options not that he had many. In fact, he had obligations that he couldn't ignore. After his parent's death, he had become the sole breadwinner, but now no one would employ him. The carpenter would blacken his name, and with a bad reputation, few people would trade with his family. They could stay in their house, but then he would have to hunt to supplement what they could grow on their patch of land. It wouldn't be too bad on a good year, but on a year when the winds blew from the North East, they would starve. In those years, the crops failed, sheep had stillborn lambs, and the old and very young died. Even the giant wolf-like wargs of the far north, sometimes ventured south to attack both flocks and villagers alike.

If he couldn't feed his kinsfolk, Stefan would have to uproot his family and go to live with distant relatives, but then they would face another obstacle. The new Overlord would ask why they'd left their home. Once he knew the truth, he would force them to move on, unless they could pay. Bribes overcame the rule of law, but he knew he wouldn't have enough money.

Lars half listened, but once they got to his friend's cottage, he jumped up on the cart outside and waited to get a word in edgeways. Stefan just continued to talk around in circles. After another ten minutes of getting nowhere, Lars finally lost patience.

"Have you finished yet?"

Stefan glowered at Lars then said, "Just thinking things through."

Lars shrugged. "That's your problem, you always overthink."

Stefan wanted to retort, yours is not thinking enough, but he bit his tongue. "Go on then what's this plan of yours."

"Now you're out of work you need to make some cash."

"That's obvious, but how the hell am I going to do that?" Stefan rubbed his face. "It's not like I can work around here anymore."

Lars grinned, and then fished something neatly creased and square out of his pocket. He took it over to the back of the cart and with care, began to unfold each leaf until it covered the whole surface.

Stefan peered down at the faded ink. "What's this?"

"A map to the city," said Lars

"A map to what city?" said Stefan as he reached out and ran his fingers over the strange material. Old but still smooth, someone had obviously repaired it a great many times.

"How old is this?"

Lars shrugged. "Well, it's a copy of a copy but the original? Who knows, a few hundred years old, perhaps more?"

Stefan looked up sharply. "Don't let the preachers see it."

"Who cares about them?"

"You should. If they told the Overlord, you'd be in trouble."

Lars shrugged again. "You worry too much."

Stefan raised an eyebrow but didn't push the issue. "Come on, get on with it."

"Oh, yeah, right. We're here." He pointed to a place on the map.

"How do you know?"

"Mura, the boatman told me."

"You bought this from the boatmen? How much did it cost you?"

Lars looked a little sheepish. "Everything I had, well almost, I bought something else as well."

Stefan rolled his eyes, wondering if the boatman had cheated his friend.

"Don't look at me like that. Trust me; it will be worth it in the end." Lars continued, "Anyway, we're here, and we want to go there." He pointed to a dot in the northeast.

"Why?"

Lars grinned and said, "Metal, lots of metal."

Stefan took a few seconds to understand. "You want to become a scavenger?"

"Yeah but not just me, I need a partner."

"Huh, who else were you thinking of?"

Lars gave him a sideways look.

"Oh." Stefan paused to take this in and then he looked at the map. "Isn't this city already taken?"

"No."

"Really?" said Stefan and gave him a dubious look.

"Well, not now they're dead."

"Oh great, that's comforting."

"They didn't die in the city."

"Oh well, that's ok then, where did they die?"

Lars noted the hint of sarcasm and replied innocently, "Various places."

"What of?"

Lars dodged the subject. "We should go upriver, take the right-hand tributary, and stop somewhere about here."

Stefan persisted. "What did they die of?"

Lars sighed and said, "Various things."

"What all of them?"

"No, one survived."

Stefan gave him a stern look.

"Well, one died from thirst, another from a snake bite and the last one of blood poisoning from something that attacked him on the plateau." He looked at his friend. "I never said this wasn't going to be dangerous."

"What about the metal?"

"They never found any. That's why the survivor sold the map."

"And somehow we're going to be successful when they weren't?"

Lars beamed. "I'm glad you asked that." He pulled out a small circular object. "They didn't have one of these."

"What is it?"

"It's a compass."

"What's that?"

"Well, see this arrow? It always points north, no matter which way you stand." He turned around, and the arrow moved.

Stefan whistled. "That's an artefact. If the preachers see you with that, you'll end up in the stocks or worse."

"Then they better not see it."

Stefan grimaced but nodded. "Fair enough, but if it shows you the way to go, how come the Boatmen didn't use it?"

"It's too much of a risk. They have a life and a family."

"And we don't?"

"Not as much. Besides, what else are we going to do? No one wants me; what skills do I have? Mucking out animals, what sort of future is that? Besides, what will you do? No one around here will give you a second look, let alone a job. What will happen when winter comes?"

Stefan hung his head and sighed. He couldn't argue with Lars logic, but this plan sounded suicidal. He barely listened as his friend chattered filling out the details. At night, they'd face bloodthirsty tumblers, during the day thirst and heat. Add into the mix, poisonous plants, wild animals, insects, and snakes.

"So," he interjected. "How accurate is this map?"

"After this amount of time, who knows, somethings will be the same, but others will have changed, I guess."

"You guess?"

"Look, the boatmen told me that this far upriver the land shouldn't have changed that much. It's not liked the sandbanks in the delta that change all the time." Lars pointed to the lowest part of the map. "The man who owned the map came from Beconsfeld, and they journeyed from there across the plateau. It's a long route, much longer than the one I plan to take upriver. We can paddle your canoe up to this point, then make a shelter and find a way up the cliff. Oh, and we will need to make a cart, winch the parts to the top and put it together up there. Once complete, we can load the cart with supplies and drag it to the city."

Stefan suddenly caught up. "Wait a sec you mentioned bloodthirsty tumblers what the hell are they?"

"Err well nasty things with long tendrils that suck blood."

"Oh, that's great, something to look forward to."

"Don't be such a wet hen."

Stefan glowered as Lars grinned.

"Look I said I had a plan. You'll need to design something on the cart that can keep us safe while leaving enough space for the loot on the return journey. Well, once we get back, we will need to lower the valuables down the cliff and leave the cart up there for next time. It should be easy enough to pack what we find into the boat and sell it downriver. Think about it, our families will want for nothing, and the carpenter and that lying apprentice can go to hell."

Lars beamed and looked expectantly at his friend, who stood thinking before he turned and walked indoors. Lars quickly folded the map and followed.

Not wanting to alarm his grandparents, Stefan sat them down in front of the fire as he prepared to speak. His grandfather, Yannis, shifted uncomfortably and stretched his leg which he had injured working as a lumberjack. Tall with a shock of white hair, his grandfather had a kindly face. Freda, his wife, sat nearby, her hands neatly clasped in her lap, her waist-length white plait draped over one shoulder. Yannis waited patiently in comparison with Stefan's tiny grandmother, who frowned at the delay, and picked up some knitting. There was always work to do.

Lars had a plan, but Stefan thought that it relied rather heavily on luck. He hesitated to tell his grandparents, not only about what had happened today but also about Lars get rich quick scheme. Once Stefan ran through his account, with Lars interjecting from time to time, his grandfather just gazed at his grandson and sighed.

Stefan looked downcast. "I never," he began.

"Hush lad, we know you would never do anything dishonourable." Yannis hobbled to his feet and put his arm around his grandson's shoulder. "I will speak with Colborn tomorrow when he has calmed his temper."

Stefan appeared uncomfortable with that suggestion. "I should be the one to speak with him."

His grandfather shook his head. "No, no, lad, there's no point in you trying. It will only rub salt in his wound. I will reason with him."

His wife snorted. "You can attempt to change his mind Yannis, but the carpenter is well-known for his stubborn attitude."

"I know Freda, but it's still worth a try."

They all knew the consequences for Stefan if he stayed in Holmfast. The fiefdom had laws, but those laws were often neither fair nor just. It valued the word of a lord or high standing member of society, more than any peasant or apprentice.

If the Master carpenter spoke to the Overlord, Stefan could be in trouble. Never mind that the new apprentice, who ranked lower than

Stefan, was the witness. If the carpenter believed him, then the Overlord believed the carpenter. They would also ignore the wife, no matter how much she protested her innocence.

If the Overlord found them both guilty of adultery, the preachers would extract their pound of flesh. While the law left the carpenter to discipline his wife, it would be worse for Stefan. Lars considered it best if his friend conveniently went missing.

Freda seemed to agree. She laid a sympathetic hand on her husband's arm. "Don't worry my love. The lad can take care of himself. We brought him up well."

The old man hesitated and then nodded.

She turned to the two younger men. "Go with our blessing and stay safe, but I suggest you pack fast. Your grandfather will keep them arguing for a while, but I have a feeling that they will come for you sooner than later."

That afternoon, they worked out a detailed plan and began to pack. Lars even managed to sneak home to speak with his sister who cried and made him promise to come back.

The two lads made the final decision to leave the following morning when Stefan's grandfather came hobbling back to the house.

Freda had never seen her husband in such a rage. "Yannis, what's wrong?"

Yannis slumped into a chair and sat fuming in silence until his rage faded into defeat.

By now, Lars and Stefan had come inside to wait for the news.

In the end, Yannis spoke, "You were right, wife of mine. I was wasting my breath! No one listened. First, Colborn ignored me and spoke to the Overlord. Then he too ignored my pleas. They have come to a decision."

Freda gasped. "So quickly, did they not want to speak with Stefan?"

Her husband shook his head. It was a done deal.

A practical woman at heart, Freda quickly recovered and began to organise.

"You must go now," she said to Lars and Stefan. "No time to lose. They will be here soon."

Stefan frowned stubbornly at his grandparents. "No, I can't leave. What will they do to you when they find me missing?"

His grandfather shook his head. "Don't worry about us lad. They can do nothing."

"But that's not true. The Overlords men can stop the villagers from trading with you. What will you do for food?"

"I said not to worry; many in the village dislike the carpenter. We will have enough to eat."

Stefan shook his head, but his grandmother intervened. "No lad, you *must* leave. It will be worse for us if they find you here. Now gather your things."

A few minutes later, they threw the last of their belongings into the long boat. Stefan's grandmother thrust a medicine pouch into his hand and made a tearful goodbye, hugging first Lars and then her grandson. Yannis simply nodded and put his arm around his diminutive wife as the lads got into the boat. Both stayed to watch, long after the young men had paddled out of sight.

For several days, they journeyed upstream without a hitch although Stefan spent his time brooding. At this time of year, before the autumn rain, the placid water flowed gently until they reached the upper tributaries. Here the river began to deepen and race between narrow banks. At this point, paddling became hard work. Not only did the eddies and ripples cause the boat to twitch, but they found that the current tried to turn it sideways. At least the journey back would be quick Lars pointed out as they puffed and strained against the rivers pull.

The worst of it came at the confluence between two tributaries. The turbulent water, one filled with silt, the other deep, dark, and cold, buffeted the boat. In front of them lay boggy ground, not somewhere where they could land, to the left and right crumbling cliffs. Lars shouted above the noise of the river that they should go up the right-hand tributary. It proved difficult to make any progress. They spent much of their strength getting to the base of the cliff and staying in a spinning eddy. After a brief rest, they pushed back into the main flow and paddled fiercely for as long as they could.

Both men began to flag when Stefan suddenly spotted a safe place on the opposite side. Here the bog gave way to higher wooded ground. It took the last of their strength to dock against the bank. Once they secured the boat, they jumped out and stretched their legs, relieved that they could finally unbend.

After a while, Lars said, "Right, I'm going to collect some wood, you unpack ok?"

He vanished off into the gloom before Stefan could reply. Half an hour later, after setting the fire for dinner, Lars heard something and froze.

"Did you hear that?"

"Hear what?"

"Listen."

"I am."

Lars could have sworn he heard something. "Quiet."

Stefan stood still, straining to hear anything above the sound of the river and the wind in the trees. "Nope, I can't hear anything."

Something howled close by, answered by a call in the distance.

Lars raised a finger and pointed. "Err, that sound."

They heard a small rustle and then out of the dark wood, two red eyes regarded them with hungry intent. Stefan snatched a burning branch from the fire and waved it in the creature's direction. Lars dived closer to the safety of the flames and fumbled at the burning wood.

"Shit," he snarled as he burnt his fingers.

Another howl echoed in the woods, and a second set of eyes appeared to their right. Stefan lunged forward, waving the brand, and yelled, "Ya, ya, get out of here."

Even when faced with Stefan's vast bulk, the creatures hardly reacted. When Lars joined in, running back and forth, yelling, they just slowly withdrew and vanished into the gloom.

Lars scrambled over towards Stefan. "Shit, wargs, they won't have gone far. Look you keep them at bay. I'll grab the stuff, and then we can make a run for the boat."

He dropped the branch at the edge of the camp and left Stefan scanning the woodland for any movement. They both sensed the wargs stayed close, unseen, and unheard, waiting for a chance to strike. Lars did not intend to give them that chance. As the firelight danced over the mooring, he hurriedly bundled up their belongings and threw them higgledy-piggledy into the boat.

"Ok, I've got everything," he said to Stefan in a low voice. "Back off slowly and let's get the hell out of here."

Stefan barely nodded, but he began to back away, keeping his eyes firmly ahead. As he moved away from the fire, the shaggy black wargs gradually emerged from the darkness. They began a low, menacing growl, which intensified with each step. The discordant sound raised the hairs on each man's body, triggered by their primal fear.

As Stefan continued to retreat, Lars waited in the boat, the oars ready, the mooring untied. They wouldn't have more than a few seconds before the wargs attacked. When his friend got within jumping distance, Lars used an oar to push at the riverbank, moving the boat slightly out into the current.

"Now," he yelled.

Stefan turned and jumped. As he twisted, he threw the burning brand at the wargs. It bounced on the soft woodland floor, sending embers splintering over their coats. Their fear of fire scattered the creatures, but Stefan had mistimed the jump. Instead of landing squarely in the boat, he hit the side with a thump; his legs knee deep in the water. The canoe rocked so violently for a moment that Lars feared that they would sink, but instead, the massive impact twisted the boat and propelled it out into the river. As Stefan pulled himself aboard, Lars rowed with all his might.

They concentrated on putting as much distance as they could between them and the bank, so much so that the two men didn't notice the boulder, until they heard a long drawn out graunch. Worn smooth by the river, it acted like a gently sloping jetty. The boat rose up out of the water and then stuck on the rock. The two men stopped rowing in surprise, but then the current began to twist the stern, threatening to overturn the boat. They quickly scrambled out and pulled it safely onto the rock.

Once secure, Lars commented, "Well we're as safe here as anywhere else."

They spent the rest of that night beached in the middle of the river, hoping that wargs didn't swim.

The next day, feeling tired from their ordeal, they continued the journey upriver. By late afternoon, Stefan spotted a suitable landing site. On the left, a landslide had created a massive scree slope that had flattened the forest, all the way down to the river. On the other side, a cliff fall had formed a sandy stretch up against the rock face. It must have been some time ago because part of it had small trees growing on the edge, stabilising the rock and soil. Between them, a single large tree bridged the river itself. It looked a safe location, so they paddled over to the island and landed. Here they pitched their camp below the dry plateau. The waters ran cold and deep, flowing fast from nearby mountains. They also needed to consider the occasional flash flood, which is why Stefan set the camp as high as possible. With just enough time before dark, they managed to create a spiked barrier over the tree, making it secure. Sure enough, they didn't see any wargs, although they could hear some howling in the woods beyond.

Over the next few weeks, they realised that the island made an ideal place to camp. Stefan immersed himself in his work and tried to avoid worrying about his family. As Lars pointed out, he could do nothing about it. Instead, his friend concentrated on making the cart. The scree broken trees provided seasoned wood. Stefan also collected then boiled local plants to make glue. It smelled so bad that Lars insisted he brewed it downwind of the camp. Lars spent much of his time hunting, gathering, and exploring during the day. By night, they kept one ear open, listening for wargs.

On the final morning, before they planned to leave, Stefan cooked breakfast, while Lars went out hunting to supplement their meagre stocks, for the trip ahead.

As he scraped up the last of his porridge, Stefan heard a whistle in the distance, a sure sign that his friend had returned. He looked up to see Lars making his way across the tree bridge with a small deer slung over his shoulder.

"Is that breakfast I smell?" he said, throwing the deer at Stefan. "Excellent I'm starving!"

Stefan gave a small sigh. He always got the job of butchering and preserving the meat with salt and herbs, which he then stored in earthenware pots. He set about the task while Lars ate breakfast and packed the final items.

Afterwards, Lars and Stefan examined the hard, red sandstone cliff that towered above them. For this plan to succeed, they would need to climb to the top and haul up each part of the cart, before assembly. Lars would scale the cliff first. He might not look much standing next to his friend's vast bulk, but his short, wiry frame made him ideal for the task. As a small child, he'd climbed trees worrying his parents with his antics, then he had moved on to greater challenges, but this would be the most dangerous of all. One slip could mean death.

Lars tied the thin rope around his waist and then nodded to Stefan. He began to climb moving one hand, one foot at a time. His friend waited nervously at the bottom as Lars gradually ascended the cliff. Even in the early morning sunshine, sweat prickled their skin. Stefan wiped his brow and watched his friend climb higher. Foot, next foot, hand, next hand, a rhythm of safety. Don't look down; don't look up; concentrate on the now.

Beads of sweat began to trickle down Lars' face. He shook them off and kept climbing. When his muscles finally started to shake, Lars felt a flush of fear rush across his skin. The surge of adrenalin that followed spurred him to the top, but once there he paused at the crumbling edge. His feet secure, he gently ran his fingers over the stone, searching for instability before choosing his final handhold.

When he crested the cliff edge, the hot, dry winds, struck his face. Lars rolled over and lay panting on his back, the sweat dripping off his body onto the red sand. Over those last few feet, he had become seriously tired. Down below, Stefan let out a great sigh as he saw his friend disappear over the top of the cliff.

It took Lars a while to regain his strength before he signalled Stefan. His friend attached a sack to the rope and Lars hauled it up the cliff. Once at the top, he opened the bag and took out some water, a few tools, a looped stake, and a thick rope. Lars hammered the stake into the ground and attached the line so that it would not fall down the cliff. Lars could not stand the thought that he might have to climb down to retrieve it and then up again. He wouldn't have the strength.

The rope now firmly attached; Stefan sent up the weighty winch arm. Lars puffed and panted as he hauled it up, then sighed, relieved when it finally appeared over the edge. As the day wore on Lars and Stefan gradually winched up the other parts, then most of their non-food supplies. Stefan would assemble the cart tomorrow after they made their final ascent. Before he climbed back down, Lars took a deep draw from his water skin. He had emptied it entirely over the afternoon. The heat made him realise how much water they would need. In this unforgiving terrain, it would be too easy to get lost and die. He could only hope that the map remained correct.

Chapter 3

Xenis

The ceremony bored Xenis. All the screaming and chanting jarred his nerves. It left him feeling irritated and annoyed. What a waste of time. Not that he allowed these emotions to show. Instead, he kept them buried deep within his mind just in case his sisters heard his innermost thoughts. Quite unlikely, but he could never be too careful. Today with any luck, all remained well and truly distracted, especially his oldest sister Valene who so obviously enjoyed the ceremony. Like the thousands of dark elves who attended, he and his brothers knelt on the polished marble floor behind his younger sisters. The rest of his house sat behind them, not including the slaves. If looked down on from above, each house would represent a triangular slice pointing towards the sacrificial hole.

His mother, the Matriarch, worshipped below in the inner sanctum with the priesthood, while his oldest sister tortured the poor unfortunate soul that hung upside down over the hole. From here, Xenis could just see the dark blood run down the victim's dusky blue skin into the long sleek white hair, so characteristic of Drow kind. He didn't know the male personally or to which house he belonged, but he did know one thing. A criminal was a socially unacceptable sacrifice. Perhaps the offender had failed in his duty once too often. It was an unpleasant fact in Mizoram that any male who made mistakes soon became expendable.

He watched his sister make the first deep cut as she chanted the ritual words.

"Ja'hai nindol or'shanse." *Accept this sacrifice.*

"Udos joros dos," chanted the crowd. *We beseech you.*

Xenis parroted the words, but in truth, they hardly registered. He felt uncomfortable in his ceremonial uniform after hours of kneeling.

He shifted uneasily and gently stretched his neck, which loosened his shoulder-length white ponytail. This small movement earned him a disapproving backward glance from his youngest sister, Larenil. Xenis ignored her but arranged his chiselled blue features in a neutral expression. If he upset any senior members of his household, he too could end up drained of blood.

Even so, he felt his mind begin to wander. Today, their plan came to fruition. Political manoeuvring had resulted in their tenure as guardians of the most sacred temple. Once again, they secured their turn to guard the byways and service the inner sanctum, although a very loose definition of turn applied. Some houses had many opportunities, while others had none at all. Many years had passed since House Zik'Keeshe had been in charge.

Valene made a new cut as she completed the next ritual move.

"Morfeth udossa rothrl." *Make us obey.*

"Udos joros dos." *We beseech you.*

A century ago, his house had fallen out of favour, lost rank, and since then they had struggled to regain power. Now, they verged on re-joining the ruling council. They would replace Faerl'Zotreth, the lowest member on the Council of Five. His house had implicated their rival in various scandals over the years, gradually bringing them into disrepute, while at the same time proving their own loyalty to the ruling house. A triumph, but not one without cost as they had earned the enmity of Faerl'Zotreth. Now it remained only a matter of time before that house retaliated. Another scream interrupted his thoughts, as it echoed around the gigantic cavern. His sister had made a deeper cut so that the blood drained into the sacrificial dish below.

"Quanth udossa xuil yorn." *Fill us with power.*

"Udos joros dos." *We beseech you.*

While their Goddess forbad open warfare, it did not stop any house from attacking in some other devious and underhand way. Zik'Keeshe had another problem. Their ancient enemy House Vlos'Killian, who did not have a seat on the Council of Five, loathed their rival's promotion. They had petitioned the ruling house to block Zik'Keeshe's ascension. The Matriarch from Mith'Barra listened, but then rejected their arguments. Ancient rivalries were not sufficient;

there had to be substantial evidence to exclude a rising star. Well, if not substantial, then at least believable.

"G'jahall udossta ogglinnar." *Defeat our enemies.*

"Udos joros dos." *We beseech you.*

From here, he had an excellent view, not that he took any pleasure in this spectacle. He didn't think that the gods actually existed and if they did, they wouldn't care one whit about the death of this male. Mostly Xenis considered religion as another excuse for power. In Mizoram, each person had their place; each had their rank. The ruling house came first, then the Council of Five and last the other houses jockeying for position below. A truth mirrored in everything else. Females came first. They were the rulers. Males came second. Royals came above commoners and then slaves the lowest of them all. The priesthood ranked higher than mages. They, in turn, ranked above warriors, but warriors came above servants. Society placed all females above any male, but even so, those that had strong magic held more respect. Sometimes it could be quite challenging to work out, who outranked whom.

As the ritual reached its final stage, Valene repeated, "Whol ilta ib'ahalii." *For her Glory*, eight times before finally plunging the dagger into the male's torso.

"Falduna ilta." *Praise her,* mumbled Xenis.

Around him, the repeated crescendo rose, drowning out the screams as they declined into a burbling reverberation. In the end, the sacrifice died quietly, the last of his life dripping onto the blood gem in the centre of the dish. The ceremony had ended.

Xenis felt only relief. Now everyone would return to his or her respective houses, hopefully without an unobtrusive stab on the way, although occasionally the guards found a stray corpse. Once the plateau cleared, the priestess would cut down the body and dissolve it in acid.

Afterwards, it would not be long before they received a summons from the Council of Five. In the meantime, his oldest sister would make the necessary arrangements, so they were ready to take control of the temple. She would choose the male guards for the outer temple and the female attendants for the inner sanctum. They would replace House Faerl'Zotreth so it would be necessary to scour the structure, for any nasty surprises they'd left behind. These could be both magical and mundane in nature so they would need a range of measures. Once Valene declared everything clear and purified, his mother, the Matriarch would visit and inspect. She would scrutinise all aspects, and they must be perfect. God forbid if they weren't.

When they were ready, the Council of Five summoned his Mother, the Matriarch of House Zik'Keeshe, to take her rightful place as the new fifth member. A proud moment surrounded by much pomp and ceremony within the house itself. Every member of the household lined the walls. Even slaves peered in wonder at the display of magic that sparkled over every surface.

Xenis watched from his position to one side of the welcoming committee as three resounding booms echoed on the outer gate. The massive carved doors swung open to admit the Mistress of Ceremonies, but instead of stepping over the threshold, she repeated the ancient words requesting permission to enter.

"I come in peace and humble supplication at the bequest of the Council of Five."

Xenis found these ironic words amusing. The concept of peace and humility remained unpopular amongst the Drow. Each house within the city behaved as an independent entity, so entering without permission could be an act of war.

His eldest sister, the tallest of the family, stood forward, her head held high and replied, "If you come in peace, then enter with the blessing of our Matriarch."

This granted permission to enter and then Valene escorted the Mistress between lines of battle-dressed guards towards the throne room. There she presented the supplicant to the Matriarch. The rest of the family stood in attendance, although males such as Xenis could only wait outside in the antechamber. The importance of this occasion did not permit them to enter the throne room. This, of course, nettled Xenis. It reminded him once again that in the end, they considered him just a lowly male. The status accorded by his royal blood meant little in comparison with the limitations of his sex. Deep in the privacy of his inner mind, he vowed that one day that would change.

Even though he couldn't attend, he knew that once the Matriarch and the Mistress exchanged their own ritual greetings, the Mistress would read the proclamation aloud. The council had summoned the Matriarch to attend her first meeting. In addition, they commanded the eldest sister to assume her duty as Overseer. This would begin their guardianship over the sacred temple, both a great responsibility and a great honour for House Zik'Keeshe.

The transfer of power over, the Mistress of Ceremonies returned through the house. The Matriarch walked by her side, with her personal bodyguard in attendance. Everyone, dressed in his or her most elegant clothes, lined the route. Even the slaves watched, albeit from a discreet distance. Once outside, the guards escorted the Matriarch to the council chamber while his sisters prepared to take possession of the sacred temple.

This put his elder sister in a good mood, although that did not mean that she would be any less psychotic than usual. Valene had grudgingly included Xenis, but he knew she only did this to infuriate him, so he quietly kept his cool. This, in turn, irritated her, so in the end, Xenis won.

When those favoured, finally assembled, they formed up with the sisters at their lead and departed. They were careful to keep their guard up. This would be an ideal time for an attack, but although many eyes watched from every window, nothing happened.

Once there, they arranged themselves in an orderly formation at the bottom of the stairs, as they waited for House Faerl'Zotreth to vacate the temple. Valene began to show anger at the delay when the outer doors finally swung open. The eldest female, followed by her younger sister and their guards walked casually, almost insolently down the stairs. Briza stopped just in front of Valene, her expression as cold as ice, and then without a word, handed over the Whip of Obedience, the symbol of the Overseer.

Valene, a foot taller and more heavyset than her adversary inclined her head. With a slight sneer, she accepted the whip and took this chance to gloat at her rivals' disgrace.

"I hope you have something interesting to do with your new-found time, perhaps teaching male infants the value of subservience?"

A lowly job, not one suited to a royal female from House Faerl'Zotreth and Briza knew it. Xenis winced internally and tensed, ready for battle, as he watched her expression change from one of disdain to outright hatred. Valene had just made another enemy for House Zik'Keeshe, a stupid move in his opinion and one that could result in bloodshed. Technically, they considered everyone an enemy, even with those that forged a temporary alliance. Every house jostled for position; however, most moves were without any significant malice. They were just part of the day-to-day routine, but this was different. Valene didn't care if she had just made another deadly enemy who sought their utter destruction. Only status mattered, hers in particular.

Briza managed with some effort to calm herself, and the tensed guards on both sides relaxed slightly. Instead, without bloodshed, she made a strange gesture, then waved for her sister and their guards to leave, although she shot Valene one last look of pure venom.

Valene waited for them to get out of earshot before uncharacteristically chuckling. "Now she will know her place."

Xenis felt glad that Briza from House Faerl'Zotreth had not heard that comment. It would have resulted in the demise of everyone present. The two females would have fought to the death over such an ill-timed remark.

Valene commanded the males to assemble, and after placing the Whip of Obedience on their heads, she muttered words of power, allowing them to enter the temple. The females, of course, could do this already, but still, the younger sisters needed a separate ritual to access the inner sanctum. Once Valene completed the rite, they climbed the wide pillar lined stairs and entered the temple itself. Xenis could still feel the residual discomfort that the doors exuded. It felt unpleasant, but only a small fraction of what he would experience if he tried to enter without permission. Society taught that attempting to pass without the 'Acceptance' spell courted not only madness but also extreme agony. As a male, he would most likely not survive the process.

Valene and her sisters stood just inside the door. They gave orders and organised the inspection.

"Fan out, search everywhere. House Faerl'Zotreth will have left traps. If you see or sense anything unusual, leave it and report its location to our brother."

When the guards left, Valene turned menacingly to Xenis. "We will leave the magical traps to you. Be sure that you find everything."

She left that threat hanging in the air, but he could also see it in her eyes, she thought him expendable. He could do nothing but accept the situation, so he cast a 'Protection' spell and went to join the search.

The guards found several reasonably standard traps, which he disarmed and that worried Xenis. There were too many traps, all of them simple, either mechanical or chemical and none that had magic. Just when he considered asking for a thorough search of the temple himself, the floor trembled. Shouts and screams echoed down the corridor. He contemplated running towards the sound but then remembered that some traps expanded to engulf all those around so he would be running into danger. Instead, he carefully approached, just as some guards came careening down the corridor.

Xenis grabbed one, but the male tried to shake him off, his eyes wild with terror. Ok, now he knew something useful. The trap contained a 'Fear and Pain' spell, but there had to be more to it than just that. A roar from the room beyond gave him an idea. He cast a 'Gather Shadows' spell and then cautiously entered the room, to see two bodies on the ground. One moved feebly, but the other looked obviously dead. To one side sat a grossly deformed ogre-like creature. It reached across, picked up the body, and then disembowelled the torso with its jaws. The blood and internal organs gushed over its face and then with a grunt of pleasure, it began feeding. While unpleasant to watch, Xenis didn't worry. This creature wouldn't fit down the corridor, and besides, ogres while strong and ugly weren't that difficult to kill for a group of skilled warriors. He backed out of the room and went to gather the guards, but instead, he found something odd.

Another roar emanated from the corridor ahead. Xenis turned the corner to find it blocked by another deformed ogre, so large that it had become wedged in place. He backed up a little only to hear a noise from behind. On entering the room, he saw an injured male on the floor, gradually twisting and deforming, screaming as he did. Now, he knew the nature of the spell. Anything caught in its radius would die or transform. With a sigh, he stepped forward and plunged his sword into the neck of the transforming guard only to have another shock. His magical sword merely slid off its skin. The blade would normally penetrate anything, but now the magic malfunctioned. It became just a sword, sharp but nothing out of the ordinary. Now, this meant real trouble. The newly formed ogre snarled as mad as hell, out for blood. Xenis quickly jumped out of the room and recast a 'Gather Shadows' spell, but this didn't work against the creature. It saw right through the shadows, but fortunately, the continuing transformation made it difficult to squeeze down the corridor.

Xenis now had a new problem, trapped between the two expanding ogres; he had nowhere left to go. His sword and magic useless, he calmly watched as both ogres struggled to get closer to him. These creatures proved not only immune to magic but also able to disrupt it, which severely limited his options. Yet shortly, their massive fists would come into range. He began to formulate a risky plan when one ogre got its foot wedged behind the other as it tried to squeeze forwards. That left some space by the crook of its knee. Xenis took the opportunity to dive through the gap. The ogre roared in frustration and thumped its fist downwards, only narrowly missing Xenis as he passed under its belly. He rolled gracefully to his feet and sped off with a satisfied grin.

After taking various twists and turns, he managed to make his way back to the entrance, only to meet another ogre as it finally squeezed out of a narrow corridor into the main thoroughfare. With a roar of triumph, it pounced, but Xenis moved too quickly. He dodged its great pounding fists, time after time before suddenly a voice cried out behind him.

"Enough!"

Valene watched the spectacle growing ever more exasperated by the delay. In the end, she decided to intervene when it became apparent that Xenis could only infuriate the disgusting creature. She did note one significant piece of information. His magical sword had lost its aura.

With her head held high, she raised a hand to cast the usual 'Pain' spell, but then considered another tactic. Instead, she narrowed her eyes and concentrated upon the ogre. More like an augmented force of will, than a spell, the power reached out. The ogre's mind crumbled quickly and then driven by his mistress's mental commands, set out to destroy its targets. It made quick work of the first few before it succumbed to its injuries. Valene then merely picked another, crushed its will, and sent it to finish the task. In the end, just a mountain of dismembered chunks remained.

Valene glared at Xenis. "Clean up this mess," she commanded. "Inform me when it's done. My sisters and I will attend the inner sanctum."

Angry at the way his sister treated him, like a drudge and not a royal, he sent runners back to the house to co-opt as much help as he could get. Even so, several hours passed before Xenis declared it not only safe but also after the 'Purification' spell, uncontaminated.

He had yet to inform his sisters, but as soon as he tried to enter the corridor that led to the inner sanctum, he felt the 'Safeguard' spells activate. A horrible feeling of revulsion, nausea along with a vicious biting pain, like the sting of a thousand insects rippled over his skin. He could hold off the sensation for a while, but with each step, the feeling mounted until he had to turn back. After a few moments, his youngest sister Larenil appeared, alerted by the proximity alarm. She brought his message to Valene, who conducted a room-by-room examination. Once complete, the oldest sister grudgingly admitted that everything passed her inspection. After which she sent a runner to inform the Matriarch.

"But unless she deems everything perfect," Valene informed her brother. "You will be the next sacrifice."

Chapter 4

Thomas and Raphael

"Give us your money half skin!"

The schoolboys crowded around him, pushing and shoving, as they laughed at his pain. They were bigger, meaner, and stronger, but that didn't stop Thomas from trying to push back. He might be small for his age, but that didn't mean he was a coward.

"Get off me!" he yelled, flailing his arms around, trying to punch anything that got too close.

They dodged back and laughed at his efforts when he missed. Again, they pushed and shoved, but this time, he managed to score a glancing blow. He smacked the fifth-year boy smartly on the chin. It wasn't enough to do any damage but more than enough to bring the bully up sharp. The others stopped, silent and still, standing in stunned amazement at the lucky hit, but also slightly fearful of what their leader might do next. Billy wiped his chin and then with a snarl, shoved Thomas hard up against the toilet stall.

"You're going to pay for that you little piece of shit."

With a nod to the left, he said to one of his gang, "Open the door."

The boys started to laugh. They knew what would happen next. Thomas could guess too, kicking and screaming, he tried to brace his legs against the sides of the stall as they began to shove him inside.

"Drown him, drown him," they chanted as Billy dragged the struggling boy over the toilet bowl.

"What's all this noise?"

In their excitement, no one had noticed a teacher enter the boy's bathroom, but Billy wasn't about to let even a glancing blow go unpunished, especially from a first year. He smacked his victims head hard on the cistern, then quickly turned away, and stepped outside the cubical.

"What are you doing?" the teacher said, responding to the strange noise.

He strode over to the cubical, pushed Billy out of the way, and opened the door. He looked inside, but it was empty. The teacher frowned, feeling mystified then turned and yelled at the boys before ordering them back to their classrooms.

****

Raphael looked up from his book. For a split second, something had disturbed his thoughts. He'd felt it tingle on the edge of his mind before it vanished. The ancient elf shrugged and dismissed it, as he returned to his reading.

Thomas lay on a soft mound blinking, dazzled by the golden light. His head hurt, but strangely, it quickly faded away. Perhaps he had died and gone to heaven or as his grandmother predicted, to hell. Afraid, he sat up and looked around. Beyond the mound of lush green moss, ferns shivered slightly in the breeze. Clumps of tiny flowers scattered the woodland floor. This couldn't be hell. Thomas sighed then leapt up and ran over the springy ground his fear forgotten. He'd never been anywhere like this before. Gone were the bullies, the dirty streets, and the rubbish blowing in the wind. He felt free, and the air smelt sweet like Jasmin. Thomas bent down, picked a flower, and examined it. Each petal faded from pink to gold, completely beautiful, so he chose another and then another. If only he could give these to his mum, she would love the colours.

At that thought, Thomas felt sad. What would happen when they told her? Would she miss him? Would his father miss him or would they argue like they always did? Each would blame the other for his death. His grandmother said that the dead could watch over the living so he would know, not that he wanted to see his mum cry again. He stood contemplating this future. The dead could not help the living, so why worry about something he couldn't change? That seemed not only wrong but also frustrating, and then a thought occurred to him. In heaven, only good things could happen, so perhaps he could just watch the happy bits. Another less pleasant thought crossed his mind. There would not be much to watch.

As a dark mood threatened to engulf him, something caught his eye. A leaf more gold than green floated down towards the ground. Thomas looked up. High above him fluttered a canopy of leaves spread wide but thin. As the breeze blew, the sunlight cast tiny shimmering pinpricks of light through the moss-trailed branches. Too far to climb, he watched for a while as the leaves cascaded down like confetti, before bending down, to pick one off the ground. The flowers now forgotten; Thomas examined the leaf. He had never seen anything like it. Not that he had seen many trees and none like this. The trees where he lived were almost grey, covered in soot and pollution, their bark peeling off until they looked like dying giants. This leaf looked alive even though it wasn't on the tree anymore. Thomas smiled and tucked it into his pocket. He would keep that for later. For now, he wanted to explore, but then he noticed that the flowers had begun to wilt.

Thomas stood listening, and there above the sound of rustling trees, he could hear water flowing in the distance. He hated the river back home. Dirty and smelly like an old tramp, it slowly oozed between its rubbish-filled banks. Unlike that river, this gurgled and gushed, an enticing sound that drew him towards the rushing water.

High in the trees, the elf Tinnueth watched the strange boy. Pudgy, awkward, and less slender than her own race, with his dark hair and brown skin, she thought him perhaps a dwarven child. Odd that the Dark Delvers allowed him outside on his own and stranger still that he ran towards the river and not the tunnels. Why would he do that? She dropped quickly from the high branches, magic slowing her descent until she landed on the soft turf. With graceful ease, Tinnueth ran silently and swiftly over the undulating ground. When she reached the boy, she found him staring intently at the water. Hidden in the shadows of a great tree, she studied his face and decided the boy did not have any Delver characteristics. What an interesting mystery. She would share this with Master Magician Raphael.

As she observed the boy's features, his expression changed as if he had come to a decision. One foot inched towards the swirling water.

"Wait."

The spell broke.

Her voice and sudden appearance brought him out of his contemplation. In open-mouthed shock, he stood still, dazzled by her beauty, and then suddenly, smiling widely, he presented her with a bunch of wilted flowers.

Tinnueth inclined her head and graciously accepted. As she projected a wave of perfect safety, she held out her hand.

"Welcome to our woods. I'm Tinnueth."

Wide-eyed, he took her hand, and she led the boy away across the mossy forest floor. Around them, birds escorted the couple, flitting from branch to branch while butterflies flocked unafraid. One landed in Tinnueth's long blond curls then flew away. Thomas laughed, trying to touch any that got close, but they always stayed just out of reach. A red dragonfly zoomed past and circled their heads before darting off. Thomas stared in wonder; he'd only ever seen them in books. An odd movement deep in the forest caught his eye, and then something strange happened. The lady waved her hand, and a young doe cautiously appeared from out of the undergrowth. Tinnueth whispered something. The doe approached and then stood still allowing Thomas to stroke her silky hide. Warm and soft, the doe trembled beneath his touch before suddenly racing off into the forest. Tinnueth smiled and indicated to Thomas that they should follow.

After a while, they emerged from the forest into a massive clearing. In the centre stood a green mound surrounded by a deep moat fed from the nearby river. Great trees, larger by far than any in the forest overhung the water. As Thomas looked up, he saw flashes of colour moving in the wind. At first, they reminded him of sails, but as they grew closer, he realised that the branches held a multitude of coloured tents.

As they both stood on the edge of the moat, Tinnueth stretched out her hand and made a strange gesture. A ladder snaked lazily down from the branches ending just above the ground. When she didn't start to climb, Thomas gave her a perplexed glance, and then he understood why. A muscular male with long brown hair called a distant warning from above and came sliding down, without even touching the rungs. When he saw Thomas, his stern face changed to one of surprise. He looked at Tinnueth, something unspoken passed between them, and then he smiled.

"It's quite a climb for one so small." He put out a hand to Thomas and then added, "My name is Aeglas."

Thomas took his hand, and to the boy's surprise, Aeglas swung him onto his back. With ease, the elf quickly climbed the ladder to the top before unloading the boy onto a walkway. Tinnueth joined them, and the two elves ushered Thomas into a large room filled with chattering people, eating their dinner. At the sight of so many strangers, Thomas baulked and stood awkwardly in the doorway. Silence descended as all eyes turned towards him. Aeglas smiled, placed a reassuring hand on the boy's shoulder, and guided him into the room towards an empty table. The chatter began again, and Thomas felt relieved not to be the centre of attention any more. His stomach took that opportunity to growl. Aeglas laughed and called out towards someone serving food. They went into an adjoining room and brought out a large tray with several dishes, which they placed in front of the boy. Not waiting for approval, he tucked in, choosing something from each bowl. When finally satisfied, Thomas pushed his plate away and looked around, then remembered his mother's comments on good manners.

"Thank you," he said to everyone.

Aeglas looked at him, his mouth open in surprise.

"You're welcome," he replied hesitantly.

Thomas felt that he needed to say more. "It was very delicious."

Tinnueth smiled. "We're pleased that you liked it."

She glanced at Aeglas, who nodded almost imperceptibly and left. He returned a few minutes later with another person, who drew up a chair next to the boy. He had an air of great age, but his features remained untouched by time. Unlike the others, who preferred woodland colours, he dressed in long black robes, which contrasted with his waist-length neatly tied platinum hair. He had such a visible appearance of wisdom and authority that Thomas suddenly felt nervous.

Tinnueth bent down and whispered to the apprehensive boy, "Don't worry, he won't bite."

Thomas smiled only marginally reassured.

The ancient elf smiled too. "My name is Raphael; what is your name?"

"Thomas."

"Do you mind if I ask you a few questions, Thomas?
Thomas shook his head.
"Where do you come from?"
"Brumham."
Raphael had never heard of a city with that name.
"How did you get here?"
Thomas frowned, oddly enough he couldn't remember. "I just woke up in the woods." He paused and then asked, "Is this heaven?"
Raphael smiled. "To some, I suppose this is heaven. Did you die?"
"Perhaps, I don't know."
"And how do you know our language?"
Thomas shrugged. "I just understood you," and then added because he was a truthful boy. "Well, after a bit anyway."
"That is a special ability."
Thomas beamed.
"I have something here. Would you like to look at it?" Raphael unfurled his hand. A gemstone glittered, its facets catching the light.
"That's pretty."
"Hold out your hand." Raphael tipped it onto the boy's palm.
Thomas gasped and almost dropped it as the gem glowed blue for a second then died.
"Thank you, Thomas. You've been most helpful. May I have my gem back please?"
Thomas gratefully relinquished the stone then sat in thoughtful contemplation as Raphael stared back at him.
"Can I go outside?"
Raphael looked at Aeglas, who nodded.
"Certainly, but stay with Aeglas we don't want you to get lost."
Thomas grinned and jumped up from his seat, looking at Tinnueth. "Can Tinnueth come too?"
She smiled. "I'm happy to join you if Master Raphael agrees."
He nodded.
She turned to Thomas. "What shall we do?"
"Explore."

Once the boy had gone, scout leader Vanya and Master Raphael, leaned against the knotted railings that ran along the outer edge of the canopy. They had known each other for more than a millennium and felt comfortable in one another's company. Tall and lean, Vanya's raven hair accentuated the magician's silver white.

As they watched the boy play on the ground below, she turned to Raphael.

"So, what is he?" asked Vanya.

"Human."

She looked surprised. "So that's what they look like?"

Raphael smiled. "What did you expect?"

"I knew they existed, but I never expected to see one. How did the boy get here?"

Raphael's expression darkened. "I don't know."

"But you suspect?"

"Possibly, there are various options I can explore."

"Do you need my help?"

Raphael shook his head, frowned, and said, "No, not for the moment. I will see if I can find the answers I seek within my books."

"And if you do not?"

Raphael's frown deepened. "Perhaps if necessary, I will refer to the library at Araothron. Either way, once I have found what I am looking for, I will speak with you again, but do not mention this to anyone else."

Vanya realised that this was far more serious than she had suspected. Raphael would never consider such an option without good cause. While not technically expelled from the capital city, the council still regarded him as less than welcome. They stood in silent contemplation for a while before she spoke.

"What should we do with him?"

"What would we do for any child?"

"But his parents won't they miss him?"

"I expect so, but that is not our problem, we will care for him until he grows old."

Vanya looked puzzled at his comment, and then asked, "How long will that be?"

"Who knows? They are a short-lived race. I wouldn't expect more than seventy years if that."

Below, the boy ran on, oblivious to his fate.

Chapter 5

Sarah

While driving, Sarah had rehearsed the lines in her head. Time was of the essence. Mr Johnson needed a doctor. She grimaced, if he wasn't already dead. If only her phone had lasted, she could have got a signal once she was on the highway.

She screeched to a halt outside the Sherrif's office, jumped out and ran up the stairs. A small breeze shivered through a gap in the wedged door, but even before she stepped over the threshold, a loud snore reverberated around the room.

Sarah pushed the door open. The grey-haired sheriff sat slumped in his chair, a newspaper over his wrinkled face. With each breath, a corner flapped slightly giving him a comical appearance. Sarah couldn't help but smile. As she stepped forwards to wake him, the floorboards creaked loudly beneath her feet.

The pudgy sheriff woke with a start. "What the hell," he slurred. "Why are you creeping up on me? Can't a man sleep in peace around here?"

He stumbled upright, groaned, and then lurched towards the toilet, clutching his head. A loud, retching noise followed. Sarah cringed as the sheriff came stumbling back into the room. He made a fresh pot of coffee and moaned about his headache while looking for something to ease the pain. After knocking back a handful of pills, he sat down holding his coffee and looked at her through red-rimmed eyes.

Sarah gave him a hard stare. He coughed and had the grace to look somewhat embarrassed.

"Well, what can I do for you?"

"You need to get a doctor."

The sheriff glared at her and looked affronted.

"I don't mean for you."

"What do you mean?"

In her haste to explain, Sarah forgot her prepared speech. Instead, it came out in a muddled rush.

"I'm really sorry, but I couldn't get a signal on my phone, then it died, so I came here to tell you that he might be dead. If not, he needs a doctor right away. I heard his dog barking and found the door locked, and I could see a body or what I think is a body through the window. Not that it was easy, the windows are grubby, so I could have been wrong, but he hadn't fed Rufus in a while, and why would Mr Johnson lie on the floor if he weren't at least very ill. I couldn't get into the house to check, but he's got funny marks on his skin. I don't know what killed him, but it looks like something bit him. Either way, he needs help, or he will die if he's not dead already."

Sarah paused when she ran out of breath and then didn't know what else to say, so she gave an apologetic shrug.

Sheriff Miller sat, sipping his coffee as if taking this all in through the fading remains of his drunken stupor.

"Sit down girl you're giving me a stiff neck."

Sarah sat on a nearby chair with an impatient sigh.

"Now run that by me again."

She repeated it, this time improving the order. The sheriff interrupted from time to time, asking questions like 'what time had she found the body' and 'why had she been there.'

When he finished, he leaned back in his chair and gave her a piercing look at odds with his previous demeanour.

"So, you're really sorry."

"What?"

Sarah frowned, perplexed at the comment. How had he come to that conclusion? Had she explained events so badly that he didn't understand?

Sheriff Miller watched her expression carefully, then asked, "Did you kill him? Because if you did, you should tell me now."

Sarah sat there open-mouthed, utterly aghast at the question. When she replied, she could hardly keep the shocked outrage out of her voice. "I would never, why would I? What possible motive could I have for killing a defenceless old man?"

"Don't get on your high horse Miss, I gotta ask, wouldn't be doing my duty if I didn't."

"Your duty," replied Sarah in a tight voice, pointing her forefinger at him. "Is not to be drunk *on* duty."

The sheriff glared at her. It had a ring of truth, but this might not be the best time to remind him. His face twisted as he contemplated a scathing retort. Just as he drew breath to speak, the front door swung open.

"Evening Sheriff Miller."

The sheriff nodded to the newcomer and said, "Evening, Hank."

Deputy Barnett sauntered in for the evening shift. He eyed up Sarah, who returned the favour. Tall, handsome with a brown crew cut hair and broad shoulders, his gormless smile, made Sarah suspect that his brains didn't match his brawn. When he opened his mouth, he confirmed her suspicions.

"You here for the evening rush, Miss?" he said.

Sarah just mentally rolled her eyes as she looked around at the empty room.

The sheriff glowered at his deputy. "No, she's here to report a possible homicide."

That got the deputies attention straight away. "Right you are boss, shall I book her?"

Sheriff Miller sighed and stood up stiffly. "No Hank, she is reporting not confessing. I am going up to Outcrop House to investigate."

"Outcrop House, isn't that old Ben's place?"

Ben must be Mr Johnson thought Sarah.

The deputy then asked a daft question, "So he's dead then?"

The sheriff shrugged.

"That's too bad."

Sarah piped up, "He might not be dead. What about calling a doctor? It'll be dark by the time you get to the house."

The sheriff appeared somewhat annoyed at her interference. "That's my business, not yours." He nodded towards the deputy. "Keep an eye on her and make sure she doesn't leave town."

With that, he grabbed a few things, then left in the one, and only police car. Sarah sat there like a lost sheep, not knowing what to do.

The deputy settled down with a coffee and his paper and then indicated with a nod that she should stay put. As she waited, Sarah got more annoyed and hungrier by the minute.

In the end, she burst out, "I could go home, and wait, you know. I only live down the street."

Hank looked up from his paper and shook his head.

"He could take ages you know, and he might not even come back tonight," Sarah added.

He ignored her, so she got up and took one step towards the door. With fantastic speed, Hank dived out of his chair and grabbed her arm before she had taken the second step.

"Sorry, Miss, but you have to stay here."

Sarah tried to pull her arm away from his tight grip.

"Let go you great lump. I'm hungry and thirsty and what about my rights. You haven't charged me with anything, so you can't keep me here."

"I can charge you with obstructing justice."

Sarah sighed in exasperation. "No, you can't."

She struggled, and he only gripped her more tightly before trying to drag her back to her chair.

"Now you sit down and wait like a nice lady else I'll have to lock you up."

"You wouldn't!"

The look on his face said otherwise, but Sarah had suffered quite enough of his attitude.

"Let me go, or you'll regret it!"

Hank dumped her back down in the chair before getting another cup of coffee and sitting down again with his paper. She noticed he didn't offer her one, so Sarah waited just long enough for him to settle down, before jumping up and diving out of the door. Sarah only just made it through before the deputy grabbed her and dragged her back, kicking and yelling. She struggled as he threw her inside a jail cell. His shins took quite a beating, but it didn't seem to worry him unduly.

"I can add assaulting a police officer and resisting arrest to your list of offences," Hank added.

Sarah fumed. "What happened to presumed innocent before proved guilty?"

From his expression, the deputy clearly didn't believe her.

As her anger built into a tight knot, she got out her phone and began to type.

The deputy looked perplexed then said, "I hope you're not trying to call anyone?"

"What about my free call?" she retorted.

Hank thought about it for a second.

"Sure," he said, then grabbed Sarah's phone through the bars, before she could send another tweet. "You just had it."

Chapter 6

Lars

That night an unfamiliar sound woke Lars with a jolt. Aware that they were camping on an old rock fall and another could come at any time; he rolled quickly to his knees.

"Stefan, wake up!"

His friend didn't reply.

"Stefan!"

Lars reached out and frantically searched the empty floor in search of a lamp. As he fumbled around cursing, he realised that he couldn't hear Stefan's snore. In a panic, Lars stood up and went to step out of the tent, only to find that it didn't exist either.

"Stefan!" he called.

His voice echoed in the night before it died away. Lars stood, silent and listening. He could not hear the river or the wind in the trees. Only a distant rumble pierced the eerie silence. It didn't sound like thunder, and it couldn't be a warg. Lars turned towards it and carefully walked forward. By now, he should be close to the river, but instead, he bumped into something hard. He reached out. It felt oddly smooth and regular like a wall. With his left hand outstretched, he began to walk, but after a few steps, his boots scraped on another hard surface. The path had come to a dead end in this narrow canyon. Out of the corner of his eye, he saw a thin, pale light, glimmering in the distance. Lars turned and crept towards it. When he finally stepped out, he stood astounded, shocked by what he saw. In both directions ran a wide road unlike any he had seen before. On either side of the road sat large buildings made of rare glass.

Along the street at regular intervals, lamps lit the night. His friend forgotten, Lars walked towards one streetlight, only to discover that someone had made it out of metal. He could not imagine anyone using such wealth to light a road, albeit a road made of such strange material. Lars bent down to touch it. Black as midnight, gritty and tough, he did not know what to make of it. Another rumble reminded Lars of his missing friend. He ran towards the sound, feeling guilty that he had paused even for a moment. The noise had come from the end of another narrow canyon, which he decided must be a street between buildings. Unlike the lit road behind him, where he could see danger coming, here, something might lurk unseen in the darkness. This caution saved his life.

As he left the confines of the lane, something huge, smelling of foul fumes, roared by at speed. The creature missed him by a few feet, but instead of devouring him, it sped off into the night. Lars felt puzzled. Animals did not run away from him, unlike Stefan. On the journey upriver, his friend had kept the wargs at bay. In comparison, they saw Lars as an easy target

Lars ducked back into the lane, but the creature didn't return. He stepped out and looked around, curious to know why. Here the wide black road had a strange dashed white line running down the middle. What special significance did the lines have? Another rumble caught his attention. Lars looked up. Something approached, its great eyes gleaming bright blinding him. It gave a mournful honk just before it pounced. Lars dived out of the way and rolled to his feet, ready to fight, but instead, it roared past. As it retreated into the distance, he could see the dark outline of a human head in its transparent belly. It had caught a person and now dragged them to its lair. With a flash of insight, he realised what had happened to his friend.

Lars sprinted after the creature, but it moved so fast that he couldn't keep up. Heart pounding, chest heaving, he slowed and bent over, gasping for breath. When he looked up, he realised that he stood at an intersection, and the creature was nowhere in sight. He'd lost the trail, and the hard black surface made it impossible to track. With a groan of despair, Lars put his head in his hands. As he wondered what to do next, a bright light suddenly shone through his fingers. Something wailed, screeched, and then pounced. Lars cried out as the impact propelled him backwards with a bone-crunching snap.

Chapter 7

Thomas

Tinnueth knew where Thomas hid. He couldn't keep quiet. She pretended she couldn't find him and kept walking past his hiding place. Each time the little chuckle gave him away, but she and Aeglas kept searching as if they hadn't heard it. This time instead of a giggle, something odd happened. A strange sensation tingled across her skin, followed by an unfamiliar sound. She ran over to the boulder where Thomas hid and looked down, only to see scuffed moss where he had once knelt.

She called out to Aeglas, "Have you seen Thomas?"

He shook his head and walked over.

"Did you hear that?"

"Yes." He looked concerned. "He hid here for some time, and I did not see him move."

They both grimaced, knowing that they were responsible for the boy's safety.

"I will search, but we should also check with Master Raphael."

Tinnueth nodded and ran towards the town. On her command, a rope snaked down from the canopy and then with practised ease, she climbed to the outer edge of the walkway. When she found Master Raphael's study empty, she moved towards the feasting hall. In the corner, she saw the magician talking to Vanya. As she approached, they stopped discussing the policies and politics of the elven capital.

"Master Raphael I'm sorry to interrupt, but Thomas has gone missing," she confessed.

Vanya appeared concerned, but Raphael took the news quite calmly. He merely nodded much to Tinnueth's surprise. He'd felt that strange sensation again a few moments ago.

"Aeglas is searching," Tinnueth continued.

"But you were wondering if I would cast a net?"
She nodded.
Raphael stood, and with Vanya and Tinnueth in tow, he walked towards his study. Once there he opened a highly carved wooden box and extracted a gem.

"I will cast the net elsewhere," he remarked nodding around the room. Raphael had a great many items, some of which might hinder the reading.

They waited while he strode off towards the furthermost vantage point. There he stood, the gem in his right hand, his other arm outstretched, his palm facing downwards. With a look of concentration, he muttered a few words. His focus intensified and then with a push, his mind soared over the woodland. A sparkling net appeared only visible to himself, but he could already see that Thomas had left their realm. All the usual inhabitants showed a tiny flicker of gold, but no human blue appeared. The boy had either gone beyond their sphere of influence or as Raphael suspected, returned to his place of origin. A concerned frown marred his ageless face.

****

Lynn Harvey fidgeted with frustration as she listened to the customer. Her shift ended at 3.30pm, but if like now, a call came in at the last moment, she left work late. She sat feeling worried that Thomas still waited outside the school gates. This time a particularly difficult man refused to accept that Customer Services could not sort out his complaint. It's not as if she didn't want to. It's just that she had no control whatsoever over how marketing worded its adverts. Yes, it seemed foolish to give new customers the best offers. Yes, it seemed daft when she couldn't give him the same deal, and yes, the company seemed to want to alienate loyal customers, so they went to their competitors. She could only silently agree and not voice her opinion if she wanted to keep the job.

When the exasperated man rang off, Lynn packed up and ran to her car. The traffic, heavier by this time, blocked her way. Once she reached the school gates, all the busses had left and the parents gone. Lynn parked and went around to the main entrance, expecting to see Thomas waiting, bored, and frustrated by her late arrival, but he wasn't there. She checked the side entrance and then began to walk around, getting more worried by the second. As Lynn turned a corner towards the staff carpark, she bumped into a young teacher.

"Thank goodness, have you seen Thomas?"

"Thomas?"

"I'm Lynn Harvey, Thomas' mum. He's in the first year."

The teacher thought for a moment and then recalled a small, skinny, brown-skinned, dark-haired boy. Yet the mother had mousey blond hair. Must take after the father she thought.

"I haven't seen him for a while, not since the third break I think but it's hard to tell with so many new students." She looked at Lynn. "Aren't you a little late?"

Lynn blushed. "Yes, I had a last-minute call."

The teacher nodded, understanding. "Well, perhaps he decided to walk home. Is it far?"

"Yes, a few miles."

"Ah well, perhaps he got a lift with a friend or something."

"Perhaps," Lynn agreed reluctantly.

She left the teacher and drove slowly taking the most likely route home that Thomas might pick. Each small boy made her heart leap with hope, but each time it crashed, threatening despair. When Lynn got back to the house, she leapt out and fumbled with her keys, as she tried to unlock the front door.

"Thomas?"

She stood on the doorstep listening, but only silence replied.

"Thomas?"

The house felt empty, as Lynn ran upstairs calling his name. Hope died, as she entered his room. Nothing had changed since the morning.

In desperation, she searched, calling out his name. An empty garden followed an empty house and then finally, an empty shed.

Lynn came back in and began to ring his short list of friends, but no one had seen him. On the edge of tears, she rang her husband, but the shift-running manager wouldn't let him come to the phone. Through gritted teeth, Lynn made him promise to let Chris know that she couldn't find Thomas. When she rang off, Lynn slumped at the bottom of the stairs and began to cry.

The trees rustled overhead, but the boy already knew that he'd returned to the world of dirt and grime. Thomas opened his eyes, yawned, and breathed in the polluted air. He recognised the park next to his house. Here and there, a few sad straggly plants clung desperately onto life, despite what humanity did to them. The view held more litter than grass and flowers.

In comparison with the other woodland, this place felt like hell, especially for a boy who loved nature and longed to explore. There he could smell the flowers, the trees, breathe air that tasted so clean and clear. He had never realised until now that this city stank of rotten eggs and tar. To know a place so full of colour and light made this world especially grey and dingy.

Even though he knew his parents would be cross with him for being away so long, he didn't want to go home. He didn't want to live here, surrounded by apartment blocks, and terraced houses, which stretched on for miles. He wanted to go back to the great golden, green woods, to see the river rushing deep and clear but above all to see Aeglas and Tinnueth again.

As he wished to go back, he remembered the leaf in his pocket and pulled it out. Even here, below the dark grey sky, it shone with life, a thing of beauty in an ugly world. He knew it wouldn't last, leaves always went brown, and horrible, crumbling into nothing, but this one he would treasure for as long as it lasted.

Thomas sighed. He knew he would have to go home, so he tucked the leaf back into his pocket for good luck, stood up and trudged across the park back to his house. Once there, he pushed open the unlocked garden gate and slouched up the path towards the house. He found the back door locked, so he rattled the handle and yelled for someone to let him in. After a few moments, his father arrived, scowling, his face like thunder. Tall, dark hair, skin and eyes, he towered over his small skinny son. Thomas stood still, wishing that he could fade into the background.

"Where have you been? You've had your mother worried sick! She's out looking for you," growled Chris.

Thomas didn't reply. He felt far too scared to speak. His father only took this as a sign of weakness.

"Where have you been? And don't lie to me!"

Thomas couldn't reply. Even if he told the truth, his dad would never believe him.

His father snarled in frustration. "Well, boy? Do I need to beat it out of you?"

Thomas mutely shook his head and backed away a little.

His father reached out and grabbed his son's arm. As he dragged him back into the house, Thomas whimpered in pain. Once inside the hallway, his father stood him up against the wall.

"You know what to do. Now stand there and don't cry, be a man."

Thomas knew what came next as he held out his hand. He shut his eyes as he heard his father undo his belt, but then something snapped inside him. He didn't need to take this; he didn't need to stand here and take the punishment. He could run, he had somewhere else to go, somewhere where no one would beat him. In an instant, Thomas dropped his hand, dodged around his father and out the back door. With all the speed he could muster, he ran like the wind out into the fading light. Thomas ran until he could not hear his dad's voice before he finally slumped on a bench at the other side of the park. There he sat brooding, wondering how he could get back to the golden green woodland.

"Hello, little boy, what are you doing out here on your own?"

Thomas jumped and looked up. He had been so deep in thought that he had not heard the man approach. Now that he took a good look at him, he didn't like what he saw. The greasy haired man dressed in brown and grey had an unpleasant smile that made Thomas feel sick inside his stomach. He wanted to run home, but he would have to face his father. Besides, he lived across the park, and he would never make it in time. The man would outrun him, but still, he had to try.

"What's that?" said Thomas pointing just behind the man.

As the greasy man turned, Thomas ran. He ran as fast and as far as he could and made it to the path that led to his house, but within a few seconds, the man caught him. Thomas screamed and kicked out, trying to bite the hand that held his arm in a cruel grip.

"It won't help; no one will hear you."

Thomas felt afraid, more afraid than he had ever been, he started to whimper and plead, but this only seemed to please the greasy man more.

"Hey, hey you, what are you doing?"

The greasy man twisted around to see a young man running towards him, an angry, concerned look on his face.

"Keep quiet," the greasy haired man hissed at the boy, but Thomas only squirmed and kicked out more.

"Little brat!"

The greasy man shoved him hard to the floor and as he turned around, failed to notice that Thomas had landed hard on the concrete, banging his head. The young man approached.

"What were you doing to that boy?"

"What boy?"

"The one behind you."

The greasy man turned, looked puzzled and then, turning back, smiled unpleasantly. "What boy?"

The young man craned his neck around the assailant, but the boy had vanished.

Chapter 8

Sarah and Cody

It had been a long night, and Sarah hadn't slept a wink. Instead, she paced around her cell, fuming at the injustice of it all. The sheriff hadn't returned, not that Sarah found this surprising. It had been late when she had reported the crime if it were a crime and not natural causes.

"Let me out!"

The deputy ignored her.

"You can't hold me, you know, I haven't done anything wrong. This is against my human rights! I demand a lawyer."

Sarah rattled the bars and stamped her foot, but again, he didn't reply. Just because she had kicked him in the shins earlier, didn't give him an excuse to ignore her now. Ok, so Deputy Barnett had added assaulting an officer of the law, to her so-called previous offence of murder suspect. Not that he or anyone else had charged her, so, in fact, the deputy had broken the law with wrongful imprisonment.

It had all seemed so straightforward. Sarah had arrived at the sheriff's office to report a possible death. The sheriff, who appeared to be just about sober, had taken down the necessary details and gone to investigate, leaving his deputy in charge. An unfortunate mistake, as the zealous deputy had taken his instructions too literally. He had translated 'don't let her leave town' as 'lock her up.' He had also taken away her phone so that she couldn't even tweet.

Sarah rattled the bars once more. "I hope you live to regret this decision!"

Hank replied with a noncommittal grunt and turned another page of his newspaper.

Sarah slumped onto the dusty bed and silently fumed. Once free, she would document her mistreatment on social media. This stupid deputy would feel smaller than an ant. He didn't know it now, but she planned to ruin his reputation unless he already had a reputation of an absolute idiot!

After ten minutes of silence, Deputy Barnett lazily peered over the top of his paper.

"Are you finally calming down now, missy?"

Sarah just glared at him, impotently wishing he would drop dead.

He smirked at her lack of response, then took his feet down from the desk, folded the paper and sauntered over to the jail cell.

"Good, now perhaps you'll be more cooperative."

Hank slouched, thumbs in his belt and gave her a condescending smile. Not that he would understand that word or let alone spell it, Sarah thought rather bitchily.

When she didn't reply, he continued his interrogation, "So, what's a girl like you, doing up in those hills alone?"

Oh my god, didn't he know how stupid he sounded? Through the long night, she had tried to reason with him but without success.

"Well, you going to reply? If not, I can just go back to reading my paper."

Sarah glared at him and slowly reiterated her story, "As I explained earlier, I am doing research for my PhD on the flora and fauna of the area, when I found a dog wandering lost and thirsty."

The deputy looked confused for a moment and interrupted, "What's a PhD?"

"A doctorate."

"You going to be a doctor?"

Sarah sighed. A five-year-old could grasp this better.

"Of ecology, yes, but it's not like a doctor of medicine, I deal with plants and animals."

"Like a vet?"

"No, I study them."

"Oh."

This seemed to satisfy him at least on some level, so she continued, "So when I returned the dog, I found the body of Mr Johnson."

The deputy grinned in sudden elation. "Got Ya! How did you know it was Mr Johnson if you didn't kill him?"

Sarah sighed, rolled her eyes, and explained patiently, well more patiently than she felt, "From the name and address on the dog's collar, so I assumed the body belonged to Mr Johnson."

"Oh."

The deputy looked a bit flummoxed, what could he say to that.

"Are there any more questions, or can I go?"

Hank looked unsure, but after some thought, he settled on the safe option. "The sheriff told me to make sure you didn't leave town."

"Yes, but that didn't mean locking me in here!"

"Well, how else can I make sure you don't leave?"

Sarah gritted her teeth. "I told you I rent a house on the edge of town. I could have gone there."

"Sorry miss you could still run even so. You'll just have to wait until the sheriff comes back."

Sarah lost her patience with a bang. "And what if he decided to take a detour via the bar on the way back? When will he be in then? Huh? Tomorrow or perhaps the next day if he's sobered enough?"

The deputy's face crinkled into sadness as he turned back towards his desk. "It's no good talking about him like that Miss. We all have our burdens."

Sarah felt a little sorry at her outburst, but even so, she had told the truth. If the sheriff didn't come back, she would have to spend the day in here. For now, she would have to put up with the deputy who wasn't talkative after that comment. With nothing to do but wait for the sheriff, Sarah sat on her bunk and stared out of the barred window.

Cody had come into town ostensibly to speak to a girl called Sarah, but also to collect the weekly groceries. From what he could find out, she rented a house on the outskirts of town. He felt a bit nervous about talking to her. As one of his MIT associates had said, men came from Mars, but women came from Venus. That meant alien, even dangerous and although strangely drawn to them, he had managed to avoid first contact so far. Today that would have to change if he planned to find out the truth.

In this small town, it only took a few minutes to find the right address. Cody pulled up in front of Sarah's house, got out, and approached the front door. He stood nervously on the porch, trying to muster some courage. His hands began prickling with cold sweat, but then Cody decided. He brushed a strand of long black hair out of his eyes, straightened up, and reached out. The bell played a happy tune at odds with his nervous state. Cody licked his lips in anticipation, but when no one replied, he let out a sigh and relaxed. Ok, so he would have to wait, in the meantime, he could pick up his groceries.

Cody turned, jumped back into his truck, and drove to the store before parking outside on the road. The doorbell tinkled as he let himself in. Stan, the shop owner, was leaning on the counter in the middle of a phone call. He nodded to Cody, his only customer, as he wandered by. Cody grabbed a shopping cart and began to pick his weekly groceries. He had only chosen a couple of items before Stan rushed over, his face glowing with excitement.

"Have you heard?"

"No."

The little man hopped from one foot to the other, almost bursting with the news. "There's been a murder!"

"Who?"

"Ben Johnson and guess what?"

Cody had a sudden insight. He could guess what Stan would say next.

"They've caught the perp! Oddly enough, it's that new girl who lives on the edge of town."

Cody just stared. Is this how it began? Could this be a conspiracy?

"She's in jail now! The sheriff is off investigating, and the deputy's guarding her."

"Oh."

Stan felt put out by Cody's lack of reaction; he had expected so much more. News, actual real news, scarcely came to this backwater town.

"Well, thanks for telling me, Stan. I'll just grab my shopping and be on my way if that's ok?"

"Sure thing," Stan sounded quite disappointed.

Cody's mind whirled with possibilities. Ominous events had entangled Sarah in more trouble than she had anticipated. Yet, if the sheriff still had to investigate, he probably hadn't charged her. Why would he lock her up? He quickly looked at his phone. Yes, she had tweeted a few hours ago but nothing since. Perhaps the deputy had taken matters into his own hands and held her against her will. Was he in league with whoever killed the old man? Sarah couldn't be guilty. She didn't have a motive. That meant someone planned to use her as a scapegoat. He needed to get her side of the story, but it didn't take a genius to realise that the deputy wouldn't let him speak to her. He needed a distraction. A cursory glance around the store gave him an idea. Cody picked up a few items in addition to his usual groceries and then paid. Once outside, he put the groceries in the truck.

He grabbed the additional items, tucked them inside his jacket, and then sauntered behind the store. Next, to the usual plastic dumpster, Cody spied something he could use. An old metal dustbin and piled up against it, a set of flattened cardboard boxes. He moved the bin further from the dumpster keeping it well away from anything flammable. After removing the metal lid, Cody placed some cardboard in the bottom, tipped on the fertiliser and sugar, and then added some crumpled paper. A less than perfect combination, but still it should have the desired effect. Cody glanced around making sure no one could see him before he lit a match. With a flick of his hand, he chucked it into the bin. It would be a few minutes before the smoke became noticeable, so he sauntered back to the truck, hid the ingredients, and then took a short walk towards the sheriff's office.

Sarah noticed a thin wisp of smoke coming from behind the grocery store. For a moment, she thought nothing of it, but when it grew, she turned towards the deputy and tried to get his attention.

"Hey, look at that."

He didn't reply and continued to ignore her as he rustled the pages of his newspaper.

"There's smoke coming from the grocery store."

Hank looked up. "You won't catch me with your lies."

Sarah became exasperated at his stupidity. "No honestly come over here and look."

After a moment of staring her down, the deputy put away his paper and looked out of the window. "Holy shit!"

He dived out of the door and raced towards the grocery store. A moment later, another man dressed in dusty jeans and a Comic-Con T-shirt, rushed into the office.

"Sarah?"

Sarah found herself staring at a lean, Native American with dark eyes and long black hair. "Yes, who are you?"

"Cody, my name is Cody."

Face flushed with success, he stared into the girl's green eyes and grinned. The plan had worked! In light of this achievement, his nerves just evaporated, and all the information tumbled out. "I saw your tweets and read your blog!"

Thank god, thought Sarah, someone knew what had happened.

Cody continued. "You're innocent. I'm sure of that, but I need to know more if I'm going to be able to help you."

Sarah felt the relief flood through her. "Sure, anything, thanks."

"Tell me everything but keep it quick because the deputy will soon realise that the smoke isn't a fire."

Sarah quickly recounted everything she had been through, including the kick.

Cody nodded, taking it all in. "Mm richly deserved, in my opinion."

"Can you get me out?"

"Not yet, but if the sheriff doesn't let you go, then I will do what I can. Do you have a contact number?"

"Sure." Sarah knew her number by heart. "I'd take your number down too, but the deputy took my iPhone. Can you find it for me?"

Cody rummaged around through the desk and fished out her mobile. When he handed it to her through the bars, she looked so grateful that his heart skipped a beat.

Once they had exchanged details, he shrugged in regret. "I should put it back."

"Thanks. You're a star. Now you'd better go, I don't want you to get into trouble on my account."

Cody nodded and almost went into hero mode. "Farewell, I will be back soon." He just managed to omit 'fair maiden.'

"Call me?"

"I will."

He exited the sheriff's office with panache. If he'd been wearing a cape, it would have swirled.

Chapter 9

Xenis

The Mistress of Ceremonies knocked on the council chamber door three times with her ornate staff and waited for the reply. After a brief pause, the golden door vibrated and a thunderous metallic voice reverberated throughout the hall.

"How dare you interrupt our deliberations?"

The Mistress and the Matriarch of Zik'Keeshe bowed their heads and spoke in unison.

"We humbly request admission."

Not that anyone would describe a Matriarch as humble, but these were the ritual words designed to remind the newcomer that they were just that, new. After another pause, the door swung open to reveal an immense sculpted room, its ceiling covered with chiselled representations of the Spider God. In the middle stood a massive ornately carved triangular stone table inlaid with gold. At the head of the table lay the Sovereign Throne, a shimmering gem incrusted metal chair draped with silk.

Each Matriarch wore their house colours, a set of protective iridescent silk robes, woven with spells to protect against mental and physical intrusion. On the throne sat the Matriarch of Mith'Barra resplendent in shimmering silver and pale blue. To her right sat the next most senior Matriarch, Zhennu'Z'ress who looked magnificent in glistening royal blue and pale green. To the left of the throne sat Fashka'D'Yorn bedecked in opalescent white and cyan. These represented the top three houses in Mizoram and by far the most dangerous. On the right, below Zhennu'Z'ress, sat Sarnor'Velve adorned with bright green flecked with sparkling silver. On the left side, next to Fashka'D'Yorn, lay an empty chair. The chair where

House Faerl'Zotreth once sat would now seat the Matriarch of House Zik'Keeshe.

The Matriarch of House Mith'Barra stood up and walked towards the Mistress of Ceremonies who gave a deep bow and waited for the ritual to begin.

"State your reasons for this interruption?"

In other circumstances, if the Matriarch deemed the reason insufficient, the supplicant faced death. In this case, she followed tradition and waited for the Mistress to respond.

"The Council of Five is but four."

"Why should that concern us?"

"There can be no consensus."

"Why should that concern us?"

"It can only lead to discord and bloodshed."

The Matriarch of Mith'Barra smiled slightly as if a little bloodshed would be a welcome sight. "Again, why should that concern us?"

The Mistress of Ceremonies stood to one side to reveal the Matriarch of House Zik'Keeshe who inclined her head and spoke in a low voice. "I humbly wish to remind the council, that open bloodshed amongst ourselves is not the will of 'She who watches.'"

Mith'Barra appeared to consider this comment for a moment then replied, "Yes, it is forbidden."

This statement was correct after a fashion. While the Drow Goddess forbade open warfare, she overlooked a quick skirmish or an anonymous stab in the back.

"Then join us so that we might avoid bloodshed."

The Mistress of Ceremonies bowed to both parties and departed closing the doors behind her with a resounding boom of finality.

The Matriarch of House Zik'Keeshe bejewelled in emerald green and gold made her way to her appointed chair and sat down. She had finally taken what she considered her rightful place on the Council of Five. Not that she showed any pleasure but merely a self-satisfied acceptance of the situation. It would be inappropriate, impolitic, or worse downright dangerous to appear overconfident in this final phase. The plans so carefully laid were gradually coming to fruition, and if all went well, eventually she would replace Mith'Barra as the ruling Matriarch. She kept these final thoughts well hidden within the depths of her mind. Others like herself had the power to extract memories and sometimes even detect random thoughts. She could not risk discovery.

The Matriarch of House Mith'Barra settled herself onto the shimmering throne and smiled without warmth. "The formalities over I would like to welcome our newest council member."

The others stared at Zik'Keeshe with stone cold appraisal as she inclined her head in gracious acknowledgement. They could only speculate on how the newcomer had engineered House Faerl'Zotreth's demotion.

Yet they could guess the truth. All houses used a standard method of advancement, but how this Matriarch had achieved such a downfall, lay shrouded in mystery. As masons, House Zik'Keeshe had once carved this very chamber, along with much of the temple. Their artisans went everywhere, albeit zealously overseen by the respective houses. They were also responsible for repairing the city walls and towers. This gave them unprecedented access to much of the city, access denied to others, yet no one had seen anything suspicious. House Faerl'Zotreth had suffered so many setbacks over the years. Their expertise lay in finding and extracting rare minerals. Yet their mines collapsed unexpectedly, essential supplies vanished, and indentured orcs and goblins died in droves. Once due to such delays, the Dark Delvers had claimed a promising vein of platinum. House Faerl'Zotreth, so angry at this assertion, had almost started a war.

Beyond their house role, Faerl'Zotreth also held the tenure as temple guardians. They oversaw religious ceremonies and organised the day-to-day running of the sanctum. Yet, nothing had gone to plan. Time after time, they botched minor rituals and misplaced religious artefacts. The city grew impatient with their incompetence. In response, the council demanded that House Faerl'Zotreth explain, but they could not, and this only fuelled their dwindling reputation. The final crunch had come during the Festival D'lil'Olath Clor. The youngest sister had inexplicably suffered memory loss when repeating her lines just before the priestess stumbled, dropping a blood chalice with a loud clang. This intolerable disgrace led to a vote of no confidence. Now, their status would fall even further, unless they somehow engineered not only a return to the council's good graces but also improved their standing in society. No doubt, the missing items would suddenly reappear with Zik'Keeshe in charge, but they would need to watch out. Faerl'Zotreth might not be able to prove anything, but they could guess the house responsible. To rise this high, would mean a fall equally far, into depths where they might not recover.

Aware of this possibility, the Matriarch of Zik'Keeshe stared back at the other council members. With a neutral air, she assessed her opponents and considered their estates just as they judged hers. Aside from their council responsibilities, each house had an inherent speciality. All contributed to the daily running of the city; many families produced food, others fashioned clothing, bone furniture, cuts gems, or created potions although, in truth, the indentured servants did the drudgework.

Every house could hunt and gather, often causing contention as one party crossed paths with another. Zhennu'Z'ress, a temporary ally of Zik'Keeshe, speciality lay in weapons training at the school of combat and were responsible for guarding the city, although they co-opted all houses into serving. They also produced weapons and armour.

Fashka'D'Yorn presided over magical training at the school of sorcery and the healing arts. Their house also cut and imbued gems with magical powers.

Sarnor'Velve excelled in the production of silk, but they were also responsible for trade, both within the city market place and the trading cavern. On the edge of the wilds, the Drow met Dark Delvers to exchange goods. Neither had any love for the other, but they remained at peace as long as their interests did not collide. While they shared an aversion to the daylight world unlike the Drow, the Dark Delvers did not hate the upper inhabitants, only viewed them with suspicion, and sometimes dislike.

Mith'Barra sat in the middle of the shimmering throne. She presided as head of the council and cast the deciding vote. Also, she had the power to overrule any decision; however, this rarely happened. Her house smelted rare metals and from the ingots fashioned magical items. Responsible for manufacturing the Drow currency, they produced and imbued the iridium coinage with magic. Their method had become a highly guarded secret that had kept them in power for a millennium.

Mith'Barra watched the display of disdainful animosity with veiled amusement, her position on the council secure. House Zik'Keeshe had a lot to learn. They were at the beginning of their journey, not the end.

She interrupted their mental fencing, which could have continued all day. "Mothers, your attention, we must begin."

The Matriarchs turned towards her.

"Sarnor'Velve, report on the Dark Delver situation."

Sarnor'Velve gave the council an account of her meeting with the trade delegation. After an exchange of threats, the Dark Delvers had finally agreed to trade at a reasonable price without any bloodshed. They would take silk in exchange for Iridium. Mith'Barra considered the offer. Their silk made the strongest bowstring, the most flexible rope in addition to the most elegant clothes. Dark Delvers prized it but loathed the spiders it came from, not exactly a problem for the Drow. Yet the Drow valued their silk highly and disliked handing it over to those that barely respected their ways.

"Your thoughts?" she said, turning to the other council members.

"That ore should be ours," replied Zik'Keeshe.

The others nodded, but Fashka'D'Yorn said, "If Faerl'Zotreth had not been delayed, it would be ours already."

A slight dig at Zik'Keeshe because everyone knew the truth. Mith'Barra inclined her head towards them. They had caused the problem, so perhaps they should be part of the solution as well.

"Do you feel that the quantity of silk is too much?"

"Yes, we should not give in so lightly. I suggest that we wring further concessions from the Dark Delvers."

This hinted that the Drow delegation had caved in too soon.

Sarnor'Velve bristled and drew breath to challenge that assertion, but Mith'Barra spoke up. "Interesting, such as?"

The Matriarch smiled and glanced slightly to her right. "They mine and cut exquisite gems; perhaps they could be persuaded to part with some of these in addition to the iridium."

Fashka'D'Yorn objected immediately. "I consider their cut gems inferior to ours."

Zik'Keeshe smirked and said, "Perhaps uncut then."

Fashka'D'Yorn glowered slightly, the gems would still have to be paid for one way or another, and they would be the ones to pay. Perhaps they should turn the tables.

"Perhaps Zik'Keeshe can offer something instead?"

Excellent stonemasons in their own right, the Dark Delvers would not need anything made by Zik'Keeshe. All the Matriarchs knew this and sneered slightly at the newest council member.

Zik'Keeshe ignored their reaction and instead seemed to consider that suggestion. "They produce fine wines and spirits, and farm different meats to ourselves."

"The produce could be poisoned."

"And face an all-out war? They would not be so foolish. In any case, we could test each batch. Make them taste a random sample or simply feed it to a servant."

"It could be a Drow only poison," Fashka'D'Yorn pointed out.

The Matriarch scoffed. "We have magic enough to reveal any spell that the Dark Delvers might leave behind. Or do you doubt the skills of your own house so much?"

Fashka'D'Yorn growled ready to launch an attack, but Mith'Barra intervened. "Are there any other suggestions? Zhennu'Z'ress you have been very quiet today have you anything to add to this discussion?"

"No, I think that alternative foodstuffs would be a reasonable request as long as we can guarantee their safety. Perhaps as the idea came from Zik'Keeshe, they would like to sample the first batch?"

This trapped Zik'Keeshe, if she said yes then Fashka'D'Yorn could poison the food and blame the Dark Delvers. If she said no, then her house would look cowardly. The Matriarch ground her teeth as the others waited with disparaging half smiles.

No, she would not let them see her as a coward, but perhaps there remained a way out. "I could agree to that with one caveat, Fashka'D'Yorn should fully check the foodstuffs and guarantee its safety."

While the others indicated their agreement, Fashka'D'Yorn glowered but then capitulated with a curt nod.

"That is settled then," replied Mith'Barra. "Sarnor'Velve you will meet with the Dark Delvers again and discuss our demands. Now, we have much to get through."

The runner waited patiently outside, weighing up the pros and cons. If he interrupted this meeting without good cause, he would incur the wrath of all within. If lucky, he would suffer an instantaneous death. If not, he shivered at the thought, the worst imaginable. Yet if he failed to deliver urgent news, he also faced death. In this case, he felt the information while important was not crucial, so he waited relatively sure he had made the right decision.

Some hours later, when the meeting ended, he stood in nervous anticipation. As the great rune carved doors swung outwards, the guards hurried to line the way. He got into a kneeling position at the end of the row along with two other runners from different houses.

Once the Matriarchs exited the council chambers in order of importance, he waited until his own emerged and walked down the line towards her colours.

She stopped. "Report?"

"Matriarch Zik'Keeshe, Mistress Valene sent me to inform you that the temple preparations are complete and ready for your inspection."

The Matriarch nodded and dismissed the runner, who departed with relieved haste to report her impending arrival. The guards gathered around their queen in a defensive formation and then marched swiftly towards the temple.

Valene and her siblings stood waiting at the foot of the temple stairs. Xenis hated this part. He could be patient, but he didn't like waiting. His mind turned over once again. Would his mother feel satisfied with their work? She remained challenging to please at the best of times. This would be the worst possible moment for her to take exception to anything he had done, or worse not done. If he had done well, his sisters would take the credit, if he had missed something he would take the fall. He sighed inwardly. Born into such a rigid caste system, he could never escape no matter how he excelled. Taught to accept their place, males simply obeyed. No amount of education or skill could make a difference. Most of the time, he tolerated it knowing that he lived in far better conditions than many others, but at other times like this when his life hung in the balance, it rankled. It might be unjust, but real justice did not exist in this city. He tensed slightly hearing the sound of marching boots. His mother and her guards had arrived.

His eldest sister Valene stepped forward and inclined her head. "Matriarch, the temple is ready for your inspection."

Her mother nodded curtly and climbed the stairs to the metal doors. Her hand extended as she whispered the ritual words claiming the temple for House Zik'Keeshe. The doors swung open in response, and she entered, her daughters trailing behind her and her sons behind them.

"Did you find many traps?" she said, turning to Valene.

"Yes, we found and destroyed them all."

"Are you sure? You were thorough?"

"Yes, Matriarch. I gave Xenis responsibility for the lower temple while my sisters, and I inspected the temple's inner sanctum."

"And the temple has been purified?"

"Yes, Matriarch to your satisfaction."

Her mothers stare unnerved Valene, but she held her gaze.

"We will see."

As the Matriarch went into each room, she paused and cast various spells to assess its state. Some to check for hidden traps, others for impurities or magical residue. She did not stop until she reached the room where Xenis had seen the first ogre.

"I sense something happened here. Even though it is purified, I can still detect a faint magical residue."

Valene nodded. "Xenis triggered the trap."

Xenis bristled but kept silent. He had not triggered the trap. After Valene's insult, Briza of Faerl'Zotreth had initiated the spell, but it had not fully activated until one of his men entered the room.

The Matriarch turned to Xenis. "Report."

He had one limited chance to redeem himself and assure his future in this world.

"I found the trap already activated by the time I reached the room. It held a powerful 'Transmogrification' spell which mutated several of my men into ogre-like creatures. I attacked, but their skin absorbed the magic on my blade, so I found myself unable to kill them. Instead, I sought to confine them in the smaller corridors where their size would be a disadvantage against a well-armed force."

"Your magic had no effect?"

"None Matriarch."

"How did you dispatch them?"

Xenis winced internally. He could see no way around this. "I could not. I was about to .."

The Matriarch held up her hand for silence. She looked most displeased. Not only had he triggered the trap but couldn't deal with the result. A double failure.

"Then how were they dispatched?" she asked, turning towards Valene.

"I suppose he did try." Valene sneered condescendingly. "But he was not equal to the task, and I had to intervene."

Xenis could see his mother considering his future, possibly one that included a great deal of pain, but then he had an idea, stepping forward, he inclined his head to speak. His mother gave him a cold hard stare and then relented with some reservation.

"We were fortunate, had my dear sister not enraged Briza of House Faerl'Zotreth, we might have not known about this threat until much later."

The Matriarch turned her head slowly towards Valene at this unwelcome news. Valene paled at her mother's penetrating stare. The temperature in the room dropped, the displeasure becoming almost palpable.

Xenis continued clearly enjoying this betrayal while at the same time disarming his sisters plan to get him punished or worse sacrificed. "I believe that her well-timed insults drove the priestess to trigger the trap earlier than previously planned. Thank the Goddess that we were the only house present. Who knows how well they concealed the trap? I expect they made it almost impossible to detect. They planned perhaps to let the spell lie dormant then activate it during a ceremony. Imagine what would have happened, representatives from every house dead. Such a catastrophe would destroy our house. As my Matriarch knows, no mere male could detect such a powerful well-concealed spell. I could never be equal to the task. Only a formidable priestess is equipped to find and disarm a trap of this magnitude. Fortunately for us, we had one available; all I had to do was find her."

Xenis loved the way he hinted that his lazy sister had not checked everything properly. To make matters more enjoyable, he told the truth as he saw it and the Matriarch understood. From her expression, albeit subtle, he knew she would let him off the hook. He smiled, disarmingly at his sister. There will be no sacrifice for you to enjoy today, he thought. Best of all she knew it and could do nothing. Yet he could tell she had something unpleasant planned for an unspecified future date. Still, he basked in the pleasure of the moment. Live for today for tomorrow he might die.

Chapter 10

Lars and Stefan

Lars woke with a sore shoulder and a splitting headache, which lasted only a few seconds. As his vision cleared, he sat up and looked around. The campsite appeared to be just the same as the night before. In the tent, across from the burnt-out fire, Stefan lay snoring his head off as usual. The roads, the lamps, and the foul-smelling creatures had all vanished. It must have been a dream, but it had seemed real.

He stood up, stretched, clicked his neck, and after walking over to the nasally vocal Stefan, he gave him a good kick. God help his wife if his friend ever got married; they would have to sleep in separate houses, not just separate beds. In fact, it would be better if she were stone deaf.

"Wake up Stefan; you're frightening the wargs."

Stefan snorted. "What? What wargs?" he slurred, "Where?"

He stumbled to his feet, only partially awake.

"I'm just kidding!" Lars grinned. "But honestly you were making enough noise to wake the dead."

Stefan stretched, yawned, and scratched his backside, before glaring at Lars.

"I had such a lovely dream. I could almost smell my Grandma's cooking," he said wistfully. "A whole side of roast lamb with herbs, crispy roast tubers, and fresh green beans, all smothered in rich, thick gravy."

"Sounds lovely, you hungry?"

"Yeah what's for breakfast?"

"Oats."

"Oats! What happened to the venison?"

"You ate it."

Stefan didn't remember eating that much.

"I only caught a small deer," Lars pointed out. "And we need to keep most of it for the journey or don't you remember what day it is?"

"I haven't forgotten; this better be worth it."

Lars hadn't seen his friend this grumpy in a while. "You're like a bear that fell on its head today."

With some reluctance, Stefan admitted. "I miss home," he said.

"More like you miss the cooking!"

"That too."

"Look you get the fire going and I'll make breakfast."

Later, as the oats began to simmer nicely, Lars spoke up, "I had the weirdest dream last night. I woke to find you missing, and I searched for you, but I got attacked by some strange creature."

"Nah, I'd have woken first and bashed its brains out."

Lars gave Stefan a dubious look. "Not the way you sleep! If you weren't snoring, people would think you were dead."

Stefan responded by throwing a wooden spoon at Lars who dodged and caught it. They both grinned at each other as they ladled out the oats and sat in silence eating their last breakfast this side of the plateaux.

After they had finished, Lars began to pack away the bedding, supplies, pots, and pans. Stefan went off to fill the skins with as much water as they could carry and set the fish traps. He'd already packed his tools although some unnecessary items were going to stay at the camp. As Stefan worked, he began to dread the climb and typically, Lars tried and failed to take his mind off it.

"Yeah, it's true, you've got more in common with an ox than a squirrel, and when did you last see an ox up a tree?"

Stefan rolled his eyes and raised a fist. "You may be a squirrel, but if you don't shut up this ox will squash you flat."

Lars just grinned and skittered out of the way. For all their banter, he actually felt as nervous as Stefan did.

Once they finished packing Stefan winched Lars up to the top of the cliff and afterwards, all the bags and most importantly the water. When he had removed the items, Lars jerked the rope to indicate to his friend that he could begin the climb.

With a big puff, Stefan let out a sigh and tied the rope around his waist. Lars held the line, but he had also attached the other end to a stake. Stefan wondered if he fell, whether it would stay fastened or if both he, Lars, and that stake, would plummet down the cliff.

Yet he couldn't put it off any longer, so he reached out and gripped the first sandstone block. At first, the climb didn't seem too bad, but as he began to tire and sweat, his hands became slippery. More than once, Stefan nearly lost his grip, and then only fear and his strength came to the rescue. At the top, Lars hauled on the rope and quickly wound it around the stake, reducing the slack. He knew if Stefan fell, the rope would run through his hands, even though he wore leather gloves. The stake, he hoped, would take most of the strain.

Near the top, Stefan entered the worst stage of the climb. Here the rock looked weathered and each handhold felt equally unsound. He had trouble choosing, but in the end, driven by impending exhaustion, Stefan just picked the nearest option. Almost immediately, he felt it tip beneath his weight, throwing him backwards. He kept his feet on the rock face, but his arms dangled uselessly in mid-air. Lars felt the sudden load slam down the length of the rope, almost jolting his shoulders out of their sockets. He gripped the line tightly, but it still ran through his gloves as the weight pulled him forwards. His feet dragged deep furrows in the sand before the remaining slack halted with a bang. Behind him, however, the stake held tight.

"Stefan! You ok?"

He listened and then heard a muffled reply coming from below the edge. "What the hell do you think? Get me up this cliff!"

Lars grinned in relief and bracing himself, started to pull. He might be stronger than he looked, but Stefan felt unbelievably heavy as he dangled on the end of the line. Besides, he had one more worry. If the rope rubbed against the cliff, it might break. After a few minutes of intense exertion, he felt some of the weight drop off. The sudden slack made him panic, but then Lars saw the top of his friend's head as he cleared the edge of the cliff. Stefan scrabbled on the broken rock and then faltered.

"I can't get up."

"Stay there!"

"Where else would I go?" asked Stefan, his voice oozing sarcasm.

Lars twisted the rope tightly around the stake then ran to help. He grabbed the back of his friend's shirt and hauled Stefan over the edge.

The big man puffed and scrambled, before rolling over onto the dirt where he lay panting.

"I never want to do that again, next time we build a rope ladder or something ok?" he said.

"Ok," Lars agreed in relief.

Both Stefan and Lars rested in the sun for some time before Stefan wiped the sweat from his brow.

"Damn, it's hot up here, have we brought enough water?" he said.

"Guess we'll find out," Lars said shrugging.

"Suppose we better put this cart together then?"

"Guess so."

Before they started, Lars rummaged through one of the packs and fished out some cloth. The boatmen had warned him that they would need head protection and now up here in the heat; he could only agree. Lars found it surprising how much the climate had changed from the valley below. From wet to dry, from woodland and bog to dust and scrub, although he realised if the river did not exist the valley would have been barren too. He knew that it hardly rained here, except for the occasional downpour, which could be very dangerous. Other than that, they faced biting sand storms, which could kill just as quickly.

By lunchtime, they had finished building. After putting everything on the cart, Lars felt impatient to go, but Stefan insisted they ate something before they moved. To avoid the sun's glare, they sat in the shade eating a few pickled sausages and some raw cloudberries, washed down with water. As soon as they finished, Lars pulled out his precious map and compass then laid it in front of the cart.

"We're here." He orientated the compass and map. "This way is north." He pointed. "Looking at the map, we will need to head that way until we hit the old road."

"Just so long as we don't go around in circles," Stefan replied dubiously, considering what he thought about Lars map reading skills.

"Hey, when have I ever led you wrong?"

Stefan grinned. "You want a list?"

Lars punched Stefan on the arm as his friend laughed.

"Hitch yourself up ox!"

"Pfft don't think you aren't going to help squirrel."

They had thought this through during the design phase. The two men couldn't have been more different. Their uneven height, strength, and bulk made it impossible to hitch their frames side by side, so they had gone for a design with one in front of the other. To begin with, Stefan took the front of the cart and pulled, while Lars pushed. After a few moments, the wheels overcame inertia and began to rattle over the uneven stony ground. Lars watched, wondering if Stefan had noticed he wasn't there, but as he waited, he realised that his friend had deliberately left him behind.

"Hey, wait up!"

He ran to catch up, only to find Stefan smirking at his arrival.

"Well if I'm not needed, I'll ride on top of the cart," said Lars.

"Over your dead body," growled Stefan as he kept walking.

Lars tilted his head, a little confused. "Hey that isn't right, shouldn't you have said 'over my dead body'?"

"No, I got it right the first time."

The cart slowed and wobbled on the stony ground.

"Get yourself hitched squirrel."

Lars sighed as he trotted around to the front and hitched himself, once attached, he pulled, and the cart leapt forward with a jerk.

"See you did need me."

Stefan replied with a 'Humph' as they rattled off across the desert.

In the heat of the day, they trudged forwards, step after laborious step until they could stand it no more. They stopped, ate their food in weary silence, with only one thing on their mind. Would they survive until morning?

After eating, they prepared for the night ahead. First, Stefan got under the waggon and brought down a hinged flap along the width of the cart. Next, he pulled down two grooved side flaps, which ran along the length and fastened them securely onto the width. At the base of all three, ran another groove into which Stefan slid a longboard, supported underneath to form the bottom of the crate. For the outer protection, he brought down three shutters from the sides of the cart. Once down, they touched the ground. Now Lars smaller frame came in handy. Someone had to squeeze down between the crate and the shutters to fasten the bolts. Both he and Lars would be able to slide into the box, bring the final screen down behind them, lock it from the inside, and then close the end of the wooden crate itself, which they could latch. The shutters didn't need any ventilation, but the box did. At both ends, Stefan had cut small holes, which allowed air to circulate. That left just enough room for two people to sleep.

They stood back and considered Stefan's handy work. A tumbler would need to attack from the side, get its tendril through the gap by the axles, bend around to the ends of the crate and in through the holes. It would be tough even for the most flexible creature, but reports from the plateaux were sketchy at best, so they should consider anything possible.

The sun had begun to sink below the horizon as Lars and Stefan slid themselves into the wooden crate. After securing the shutter, and finally locking the end of what Lars thought of as their coffin, they settled down. Two men cramped in a tight space isn't a recipe for a good night, especially if Stefan did his usual and snored. Yet even after a tough day, neither of them felt tired, just anxious.

To lighten the mood Lars joked. "For god's sake, don't fart in here. It could kill us both!"

Stefan smiled weakly but didn't reply. Lars sensed that his friend did not like the enclosed space, not that he relished it either.

They both waited nervously, their ears straining for any noise, but when nothing happened, they began to relax. Stefan had started to doze and snore when a slight scratching sound alerted them to the presence of a creature. What sort, remained a mystery, for shortly afterwards the noise faded into the distance.

"I don't think we should have lit a fire," whispered Lars. "Perhaps it's the embers that drew it here?"

"More likely, our smell."

"Don't you mean your smell?"

Lars grinned in the dark. Even in situations like this, he could hardly resist a dig at his easy-going friend.

"Humph."

Lars smiled at his friend's usual reply.

Not long afterwards, they heard another noise, it sounded like something investigating the camp, but then suddenly it left. Stefan thought that didn't bode well. What could have scared it away? They soon found out, as a rattling clatter, echoed through the wood. First, they could only hear one, but then more joined, scratching at the shutters as if searching for a way in.

They listened, and Stefan finally whispered to Lars. "If we don't make it through this," he said.

His friend never finished what he had been about to say, but Lars could guess. He interrupted, although he thought the same thing, he would *never* have said so.

Instead, he whispered back, "We will, you're a great carpenter, this will work."

Their voices only encouraged the things outside to redouble their efforts, so both men kept silent from then on. Yet it remained a mystery how the tumblers still sensed them. The constant scrabbling seemed to go on forever. The friends kept quiet, tense, but ready, just in case something broke through, but as time stretched, it became apparent that Stefan's design worked and that they were safe. As night finally turned to daytime and light began to filter through the air holes, as quickly as it had started, the noise ceased.

Chapter 11

Glen and Cody

The sun streamed through a gap in the curtains. Glen groaned and turned over. He'd been trying to sleep, but a voice in the other room made it impossible. He sighed, staggered upright, and wandered into the living room. Still half-asleep, it took a few seconds to register that the voice came from the TV, some history program about CERN. The presenter interviewed a scientist. Back in 2008, the media raised concerns that during experiments, micro black holes might form and grow. The scientist laughed and predicted it as a one in fifty million chance, so nothing had happened. Instead, they discovered new particles not seen since the Big Bang. Glen yawned, indifferent. Ancient not modern history interested him, so he switched off the TV.

"Cody?" he called out.

He waited but heard no reply, so he knocked on his friend's bedroom door.

"Cody, are you there, mate?"

He listened, but when nothing happened, he checked outside. Light blasted his face with eye-watering brightness. For a second, he blinked until the landscape came into focus. Cody's truck had gone. Glen shrugged. His friend had probably gone out for groceries. With relief, he closed the door and slouched off to make a cup of tea.

As he waited, Glen felt a stab of nostalgia for mild, wet England. Who'd have thought it? Something he never missed, before living in Arizona.

After the death of his parents, he'd been directionless until he'd gone to Comic-Con. That's where he'd met Cody. They were polar opposites. Glen was British, tall, skinny with a mop of brown hair, blue eyes and had skin so white some called it translucent. Cody was part Navajo, lean and fit with long black hair, dark skin, and eyes.

Cody had gone to MIT while Glen studied Ancient History. His friend came across as so geeky that Glen could easily imagine him dropping from his mother's womb complaining about the design and the need for an upgrade. Glen worked in a call centre while Cody made money as an ethical hacker. He also loved conspiracy theories, but Glen thought that Governments and corporations just tried to ignore anything inconvenient. He didn't expect them to be truthful, but he couldn't imagine they followed a single world plan. Cody, however, insisted he knew the truth. Like some digital superhero, he stood tall and proud against their tyranny. Glen found that image somewhat marred by the ketchup stains on his friend's T-shirt. Even though they disagreed on almost everything, they became friends chatting about their favourite graphic novels, so when Comic-Con ended, Cody invited Glen to stay. Now he lived in his eccentric friends' trailer surrounded by computers and outside, the desert.

Something out of place brought him back to reality from down memory lane, a post-it note on the fridge. He read it, shook his head, and re-read it just to make sure.

"He's dead, gone to investigate?" Glen read aloud.

His friend had run off like some geeky version of Miss Marple to solve something that would turn out mundane and not a mystery. Even as he thought this, he heard the sound of a truck breaking noisily in the dirt outside. Cody darted into the trailer and began pulling down the blinds, cutting out most of the light.

Glen stood bemused. "Err hi, where have you been?"

Cody crouched down and peered out through a slit in a blind.

"Shhh get down," he said. "They might be watching."

Glen sighed and asked, even though he could guess the answer, "Who might be watching?"

"The government, haven't you listened to anything I told you?" said Cody all the time keeping a firm eye out for any government agents approaching the trailer.

Glen realised that this might take a while, so he sat down on the couch and decided to go along with it. "What happened?"

Cody turned, assured that they were safe for a moment, and sat with his back to the wall.

"She found his dog wandering hungry and thirsty, you know he never goes anywhere without it," he said.

Actually, he didn't so Glen just looked confused.

"Whose dog," he said.

"Mr Johnson's dog," said Cody, slightly exasperated. "She went up to his shack and found him dead, so she reported it. Now he's gone to investigate."

"Wait a second, who's he, who's she?"

Cody beamed. "The sheriff and Sarah," but then he frowned. "Are you sure you want to get involved? It could be dangerous."

Glen leaned forward, keeping a straight face. "Well I'm involved already aren't I just because I know you?"

Cody nodded. "True, I guess. Alright, then I'll tell you everything once I've secured the site."

First, he checked around the perimeter of the caravan by peeking out of each blind and scanning the horizon for operatives. Once he had made the 360-degree circuit, confirming an all clear, he switched on the TV to cover their voices.

"It's the best I can do at short notice," he said before dragging Glen to sit on the floor. "Do you remember last night?"

Glen shrugged his mind a blank. He couldn't remember anything specific.

"Well, it might have been after you went to bed." Cody tipped his head and reconsidered, after a moment he added, "Ok well a long time after you went to bed. I came across a tweet from Sarah Bard."

"Ok"

"'Omg I've just found a body! I'm going to the sheriff's office to report it.' It sounded interesting, so I looked around and found her blog. She's studying local flora and fauna for her PhD, something about the difference in elevation, preventing them from mixing with other ecosystems. It all seemed rather dull to me."

Glen shrugged if it didn't have chipsets Cody didn't find it interesting.

"I read all the usual stuff about plants then she went on to say that, she had found a dog wandering on its own. Its tag said it belonged to Mr Johnson at Outcrop House, but and this is the weird bit." Cody gave Glen a meaningful look. "When she took the dog back, she found the old man lying on the floor, in a locked room. Sarah thought he might be dead."

Glen frowned unimpressed. "You got that from the blog?"

"Some of it but not everything," said Cody then grinned. "I found her this morning, locked in the county jail."

"They arrested her?"

"They made a mistake." Cody looked smug. "But I got to talk to her. I set off a smoke bomb behind the store and distracted the deputy. What she said won't be in any official report."

"You did *what*?"

"Don't worry no one saw me."

"Except eyes in the sky?"

Cody grimaced. Glen had a point.

"Never mind it's too late now. Anyway, this is what I found out." Cody paused for dramatic effect. "Puncture marks covered the body."

Glen almost rolled his eyes, but he smiled and suggested, "Not vampires surely?"

For a second Cody looked thoughtful, then he realised that Glen wasn't taking him seriously.

His face clouded over. "Hey, don't mock! It could be, you don't know what goes on, could be anything. If you don't believe me, let's go and see her, if they let her out."

"What do you mean if they let her out?"

"The deputy locked her up, but she said it might be ok when the sheriff got back. If not, then it's up to us to prove her innocence."

Chapter 12

Thomas and Raphael

His head hurt, but it faded almost as if it had never happened, then Thomas remembered the park and that man. He never wanted to go back there again. He stifled a sob. His dad always told him not to cry and be a man. Thomas felt his fear fade as he pictured his father waiting for him by the kitchen door, the belt wound around his hand. He felt a surge of anger. Let him stay there forever; he wouldn't come back. A tinge of sadness replaced the anger. He hadn't died and gone to heaven.

Since Master Raphael could not locate Thomas, Tinnueth went to find Aeglas. She ran back to the boy's hiding place and called out. After a few minutes, Aeglas jogged over the mossy ground towards her.
"Any luck?"
"None."
"Strange."
"What should we do now?"
Aeglas shrugged. "Go back home and wait."
As they both turned to leave, they heard a sound followed by a sob. Tinnueth turned and ran towards the sound. Not far away, she found the boy. He sat hugging his knees, staring intently into the distance.
Tinnueth bent down and saw that something had frightened him. "Thomas, are you alright?"
A voice like smooth silk made him look up. He saw concern mirrored in a set of perfect blue eyes. He nodded, still feeling a mixture of anger and sadness, but she must have sensed his inner turmoil because she held out her arms, offering comfort. For a moment, Thomas hesitated, not wanting to seem like a child. Yet when she tilted

her head in understanding, he relented and hugged her. Warm and soft, he held her tightly as her presence soothed him. Thomas sighed and relaxed. He could smell Jasmin in her hair. In that moment, he felt complete contentment. She would always be there for him. Thomas looked up to see the golden leaves rustling in the breeze. He smiled. Just like her, this wood was perfect.

She felt the boy relax, so she pulled back a little to look at him. "Thomas. Do you want to talk about it?
He shook his head.
"Perhaps later?"
He shrugged.
She tried another approach. "Are you hungry?"
Thomas considered her question. He had eaten a while ago, so he nodded. They joined Aeglas, and together they walked towards the town. This time Thomas studied the diverted river that flowed around the village in a wide trench. So clear, it seemed shallow, but as he leaned over, he realised that it dropped deeply down onto a gravel bed. The water looked so enticing that he wanted to jump in, except for one thing, the sheer sides would make it difficult to get out. From the opposite edge, the bank rose steeply but then flattened out into a shallow incline on which grew the great trees. After looking both ways, he realised he couldn't see a bridge or another way across. A moment later, he understood as Tinnueth muttered a word. This time a rope and not a ladder snaked down from the canopy above. It had a single loop at the end and no rungs. Tinnueth put her foot into the coil and indicated to Thomas that he should do the same, and then she showed him how to wind the rope around his body. The cord seemed to hold him almost as if it had a mind of its own.
"Hold on tight."
They ascended rapidly only to stop when they reached a small balcony. Aeglas helped Thomas climb out of the rope, albeit a little awkwardly, while Tinnueth gracefully alighted onto the wooden ledge behind him. Together they strolled slowly along the walkway as Thomas gawked in all directions. Last time it had been too much to take in, but now, he realised that someone hadn't built the town. Instead of planks held together by nails and screws, the trees looked

as if someone had persuaded them to grow into walkways, railings, rooms, and even stairs. Coloured canvas painted with birds and animals shielded the balconies and open spaces. The pictures looked so real that Thomas expected them to fly away when he tried to touch them.

Below the great trees, grew all manner of plants, covered in an abundance of fruit and vegetables. Some grew in dense mats while others wound their way up the trunks. In between the patches, Thomas could see distant figures walking on narrow paths tending the plants.

When they arrived at the feasting hall, Aeglas went to find Raphael, but it took a while before they returned. The boy had managed to eat several plates of food, a feat that quite impressed the elves.

Raphael sat down and stared at the boy as he waited for him to finish. "Thomas?"

The boy looked up. "Yes?"

"Do you remember how you left us?"

The boy nodded.

"And how you returned?"

Thomas thought about that and shrugged.

"Can you tell me?"

"I think I fell asleep then I woke up in the park."

He stopped as the frightening memory re-surfaced. "When I got home, my dad was angry, so I ran away. Then some creep pushed me over, and I hit my head," he said, then paused. "But I'm ok now."

Raphael nodded. "And that's when you found yourself back here?"

"Yes."

"Thank you for answering my questions, Thomas."

The boy smiled and managed to eat a little more even though he felt full to bursting.

Before the elf left, Thomas, who had been mulling over an idea while he ate, blurted, "Can I bring my friends here?"

Raphael smiled and considered the question carefully. "Are you able to bring them with you?"

Thomas frowned, feeling confused. "Am I allowed to?"

"If you can bring them with you, we will allow them to stay."

The boy looked happy for a moment, then frowned. "But I don't know how."

Raphael just nodded and turned away. His smile faded as he left the room. If his suspicions proved correct, history could repeat itself.

Thomas pondered that question. How would he bring his friends here? If he told them the truth, they might not believe him. Yet if he went back home, he definitely couldn't explain everything to his mum. She would just tell his dad, and he would never understand. To make matters worse, the supposed lie would only make his dad furious. Perhaps it was best to keep this place a secret. Thomas smiled. He liked that idea. It made him feel special.

He looked up at Aeglas. "Can I explore again?"

Aeglas shrugged, wondering if the boy would vanish like last time, but Thomas didn't let him say no. "Come on!"

Thomas jumped up and ran out of the room, almost knocking into another elf as he raced along the walkway. Aeglas followed as the boy bounded fearlessly from branch to branch. This new and sudden level of agility surprised the elf. Vanya had explained that the boy was human and therefore wouldn't move with such confidence. It took several hours for the boy to explore the upper reaches of the town and Aeglas had to stop him descending to the ground as dusk settled over the woodland.

"Tomorrow," he said when the boy objected.

Thomas scowled a little, and then his face lit up.

"Food?" he said.

Aeglas shook his head in wonder. The boy had a bottomless pit for a stomach, but he relented and took him to the feasting hall.

Tinnueth sat waiting for them, and she smiled when the boy tucked into yet another bowl of food, but she could tell that something troubled Aeglas.

"Did you enjoy your afternoon?"

"Yes," blurted Thomas with his mouth full.

Aeglas gave him a pointed look.

"Sorry," said Thomas after swallowing and then proceeded to tell Tinnueth about his daring exploits in the trees.

"You were able to jump from branch to branch?"

"Yes, it was easy!"

"You didn't fear that you might fall?"

"No, that would never happen."

Aeglas gave Tinnueth a look, a look that said, only elves have this type of confidence. He stared at the boy pondering what had happened. Perhaps Raphael would have some answers, but he wondered if the master magician would share them with anyone.

Once Thomas finished eating, he stood and asked to leave the table. He wandered out of the feasting hall and took a direct route across town. Tinnueth followed and found him sitting on a walkway, dangling his feet into thin air. At this height, he should be worried, but again Tinnueth noticed that he seemed quite fearless. Curious, she sat down and waited as they watched the sun sink below the horizon.

After some time, he spoke, "I don't want to go home."

She considered that statement and asked quietly, "Why is that?"

He didn't answer her, partly because he couldn't be entirely sure. After some thought he decided, it could be because of the bullies, his dad, or the grey boringness of life but that didn't include everything. He overlooked something important, something just out of reach.

He sighed a deep sigh for one so young and then turned to Tinnueth. "Will I have to go back?"

She shrugged. "Perhaps."

"If I do, will you wait for me?"

Tinnueth smiled. "I will always be here for you."

He moved closer and rested his head against her arm as a great warmth spread through his heart. At least he wouldn't be alone.

****

Chris woke with a snort and turned over as a twinge of pain shot through his back. Once again, he had fallen asleep on the couch, and Lynn hadn't bothered to wake him when she got back. With a groan, he staggered upright and stretched. Somewhere in the house, a clock chimed four, far too early to get up. After lurching down the corridor, he climbed the stairs to bed. Almost as an afterthought, he looked in on Thomas. He expected to find the boy sprawled across his bed, but instead, the room lay empty, the duvet still neatly made. Chris felt a moment of panic, and then a surge of annoyance quickly replaced by relief. The boy had run off and not come back. Perhaps he'd slept at a friend's house and not bothered to let them know.

He slouched into his own bedroom to see his wife curled up in bed. Her boss had called asking her to cover for absent staff. With their mounting debts, she could hardly say no to another shift. He had promised his tearful wife to keep looking for Thomas, but after finding him outside the kitchen door, his temper had got the better of him. Chris faltered as the feeling of relief, turned to guilt, and then dread. He would have to wake Lynn and tell her their son wasn't home and worse why. He had promised her those days were over.

Chris bent down and shook her gently. "Lynn," he whispered.

She stirred a little but then fell back into a deep sleep.

He shook her again, and she gradually roused.

"What?" she asked irritably.

"Lynn, Thomas isn't in his bed."

"What?"

She sat up, and even in the dim light, he could see fear mirrored in her pinched face.

"He didn't come back?"

Chris hesitated. She saw his reaction. "Oh, Chris, what did you do?"

Now on the defensive Chris glowered. "I caught him trying to sneak in through the kitchen door."

"And?"

"He didn't seem to care that he'd made you sick with worry."

Lynn's face-hardened. "What did you do?"

"Nothing, he ran off."

"If you did nothing, why did he run?"

Chris shrugged.

"Did you hit him?"

"No." He replied sullenly.

"Then what did you do?"

"I just undid my belt, as a threat."

"And you wonder why he ran."

An awkward silence followed before he scored a point.

"Well if you were so worried about our son, why didn't you check in on him when you got home?"

A guilty look spread across her face. Almost zombie like when she came home, she had climbed the stairs and fallen into bed without thinking.

"Well, you promised to look for him, but instead you drove him away," said Lynn.

She stifled a sob, but then pulled herself together. "Well, I'll ring his friends while you go and look for him first in the back garden and then in the park."

Chris glowered at her. He didn't like his wife giving orders.

"If we can't find him," she said and then broke off. "We should ring the police."

Chapter 13

Sarah

The morning sunshine streamed through the window, bathing her face with the light. Sarah groaned and rolled over. She had slept, albeit poorly on the uncomfortable bed. The dusty hard mattress felt unused in a town where crime rarely happened. Every muscle ached when she sat up as if a personal trainer had put her through the wringer. Something she had tried a few years back and vowed never to repeat.

"You can be any shape you want," he'd said. "As long as you are willing to put in the effort."

After that, she had decided she wanted to be short and slightly dumpy, which required no effort at all. Now though, she would have given her right arm for a shower, a fresh change of clothes, and above all some toothpaste. Her mouth tasted horrible, and she felt dishevelled. To make matters worse, an enticing smell of fresh coffee wafted into her cell.

Deputy Barnett sat at his desk, drinking from a large cup. He looked as fresh as a daisy, whereas she looked like something rolling around at the bottom of a mouse cage. A sense of loathing engulfed her, but she tried to suppress the emotion in the hope that she might get breakfast.

"Err morning, any chance of a coffee?"

He didn't reply, so Sarah repeated it louder this time. He just hunched his shoulders and ignored her, obviously still irritated by her behaviour the night before. She felt her indignation intensify.

"Ah come on I'm thirsty!"

The deputy stood reluctantly, went over to the water cooler, poured a cup, and brought it to her without a word. At first, she drank gratefully, gulping it down as he walked away but then realised that he did not intend to bring her anything else.

"Is that it? What about breakfast?"

As if to emphasise this comment, her stomach rumbled loudly, but Hank looked at her without replying.

"Hey you can't just ignore me, what about my rights?"

He shrugged and went back to his work, infuriating Sarah to bursting point. She didn't care if she annoyed him. Sarah grabbed the bars and tried to rattle them.

"This is inhumane! A prisoner has rights you know, the right to food and drink, and that's more than half a cup of water every so often. In fact, my human rights are part of the constitution. Do you know what they are?" She didn't wait for his reply. "It's the right not to be imprisoned without charge, hey you heard me, you locked me in here, but you haven't charged me with anything. Where's your evidence? I have a right to due process! Then you have my stuff, I have the right to personal property, and if that wasn't enough, I have the right to food, drink, and the right to bathe."

Now that she thought about it, she felt a definite desire to pee. How could she be so thirsty and yet need to go? It just didn't make sense.

"No access to the restroom, that's a cruel and unusual punishment, and for what? I've done nothing wrong, and this is tantamount to torture. When I get out, I'll make you regret this! Let me out now!"

He snorted. "Are you finished yet? If you've got enough energy to yell like that, then you can't be that hungry." He relented a little at her expression. "Behave, and I'll let you go to the restroom."

Sarah almost screamed with frustration, but she bit her tongue.

"Fine," she said through gritted teeth, so he let her out.

A few minutes later, she emerged from the restroom feeling somewhat fresher than before. "Can I at least have some food and my phone back?"

"Don't have any food here, but you can have another cup of water."

Sarah accepted the offer although she sulked when he wouldn't give back her phone. She wondered if anyone had missed her. By this time each morning, she would be tweeting, blogging, posting on Instagram and generally messaging. Surely, someone would notice that she hadn't done that since yesterday.

A knock on the outer door interrupted her deliberations. The man from the store strolled in and put a paper, plus a breakfast bagel on the desk.

Stan smiled and nodded. "Morning Hank, hear you've got a dangerous criminal locked up."

Dangerous criminal, Sarah nearly skyrocketed. "I'm innocent and illegally detained!" she shouted through the bars.

Stan turned and backed off smartly when he saw her angry face.

"Quieten down," yelled the deputy. He turned to Stan. "This is police business, nothing for you to worry about."

Stan however didn't look like he would take that advice. In fact, his face crinkled in worry as he stammered his apologies and made a quick escape.

"You're going to have to let me out sooner or later," snarled Sarah.

"I'll let the sheriff decide that."

Sarah raged. This stupid deputy could ruin her reputation. Her name would be mud in this town. No one would trust her anymore, and then a thought occurred to her. Oh my god, what if the university found out? Would they believe the lies? Would they terminate her studies? Would they end her PhD and then her career before it even started? The realisation struck home, and she sat down trembling. The deputy took this as a good sign. He stood thinking through a new line of questioning when Sheriff Miller came in, dusty and tired.

He scanned past the cell. At first, it didn't register, and then he stopped, shook his head, and finally groaned.

"What the hell is she doing in there?"

The deputy grinned. "I've kept her safe just like you said, figured she couldn't leave town this way."

The sheriff stood, hands on hips, shaking his head in mute frustration for over a minute before he finally exploded.

"Hank Barnett, you damned numpty!"

The deputy looked shocked.

"When I said, don't let her leave town, I didn't mean lock her up!"

"But she kicked me."

"I don't care if she pinched your butt and slapped you around the face, you don't lock people up without a good reason. Now give me the keys!"

The deputy fumbled with the tangled bunch and tried to hand them over but the sheriff, by now so exasperated by his subordinate, didn't wait. He snatched the keys, went over to the cell, and unlocked it.

"Sorry about this miss. I hope you don't take this poor treatment to heart. He didn't mean anything by it."

Sarah, however, did not feel in the mood to forgive and forget.

"Nothing by it? Nothing by it? He took away my phone as he shoved me into this cell, and then he locked me up without charge."

Her stomach took the opportunity to rumble. "I've been denied my basic rights. No food, only water and I had to beg to go to the restroom."

Sheriff Miller looked extremely worried. This could be worse than he thought.

"Then to top it all Stan came in and accused me of being a dangerous criminal. My reputation is in tatters! If my university finds out, I could lose my place. I have every right to sue you, and I would win." She jabbed her finger at Deputy Barnett and then at Sheriff Miller. "It would ruin your reputations, and you'd lose your jobs. It would be the end of you both."

The sheriff shook his head in dismay. "Miss Bard, I am very sorry." He turned to his deputy. "Now get her a coffee!"

He gently took her arm. "Please sit down. Can't we discuss this?"

"What's there to discuss? He ignored my human rights, and you know it."

The deputy brought her a coffee. "Milk? Sugar?"

Sarah shook her head.

Sheriff Miller glowered at his subordinate. "Now go get her a bagel." He turned to Sarah. "Anything else you want? It's on us, of course."

Sarah felt too tired and hungry to think for a moment, so she just replied, "Anything is good, I'm starving."

Hank nodded and then dashed out of the room, glad to be out of the way.

The sheriff turned back to Sarah and leaned forward. "You have every right to feel abused. I know Hank isn't the sharpest knife in the drawer and if you want to press charges, I'd understand." He hesitated. "But if we can find another way to make it up to you, we will."

Sarah considered his offer in silence. A few minutes later, the deputy turned up with a bundle of food in his arms.

"I didn't know what you liked so I got all sorts of stuff," he said fumbling the items on to the desk. "Take what you want."

Hank stood up and smiled awkwardly, a worried but hopeful look on his handsome face.

Sarah mentally groaned. Hank had the look of a puppy caught next to a big pile of poo on the carpet but still hoped that its owner would forgive it because it looked cute. She felt herself weaken. Perhaps she could use this to her advantage, as long as the sheriff and his deputy agreed to clear up some of the mess.

Sarah sighed and then picked up a cream cheese bagel. The two men waited in awkward silence as she ate. Once she had finished that and her coffee, she started to feel a bit better. Over a blueberry muffin, she formulated her response. Sarah considered her reputation tarnished. The university would have a head fit if they found out. Other than that, Hank would need to clear her name around town, although she knew that some people wouldn't believe it. Perhaps a show of forgiveness would work in her favour.

As Sarah sighed again, both men looked increasingly worried. "Ok, I won't press charges." They smiled and looked relieved. "But and I stress this, you'll need to make amends. I have two conditions."

"Ok, what can we do?" asked Sheriff Miller.

"First, I need your deputy to clear my name. Stan speaks to everyone who comes into the store. Hank here needs to tell Stan and anyone he meets the truth. He will need to say that I'm not pressing charges over this wrongful arrest. It was all a terrible misunderstanding brought about by bad communication and stress."

The statement contained enough truth to be believable, but also it meant the deputy would have to eat humble pie, and in its own way, that felt quite satisfying.

"I could ask for a written apology, but I think it best that we keep paperwork out of this." She looked up at Hank. "Have you done any paperwork?"

Hank shook his head as the sheriff rolled his eyes. Clearly, paperwork was not his deputies' strong point.

"Then and this is my second condition, that I am kept in the loop over Mr Johnson's death."

Sheriff Miller looked surprised and a bit dubious.

"I've been accused of all sorts by him," she said, looking at Hank. "The very least you can do is tell me the truth."

That way, she could keep Cody up to date, and it would satisfy her abundant curiosity.

The sheriff hesitated and then leaned forward. "Look I shouldn't be telling you any of this, but if you agree not to press charges, we'll keep you in the loop, agreed."

Sarah leaned forward. "Agreed."

Sheriff Miller didn't exactly feel happy but if he could avoid a lawsuit, he would, and fortunately, for once his deputy's inability to file any paperwork had come in handy.

"Ok, this is what happened."

Sarah listened as the sheriff recounted events.

After calling the local doctor, he'd gone up to the outcrop the night before last. Just as she said, he'd found the dog, waiting on the porch, which he put in his truck. After a brief look around the outside of the house and environs, he decided that nothing seemed to be amiss. Yet he found the front door locked. When he shone his torch through the window, he saw Mr Johnson lying on the floor, apparently dead. Not wanting to break down the door and destroy any evidence, he went to where he could get a signal and called the county sheriff's office and local CSI. While he waited for them to arrive, the sheriff made a few phone calls to anyone who might have last seen Ben.

A little later, everyone showed up along with a few unwelcome onlookers, which the county sheriff ushered away. Those with permission to stay took a good look at the site and then the body. Yet something odd happened. After the doctor confirmed that Mr Johnson was dead, the sheriff noticed some odd behaviour. The CSI had rechecked everything twice, apparently confused and then chatted in a low voice with those in charge. After that, no one had given much away. The crime scene, if they decided that one existed, showed some inconsistent results. The CSI used the word anomalous because nothing made sense. He could not determine the exact time of death because the evidence conflicted. No one could decide what had happened. With no evidence of murder but no clear-cut proof of natural causes, they'd taken the body away for a full autopsy.

Sarah sighed, at least that backed up most of what she had already said.

It had been late when they finally left, so the sheriff took Rufus home. He gave the dog to a neighbour who said she would be happy to look after it for a while.

The sheriff said, "I don't believe you had anything to do with the death of Mr Johnson but…" He looked apprehensive. "I have to ask. Where were you Thursday night to Friday morning?"

Sarah narrowed her eyes. "I thought you said the CSI couldn't determine the exact time of death.

"True, but given the fact that Mrs Edward chatted with Ben that afternoon and that he didn't turn up for his usual meal at Sam's diner on Friday, the time frame had to be somewhere between those two meetings."

Sarah thought back. "Thursday evening, I had a snack at Sam's, and then I went home to watch TV. I went to bed around 10.30pm. Friday morning, I filled up with gas at Sam's then went out to check my cameras. I downloaded information from each and then moved onto the next. I can provide you with their time stamps."

Sheriff Miller nodded. "Thank you. I appreciate your help. Enquiries are ongoing, so with any luck, we will find out the truth. Once again, I want to say how sorry we both are for our mistakes and that you are free to go."

Hank mumbled an apology too and handed back her belongings.

Sarah gave him a haughty look before accepting them. "Don't forget what I said. I will check to see if everyone knows the truth."

The deputy hung his head. In this small community, he knew it would get around that he had made a mistake. The town's folk would laugh and mock him for a while.

With that, she left the office and replied to Cody's messages as she walked towards her truck.

Chapter 14

Lars and Stefan

The noise stopped. Light filtered through the air holes. Morning had come, and they still lived. Stefan waited, reluctant to leave the cart. It might be a trap.

Lars grew impatient. "I doubt the tumblers are smart enough for that sort of tactic."

Stefan turned to him. "Do you really want to find out the hard way?"

Lars shrugged. His friend made a good point, but in the end, his bladder clinched the argument.

"We can't stay here all day," he said.

Stefan sighed and shook his head emphatically. Lars quietly unbolted the inner box, then stopped and listened. When he heard nothing, he grabbed the shutter and unlocked it. With Stefan's help, he opened up a small crack. The bright morning sun streamed in, but outside, nothing stirred.

"I think it's safe," whispered Lars.

"Then why are you whispering?" asked Stefan with a grin.

Lars made a face at Stefan as they both hauled the shutter fully open and emerged into the sunlight. Stefan sighed with satisfaction as he immediately relieved himself in the nearby bushes, while Lars did the same. Afterwards, he checked the cart and its condition while Lars examined the surrounding area. The creatures had spread the blackened remains of the campfire over a wide area. Beyond, long sinuous tracks led away into the brush. He followed, counting them as he walked and then stood thinking. It looked as if eight had attacked the cart last night. Only eight made that terrible noise and scared them half to death. What if more came tonight?

"Hey, Stefan, what's the cart like after last night?" he called out.

"Not as bad as I had expected. I chose hardwood instead of softwood, good thing too because if I hadn't, I don't think we'd have made it through the night. Look here."

As Lars wandered over, Stefan pointed at the scratches in the surface. Some looked deep enough to qualify as gouges.

Lars frowned, concerned by the damage. "Do you think this will last the trip?"

Stefan pondered before replying with a long drawn out, "Mm, well Yes."

"You don't sound too sure."

"Well, we will have to see. I can cannibalise parts of the cart to make repairs if necessary. Shame we don't have metal to make the shutters."

"Well if we get lucky, we should find plenty."

"*If* we get lucky."

Lars rolled his eyes and shook his head. "Always the optimist."

They were just about to argue when Stefan's stomach interrupted with a noise like a badly blocked drain. They both stared at his belly in mild horror.

"Cor, I'm starving!" he said.

"What a noise! Well if nothing else we could use your stomach to frighten them away."

"Or we could use you as bait squirrel." Stefan gave an evil grin

"Yeah right," Lars smirked.

Breakfast consisted of oats with chopped venison sausages and a few wild onions. They needed something substantial for the journey ahead after the exhausting day yesterday, followed by the lack of sleep last night. Once they completed breakfast, they packed, hitched the cart, and then followed the compass point in the same direction as yesterday.

After a couple of hours of hard slog, Lars yelled in excitement. "I think I see it!"

"See what?"

"The old road. It means we are on the right track. No pun intended." He grinned.

Stefan rolled his eyes and shook his head.

After a few minutes more, they came to the edge of the road. The lads unhitched themselves, and while Stefan rested, Lars marked the spot with a pile of stones before going across to examine the road. He stood staring at it, astounded. It looked the same black colour as the one in his dream although when Lars bent down, it felt sticky and crumbly unlike the other. He looked along its length and saw something odd. The road appeared to bend and crumple, shifting, and twisting as he watched.

"Hey take a look at this."

Stefan groaned, stood up, and came over. "What?"

"Look along the road."

"Yeah, it's a heat haze."

Lars looked surprised. His friend knew something he didn't. "What's a heat haze?"

"It's when the sun reflects heat off a surface and warms the air unevenly above it so that it distorts your vision."

True enough, when Lars peered at the air above the road, it shimmered and danced in the heat. "How did you know that?"

"A travelling teacher visited the village a while back."

Another thing he had missed while indentured thought Lars sourly.

"Let's get going."

Without a word, they went back to the cart, hitched up and tried to pull it onto the road. The men found the crumbling edge awkward to mount but eventually, after several tries; they rolled forwards. After that, it became easy going, well easier than before anyway. The road had some big potholes, which they tried to avoid and they found that the edge tended to crumble if they got too close. Other than that, they just went around or through any plants growing in the loose surface and then over minor lumps and bumps.

As they travelled, Lars considered last night. Like the streets in his dream, someone had built this road. Sure, it looked older and worn, but it couldn't be a coincidence. He wondered if he had dreamt about the past.

After a while, they pulled off the road and stopped for lunch. Lars looked at the soles of his boots and wrinkled his nose. The black sticky substance coated everything. Stefan examined the cart and sighed at the state of the wheels.

"We'll have to leave our boots outside tonight," said Stefan. "I don't think I can stand the smell."

"Now you know how I always feel about your shoes."

Lars smirked, and Stefan replied by punching his arm. It took a few moments for the feeling to return. When they hitched up, Lars pretended that it hurt too much for him to help. Stefan didn't believe him for a minute.

That afternoon they made excellent time. For the most part, the road remained flat although the occasional small hill did cause a problem. After the first rise where they had struggled to get to the top, Stefan suggested another tactic. Lars stayed hitched while Stefan pushed to get a good run-up. The plan worked. The momentum carried them almost to the top. Only the last few feet required a massive push from Stefan as Lars strained in the harness. After the third hillock, both men sagged, utterly knackered. Neither could stand another hill, so they stopped and camped for the night. After a decent dinner, they packed up, got the crate ready, and settled down this time to sleep. They stayed in their clothes but left their boots on top of the cart. The tops covered by a set of socks, an old trick to keep out the indigenous wildlife. This time when night fell, they felt more relaxed knowing that Stefan's design worked. Not even Stefan's snoring could keep Lars awake as the tumblers scrabbled ineffectually outside.

Chapter 15

Thomas

At first light, Chris searched the park but returned home when he couldn't find his son. His wife, distraught to the point of hysterics, finally rang the police. In response, they sent two police officers' round to their house and took a statement. She told them that her son's friends had not seen him recently and that after a thorough search of the park, her husband could not find him. Lynn decided not to mention the confrontation between Chris and Thomas or the argument later, but this didn't fool the officers. They had enough experience to know when someone withheld vital information. At the end of the interview, they asked both Mr and Mrs Harvey to bring some information and a selection of recent photographs down to the station. Once there, they split the couple up and questioned them further. It didn't take long for Lynn to break down and confess the truth. The truth that Chris confronted Thomas just before the boy ran away.

She sat crying, her head in her hands as the policewoman waited patiently.

Through gulps, Lynn spoke, "He said… he… didn't hit him."

"Do you believe him?"

The policewoman noted the mother's hesitation.

"Yes."

"Has he hit Thomas before?"

Lynn began to cry harder and then nodded.

"Does he hit you?"

This time, she emphatically shook her head.

"Just Thomas?"

Lynn nodded.

"Thank you for being honest, Mrs Harvey."

She leaned over and whispered something to the other detective in the room before turning back to the suspect. "Can we get anything for you, Mrs Harvey, a cup of water perhaps?"

Lynn nodded.

The other detective stood up and left.

In the other room, Chris sat straight in his chair, his arms folded. They'd asked him about his son, his friends, how he got on at school and about family life.

A knock on the door called away one of the detectives, who returned a few minutes later.

The man sat down in front of him, shuffled some papers, and then dropped the bombshell. "Do you hit your son?"

Chris stiffened, trapped by the question.

The detective looked up and waited for a reply.

Chris scowled. "Sometimes, the lad needs discipline."

"And how do you discipline him?"

"What do you mean?"

"Do you punch him?"

Chris rocked back in his chair. "No, never."

"Then what do you do?"

"I believe in good old-fashioned punishment."

"Such as?"

Chris felt his face flush scarlet. Somehow, when he spoke openly about his actions, it didn't seem quite as right. "I use my belt."

"You beat him with it?"

"No, I don't beat him. Sometimes I slapped him across his palm or legs."

"Right."

They didn't believe him.

Chris leaned forward. "When he was younger, he could be a bit of a hand full, getting into trouble all the time. I have to keep him on the straight and narrow because I want him to grow into a responsible adult."

"So, in the past, you slapped him."

"Yes."

"What changed?

"My wife, she didn't like it, made me promise to stop."

"Did you stop this time or did you take your frustrations out on the boy?"

It took him a few seconds to realise that they thought he had killed his son.

"I would never, I could never. He's my boy," he stuttered.

Yet Chris couldn't bring himself to say he loved his son, not in front of strangers. "I demand a lawyer."

By then, it was too late. The officers felt that they had their man. Now they needed the evidence to prove it.

****

Raphael watched Thomas for a while before returning to his books. Other elves watched too, joining in with whatever games Aeglas devised. Tinnueth stood on the sidelines, laughing, and smiling at their antics before joining in as well. Children were rare in their society and therefore cherished, but for Raphael, the boy's sudden appearance raised concerns. In an attempt to find the truth, he considered every idea however unlikely.

He ran his hands along the shelves, and then picked out a book as he considered the first question. How did the boy arrive and depart unseen? Raphael read for a while contemplating the options and decided that he should consider each possible method, in partnership with each mechanism. Likely spells or magic fell into the invisibility category. Some spells dealt with the real world while others concentrated on the mind. Material incantations could bend light, gather shadows, or blend a body in with their background. Mental spells affected the minds of others by merely making a person go unnoticed or presenting that person as someone friendly and familiar.

Raphael reflected upon each possibility before putting away the book and choosing another. Next, he should consider cloaks, rings, or necklaces of invisibility. Rare or problematic to make, they did not muffle sounds or remove imprints on the ground. It was almost impossible to use those items in conjunction with either a 'Removal' or a 'Levitation' spell, in addition to a 'Dampening' incantation. It would take a sorcerer of incredible skill. If a person had that much power, they would be able to achieve their ends without using a small boy.

After rejecting that idea, he put the book back on the shelf and delicately pulled out another. On the outside, it appeared entirely new, but inside it held another book, so ancient, only magic kept it from crumbling. He read a few pages. If he rejected invisibility that only left local, temporal, or banned 'Universal Transference' spells. Apart from this book, any reference to these spells resided in the restricted section of the library at Araothron. Few even knew such enchantments existed, but he understood the basics. His master had devised them when Raphael studied as a young apprentice. In the distant past, Master Magician Aeneas had presented a scholarly paper, which caused a great uproar within the magical community. After significant debate, the ruling council then banned such knowledge citing its potential dangers. Nevertheless, his master had continued his research in secret with all the ramifications that entailed. After what occurred, the authorities destroyed or hid any reference to that knowledge.

Another thought occurred to him. He placed his current book on his desk and then scanning along the shelves, picked out a few more. After flicking through the pages, he sighed, frustrated. He couldn't find what he needed within his library. Even though he had an extensive collection for a backwater town, nothing compared with the library at Araothron. Raphael settled back to read the remaining books. Once he had completed his study, he stayed deep in thought until the light began to fade.

After the games, Thomas did not feel tired. Instead, he'd climbed the tallest tree and then lay down on his back to watch the night sky. So brilliant, so beautiful, a trillion pinpricks of light speckled the heavens and so unlike home, where only the pale glimmer of the brightest star showed on a cloudless night. He marvelled in awe at this timeless wonder until Aeglas joined him.

They sat in silence, staring into the night until a meteorite shot across the sky, leaving a short trail of light.

"Does that happen often?" asked Thomas.

"At this time of year, yes. Our world passes through the tail of a comet, and small fragments rain down upon the planet."

"Do you ever see anything larger?"

"There have been times when other celestial bodies have been caught by our gravitational field."

Thomas sat up and stared. He'd thought because elves lived in trees that they knew nothing about how the universe worked. He knew a little from his school of course, but to hear his friend talk of gravitational fields sounded so odd and out of place.

Aeglas smiled as if reading his thoughts.

"Just because we live as we do, does not mean we do not seek knowledge. In fact, during our life span, we learn a great many things."

"How old are you?"

"I am young."

"I'm eleven."

"Ahh, a great age."

Aeglas looked solemn, but Thomas could see a twinkle in his eye.

"Don't tease. Go on, how old are you?"

"One hundred and nine."

Thomas gaped. "How old is Tinnueth then?"

Aeglas laughed. "I would never reveal a ladies age and do you think it would be appropriate to ask her?"

Thomas considered and then shook his head, but he couldn't help feeling curious. "Is she older or younger than you? You can tell me that can't you?"

"We are of a similar age."

Thomas nodded and then blurted, "Who's the oldest?"

"Master Raphael, he is a great age."

"Can I ask how old he is?"

Aeglas laughed. "You can ask, but I cannot answer because I do not know. Once we get past a certain age, counting yet another year seems almost irrelevant."

Thomas accepted this and lay back once more to watch the night sky.

They stayed in silence for a while before he asked, "Did you come up here to check if I'd fallen asleep?"

"No, I came to keep you company."

"I'm quite safe. If I slept, I would wake up at home."

"Ah but if you just fell out of the tree, what would happen?"

Thomas hadn't considered this option. If he fell, he might hurt himself and perhaps even die. "Don't you need to sleep?"

"Not today."

That reply surprised Thomas. He sat up, dangled his legs either side of the branch, and thought about how different elves were from humans. They were so graceful, lived such a long time, knew so much, and didn't need to sleep every day. They were everything he wanted to be. While he swung his legs slightly, it didn't occur to him that he sat over a hundred feet in the air and yet felt entirely at ease. His carefree attitude intrigued Aeglas, who watched him for sudden signs of discomfort but they never came. Instead, a thoughtful look passed across the boy's face.

"How often do you sleep then?" asked Thomas.

"Every three to four days, but we can go without sleep for much longer if we meditate."

Thomas looked confused. "Why should that work? Can't you just rest if you're tired?"

"Resting helps, but sleep is more than just rest. During sleep, we heal and dream. If we never slept, then we would eventually go mad."

"Why does that happen?"

"Dreaming is the minds way of making sense of everything. It sorts through experiences, problems, emotions even desires."

"Is meditation like sleep?"

"For us, yes, it is similar."

"What do you do?"

"First, we relax, clear our minds, and then focus on healing the body."

"How do you know it's working?"

"A feeling of warmth flows through our muscles."

"Do you dream when you meditate?"

Aeglas tilted his head and replied, "Not really, but we try to help the mind do something similar. After healing, we switch our minds focus to the preceding day's events. We specifically concentrate on anything that has troubled or challenged us. This helps the mind deal with how we feel. When the process is complete, we experience a sensation of wellbeing."

"How long does it take?"

"That varies depending on the person and their skill, but it can take as little as half an hour although like sleep, the shorter the meditation, the less effective the results."

"Can you teach me?"

Aeglas laughed then realised that Thomas genuinely wanted to know. Could a human learn such a skill, besides why would he want to? He frowned and asked although he already suspected how Thomas would answer. "Why would you wish to learn?"

Thomas shrugged unwilling to reveal the real reason. "Dunno but it could be useful."

Aeglas nodded. "That is true; however, it is a difficult skill to acquire. Even with practice, it takes years to perfect."

Thomas surprised him. The boy grinned. "Nothing worth having is easy, and it's not like I have any homework to do here."

"Homework?"

"Yeah, you know extra study after school."

Aeglas smiled and acquiesced. "I don't think I will be much of a teacher, but I will try."

Thomas looked at him, expectantly.

"But not now, we'll start tomorrow."

****

Chris waited for hours before the lawyer arrived. Unable to pay the going rate, he had to rely on those that volunteered their services. When he finally turned up, he turned out to be a she. At first, the diminutive woman didn't exactly inspire confidence, but she cast such an air of authority that his worries quickly faded.

After listening to his story, including the part when Thomas ran away after the argument, he asked her shamefaced, "Do you think they are going to charge me?"

"Well, although the evidence is circumstantial, you did admit to having an argument with your son and threatening to beat him with a belt. However, you hotly denied actually hitting him before he ran away. Nevertheless, there is no evidence to corroborate or contradict your story. No one has heard from or seen Thomas since."

Chris slumped and nodded.

She stood up and walked towards the door. "I will talk to the officers in charge."

He waited deep in misery for her return. When she came back into the room, he could hardly stir himself from the profound depression that threatened to overwhelm him.

"They will release you without charge, but with a caution, however, I would advise you not to do or say anything unwise."

The ray of hope died as he realised what that meant. "What's going to happen about my son? He's still missing."

"The police intend to organise a search of the local park and surrounding streets tomorrow, although it may take a few days to complete."

"Could I help?"

"If they need public assistance, they will ask."

He nodded, understanding that his involvement would only make things worse.

She tilted her head to one side and stared at him shrewdly. Over the years, she had defended a great many people. Some proved innocent, some proved guilty, and some got away with their crimes. Her instincts told her that this man fell roughly into the first category even though she would hardly call him innocent. Abusive would be a better description but not a murderer. He did care for his son, although she doubted that he knew how to show it.

Chapter 16

Xenis and Valene

Her mother listened as Valene paced, venting her frustration, but the tirade kept going in circles. Now the endless repetition that echoed through the throne room began to annoy the Matriarch.

"We cannot let them get away with this! They should fear and respect us, but do they? No, they do not! Even though only males died, we cannot ignore the insult to our house. Our reputation is now in question. We need to act immediately; otherwise, we will become a laughing stock across the city."

Valene drew breath to continue, but the Matriarch interrupted curtly, "What do you suggest we do?"

"Attack now, destroy their mines, and slaughter their slaves."

The Matriarch leaned back and snorted with derision, her patience wearing thin.

"Is that the best you can come up with?" she sneered.

Her youngest sister Larenil then made matters worse, when she dared to interject.

"Yes, that tactic is too obvious. Everyone will know that our house instigated the attacks. We need to be more subtle. We can't *just* react to this disaster," she said, casting a disdainful glance at Valene. "It would be like admitting *you* failed."

Valene could hardly believe what she heard. How dare Larenil blame her for this misfortune? As a lesser royal, her youngest sister should not presume to speak! She should know her place and remain silent.

Xenis watched his eldest sister's face with well-concealed amusement. Valene looked about to explode. He wondered how much more his mother would tolerate, by the look on her face, not much.

Valene leaned forward, trembling with fury as she pointed one menacing finger at her sister. "How dare you even..."

The Matriarch suddenly lost her temper. "Enough!"

Valene settled down into a simmering rage as the Matriarch glowered in her direction. In the silence that followed, the ruler of Zik'Keeshe considered the options. What should they do? If they reacted, the other houses would see this as weakness or worse. Yet if they did not, they would judge the house cowardly, making them vulnerable to attack.

"We need to formulate a plan, but I have yet to hear any suggestions worthy of consideration."

She leaned forward and pointed her forefinger at Valene.

"I will hold you personally responsible for this humiliation if we do not have a satisfactory outcome," she growled.

Valene almost gasped at that threat before going silent.

In that moment of respite, Xenis took the opportunity to speak.

"Let them wait," he said quietly.

"What?" the Matriarch snarled at his interruption.

"With respect mother, let them wait. Why react? Why do what they want? Why should we be the ones to break the rules with a direct attack? No, instead we should take revenge at a time and place of our choosing, not theirs. Let them prepare for our attack, let them plan, let them worry, and when they grow complacent and drop their guard, that will be the time."

"And in the meantime, what should we do? The city will think we are gutless," spat Valene, unwisely interrupting.

The Matriarch gave her daughter a penetrating look and indicated for her son to carry on.

He stared at his sister. "We should use a many-pronged *subtle* and indirect method of attack."

Valene glowered.

"We will do enough so that others will guess we are behind events but not so much as to cause open warfare. After all, we do not want to draw the council's attention so soon after gaining a seat."

He paused to let the implications sink in before he continued. "At the moment, House Faerl'Zotreth is vulnerable. They have suffered a major loss of status, but we want to turn that into a catastrophic loss."

Valene spat out her words in contempt, "And how will we do that, brother?"

Xenis turned and smiled smugly. "First, we must keep an eye on events and where ever possible, manipulate them. Then it is just a matter of timing and of course, some lateral thinking." He bowed slightly. "May I humbly submit that I have some talent in that direction?"

Valene scowled. Xenis was anything but humble.

Nonetheless, the Matriarch indicated that she would listen. "Go on."

"House Faerl'Zotreth needs not only to boost its status but retain what little it has left. As it stands, they will live in fear that another house might surreptitiously decide to eliminate them as a rival. We need to manoeuvre their enemies into making that decision, thus doing our dirty work. First, we persuade their allies to distance themselves by making any association toxic. Our spies and contacts will spread rumours about House Faerl'Zotreth. That they are involved in something despicable and hint at how they have voiced contempt towards the Council of Five and even the ruling house. If you consider recent events, everyone will believe this is true. Then become allies with their allies. Insist that our new friends drop other allegiances for a greater house, which is on the rise. I suggest targeting Renor'Zilisto."

The Matriarch frowned slightly, sat back in her chair, and contemplated his idea.

"They are nothing but a bunch of witless farmers, far beneath us," hissed Valene.

"Those witless farmers produce most of the food for House Faerl'Zotreth. Without them, how will they feed their slaves and the lower members of their household? They will need to hunt and gather in the caverns to supply their needs. To do this, the Matriarch will order more warriors out in the open. Their house will be vulnerable to attack. We will accidentally cross paths with them and claim that the resources they seek, are ours. Such action is justifiable within the law, and we will win because we will be prepared, whereas they will be hungry and perhaps by then, even desperate. Meanwhile, their castle will have fewer guards, while we can't attack them directly, it will allow us to infiltrate their defences. We can place spies who will hide traps or monitoring devises in place."

"What of their other allies?"

As the status of House Faerl'Zotreth wanes, we should encourage them to distance themselves from their former ally. The information gathered from the listening devices should give us an idea of how to achieve this. It may be something quite simple, such as the patronage of a higher house, a better deal for goods or we might resort to bribes or threats. Remind them that they might go down, along with their ally. Then finally, once we have compromised House Faerl'Zotreth, we can choose a time and place to cause maximum devastation. Their failure will be inevitable."

The Matriarch smiled slightly, clearly intrigued, a rare event.

"Finally, an idea with some merit, see to it, Valene. You need to prove your worth after this fiasco, your sisters, and even your youngest brother will be happy to assist, I am sure."

Valene bowed her head in acceptance, all the while fuming inside.

The Matriarch waved her hand. "You are all dismissed."

As Xenis bowed and turned to go, Valene saw the expression on his face. A slight smug smile twisted his lips as he glanced in her direction. How she hated him.

Chapter 17

Cody

The bed creaked ominously as Cody turned over. The mattress had long seen better days. Instead of fitting the contours of his body, it dipped deeply in the middle. It felt more like sleeping in a paddling pool, especially on hot nights like tonight. Cody had long since learnt to ignore the constant whir of the old air conditioning. Its absence indicated it had broken down once again. Half asleep, he turned over and reached for the light pull. As he groped ineffectually in the darkness, he sighed. There must be another power outage. He would have to get up and open a window if he wanted to sleep.

With a groan of disgust, he swung his legs out of bed and stood up, yawning. Eyes half shut he stumbled forwards into a wall. He turned and walked the other way straight into another wall. Cody swore, shook his head, wiggled his toes, and tried to wake up. It took a few seconds to register that the caravan had carpet and he stood on bare floorboards. That didn't make sense, so Cody took another step forward and this time bashed his shins on something hard and cold. He bent down and ran his hands across the object. It felt like an old-fashioned bedstead. Memories sprang to mind and with those a few disturbing words. Words like, dormitory, hospital ward, or worse, prison.

What had he done yesterday? Set off a smoke bomb, talked to Sarah in jail and got her message to meet up once freed. Yep, he could be in trouble, big trouble with the authorities.

He didn't dare call out. What if someone came, but then he considered the alternative, what if they didn't. Perhaps they would return or just leave him to rot. Cody decided it didn't matter. He didn't plan to stick around. With his hands on the bed, he inched forward and reached out into the darkness. His fingers touched metal. Another bedframe, and fortunately, found it unoccupied. He reached out again and felt yet another bed. After a few more beds, he patted a wall and then to the left a door. Tense and ready to run he reached out, grabbed the doorknob, and turned, only to have it come off in his hand. Somewhat surprised Cody fumbled and dropped it with a loud clang, cursing his stupidity. He waited as the sound died away, but no one came. No shouts of 'stop him he's trying to escape,' or 'kill him he's seen too much.' Just silence and in an odd way, that came as a bit of a disappointment.

Now that Cody knew he didn't have to worry about how much noise he made, he put his fingers in the door hole and pulled hard. The stiff hinges offered some resistance then it gave way with a loud rusty creak, revealing a corridor. At the far end, a stairwell wound down into a shaft of light. When he got there and looked down, he saw no stairs only a hole that fell several stories. Cody understood. They, whoever they were, had left him in an abandoned building. The authorities, a government agency, black ops, corrupt corporations, or even aliens, any of these were possible.

Cody backtracked a little, keeping his hand on the wall and passed the door into the dormitory before turning a corner into dense darkness. What sort of building didn't have windows? He inched forward and then leaned left to touch the other wall, only to encounter something metal. It felt ribbed like a shutter, so he tried to open it, but it refused to budge. After straining for a few minutes, Cody gave up and moved on. With each step, the sagging floor creaked unpleasantly making him paranoid. He rounded the next corner only to see another glimmer of light. The corridor ended in a window. It still had a shutter, but it hung partly off its hinges, letting in not daylight as he first thought but moonlight. Cody got his hands under the gap and heaved. With a loud squeal, it moved, and he looked out. He could have cheered. A spiral fire escape ran down to the ground. He swung his legs over the window ledge and climbed onto the staircase. It shuddered which didn't inspire confidence, so taking care, he began to walk down the steps. After a few seconds, Cody stopped. The movement had started some sort of resonance. As he stood still, it subsided, but as soon as he moved again, it began to quake and this time it didn't stop. Cody ran hell for leather down the stairs as it swayed from side to side and then hurdled the bannisters. He landed badly and rolled, scrambling to get away as he heard a massive crack behind him. The staircase gave one final shudder, pulled away from the wall and then collapsed only yards from his feet, churning up an enormous cloud of dust.

Cody slumped into a heap, panting, and coughing as he waited for the cloud to subside. When he could finally breathe again, he stood up and brushed himself down. His captors had left him to die in some deserted city. Perhaps they'd left him in the US or drugged him and flown him somewhere else. Even in the low light, he could see that the buildings around him lay derelict. Some had their roofs missing. Others had crumbling walls covered by shifting sand. It reminded him of small abandoned mining towns in Arizona but on a massive scale. If he didn't know better, he would have said this could be the suburbs of some industrial city, but even parts of Detroit didn't look this bad. With no particular plan in mind, he just picked a direction and walked. Underfoot, the ground changed from sand to rough road as he moved out of the industrial area into something more residential. Each house had differences, some small, some large. Their front gardens now dead, their driveways crumbling, it filled him with curiosity, so he picked the next house to his left.

The front door hung off its hinges, but he still felt strange as he went in. It felt like trespassing, but he doubted the owners would mind, even if they still lived. The house like the rest of the city had that eerie abandoned feeling. In the hallway, the hooks held the frayed remains of children's coats. He reached out and gently touched one. Cody shivered as it crumbled to dust beneath his fingers. The living room fared no better, retaining scattered remnants of family life. A couch next to an overturned chair, a lamp, a teddy bear in the corner of the room, a newspaper on the floor. He turned to go into the kitchen and then stopped. He'd just seen a paper, perhaps a vital source of information!

Cody knelt down on the dusty carpet. He didn't dare pick up the publication. It would crumble instantly. He blew gently trying to puff away the dust, but even that caused one corner to disintegrate. Besides, he couldn't see the text in this light, but he could see a picture. It looked like a team of people standing next to a large round object, but he couldn't see much detail. When the sun rose, he would be able to read it, but Cody didn't fancy staying here that long. The whole place gave him the creeps. It felt as if everyone had been going about their business one minute and then vanished the next. It reminded him of pictures after the Chernobyl disaster. Cutlery and plates left on the kitchen table, children's toys still scattered around the room, and shoes left waiting for their owners to return.

Cody shuddered in revulsion as goosebumps rippled over his body. All these familiar objects made this situation seem so real. Up until now, he'd felt detached, more like watching a history documentary than reality, now it felt up close and personal. He stood and shook off his unease before hurrying away. He would remember this location, and when daylight returned, he would read the newspaper. If of course, they'd written it in English and not another language like Russian.

Outside the house in the bright moonlight, the city looked bleak and broken but somehow less terrifying. Here it seemed like any run-down city and not a personal tragedy. He could think of it in objective terms. Cody studied the buildings as he walked past, etched in deep shadow and silver light he could see that the brickwork looked weathered. He knew that while the desert preserved somethings, others eroded quickly. Cold nights, hot days, split rock, pealing it off in sheets like the skin of an onion. Some buildings were grand with pillars and columns, while others looked modern, made of steel and glass, yet all appeared in such a state of disrepair. It made it difficult to calculate their age and more importantly when the inhabitants had abandoned the city.

Cody carefully picked his way across the broken pavement as he moved towards the heart of the city. Here the sand had not covered the deteriorating road. Debris littered the streets, sometimes barring his route. As he picked his way around chunks of twisted steel, brick, and concrete, he kept glancing upwards, aware that the buildings were crumbling and unsafe.

Another thing he noticed, there weren't any vehicles. At first, this seemed strange, but then he thought perhaps there had been a warning. Cody couldn't see any bones, so people must have fled. Where had they gone, to shelters, to another city, perhaps?

As he approached the centre, the buildings rose higher. They looked like the remains of skyscrapers; their metallic skeletons thrust upwards toward the sky. There were no recent signs of human activity, although the dark canyon of buildings limited his vision. He could just see enough to step over fallen girders as he made his way to the central intersection. Once there, he could see straight streets in all directions, marred by crumbling facades and fallen debris. There must be someone alive. He couldn't be the only one.

"Is there anyone there?" he shouted.

The sound of his voice echoed off the buildings, repeating itself into eternity. Lost and alone, with no idea what to do, Cody sat down on a wall and put his head in his hands. For a while, he sat brooding until a small rustling sound caught his attention. Cody looked up and saw an odd sight. At first, he couldn't identify what he saw and then when he could, he didn't believe it. In the windless night, a ball of tumbleweed rolled down the street towards him. It looked so strange; its movement purposeful as if it had a mind of its own. Cody just sat there staring as it came closer and then he heard another noise. He looked to his left. Another tumbleweed travelled towards him, rustling slightly as it bumped over the uneven surface.

It took him a few moments to realise the impossible that they were heading directly towards him. Cody leapt up and started to go around, giving it a wide berth. He didn't consider it a threat. After all, it was just some shrub, but when he moved, the tumbleweed changed its angle to intercept him. Cody shivered in revulsion and backed away, but he couldn't take his eyes off it. As it approached, it seemed to unfurl revealing long barbed tendrils. With an adrenalin-fuelled leap, he jumped over it, and as he landed, he felt something sharp swipe against his jeans. It had just tried to grab him, but plants couldn't do that could they? Cody raced away, wanting to put as much distance between himself and his attacker. He didn't dare look back or stop. They did not move fast, but they had an unrelenting quality about them.

As he rounded a corner, he almost crashed into yet more tumbleweed. One made a mad slash at his legs, fortunately missing as Cody stumbled past. He didn't know what attracted them. It might be his voice, the vibrations from running, or perhaps his heat, or smell.

Either way, they tracked him from all directions like a Satnav. They had cut off every avenue but one. Cody jumped over a pile of rubble and made for the nearest building. If he could climb high and wait for dawn, perhaps he would stand a chance. Once inside, Cody slowed and took a quick look around. Across the room in the limited light, he could see a set of stairs. He ran forward across the shadowed foyer, then with heart stilling terror, realised his mistake. Grown unstable with age, the floor began to buckle and collapse beneath his feet.

Chapter 18

Lars

Lars woke as the sun sank below the horizon. Still sleepy, he looked around and realised that he stood in the middle of a black road. A memory flashed in front of his eyes. With a remarkable turn of speed for someone who had just woken, he reached the edge of the building. Once there, he relaxed and allowed his natural sense of curiosity to nudge him. In his mind, he could almost hear his mother sigh with exasperation. A rebellious streak surfaced, she couldn't stop him, so Lars explored until another sound caught his attention. Oddly different, more like a buzz, he crept towards the noise. It came from the end of a narrow alleyway.

In the distance, he could see bright lights partially obscured by coloured boxes and crates on wheels that lined the wall. They gave excellent cover as he crept toward the noise. When he reached the end of the alley, his view expanded to encompass something he could hardly grasp. All around pictures and colours flashed. The walls had bright lights, luminous and dazzling, and an unbelievably large woman talked on the side of a building. The appalling noised nearly overwhelmed him. He stood staring, dumb and in awe. Creatures of all sizes rushed up and down the street, and people walked by unmolested on little raised sections of road. As he watched, something even more peculiar happened. A red light appeared, then all the creatures stopped and waited in a line. In time with a beeping sound, both men and women, crossed the street unharmed, and once on the other side, it all started again. Lars could see people sitting inside the creatures quite calmly, well more or less. He had to consider the possibility that these creatures were beasts of burden and not predators.

As he stood, everyone walked around him. Some glanced in his direction, while others gave him a strange look but most ignored him. Some held odd bricks up to their ears and talked. Could it be some bizarre religious ritual? Lars avoided religion back home. The preachers taught that the old world had been wicked. For their sin's, the punishment had rained down from on high. Yet Lars couldn't believe everyone had been evil. He also didn't understand why any god should punish the good along with the bad. It didn't make sense to him, so he hadn't bothered to think about it.

Just as he wondered what to do next, something incredible happened. One of the creatures roared up and stopped in front of him. To his amazement, a flap opened up, and then a man and a woman got out of its stomach. They closed the flap, chatted to each other, and as they left the man gave a flourish. In response, the creature flashed its eyes and beeped as they walked away. It allowed Lars to see one of these creatures up close. With exaggerated care, he approached the beast so as not to frighten it. Whatever he did seemed to work because when he reached out to touch it, the creature didn't move. He peered inside its stomach, and the more he looked, the more he realised that it wasn't alive. It had seats, a wheel and raised things like toggles on a shirt. This must be a cart. Lars grinned. He couldn't resist the challenge. Perhaps this thing on the flap might be a handle of sorts. Just as he reached out to grasp it, a loud voice yelled out.

Lars turned to see an angry man bearing down on him. Yes, of course, they thought he had tried to steal their cart, how stupid of him. Lars apologised even though he couldn't understand what they said. The man only shook his head, pointed, and shouted some more. A woman in a strange dress came over to the man, said something, and then patted him on the arm. She spoke again, but this time Lars understood her.

"Eddie love, can't you see he's a tramp and a foreigner, just leave him be."

"He tried to steal my car!"

"Look at him; the way he's staring, he's not right in the head."

"He could be dangerous then!"

She smiled and asked Lars sweetly, "Are you dangerous?"

Lars just shook his head in shock.

"There you are, Eddie. He's just a crazy man; don't worry yourself about him."

This seemed to calm the man down, but as he got into the cart, he glared at Lars.

"Bloody care in the community!" he yelled.

Lars understood the words but not the meaning, so he just smiled vaguely and waved as they sped off in their cart. He found it interesting how it had no horse or ox; perhaps they used those peddles he had seen to make it go, although he didn't know how it worked.

A short laugh then a fit of coughing echoed behind him in the alley.

"Well, you sure know how to make yourself visible," coughed the voice.

"Hello?" replied Lars.

There at the entrance, sat a man dressed in dark rags with his lower body covered by a brown blanket. Lars realised that once the lights had drawn his attention, he must have walked right past the man without seeing him.

"What do you mean? Make myself visible?" Lars asked.

"Well, you didn't see me once you saw the lights, did you?"

Lars nodded. He had to admit to his shame, he hadn't.

"And you notice how people step around you? They don't talk to you unless they have to?"

"Yes." Lars had noticed that as well.

"Well that's the life of a tramp," the man said then he lowered his voice. "We're almost invisible. People do their best to ignore us."

"Why?"

"Because we are different."

Lars understood. He had always felt different and now more than ever before. "So, being different is bad?"

The man stroked his straggly brown beard for a moment and thought.

"Can be," he said. "But in some ways, I got more freedom than those poor sods out there. They don't even realise they are slaves to the system."

"They're slaves?" Lars gasped, horrified by this revelation. "But slavery is bad."

"Yes, but they don't know it."

Lars felt sorry for them. "But they seem so well fed, and they're all dressed in fine clothes."

"Ah, but do they look happy?"

"No, no, not really." He hadn't seen many of them smile.

"That's the system for you. It looks after people most of the time as long as they conform. Isn't good for anyone though if they speak out of turn or something goes wrong, then they fall through the cracks and end up here."

Lars looked confused. "In this alley?"

The man laughed. "No on the streets like me."

"And that's bad?"

"It's not good if it's cold, but I have a place in the Western Ham shelter most of the time. I beg a little and those that feel bad enough give me money, so I get enough to eat and drink."

A shelter sounded fine to Lars, somewhere quiet out of the noisy chaos of the street. The man must have sensed Lars thoughts.

"It's a warm night, so I wasn't going to bother, but since you are new in town, I'll show you around," he offered.

Lars felt grateful. "Thank you; I feel a bit lost."

The man laughed. "And it shows."

He got up and held out a grubby hand. "Names Ted, my mother named me Theodor; she had great hopes for me, never lived up to them mind you."

That sounded all too familiar to Lars. He grasped the hand, and the man shook it, in some sort of ritual greeting.

"My name is Lars."

"Nice to meet you, Lars, let's get going, the shelter fills up pretty quickly even on a warm night. There will be soup if you're hungry."

"Soup sounds good."

Lars followed Ted back down the alley and then through twists and turns until they came to the community centre. Across from that stood a large squat building with a set of double doors, which lay open to the world. A line of people shuffled inside, and Ted ushered Lars to the end. After a few minutes, they were at the front, and Ted indicated for Lars to take a bowl, which a young lad obligingly filled with a chunky vegetable soup. Once he'd scooped up his portion, Ted showed Lars that they could pick a bread roll as well. Lars really looked forward to the bread. He hadn't eaten any for several months, and sure enough, once they found some seats, he broke it open. A hot crusty roll dipped in soup tasted like heaven.

"You're hungry," commented Ted as he watched Lars wolf down the soup.

Lars waited until he had finished before replying, "Haven't had any bread for months, and the soup is delicious."

Ted eyed up, Lars with surprise. "You look pretty healthy all considering."

"I've eaten what I could catch," explained Lars.

"Ah, living off the country."

Lars nodded.

"Well, you'll find the big city different then."

"Too true." Lars undoubtedly found the city amazing, albeit a little scary at first.

Ted must have seen someone he knew for he waved in the direction of a tall, well-dressed young man with a neatly trimmed dark beard.

"Hey, Phil we got a new one here."

The man came over. "How are you doing old timer, not seen you around for a while."

Ted shrugged. "It's been warm, and I get enough to eat most of the time."

"So, who's your friend?"

"Phil this is Lars, he's new to the city, been living off the countryside."

"A man of many skills then." Phil grinned.

"Yes." Lars knew that he had become a skilled hunter.

"You plan to stay long?"

Lars had no idea how long so he just replied truthfully, "I don't know."

"Well, as long as you get here before 8pm there are usually beds for the night."

Lars felt pleased to have somewhere to stay. "Thanks!"

"No problem."

Phil turned and walked away when the serving lad called for some help.

"I'd get here a bit earlier in winter," added Ted in a low voice. "If it gets cold people will be queueing up at the door even though they don't open till 7pm."

Lars nodded at this sage advice feeling pretty tired already. A full stomach and the warm shelter made him feel sleepy.

"Can I get a bed for the night?" he asked.

"Don't see why not," replied Ted.

After they put their bowls on the dirty dishes tray, he took him over to the sleeping area.

There were rows of simple cots. To Lars, who often slept on the ground, this looked like a complete luxury.

"Once you got your bed, don't get up for a pee, until the shelter closes for the night, else you'll lose your spot."

This too made sense to Lars.

"Well pick a bed and don't sleep in your shoes, they don't like that but keep them close. You don't want someone else walking off with them."

Lars thanked Ted for the advice before picking a cot in the darkest corner. He took off his shoes and tied them to his belt before lying down. The sound of people chatting in the canteen soothed him like a bubbling stream as he drifted off to sleep.

Chapter 19

Adam and Ceola

The pleasant electric shock passed across her body, disturbing her sleep. Awake now, a malicious smile spread across her face as she stretched and arched her back in wicked anticipation.

"I sense a little fish caught in my net."

Ceola always loved this part, not knowing what she had caught, until she saw them. By then, of course, it was too late, well too late for them anyway. She slipped on a sheer robe and stepped out of the skin-covered yurt. The air shimmered around her as she closed her eyes and breathed deeply, drinking in the scent of the forest. Its earthy aroma blended nicely with the light metallic overtones of water. She could not catch the scent of her prey, not at this distance, but she would taste it soon enough.

With graceful ease, Ceola began to work her way through the woodland towards a boat moored on the beach. As she walked, she sang, the melody tugged, then pulled, twisting, and tearing at the world as it echoed outwards.

As she sang, Ceola felt another disturbance in the net as the prey kicked. It struggled, unknowingly caught, trapped and unaware of its perilous situation. Yet it felt different from her usual quarry. She sniffed the air. Not magical, she decided, but something strange, something new.

"What delicious morsel have I snared today?"

She delighted at the building anticipation as she emerged from the woodland. Here the dappled forest light gave way to a pale pre-dawn glow that settled over the water. By the shore, its prow roped to a post, lay her boat. It offered the only escape from the island unless she swam through the deep dark waters.

Ceola stepped off the green turf on to the beach. With each step, the sand crumbled beneath her feet as she made her way towards the boat. Once untied, she pushed it out into the lake and then leapt gracefully onto its deck. As she rowed, she sang another song, twisting the notes to carry further. She could sense the creature now, a human male, healthy and young, that felt good. He would do well in her experiments and then once complete; she smiled cruelly to herself, well, that would be another stimulating day.

Adam frowned, eyes slightly open and only half-awake. He shivered and groped for the duvet, which must have fallen onto the floor. Instead, his hand touched... grass. He patted it and ran his hand over the surface. It couldn't, could it? He sat up, rubbed his eyes, and looked around in disbelief. "What the hell?"

Adam sat on a small grassy patch between a moss fringed log and a gnarled tree. Around in all directions, stretched patchy woodland. He could hear birds calling to one another, the sound of rustling leaves and creaking branches. "Oh shit."

Had his drinking mates pranked him? Yet he couldn't see any tyre tracks, nowhere to drive a 4X4, they must have carried him. He looked down. "Oh shit, shit and double shit." They hadn't left him any clothes.

Adam stood slowly and peered over the fallen log. In front, lay a small path so he took that in the hope that it might lead somewhere useful and not too public. He didn't want the police to arrest him. Ferns and brambles brushed against his skin as he hobbled over the stony ground. Ahead Adam could see a break in the woodland and the light began to grow. A sudden noise caused him to freeze, followed by a grinding sound and a small splash like someone jumping out of a boat.

"Hello?" he called.

When Adam heard no reply, he edged carefully forward towards the sound. As the woodland thinned, it revealed a sandy beach and beyond a vast dark lake tinted gold, which rippled gently in the breeze. To his right, on the shoreline, he could see a woman pulling a boat out of the water. Adam had a problem. Any moment now, she would turn, see him, and then scream. He glanced anxiously around. Should he hide or try to cover up, then he spied a large fern leaf. Yes, that would do at a pinch, so he broke it off, only to hear a snigger.

Adam turned back and met her gaze as she eyed up his chiselled jawline and muscular body. Head tilted to one side, she smirked, clearly amused at his poor attempt at modesty. Apparently, *his* nudity didn't bother her. As she looked him up and down, he returned the favour. With tawny gold skin, the woman looked incredibly beautiful. Her honey brown hair cascaded down her shoulders, reaching her waist. She wore a simple translucent shift, which left hardly anything to the imagination. It barely covered her pert, curvy, and amazingly sensual body.

He felt himself respond and smiled sheepishly. "Well, this is awkward."

She didn't reply. Instead, the woman smiled and traced a strange pattern in the air with the forefingers of her right hand. Adam frowned, was this a greeting? He decided to return the gesture, but then he realised the pattern hadn't vanished. Instead, it began to form a glowing shape. His eyes widened, and he tried to back away but found he couldn't run. He remained rooted to the spot as a shimmering red symbol formed and expanded in the air. Without warning, it raced towards him, striking him squarely in the chest. As it passed into his body, his mind fogged and became calm.

When the fog began to clear, Adam found himself lying in a boat. Somehow, he realised that the woman had kidnapped him, which he should find alarming, but strangely, it didn't matter. He smiled slowly, taking a deep breath, happy and content as he looked at the sky above. Brilliant blue, with fluffy white clouds scudding gently in the breeze, the day felt perfect in every way. He could have stayed there forever, seeing patterns in the clouds, but he sensed her call. Now compelled to obey her command, Adam sat up and found his gaze drawn to the surrounding water. It matched the colour of the sky, azure and clear. To his right, the white sand sparkled in the sunlight and around the boat; tiny waves glistened as they broke upon the shore. How strange, he knew she had brought him to her island home. At that thought, Adam turned and saw his goddess waiting for him. He stepped out of the boat and walked up the beach to greet her. As he looked into her green eyes, Adam felt his heart swell to bursting point. More beautiful than before and flawless in every way, he couldn't imagine a more exquisite woman. He would worship her now and forever more.

In silence, she took his hand and smiling shyly; she turned and led him into a moss-covered wood. As they walked hand in hand, he could see the dew glistening on each plant like little diamonds. The air felt damp but sweet, made even more so by each other's company. The trees slender with silver bark shook gently in the wind, leaves falling silently like shimmering confetti. The air itself seemed rare and magical, and he found himself almost giggling in drunken delight.

When they finally came upon a woodland glade, he saw a tent made from overlapping coloured animal skins. The woman stood at the entrance, opened a flap, and waited. When Adam ducked inside, the air smelled sweet like cinnamon and vanilla, but other than that; he could sense very little. His goddess entered behind him and closed the flap, cutting out the sunlight. When she moved past him, she brushed against his skin, causing a flare of desire, but somehow, he knew that his goddess wasn't ready for him.

As his eyes adjusted to the dim interior, a light revealed strange objects hanging from the ceiling in nets. Translucent pots dangled in little clusters amongst herbs set to dry. Some vessels contained seeds or liquid, while others gave off a faint glow, but it was the giant bed covered in animal furs, which caught his attention.

She smiled, held out her hand, and he responded by taking her hand in his. Adam felt drawn to her like a moth towards a searing flame, but he couldn't resist, not even if he'd wanted to. Yet behind his eyes, a tiny part of his mind screamed faintly, beating for attention at the barrier placed in its way.

His goddess put her hand against his face and traced her fingers down his jaw, neck and then across his rippling torso. He shivered in delight, awaiting her command, which he knew would come soon. With one finger, she pushed him gently onto the fur-covered bed. He didn't resist, why would he? She meant everything to him. Any man would be happy to find himself in this compromising position. He loved her more than he loved life itself, and he would do anything for her.

Adam lay back and waited in delicious anticipation; any moment now, she would join him. When she didn't, he felt confused by what he saw as mixed signals. He raised his head in search of her. In the dim light, he could see her standing now naked, one arm resting on her elbow as she traced her bottom lip in contemplation. With a sinister smile and a flash of her eyes, she jumped across the room, mounted the bed, and straddled her legs across his abs. He found her strangely heavy and stronger than anticipated. As she ran her hands through his spikey blond hair, Adam began to trace his fingers across her breasts, but she took his wrists and held him down. Instead, he found himself at her mercy, trapped beneath her weight. She stared intensely into his eyes and then smiling, bent down to nibble at his neck. Her lips felt magnificent, silky smooth and soft, but as she kissed him, it dawned on Adam that the sensation had begun to change.

He lifted his head so that he could see her beautiful face only to stare in mute horror as her eyes changed from sea green gradually through to glowing red. He almost panicked for a moment, but the glow bored into him, filling him with calm. It would be all right. It was all right. She would be with him now and forever.

He watched, filled with pleasure as she gradually changed. Her nails elongated; her skin became tawny brown fur. Her mane of hair became an upstanding ridge, which lay between two long pointed ears. After her body transformed, her face began to change. The last vestige of her false humanity vanished as her nose and mouth extended forwards to become a fang-filled maw.

Without warning, she tilted her head back and howled before she bent swiftly down to bite his neck. Her teeth nipped the skin just enough to draw blood, but he didn't flinch. She seemed pleased that he had not resisted and took a bigger bite this time before pulling back, a look of satisfaction on her wolverine face. He wanted to struggle against the pain, but she held him fast.

"Just close your eyes and relax, there's no need to resist me. All will be well." The voice bypassed his ears and went straight into his mind, but somehow, this didn't surprise him.

Unable to resist, he did as the woman commanded. On the surface, he felt that everything would be all right, even though a small distant part of him silently screamed. Deep in the pit of his soul, he knew that he should get up and run, but then a wave of pleasure overtook him. It didn't matter that one day soon he might die; for now, he would enjoy it all.

Chapter 20

Thomas

In the oppressive darkness, the park felt vast and scary. Thomas found himself in some distant part surrounded by skeletal trees that loomed out of the deep shadows. They creaked and shifted in the wind, making him feel uneasy. To make matters worse, in the distance, he could hear laughter. It sounded like a bunch of older kids. He wanted to avoid them, but at the same time, he didn't know where else to go.

With increasing trepidation, he walked uphill towards the noise. As he crested the hill, he saw them and stopped. They were sitting on a bench under a lamp, drinking something from a large bottle. One jumped off the bench and started to muck around pushing another boy and laughing. Alone and frightened like a rabbit caught in car headlights, he froze afraid that they might see him. When they didn't, he turned and quickly walked away. As the darkness engulfed him once more, his senses seemed to heighten. Around him, the trees groaned and swayed, the leaves rustling with every gust. He could hear every little noise amplified by his fear. A squeak of something metallic that turned in the wind joined the cacophony. In the flickering light of another lamp, a playground emerged from the darkness, but instead of finding this comforting, it made Thomas terrified. It looked like something out of a clown filled horror movie. Any moment now, something nasty would leap out and carry him off to its own private hell.

He backed away and ran wildly in the opposite direction. Thomas kept running, not caring where he went only that he needed to get away. When he began to run out of breath, Thomas saw a solitary lamp. His heart leapt; he knew this place. He wasn't far from home. Thomas sprinted all the way to the back gate and rattled at the latch. It came open, so he dived through and closed it behind him. He leant against it with a sigh of relief. His dad regularly forgot to lock it, much to his mum's displeasure. As usual, it would result in an argument and then ramble on to other slights, both real and imagined. Thomas rarely listened to them once they got started. Always about the same old things, tired arguments repeated without resolution. Why didn't they just kiss, and make up? He would sit in his bedroom with the door closed, pull the pillow over his head, and imagine magical places, which he now knew *really* existed. Places better than this dull grey world.

Thomas tiptoed through the back garden towards the kitchen door. Unlike the back gate, he found it locked. He scratched his head and thought for a moment. Thomas wasn't supposed to know about the spare key, but his parents weren't very good at hiding things from him. He was smart, or so his teachers told him. Yes, he remembered, he would find it in a pretend stone somewhere at the end of the rockery.

The stone had a plastic base, which he unscrewed with some effort, and after unlocking the kitchen door, he put it back in the hiding place. Thomas chuckled, they would never know, but then he hesitated. Would they be pleased to see him or would they be angry? Thomas bit his lip at the thought of his dad's anger. His father could be so frightening at times even when his mum hovered close to calm him down. Thomas wondered if he should turn back, go to sleep in the shed and return to his new friends, but only his mum's smile made him stop. She would be glad to see him, so Thomas plucked up courage and opened the door.

At first, he couldn't see anyone, but a light in the living room indicated that someone had come home.

"Mum? Dad? I'm home!" he called out.

He waited, then yelled, "Mum?"

Thomas could hear the TV on in the other room, so he went towards the sound and peered around the corner. He could see his dad sprawled on the sofa and as per usual, he snored. Thomas rushed over, happy to see his father even if he faced his usual punishment.

He shook him. "Dad, wake up!"

The snoring stopped for a second and then resumed.

"Dad," said Thomas more insistently, but his father just snorted and turned over.

Thomas felt quite disconcerted. Where was his mum and why wouldn't his dad wake up? Hadn't they missed him?

"Dad!" he yelled.

"What?" mumbled his dad, his voice slurred and barely awake. "Go to your room." After another snort, his father went back to sleep.

Thomas couldn't believe it, he ran upstairs, but by the time he got to his room, he sobbed. He flung himself down on his bed, feeling numb. They didn't care, they didn't miss him, and he wished in the depths of his soul that he could return to the elves and never come back. That forest would become his new home. He could finally live in a place where someone wanted him.

Downstairs, keys rattled at the front door. Mrs Lynn Harvey slowly pushed it open and then sighed as she closed it behind her. She wanted to continue her search, but the policewoman had insisted that she return home. It had become too dark to see. They would resume their work in the morning. The police had taken her home rather than let her drive and fall asleep at the wheel. Lynn felt exhausted but determined to continue, although, in the back of her mind, her hope seeped away. She shook her head, no, she couldn't think like that. She wouldn't give up. They would find him although Lynn knew what the police thought. The more time passed the less chance they had of seeing her son alive. Close to tears, she hung up her coat and threw her bag on the hallway table.

In the lounge, she could hear her husband breathing heavily in his sleep. Lynn had taken time off work, so he had pulled another double shift. While her employer understood the situation, his employer didn't care. She could take unpaid leave, but they offered him more work or nothing at all. Not even a job, if he took time off to help his wife search. Financially, they had to keep their heads above water. They couldn't sink into any more debt, else they might lose the house, so her husband kept working every hour that he could. As she wandered listlessly into the room, he turned over in his sleep and muttered something.

"Honey," she whispered.

"Go to your room," he murmured.

"What?" she paused, looking puzzled then she shook him. "Chris, wake up!"

He snorted then opened his eyes and looked at her. "I dreamt that he was here."

"Then you sent him to his room?" From her expression, he knew he'd already made a mistake.

With a sigh, he sat up and ran his hands through his black hair. "I know this is all my fault."

His wife sat down and put her arm around his shoulders.

"I've always been too tough on him. I'm just like my father, and I hated that bastard. Haven't I learnt anything? Don't cry, be a man, what eleven-year-old is a man yet," his voice cracked in despair.

He buried his face in her mousey hair as she comforted him but secretly part of her couldn't help but agree.

Chapter 21

Glen, Sarah, and Cody

The trailer shook violently. Glen woke with a start, leapt out of bed, and raced into the main room thinking of earthquakes or explosions. Instead, in the dim light, he saw Cody lying on the floor twitching and shaking in some sort of fit.

Glen dived over to check his friend. "What's wrong? Are you ok?"

"Switch the light on," groaned Cody as Glen helped him sit up. "Everywhere, all around me, and then the floor collapsed."

Glen flicked the switch and blinked furiously, blinded by the light. As his vision returned, he saw the computer chair tipped on its side, resting against the wall.

"It sounds like you had a nightmare," he said. "I'll make you a nice cup of tea." Except that, Americans didn't have a tea fixation. "Perhaps a coffee instead?"

"Yeah, please."

By the time Glen had made the drink, Cody had sat on the floor still feeling a little shaken but calmer. He drained the cup, handed it back and then shook his head.

"It felt so real. I could swear I was actually there." As he tried to stand up, he swore and rubbed his leg. He looked closer. "Hey, I've ripped my jeans!"

Glen knelt and looked between the rips. "It's not bleeding."

He helped his friend to his feet, and Cody hobbled towards the couch where he sat frowning and rubbing his leg. Glen picked up the computer chair and placed it back in its usual location, before sitting down. He yawned. He really wanted to get back to sleep.

"Look any pain is probably just psychosomatic. I know it seemed real, but the skin isn't even grazed." Glen gestured towards the computer grinning. "As for the nightmare, I guess you fell asleep at the keyboard again."

Cody nodded. "I found some odd stuff, though."

Glen laughed and stifled a yawn. "When don't you? Anyway, I'm off to sleep again."

Cody nodded and sat down at the computer. He hadn't told Glen about what he had found. Perhaps considering his friend's scepticism, he should keep it to himself. Just now, he didn't want to sleep. That nightmare had felt as real as sitting here, in some ways even more so. He had sensed the cool night air on his face, the broken road beneath his feet and the fear as those things chased him. It seemed too real for comfort. Cody shivered and tried to think of something else, something not quite so horrible, but one thought went round and round in his brain. There must be other people in the same situation. His original idea started with an experiment in area 51. He shook his head. In light of his recent experience, he didn't think so. Cody thought uneasily back to his dream and Glen's comment about psychosomatic pain. Could dreams feel so real that the dreamer would get hurt or even die? It led to another thought. Why did it start after Mr Johnson's death? Was this just a coincidence? It seemed unlikely.

From Sarah's description, it sounded as if the old man had perished locked in his own house, which had no signs of forced entry. He had small punctures all over his body, but were they enough to kill him? Perhaps the government researched new ways of eliminating their enemies. Could Mr Johnson be a victim of research into death by dreaming? It would be a valuable tool if the government needed to target either a specific individual or even enemy troops. After all, everyone needed to sleep. If they could kill an enemy in his dreams, it would seem as if he had died of unknown or even natural causes. Apart from the wounds, Cody saw at least one other flaw in his reasoning. Why choose the old man? As far as he knew, Mr Johnson didn't present a threat to anyone. His original instincts might be correct, an experiment that had gone wrong. Ok, so he should search for people who died in unusual circumstances with no known cause of death or seemingly natural causes. That could cover a multitude of options, so he narrowed the parameters.

What he eventually found sparked his interest. A few recent reports listed people dying in unexplained circumstances with the cause of death listed as unknown. He noted that agencies had recorded more than the usual number of missing people. As he glanced down the page, his eyes rested on a hacked internal police report from England. A man had gone missing from his home. His wife had returned to find the door locked and no signs of forced entry. The police confirmed that all his keys and possessions remained in the house. The man seemed normal, with no personal or financial problems. From all accounts, he appeared to have vanished while snoozing in front of the TV. The police couldn't find a body and no one had seen him recently. They had hit a dead end. The forums suggested government experiments or alien abduction, but Cody didn't want to rule out any possibilities.

He trawled through the information. Each case seemed to have a similar pattern. Someone went missing or died without reason. No enemies, no motive to leave, no forced entry, no personal items missing, no financial, physiological, or mental problems, unquestionably a mystery. For now, he would have to collect more data, so he brought up his geographical program and plotted the case locations around the world. They seemed random, but in time, perhaps a pattern would emerge.

Cody yawned and stretched back on his chair, time for coffee. As the pot simmered, he could see the sun shining through a crack in the blinds. He often watched the sunrise from the wrong side of the morning. He had become not an early bird, more of a never gone to sleep lark.

As the morning progressed, Cody became annoyed as Glen failed to get up.

He banged on his friend's door and shouted, "Wake up!"

A groan followed, but then the snoring began again.

"Glen, wake up."

"Arg what is it?"

"Time to get up."

"What already?"

"Yes," said Cody impatiently. "I want to see Sarah now."

The trailer rocked a sure sign that Glen had just turned over and fallen out of the narrow bed. Cody waited impatiently as Glen got ready and then with little more than a sip of coffee, he hauled him outside.

The truck bumped along the desert track before turning onto the scenic route. Cody took the rough but straight road that ran through the countryside towards the distant mountains.

"So how long will it take to get where we're going?" Glen asked. He had a growing empty feeling in the pit of his stomach.

"Don't worry. It's not far. Sarah has rented a house on the outskirts of town."

Glen noted the 'not far' comment. The English didn't understand the American concept of distance, who considered a hundred miles a quick trip. With little to do apart from watching the scenery, he twiddled with his phone. It took a while to get a signal and Google the town, which turned out to be rather mundane. It had approximately three hundred inhabitants, most of whom were well over sixty-five. Apart from the sheriff's office, they had Sam's diner/garage and Stan's local store, which doubled up as a post office. That was about it. He couldn't describe it as a one-horse town more of a one-horse and a mule town. Once a prosperous mining settlement, it had gradually faded back into the desert when the copper had run out sometime last century. Now the inhabitants lived off passing trade and some local ranching, but the poor desert soil provided little in the way of good fodder for their cattle. Glen stared at a few pictures. This place seemed an unlikely centre for events. With a sigh, he realised that it would take a while to get there, so he rested his head against the side of the truck and decided to watch the world go by. Instead, he woke with a snort as Cody thumped his arm.

"Hey wake up we're almost there. By the way, you were snoring," he said grinning.

Glen yawned, bleary-eyed and stiff. He stretched, rubbed his neck, and blinked as the truck rumbled into town. White wooden buildings topped by slate grey roofs lined a wide dusty road. Just like the pictures.

"She's at the other end of town," said Cody.

A moment later, they pulled up in front of a wooden house with a blue door. Cody parked and not waiting for Glen, jumped out and ran up the path. Glen, on the other hand, slowly creaked out of the truck, his muscles aching from the journey.

Cody rang the doorbell several times and stood, tapping his foot as he fidgeted with impatience. After a few minutes, Glen shrugged at Cody.

"Perhaps she's out?" he suggested.

"But I sent her a message," Cody protested.

"Ok, well then let's look around."

Glen felt awkward, like some burglar casing out a joint, but he glanced around anyway. A jeep sat parked in front of the garage. Through the gate, the back garden itself looked little more than a patch of grass, a patio with a BBQ and a storage shed. "Guess she could be in the shed or the garage. I'll try the shed. You try the garage."

Cody nodded and headed towards the garage.

Glen walked over a manhole cover towards the shed and tapped on the door. "Anyone at home?"

No one replied, but Cody had more luck. When he knocked on the back door, he heard a crash and the sound of muffled swearing. Glen thought that they had probably found Sarah, either that or some mad scientist making a fiendish creature out of body parts. This impression didn't improve when echoing footsteps approached the door. It opened slowly with a menacing creak. Glen held his breath in anticipation. He felt mildly disappointed when it revealed not a nightmarish apparition but a woman dressed in a lab coat. Both men stood grinning awkwardly, unable or unwilling to speak. In the end, Glen elbowed Cody in the ribs.

Cody nodded, then spoke, "Hi, Sarah, did you get my message?"

She smiled. "Yes, sorry, I forgot! I didn't realise the time." She glanced around. "Err what time is it?"

"About lunchtime, I think."

"No wonder I was feeling hungry! Time flies when you're having fun." She smiled cheerfully.

Glen didn't understand her concept of fun but peeking into the garage, it looked like it consisted of flasks, microscopes, camera equipment, and an awful lot of small boxes.

Sarah noticed his apparent interest. "Welcome to my humble lab. I'm working on my PhD. Do you have an interest in ecology?"

"I'm more of a history man myself." He put his hand out. "By the way, my name's Glen. I'm staying with Cody."

As they shook hands, both men missed the look that Sarah gave. Friend or partner, she wondered.

"Cody told me about your recent experience," said Glen. "And I wanted to hear about it from the horse's mouth, so to speak."

They didn't miss her next expression. Cody tried to rectify his friend's mistake. "Not that you look like a horse or anything."

They stood in awkward silence before Sarah dismissed that comment and shrugged. "Look I'll just get changed and take you there. Then you can make up your own minds."

Cody grinned. "Good idea, we can see the scene of the crime."

The truck bounced along the uneven track. Cody stared out of the window while Glen occasionally glanced at Sarah. She looked average, neither pretty nor ugly, mousy brown hair, medium build, but unusually, she had startling green eyes.

"So," she said finally. "I thought you guys wanted to hear what happened?"

Glen nodded. She filled them in on the details and then pointed. "Ah well, we're almost there you can take a look for yourself."

They drove off the road and up a heavily rutted track, which wound around the hillside. As the truck turned the corner, Glen could see a house tucked into the hill, below a rocky outcrop. It looked so ordinary, not the place for a strange death. They pulled up outside the home and looked around. The cops had put a no entry sign on the door and barred their way with tape. Glen waited and wondered what to do, but Cody just ignored the warning, opened the door, and ducked underneath the tape.

"Hey, where's the outline of the body?" he said, sounding disappointed.

Glen looked inside. "Do they still do that?"

"Dunno but I expected something at least."

Sarah joined them and pointed to the floor. "I found him there."

They peered at the spot as she walked around the room. "See what I mean? No blood stains, no signs of a struggle or break-in."

Glen looked at the scuffed marks on the floor. "What about these footsteps?"

"I think they're new."

"Did you get a good look at the body?"

"Well, as good as I could."

"What about the bites you mentioned?"

"It's my guess they weren't bites, well not any insect bites I've ever seen, more like puncture wounds. Besides, Mr Johnson's skin seemed too wrinkled. I mean sure he's an old man but he appeared almost shrunken."

Sarah looked sideways at Cody, who hopped from one foot to another.

"Is he ok?" she asked, unsure if this was normal behaviour.

Glen gave an embarrassed shrug. "He likes a mystery."

Cody grinned. "A mystery, more like a cover-up! They must have killed him elsewhere and moved the body."

Glen and Sarah looked at each other.

"It's possible," she agreed and then asked the dreaded question. "Who would do that?"

"It must be the government in collusion with local law enforcement or big business. Perhaps to cover up an experiment in area 51 that went wrong." He paced the room. "Yes, they mutated local wildlife to feed on blood. The government knows but considers that the mutations might be useful in warfare or the biotech industries. Government agents infiltrated local law enforcement, in an attempt to conceal the evidence by moving the body."

Sarah stood open-mouthed, dumbfounded, not quite believing what she had just heard.

Glen winced, but not wishing to contradict his friend in front of anyone he said, "Well that's one theory at least. Shall we go outside and see what else we can find?"

They ducked under the tape and fanned out. Sarah went around the side of the house. Glen and Cody moved towards the opposite corner at the back of the property and then stood surprised.

"Hey, Sarah," called Glen. "Come and take a look at this."

She rounded the corner and stared at the back yard. Tumbleweed filled the corral. "Creepy."

Cody put his head on one side. "Careful," he cautioned. "Perhaps the threat comes from flora, not fauna."

Sarah looked at him, sceptically. "You mean mutated tumbleweed?"

He shrugged. "Well, maybe not these specimens but others, who knows."

As they stood in contemplation, Sarah stared at Cody. Was this guy crazy and off his meds?

Glen noticed and frantically sought for something interesting to say. "Did you know that Tumbleweed isn't native to Arizona? Ukrainian farmers accidentally introduced it, and its real name is Russian thistle."

Sarah raised an eyebrow. "You don't say."

He pushed on in desperate hope. "It moves by tumbling in the wind and can spread up to a quarter of a million seeds." He blushed at her piercing stare. "Sorry, I'm babbling. After all, you're the ecologist, you know these things."

She sighed. "Well, crazy as this all sounds, it's probably worth taking a few samples." Beneath her breath, she added, "If only to shut you both up."

It didn't work. The drive back numbed Glen and Sarah. Both excited and worried about being part of a conspiracy, Cody concocted scenarios that were ever more bizarre. Once home, he vowed to Glen that he would find anyone connected with this heinous crime and bring them to justice.

Chapter 22

Karen

That lazy weekend after returning from holiday hadn't been a good idea. Karen rushed around, desperately trying to get dressed, but after the random unpacking, she couldn't find a thing. Skirt askew, blouse half-done up, one stiletto on, the other missing, she searched the house getting more frustrated by the minute. At only five-foot-tall, Karen never went out without a pair of six-inch heels. When she finally found the missing item, she sighed and reluctantly put on her make-up.

It's a shame that holiday's didn't last because now it was back to reality. Not that Karen found life tough, but sometimes it could be tedious. At least she had decent pay, and her colleagues weren't humourless zombies, unlike her last job. That should make her grateful, but somehow it didn't seem enough. She needed some excitement or at least a challenge. That reminded her of the old adage, be careful what you wish for. With a sigh, Karen smoothed down her long blond bob and hurried out of the door towards the train station. She just managed to catch the eight o'clock to Bristol.

Once at work, Karen checked her emails. After two weeks away, it became a mammoth task. Just separating the essential letters from the usual semi-spam took all morning. The two most interesting concerned an IT project and another about the Annual Business Performance Conference next week. Karen smiled. She always enjoyed the conference, and it reminded her to email Rebecca to confirm her attendance. After that, time dragged, and by the end of the day, Karen couldn't wait to go home.

A misty autumn night settled across the city. As she stepped outside, a chilly wind swirled around her, so she gathered up her collar and walked briskly across the square. Her heels clicked on the stone pavement while her mind ticked-over in the background.

"A penny for your thoughts, dear lady?"

The nearby voice made Karen jump.

An old woman in rough clothing held out a small posy. "Will you buy a lucky charm?"

Karen often dropped her spare change into a charity box but buying a spray of heather, sounded more like a scam. Yet, part of her took pity on this old lady, while another part cursed for being a soft touch.

In the end, she passed over a small note. The old woman stared at it for a moment and then snatched the money, before handing Karen the heather. A shrewd, calculating look then passed across the gipsy's face judging, probably quite accurately, that she could extract more money from this easy mark.

"What about a palm reading my sweet?"

Karen sighed at her own stupidity, but she indulged the woman anyway. The gipsy took her hand and moved into a singsong storytelling voice.

"You will meet a tall, dark, handsome stranger."

What a surprise thought Karen cynically, but then something rather odd happened. The 'would be' palmist reacted unexpectedly and if Karen guessed correctly, quite out of character. The old woman's face wrinkled in surprise and disquiet.

The gipsy dropped her artificial tone and returned to her own voice. "Hum, stranger and darker than I have ever seen before." She looked closer, tracing the lines with her finger. "You will be going on a long journey, far, far away."

At that, Karen laughed. "I've only just come back."

The old woman squinted as if searching for something. "No," she whispered. "No, that can't be right."

In distress, she pushed Karen's hand away before taking a step back. "You'll need that lucky charm girl."

Karen stared, astonished, wondering if this was part of the act. She went to hand over another donation when the old woman made a decision.

"Keep it," she said, waving the money away.

With a shake of her head, the woman turned and hurried off across the square as if trying to put as much distance between them as possible. When she reached the other side, she glanced back at Karen and muttered something under her breath, before fading into the misty night.

Karen watched her go and then shrugged. "What strange behaviour."

After all, she didn't believe in palm reading, but a small doubt lingered in her mind as she took the train home.

Chapter 23

Lars and Stefan

Stefan rolled over and banged his head on the wall. "Ow!" He rubbed his forehead and tried to sit up only to bang his head on the underside of the cart. "Stupid idiot!"

He felt tired and clumsy because he'd slept poorly, not a good start to any morning. Stefan rolled over, and then it dawned on him. Why hadn't he squashed Lars? Lars should be complaining like hell. In the dark, cramped space under the cart, he couldn't see the outline of his friend only his bedding. Stefan fumbled for the internal lock and then tried to lift the shutter. After some frustrated swearing, he remembered to undo the outer bolt, and then, of course, it opened quickly enough. Light flooded into the little room blinding Stefan with early morning sunshine. He crawled out, shading his eyes, and looked around for his friend.

Lars!" he yelled. His mind whirled as he searched the area. Something had scuffed the ground, but he couldn't see any blood. "Lars!" he yelled again.

He couldn't see any signs of a fight, but Stefan felt a stab of guilt. He knew that he could have slept through the noise. Other people complained about his deep sleep. He didn't remember anything, but they swore that he slept all night and grunted like an angry boar. Stefan winced. What would Asta say? He knew that she depended on him to look after her brother.

"Lars!" he bellowed. "Where are you?"

Lars emerged from the scrub. He sounded tired and irritated. "What?"

Stefan grinned, overjoyed to see his friend alive. He picked him up and hugged him tightly. Amid the iron grip, Lars found he could do little more than gasp and splutter.

"Let me go you great lump," he croaked hoarsely.

Stefan dropped him immediately looking contrite, but then his face began to change from joy through concern to anger. Now over the shock, Stefan became irate.

He leaned forward, grabbed Lars by the shirt, and began to shake as he yelled, "Where the hell have you been? I've been worried sick. I thought you were dead and I would have to tell your sister. What could I say? That I had left her only brother to die alone in the desert. She would never forgive me. I could never forgive myself!"

Lars felt his teeth rattle as Stefan continued to rant.

"P-Put me d-down!" he stammered, and sure enough Stefan did, but he continued to glower at his friend in righteous indignation.

Lars simply smoothed down his clothes, gave a cheeky smile, and said coyly, "I didn't know you cared so much."

That did not go down well with Stefan who glared and stomped off with a, "Humph!"

Lars chuckled at his friend's response. He would get over it soon. Stefan didn't hold a grudge. Anyway, what could he say? Oh, by the way, I spent the night in a shelter in the past, or perhaps the future or somewhere else. One thing Lars did know, it did not happen in the here and now.

From the noise at the campsite, Stefan had begun to take his ire out on the cooking pans. God alone knows what he would make for breakfast, but Lars didn't fancy eating it. In the end, he got the silent treatment over a cup of lukewarm tea and some cold sausage.

Not until later, after they had packed everything away, Stefan said, "Don't do that again ok?"

"Ok."

Lars had to agree, but something inside him made him realise that he wouldn't be able to keep that promise. As it turned out, he'd got lucky. He must have spent part of the night outside. A cold shiver of realisation ran down his spine. He wouldn't stand a chance if the tumblers caught him out in the open and next time if that happened, his luck might run out. Lars smiled weakly at Stefan, who slapped him on the back. At least all seemed forgiven for now.

Once hitched up, they continued along the black road again travelling over hillocks and around potholes. The way seemed to be getting worse, and the progress slowed but eventually over a small rise, they could see buildings on the horizon. Stefan squinted, trying to estimate the distance. Perhaps they would get there an hour or two before nightfall. The hard slog had taken its toll but as Lars reminded Stefan, better than shovelling shit, although Stefan didn't entirely agree. For the most part, he'd enjoyed *his* apprenticeship.

By now, they were nearing the buildings, and from what Lars could see, they appeared taller than anticipated. It reminded him of the city in his dreams but older and more broken. They would face danger from falling masonry, unstable floors, and creatures that lived in the dark, cool depths.

Stefan must have been thinking the same thing because he said, "We should camp outside the city and make a fresh start tomorrow."

His friend nodded. "I agree."

Chapter 24

Adam

Adam stretched and thumped his alarm clock. That dream had been good, although very strange in parts and so real. Unlike most people, he could remember his nightmares, and when he got ill or hot, they became vivid. Sometimes he could take control and steer them, but only a little. He'd also debunked the myth that dying in dreams killed you in real life. Once he had fallen off a cliff. When he hit the ground, he had a surprise. The fall should have killed him, but it didn't. Instead, the earth had become soft, his rational mind explaining away the anomaly. Like now, he'd woken in sweat, slightly terrified but this time also disturbingly aroused.

Adam sighed; it had been one of 'those' dreams. His married friends would laugh and tell him that deep down he feared relationships. Any woman he dated would turn into a monster, and he did have a nasty tendency to pick psychos. On a night out, he drank too much and chatted up the nearest pretty girl. Once both sober, they found they had nothing in common apart from sex. The gym had become much the same. He liked to watch the girls during their spin class. He'd been through most of them, and every relationship had fallen apart, but he didn't mind. He could usually persuade them when he felt in the mood. It usually ended when the clingy female went entirely off the rails, but having learnt this lesson; it wasn't much of a problem. Nowadays he didn't stay with them long enough to get to that stage.

Adam rolled over, climbed out of bed, and looked into the massive mirrors on his fitted wardrobe. Tall, muscled, his short blond hair framed high cheekbones and a chiselled jaw. He also had deep and dreamy hazel eyes or so countless women had told him.

"That's odd."

He moved closer to the mirror and tilted his head to one side. A graze ran down his neck. He must have scratched himself in the night. As he stared, it started to fade, so he smiled and dismissed it. Hell, he felt fine today, in fact, better than fine.

After a shower and a cup of coffee, Adam listened to the TV. The media kept banging on about a missing boy when he wanted to listen to the business news. Adam shook his head in disgust and glanced at the clock. He couldn't risk being late, so he grabbed his briefcase and walked to catch the train.

Adam had joined Redfern & Brewster just over a year ago. Since then, his good looks and charm had served him well. Now his manager considered him the new hotshot. The downside of which meant his work colleagues thoroughly disliked him, but he didn't care. Most of them just coasted with little or no ambition past the next pay cheque. They fixated on their holidays and family life, but Adam wanted so much more. He wanted to be top of the pyramid, the boss of his boss, the top dog. He wanted the high life, the power, and prestige that went with being a CEO, and finally, he had the chance to prove himself.

Rumours circulated that the sports retail giant, Lomax had started to look for a new marketing representative. Mr Hall, Adams boss, approached them and suggested that they might consider Redfern & Brewster. The representative of the Lomax Corporation tentatively agreed, and they had set a meeting date. Along with other representatives, they intended to send Mr Knox, who had a reputation of being a perfectionist.

Adam arrived at work on time, sauntered through the large double doors and smiled at the reception staff as he passed. "Good morning, ladies."

"Good morning, Adam," they replied in chorus.

A lot of chatter went through reception along with most of the phone calls. The reception staff turned out to be an excellent source of information and keeping them sweet meant they often told him the news before anyone else.

On a typical day, he would take the stairs up to the fourth floor, but today he took the lift. Samantha, from accounting, smiled and asked if he was going up. He smiled back and thanked her. As they travelled upwards, he idly considered the possibility that she might be interested in him. While married, she was hot and an easy target, bored as she must be by that tedious husband of hers.

Adam got out of the lift and ambled across the open plan office. As he passed, he glanced at his work colleagues with barely concealed disdain. Soon this sorry lot would have to look up to him. On the one hand, they were useful. On the other hand, they *shared* his success. They needed to see him as their natural leader, but their growing jealousy could be a problem.

Along with the office rank and file, he gradually made his way to his desk behind the eye height dividers, which afforded little privacy.

As he put down his case, Mr Hall called out across the office, "Adam, I'd like a word with you."

"Certainly, Mr Hall."

His boss walked over and clapped him on the shoulder.

"I've been thinking, and I have decided that you are the best person to make the Lomax presentation. I'd also like you to lead the team in the final stages of preparation both today and tomorrow morning before the client arrives."

Adam carefully portrayed humble acceptance. "Thank you, Mr Hall. I appreciate your confidence in me."

"I think that you have shown tremendous commitment in bringing this new client on board and I understand how hard you've worked."

A grunt of disbelief from someone in the office marred the moment.

Mr Hall frowned and raised his voice, "Unlike others, I know you have the best interests of this company at heart."

"Thank you, Mr Hall. I will do my best to live up to your expectations."

Mr Hall clapped Adam resoundingly on the back. "I'm sure you will, as always you are the best we have. After this Lomax client is on board, we must have another little chat."

Adam beamed. "Certainly, Mr Hall."

They would need a new section head in the winter once Andrea retired. She had been on extended sick leave, so Mr Hall had seconded Amos to fill her position. He hadn't done well. If the rumours were true, he would happily slip back into his old job, leaving the vacancy wide open for Adam.

"Well I should get back to work Sir, there's a lot to do today if we are to hook this fish."

Mr Hall smiled and nodded in satisfaction. "That's the attitude, always an eye on the prize."

As his boss walked away, Adam looked over the office staff and saw emotions dance across each face. Some seemed bewildered; others resigned, while a few fumed with impotent fury. That praise had swallowed all their hard work. Adam had taken their thunder and turned it into dust. He would have to do something about their attitudes once he got a promotion. While Adam could ignore some insubordination, he wouldn't let it develop into open rebellion. Some he could charm, others he would threaten, or sideline if needed. They had better learn to co-operate, or they would find themselves doing endless, pointless paperwork in the basement filing room.

Chapter 25

Thomas

Thomas woke once more on the soft green carpet of moss and ferns. Even in this beautiful place, he felt sad. His parents didn't miss him. They didn't love him. He lay staring up at the enormous golden green trees, watching their leaves cascade gently down. In the distance, he could hear the rush of water and above him the sound of foliage rustling in the wind. Birds flitted from branch to branch announcing their territorial claims, while nearby a small deer bounded over the mossy ground towards some unknown destination. Thomas felt the sadness gradually drain away. He wanted so badly to belong here, but he felt small and clumsy in comparison with Aeglas. As for Tinnueth, Thomas had never seen anyone more beautiful and perfect. He wanted to be just like them. Maybe if he wished hard enough, it would come true.

Tinnueth stopped and listened to that strange sound. She had heard that before. Curious to see if Thomas had come back, she slid gracefully down a rope from the platform towards the ground. After a hundred feet, she jumped the rest of the way and landed quietly on the earth. The noise had come from the west, so she ran silently in that direction. The boy wasn't far away, so it only took a few moments to find him. He lay on the ground staring silently up into the trees, apparently upset.
She knelt down and looked at him with concern and sympathy. "Child, what is the matter?"
He turned his head and scowled. "I'm not a child."
Tinnueth smiled at his defiance, by any measure he was a child, but she didn't want to upset him, so she agreed, "No, you're not; you're a boy."

The scowl faded, replaced by a shy smile. At least Tinnueth cares, he thought. Without a word, Thomas jumped up and put his arms around her. She smiled and hugged him as he hugged her tightly. After a while, he let go and looked at her.

"I love you," he announced.

This surprised Tinnueth, but she didn't show it.

He waited for an answer; then asked, "Do you love me too?"

She could tell he was quite sincere, but no one had ever asked her this question before. Did she love this child, a human child that she barely knew? Yet she couldn't say no, it would hurt him, so she evaded the question. "Thomas, what happened?"

He hung his head and whispered, "I went home, and they didn't care."

"Who didn't care?"

"My mum and dad didn't care. My mum wasn't even there, and my dad snored on the settee like a warthog, but you missed me, didn't you?"

That question she could answer with a clear conscience. "Yes, I missed you."

"And you care?"

"Yes, I care."

Thomas smiled shyly and gave her another hug before he decided. "I'm hungry!"

Tinnueth laughed. "You're always hungry."

She held her hand out to him, and he took it. Together they made their way towards the town. He looked forward to dinner already. Thomas liked the feasting hall with its great gnarled tables, metal stove, and crystal lights. It reminded him of old-fashioned pictures of winter fest, but best of all he liked the food.

When they arrived at the town, she summoned the ropes from the trees.

Tinnueth bent to help him, but Thomas declined. "I don't need help from anyone."

"Except Aeglas?"

Thomas considered that comment and conceded. "Yes, but he's special." He thought about it. "You're special too, but in another way."

"Good, I'd hate to be outdone."

Thomas hooked his foot into the loop and ascended without fear. Once at the top, he dashed nimbly across the walkways towards the feasting hall.

"I'm back," he yelled as he pushed open the door.

His exuberant entry amused those in the room. They smiled and muttered to one another. His behaviour made a welcome change. Thomas looked around and spotted Aeglas sitting at a table near the fireplace. He grinned as the boy ran over.

Aeglas looked him over with a critical eye. "You're getting bigger each time I see you."

Thomas grinned. "Hi, Aeglas." He looked hopeful. "When's dinner?"

Aeglas chuckled, amazed that the boy had such a bottomless pit for a stomach. "The cooks are almost ready. If you sit down, they will bring the dishes out any time now."

Thomas sat and fidgeted, hunger gnawing at his stomach. He almost pounced on the food as they put it on the table, but then he remembered his manners and waited until others had taken their portions.

Aeglas noticed his reticence. "It's alright to help yourself. You can take as much as you want."

"Thanks, Aeglas."

Thomas piled the plate high and then tucked in. He only took a few minutes to clear the plate before he reached for another helping.

"Soon, you will be as tall and strong as me if you keep eating that way. That or you'll burst."

Thomas laughed. "Imagine the mess!"

This time Thomas ate slowly savouring each bite. There were so many dishes to choose from each one different from the last. Some creamy, some spicy, others crunchy but all tasted delicious.

Tinnueth smiled at the boy, at least he was happy, but once again, his arrival troubled her. She could see it troubled Aeglas too, although the signs were subtle. She slipped silently out of the feasting hall and made her way to Master Raphael's study. There Tinnueth found him sitting behind his great desk talking to Vanya.

"Sorry to disturb you, if it's important I can come back later," she said.

"No, it's alright. How can I help?"

"Thomas is back."

Vanya glanced at Raphael, although their people were patient, they had expected questions sooner rather than later.

"I heard an odd noise and found him lying on the ground. Yet I know that he won't stay, he will vanish again. I would like to ask how this happens and more importantly, why?"

Tinnueth had asked an unusually direct question for one of the people.

Raphael chose to answer her less directly. "I've been refreshing my memory."

He picked up a weathered leather-bound book and gently turned over the delicate pages. "This book is one of my most treasured possessions. It is extremely old." He looked up. "Can you read the title?"

Tinnueth peered over his desk. "'The Origins of the Elven Empire.' Does that include the Great War?" she asked.

Raphael raised an eyebrow in surprise. "And how do you know of such things?"

Tinnueth stared awkwardly at the floor. "I'm sorry. I spoke out of turn."

"Yes, many would think that. I know the law forbids us to speak of those times, but somehow, you know."

When she didn't answer, he said more gently, "Don't worry, I won't betray you."

Only partially reassured, she mumbled, "My family."

He nodded, but he could tell she had something else on her mind.

"Why have you not relinquished this book?" she asked.

"It is my personal copy."

Tinnueth frowned. "Master Thaumaturge," she said using his official title. "Shouldn't it be in the library in Araothron?"

Raphael shrugged. "Perhaps but what they don't know won't hurt them."

His comment shocked Tinnueth. She had never understood why someone of his standing chose to reside in this backwater town. Perhaps this was the reason.

Raphael leaned back in his chair and mused, "I wonder what else your family has told you."

Again, she chose not to reply.

"I hope you understand that in showing you the book, I have placed great trust in you. Do you know what would happen, if anyone else were to find out?"

Tinnueth nodded.

"And you know what would happen to Thomas should the council learn of his existence?"

Tinnueth could only imagine.

The master continued, "He is too young. He will not be able to answer their questions. Well, not to their satisfaction."

"What will happen to him?"

Raphael leaned back in his chair; his hands clasped together in contemplation. "I have contacts, but I am not sure if they would aid or betray me." He sighed. "I must study the old texts and come to some decision. For the moment, keep Thomas close and safe, until I know how to proceed."

****

The news report flashed before the young man's eyes as he ate his dinner, but he didn't pay much attention. The TV had become just background noise to drown the silence of an empty house. Later that night, slumped on the couch, he flicked through the channels and came across the news story once more.

The newscaster updated the current situation. "And the police are continuing to search for the boy missing since Friday night."

A picture of a familiar face flashed across the screen, and the man froze. Could he be sure? The image vanished. He thought about it. Perhaps that could be the boy from the park. He'd seen them running across the grass, and he'd confronted the greasy man, but strangely, the boy had vanished. That would be a problem. How could he explain it? The police might not believe him. He sat, trying to decide whether he should ring them or not.

The newscaster continued. "A source confirms that the police have questioned the boy's father on suspicion of murder, but they released him without charge. The police have chosen not to comment on this only saying that enquiries are ongoing."

The father questioned, of course, they would want to eliminate the family from their investigation, but had he seen the father in the park or someone else?

"The police ask that anyone with information should contact them." The presenter gave the number.

The man sat in a numb stupor for a while, mulling over the idea. He couldn't decide whether he should call them or not. In the end, he decided that he felt too tired to talk to anyone this late, so he went to bed. Perhaps he'd call in the morning.

Chapter 26

Karen

The night sky had fallen from heaven to earth. Tiny twinkling points of light flickered in a dark abyss. Such beauty astounded her. High above the glow, Karen noted shades of red and purple, dotted throughout the mass of glittering starlight. The pure magnificence captivated her mind as an irresistible desire welled deep inside. Karen felt that she would never feel satisfied unless she could reach out and touch them. She didn't even realise that she had stepped forward until the freezing pain in her bare feet brought her back to reality. Beyond her toes, the darkness deepened. One more step and she would have plunged off a cliff.

Karen backed away, giving an involuntary shudder at her narrow escape. Cold and shivering, she pulled her dressing gown tightly around her shoulders and remembered a documentary on the ocean deeps. In the depths lived an anglerfish. It dangled a lamplight lure attracting little fish who died in a mouth of razor-sharp teeth. Was she that little fish? Had others perished in their overwhelming desire to see the lights? She shivered again and turned away.

Behind her, a wide tunnel stretched off into the darkness. A place that Karen subconsciously sensed she should avoid. To her right nothing but a sheer drop. To her left, the dim outline of a sloping path, it's back wall reflected in the starlight. She gingerly took a few steps towards it and reached out to touch the vertical stone. It felt smooth beneath her fingers as if a million hands had caressed the rock as they passed. Beneath her feet, the floor like the wall felt worn and even. It might be a well-trodden path, but it seemed stupid to follow it. Yet move or freeze, remained her only two options. With small shuffling steps, Karen hugged the wall and walked down the slope. She kept her head turned away from the dark edge and the intoxicating lights.

After a while, the path got steeper then swept right. Karen inched her way down towards the corner, which then flattened out. Once safely there, she sighed quietly with relief and rested against the wall. Nearby, Karen could hear rushing water that echoed in the darkness. Down here, the stars did not cast their light. If something lurked in the gloom, then it did so silently, waiting perhaps for her to move closer. For a moment, she struggled to keep herself from panicking. A practical person at heart she preferred to rely on logic whenever possible, but this did not feel like a logical situation. Her choices remained stark, go back up the path into the darkness, or move on. A random thought popped into her mind, girding her loins, a phrase, which made her laugh. The chuckle had a slightly hysterical edge.

The roaring water drowned the sound of her bare feet, but that didn't stop Karen from listening with intense concentration. As she crept forward, her left foot clipped the edge of something hard. When she looked down, she could see nothing, so she looked up. A tall shape loomed out of the darkness. For a second, Karen froze, not knowing whether to run or hide. When nothing happened, she relaxed and gingerly touched the object. It felt like the edge of a great-carved chunk of rock and realised that it was a massive statue. When Karen looked up and squinted, she saw a long-eared humanoid head glowing dimly in the reflected starlight. Karen shuddered. Who had carved the figure?

A noise made her spin around, her heart thumping in panic. Frozen like the statue, she listened intently. Over the sound of the river, Karen swore that she could hear voices echoing in the darkness. Maybe they were friendly, but she couldn't risk it. She couldn't run, but perhaps she could hide. The statue offered the only option. Karen stretched out her hands and felt her way around the side, towards the back. Here she found her access blocked by a wall, so she hunkered down where it met the statue. As Karen finally settled, a strange vibration emanated from the base. It tingled through the soles of her feet, setting her teeth on edge. A shout went up, and footsteps advanced towards her. As she scrambled to rise, her foot slipped on what turned out to be a damp, narrow ledge. With a small shriek, Karen fell into the roaring darkness below.

Chapter 27

Lars

The area behind the shelter looked filthy. Wet cardboard and paper stuck to the ground, while empty food cartons and plastic bottles rattled in the wind. If this was civilisation, Lars wanted nothing to do with it. For the first time, he had a window into the preacher's mind. These people were not evil, but in many respects, they didn't care. They had so much but didn't appreciate it enough to keep their streets clean.

The rain splattered down his neck, and he shivered in the gusty wind. The abrupt change from the desert heat shocked him, and he desperately wanted to get out of the rain. Lars pulled his thin collar around his neck and walked towards the shelter as the wind buffeted his body. When he rounded the corner, he bumped into Phil the night shelter worker.

The man recognised him. "Hey here already?"

Lars nodded.

"Well, it's going to turn into a wet and windy night."

Phil rattled the keys in the lock and opened the night shelter door. He turned towards Lars with an apologetic look on his face.

"It's only 6pm. I really shouldn't let you in yet," he said.

Lars understood. "That's ok," he replied amiably.

At least if he stood close to the door, he could stay relatively dry. The canopy provided some shelter although the occasional strong gust blew the rain onto the mat.

Phil peered at the foul weather with a guilty look on his face and then relented. "Well, you can come in if you are willing to help me out."

Lars looked surprised. "Sure, what do you need?"

"Well once some of the volunteers arrive, I'll need to go out to the local supermarket and collect the out of date food. They let us have it rather than throwing it away."

Lars didn't understand Phil. Words like, 'out of date' or 'throw away' did not apply to food, unless it became green and runny, but he didn't question him. Instead, he just nodded.

"Great!" said Phil.

A noise behind Lars indicated that a cart had arrived. Two people got out and scurried over to the door, shaking the rain off their clothes as they came inside. "Cor foul night Phil."

"Hey Ian, hey Silvia, yeah it's getting worse. I think we'll have a full house tonight." Phil turned to Lars. "This is," then he paused. "Sorry I've forgotten your name."

"Lars."

"Lars? Sounds northern are you from the north?" asked Silvia as she took off her coat and hung it up.

"Yes, I am."

He didn't say which north. They would hardly believe him if he told the truth.

"If you guys get started Lars and I will go and get the food if that's ok?" said Phil.

"Sure." They both agreed.

"Ok, let's take the van," he said, turning to Lars.

Lars didn't know what 'take the van' meant either but he was intrigued to find out. Phil led Lars across the space in front of the night shelter and into an adjacent alleyway. Next to the wall sat a large white cart. When Phil unlocked it and jumped inside Lars surmised that this must be 'the van.'

He paused for a moment unsure what to do, but Phil leaned across, opened the other door, and yelled from inside, "Get in!"

Lars felt like an intrepid explorer, discovering the unknown as he grasped the handle and slipped inside the van. Soft and amazingly comfortable, the seats moulded to his body, unlike anything he had encountered before. His feet rested on some strange black spongy material, designed by the looks of it, to repel water.

Phil interrupted his thoughts. "Well close the door and buckle up."

Ah yes, he would have to close the door to shut out the rain but what did buckle up mean? Lars grasped the door handle and with a gentle pull closed it.

"How do I buckle up?" he asked.

Phil looked surprised. "You've never been in a car before?"

"I thought you said this was a van."

"Pfft car or van, they are pretty much the same."

"Ok then in answer to your question, no I have never been in a car before."

Phil gave Lars a very odd look but relented. "Ok well, you take this." He pointed to the belt. "And put that metal clip into that holder there." He pointed to a strange aperture.

Lars did as Phil instructed, but unlike the seat, it didn't feel very comfortable. "What's this for?"

"It's to stop you flying through the windscreen if I have to stop suddenly."

Lars didn't know what he meant by windscreen but flying through it didn't sound like a good idea. "Ah, thanks."

Phil gave Lars another odd look. "Are you sure you're not pulling my leg?"

Lars had not pulled his leg or any other part of Phil's body, so he just answered. "No, I'm not."

"How come you have never been in a car before?"

"They don't have them where I come from."

Phil studied Lars as best he could while driving. He appeared to be a blond Northman as far as Phil could tell. They were as advanced as the rest of the developed world. He knew he shouldn't pry, but his curiosity got the better of him.

"Where do you come from?" asked Phil.

"Holmfast, it's in the north along the banks of the river Mersyn."

"I've not heard of those before."

Lars hesitated. He began to doubt that he had travelled into the past. This world had attitudes too different from his own. Perhaps he had visited the future or even another planet.

"No, you wouldn't, it's not around here. I'm a traveller. I'm not sure if this is the past or the future or if I am just from another world, but it's very different here. Your world is so full of marvels that people take for granted."

Phil just smiled, now he knew that Lars was taking the piss. "Sure, you are mate," he replied, humouring his travelling companion.

Lars could tell that Phil didn't believe a word, even though he'd only voiced the truth. Oh well, at least he had tried.

The van began to slow and turn on to a large black area covered with many white lines, some of which contained cars. Phil turned gently into a space at the back of a large building and stopped.

He turned to Lars. "Well, Mr Traveller, we are here. Now you can help me load the food into the back of the van."

Phil got out and knocked on a large set of double doors. As Lars joined him, a man wearing some strange brightly coloured clothes answered. He invited them just inside, out of the rain and told them to wait for the duty manager. At first, Lars thought the man looked like a jester in his brightly coloured clothes, but then he saw other people wearing the same outfit, which troubled him. It reminded him of the Overlords men but without the weaponry. Phil though seemed quite relaxed, so Lars tried not to worry.

Soon a man more sombrely dressed came over and shook Phil's hand. "Good work you are doing on such a foul night. There's a full cage tonight, trading's been slow today, and there are plenty of packages on their end date. I'll just get one of the staff to wheel it out for you, ok?"

"Sure, thanks, we appreciate this," Phil replied with a smile.

"No problem, nice meeting you again," replied the duty manager and they shook hands once more.

They waited until Lars heard an odd rattling noise. Around the corner, emerged a tall metal cage on wheels, containing assorted boxes of many shapes and sizes. It stopped, and a face peered out from behind the cage.

"It's all yours; let me know when you've finished unpacking," said the man.

"Sure thing," said Phil.

Phil opened the van and indicated to Lars that he should start to untie the straps on the cage so that they could unload. Lars couldn't resist running his hands over the bright metal. So much wealth to move food, he found it amazing!

"Hey," yelled Phil. "It's raining cats and dogs out here! Are you going to help or just stand there like a lemon?"

Lars looked up, the rain hammered down, soaking Phil but stare as he might; he couldn't see any animals falling from the sky. The words made sense, but somehow, he didn't understand their context, yet another confusing aspect of this place.

Phil reversed the van so that its rear end backed up against the cage, out of the weather. He leapt out and together they bundled the boxes into the back. Lars noticed the neat packaging around each piece of food. He could see nothing wrong with it.

"Is this out of date food?" he questioned cautiously.

"Yes," Phil replied, stacking more boxes.

"What does out of date actually mean?"

Phil had to pause for a moment to think. He had taken the concept for granted so he couldn't come up with an immediate answer. "I think it's when the quality starts to deteriorate, some of it you need to eat before a certain date for safety reasons, but other stuff is ok but not at its best."

Lars found this a strange concept. "Out of date food where I come from, is when it goes green and runny," said Lars.

Phil chuckled. "Not everyone has the same standards."

A thought occurred to Lars. "Does this mean that people waste a lot of food?"

"Yeah, they can do."

To Lars who lived in a country where starvation could happen if the harvest failed, the idea of wasting food appalled him. These people seemed so rich that they could afford to throw it away, and yet he had seen other people, like Ted, who weren't wealthy at all. Like so much, this made no sense to Lars.

They finished loading the van. Lars went back into the warehouse and called out that they had finished. A member of staff came out and pushed the precious metal cage back into the store. On the journey back to the shelter, Lars sat in silence, wrapped up in his own thoughts. He felt tired from his days on the plateau, which seemed more than a world away, and confused by all he had seen.

When they pulled up outside the shelter, Phil turned to him looking concerned. "Something on your mind?"

Lars just shrugged too weary and unwilling to discuss what he felt, even if he could have put it into words. Phil sensed his reluctance and didn't push for information. Instead, he leapt out and wedged open the shelter door before unlocking the back of the van. He started to unpack.

"Hey Lars, are you going to help?" called Phil. He continued to work, and then called again, "Lars?" Phil went around to the front of the van, but Lars had gone.

Chapter 28

Adam and Faxon

Adam found himself lying on a bed of soft furs. Warm and comfortable, he remained there in contented lethargy. He could see little detail inside the dark tent, but his sense of smell ran riot. Sweet, fragrant herbs, the deep rounded smell of earth, and the slightly acidic odour of water clashed with the tang of cured fur. Each jostled for his attention. Outside he could also hear the aspens whispering in the wind and the sound of lake water as it lapped against the shore. Adam felt as if he could hear and smell the world for miles around. When this combined with the overpowering fragrance of the tent, it suddenly became too much. He needed to breathe clean air, to stand under the open sky. Adam rolled off the bed and fled outside.

Bright moonlight filtered through the trees turning the world to mottled silver. Yet something else had changed, more than just the lack of sunlight. He raised his head, concentrated, and found that he could stretch out his senses. The island felt like discarded clothes. The person had gone, but their smell, their warmth still lingered. He found that he could identify where she had moved. In fact, following her scent was as effortless as following a trail marked on a map. It ran along the path and through the air in front of him, almost like a ghostly image of her body. Without knowing why, Adam felt compelled to follow, drawn almost against his will. As he walked, he felt light-headed. He knew that like the island, he had changed but how he knew this fact, remained a mystery.

Beyond the wood, he could see a break in the trees as the path began to slope downwards towards the beach. As Adam stepped out of the dappled woodland into the moonlight, he slowed and stopped. In front, lay a great lake. Above the moon caught his attention. Adam became aware of a strange feeling, almost like a premonition. Without thinking, he ran across the beach and plunged into the lake, enjoying the fresh and soothing sensation on his skin as he swam beneath the surface. Adam found that he could hold his breath for a long time, longer than ever before as he powered through the depths. When his breath finally ran out, he surfaced. Adam swam with quick, powerful strokes across the lake. Once he reached the shore, he stood, water dripping down his body before he shook off the tiny droplets like a dog.

Across the silver sands, lay dense woodland. Fallen logs and undergrowth blocked his way. Almost on autopilot, Adam turned and jogged along the edge of the wood searching for a path. He could run along the riverbank, which fed the lake, or he could make his way through the woods. In the moonlight, Adam saw what looked like an overgrown animal track. He could thrust his way through with brute force. The urge to destroy took over.

Adam accelerated and charged through the gap, breaking off the vegetation. Branches and stems snapped off, flying in all directions as he crashed through the wood, creating a path of his own. Utter destruction lay in his wake. Adam could feel great strength swelling within him. He had become power incarnate, stronger than ever; he could take on the world, and it would cower at his feet. As if to prove his might, he picked up a tree trunk and threw it crashing into the undergrowth.

Adam stood panting, strangely drained but smiling, content with his fun. In a moment of reflection, he realised he had lost her scent. He had forgotten to check for it when he left the lake. Somehow, the cold water had washed it from his mind.

Adam tilted his head in consideration, did it matter to him that he had lost her? He remembered the intoxicating pull and shivered. She would have controlled him, utterly making him a slave to her will. He didn't want that. Yet even though he had become free, another part of him longed for her embrace. Adam shrugged. Never mind, there would be other females. Not control freaks, but women more amenable to his needs.

The brief rest allowed his strength to return, and Adam resumed the destruction as he forged ahead. When he finally broke into a glade, the bright moonlight illuminated deep grass and beyond a figure.

There on a fallen log sat a curly-haired man, his bare rippling muscles clearly etched in the light. The spell broke.

Adam came to his senses and became aware for the first time that he stood naked. Although he felt capable of defending himself, this stranger made him hesitate. He oozed confidence and hidden strength. The man cynically eyed Adam and said something unintelligible. When Adam didn't reply, the man repeated the sentence and then sighed. He muttered something under his breath before repeating the words louder and more slowly as if talking to someone dim-witted. "The -whole –world- could -hear -you -crashing -through -the – forest."

Adams jaw dropped, astonished that he could now understand, but then he shrugged as if indifferent. "So, what's it to you?"

The man sneered. "You want *her* to take you back?"

Adam understood but just folded his arms and glared insolently, nettled by the man's attitude.

The man shook his head. "So naive."

He sighed, strode over, and clipped Adam around the head like some unruly puppy. This thoroughly irritated Adam. He pushed back, but he might as well have tried to push over a solid brick wall. He felt total resistance, no movement at all. The man just laughed and with one swift kick, knocked him to the floor. Adam lay shocked for a second, then leapt up and with a snarl swung at the man who neatly stepped out of the way. Adam turned and charged trying to knock him over or hit him, but each time the man moved swiftly and economically out of the way. After several frustrating, fruitless minutes, Adam realised that this wasn't going to work.

Now aware that this challenger could have floored him at any time, he asked, "So what's your game?"

The man shrugged and grinned. "No game, just an education."

Adam didn't like the sound of that, and it must have shown because the man looked at him with amused condescension. "Well, are you going to answer?"

Adam growled. "No, I don't want to go back to her."

The man snorted. "Not quite as stupid as you look then."

Adam glowered and considered his options. Part of him wanted to punch his way out. Another part wanted to turn around and leave. The disciplined part knew both were stupid, besides he wanted to know more about that woman. "Who is she?"

"Her name is Ceola. She is one of us," the man replied. "But twisted and evil, a witch creating new forms and then feeding off their energy to increase her power. You were her latest conquest."

Adam sneered at the word witch. "How do you know? And who are you?"

The man shook his head as if amazed by this stupidity. "My name is Faxon. What should I call you?"

"Adam."

"Well, Adam, each pack whose territory borders the lake keeps an eye on the witch and protects its members from her magic."

Adam snorted and shook his head. "Magic doesn't exist."

"I've changed my mind; maybe you are as stupid as you look. What do you think you felt back there?"

Adam didn't know. He didn't want to know, none of this made sense, so he shrugged and changed the subject. "Will she want me back?"

"Probably, if you let her, that's why we avoid the island and the area around the shore. She's powerful on her home ground; that's the reason why we don't attack her. If she stays there, she's safe," He growled. "Look closely," he said and pointed to his nose.

Adam peered. "Nose plugs?"

Faxon smiled. "Yes, some of her enchantments rely upon scent, if you cannot smell her, then you can resist. Apart from that, we have learnt to avoid her magic. Do not look her in the eyes. Keep your mind off her voice and on something important to you; it will act as an anchor. Then either attack or flee, but I suggest you flee. I doubt you could deal with her combat magic."

Adam felt uncomfortable about the concept of magic, until recently, he would have regarded it as a foolish superstition, but now the doubts crept in.

Faxon looked at him as if reading his mind. He regarded Adam, as a sergeant would eye up a raw recruit, assessing his strengths and his weaknesses. Adam didn't like the expression. It said, 'I can see more weakness than strength.' He wasn't accustomed to *that* attitude.

Faxon continued. "The other night, I heard her howl in the distance, a howl filled with bitter frustration and boiling rage. With care, I walked towards the edge of the woodland and looked out across the lake. I could see her in the moonlight searching the shore of the island hissing in disappointment when she couldn't find her quarry. I guessed then that someone had escaped, yet it seemed impossible that anyone could do that. No one we know has returned from that island once there. I watched her movements for many hours. She obviously returned to her dwelling, collected some items, and then rowed the boat out across the lake to the opposite shore. She left it there, after casting her magic upon it and then searched the woodland. Conscious of her enchantments, I kept my distance. The magic only brushed gently against my mind, as I wasn't her intended target. After she moved beyond our borders into human lands, I left the hunt and began to search for the person who escaped. I waited here all day before you came crashing through the woodland. I thought that this time she had bewitched a giant cow." Faxon smirked. "But in the end, it was just a man."

Adam glowered but then realised what he had heard. "Human lands? Whose lands are these then?"

Faxon smiled. "You will find out soon enough. In the meantime, I suggest that you follow me well away from here. We are camped just beyond the tributary."

The cryptic reply irritated Adam, but it made sense to leave before the so-called witch returned. The man turned and jogged down a path that led from the glade. Adam followed. Faxon picked up considerable speed, jumping over fallen logs and dodging vegetation that blocked his way. Silent in his movement, his breathing quiet, he ran with graceful ease.

In comparison, Adam crashed through the undergrowth, panting like a dog on a hot day. He managed to keep up, but it took effort. Gone were the feelings of great strength, leaving unwelcome humility. He realised that this man was his superior. It gave him cold comfort to know that Faxon didn't intend any violence and dealt with him in a teacher like way.

After a short while, they broke out of the forest and came to the edge of a river. Faxon pointed west and north in a broad arc.

"That way lies human lands. Our journey passes not far from a few of their villages, which border the main river. However, we will cross the tributary here." He pointed at what looked like a deep ford.

"We are not going to the village?"

"No, mostly, our kind stays away."

Adam wanted to ask why and what Faxon meant by 'our kind' which sounded somewhat ominous but he hesitated. Instead, the moment lost, he nodded and turned to follow the man as he jumped into the water.

"Follow my path exactly, the edge is treacherous," called Faxon as they waded through the water.

As Adam reached the middle of the river, something glinted in his peripheral vision. He glanced sideways and realised that light came from a distant village. The sight distracted him for a moment, and he missed his footing, stumbling sideways. The edge of the underwater causeway gave way under his weight. With a yelp, he plunged under the surface as Faxon called out his name.

Chapter 29

Xenis and Valene

Xenis felt the vibrations through his boots before he heard the sentinels wail. Someone had tried to enter the city without permission. Only known Drow could come and go with impunity. Anyone else faced capture and torture, an excruciating death was the only form of release.

Xenis wanted to see someone mad enough to tempt fate. The highest tower opposite the main gate overlooked the bridge and offered the best vantage point. From there, he could look across much of the city in addition to the main causeway. With few places for an intruder to hide, he anticipated the whole spectacle would end quickly, so instead of walking with dignity, Xenis ran. In the corridors, goblin servants busied themselves, going about their usual duties. He considered them minor obstacles as he dodged around them, sending the hapless creatures into a tailspin as they dropped their burdens with a clatter. Not that Xenis cared. They would suffer for the mess, not him.

When he reached the vantage point, he nodded to the two guards who watched events with interest. Xenis joined them only to see sentries standing by the left statue, at the end of the causeway, while members of House Zhennu'Z'ress, surveyed the area.

"Have they caught anyone?" he asked.

"Not that we've seen, Xenis."

Technically, they should have referred to him as 'my lord' due to his royal birth, but Xenis insisted that they drop any formal title. He found the convention hindered the development of beneficial relationships. His sister might command them by default, but their loyalties lay with him.

He nodded towards the crowd. "Have they been milling around like that for long?"

"Pretty much since the alarm went off."

"Did you see anything before that?"

Kasen shrugged. "Mm not really."

"Not really?"

"Well it could have been legitimate, but I thought I saw a heat source move down the ramp, but it vanished behind the Sentinel."

Xenis considered that intriguing news. The fact that Zhennu'Z'ress didn't run in hot pursuit through the Under Dark could only mean one thing. The intruder had dived into the water to avoid capture, a foolish move. The river went underground at the edge of the city before emerging in the agricultural caverns. The chance of surviving became unlikely even with powerful magic, but the intruder would anticipate that problem. With steep sides and fast flowing water, they would need help to escape before the waterfall. Who had helped them?

Xenis surreptitiously moved behind a stone pillar, cast a 'Blur' spell to avoid anyone seeing him clearly, and then a 'Far Seeing' spell before stepping back out. He surveyed the other houses. Now he could see minute details, even lip-read. Even so, he had to limit the spell's magnitude. What he did wasn't exactly illegal, but the other houses would consider it an aggressive move, and they would answer in kind.

First, he regarded their ancient enemy House Vlos'Killian. He noted that the guards remained vigilant but unworried. They were not able to help the intruder unless he or she could swim against the current, although Xenis did not dismiss that possibility. On the other side of the gate, he viewed Zhennu'Z'ress and smiled unsurprised. They had become a hive of activity. Yet he didn't think they would undermine their own security arrangements unless they had a purpose, like framing someone else for the intrusion. Next, he focused his attention on their current enemy, House Faerl'Zotreth, just as the royal siblings emerged onto the roof. Xenis ducked quickly behind the pillar and shut off the spells.

"Are they looking in our direction?"

"One of them gave me an irritated glance," replied Kasen. "But she turned back quickly. I don't think she cast a spell."

Xenis sighed and waited a few moments before recasting the spells. When he looked out, he considered the next houses carefully. Sarnor'Velve, a major player, stood next to Bel'La'Thalack a mid-level house. Each had some activity. An intruder might be a rare event, but nothing stood out as unusual. As he could read their lips from this distance, he knew they only engaged in idle speculation.

From this angle, he couldn't see much of the inaptly named minor House Har'Luth'Jal, who had delusions of grandeur or House Venorik'Sarg. Lastly, when he looked at House Renor'Zalisto, a farming house situated next to the waterfall at the back of the city, he saw something else. All their guards lined the ramparts, not only strange but also suspicious. Xenis wanted to learn more, but maintaining two spells across this distance proved difficult. He had begun to tire dangerously, so he broke the incantations and considered this new information. Even though Faerl'Zotreth had lost their place on the council, their ally Renor'Zalisto might still do their patrons dirty work. If his spy ring could prove their involvement in today's event, he could use that information to his advantage.

The youngest sister of House Faerl'Zotreth frowned. "Did you feel that?"

"Feel what?"

"I felt something; a spell aimed in this direction. It brushed past the edges of my mind."

"Then I'm amazed you felt anything at all."

Sabal glowered at her older sibling. "Unlike you, I took precautions; I cast a 'Shield' spell."

"Precautions." Briza sneered. "You mean an unnecessary expenditure of power. Who would dare attack us here within our own house?" Her expression darkened. "Even though we are no longer members, the council would still deal harshly with that behaviour."

Her younger sister shrugged, thinking that it wouldn't stop anyone. If they thought they could get away with it, they would still try. "Zhennu'Z'ress are in trouble," she said, changing the subject.

"Good."

Sabal sensed her sister did not feel in a talkative mood. Ever since they lost the Temple guardianship, House Faerl'Zotreth had been tense. To make matters worse, Valene had managed to rile Briza so much that she had detonated the 'Transmogrification' spell early. Instead of creating maximum damage at a time of their choosing, their spies informed their Matriarch that it had a minimal effect, only killing and injuring a few males. Her mother, most displeased by this lack of self-control, vented her anger on Briza. From the screams, Sabal knew the pain must have been excruciating, but it served a purpose. It allowed the Matriarch to regain her composure. Once calm, she ordered preparations to begin. It was only a matter of time before the house suffered reprisals, but after a few days of waiting, nothing had happened.

"I tire of this spectacle." Briza spoke to the nearest guard, "Report to the throne room if anything interesting happens."

She turned and motioned curtly for her younger sister to follow.

My sister behaves as if the thrashing never occurred. As if I would forget, thought Sabal. She had kept a straight face and a tightly closed mind, while all the time enjoying her sister's humiliation.

The two Drow females walked down the spiral staircase and made their way to the throne room. Their mother sat conferring with her advisor to the guard.

The Matriarch dismissed her advisor and then enquired, "Well? Did they catch the intruder?"

"They couldn't find anyone."

"But something triggered the sentinels."

"They searched around the left statue but without success."

"And you know this how?"

Briza drew breath to answer her mother, but Sabal interrupted. "I think they jumped into the water."

Briza glowered and allowed it to pass, but then Sabal added, "Well, that's the only way out of there. If they had caught someone, we would have seen."

"Unless another house helped them escape," Briza replied exasperated.

Sabal shrugged and conceded that point, before asking, "Who would benefit?"

"We might if we can discredit Zhennu'Z'ress and with them their puppet Zik'Keeshe."

Their mother tilted her head in interest.

Sabal rolled her eyes. "Yes, those two are obvious. I meant apart from that alliance."

Briza scowled. Her younger sister would never have dared speak like that until recently. Her humiliation at the hands of her mother had emboldened Sabal, a development that Briza planned to crush.

"I can think of House Bel'la'Thalack. They now supply Zhennu'Z'ress as we once did."

Since the schism with Zhennu'Z'ress over ingot prices and late delivery, House Faerl'Zotreth had lost custom throughout the city.

"Yes but we all know who was responsible for that, House Zik'Keeshe."

"But ultimately they did that on the orders of Zhennu'Z'ress."

The two sisters glared at each other. Sabal broke the antagonistic silence. "What should we do? Sit and wait for reprisals? No, I say we should take the fight to them."

"And what would you have us do? A direct attack will bring the council down upon our heads."

Sabal sighed at her sisters' stupidity. "No, of course not, first we should imply that Zhennu'Z'ress are incompetent. After all, if they don't find the intruder that will be entirely true. Secondly, House Zik'Keeshe has a vulnerability you won't have considered. They accept advice from a male. I suggest that we send them a message by eliminating him. The council would not worry about his death even though he is of royal blood."

Her sister snorted in contempt. "I heard that their males have too much influence. Imagine relying on a male for information."

The Matriarch interrupted. "A sound suggestion. See to it."

Zilva felt worried although she took pains not to show any distress. Zhennu'Z'ress had responsibility for guarding the city, but today they had failed. The sentinels had detected an intruder, but the guards had not captured anyone or even identified who had tried to enter the city without permission. No one had attempted such a thing in a long time. Who would be mad enough to suffer the consequences?

They had however found something, but no one recognised its source. It wasn't even magical just different, not an orc, goblin, a dark delver, drow or even the drow's ancient enemy. Zilva considered another option. Perhaps one of them had sent this strange creature knowing that the dark elves would not recognise its signature. She thought that once she had isolated the trail, her guards might be able to find it again. Yet apart from next to the statue and up the ramp, she learnt nothing. It started as it finished, in a dead end.

Chapter 30

Cody

The light glinted off the broken glass casting flickering diamond specks across the stone. Cody stretched, yawned, then staggered to his feet and looked down. He had been sitting uncomfortably on a broken paving slab. Still disorientated he looked around and saw a broken city of crumbling stone and corroding metal sinking gradually back into the desert. In the distance, a skyline filled with tall twisted buildings. Close by, the remains of houses, their roofs gone, their rooms filling up with sand. A cold feeling crept over his skin. Even in the heat, he shivered. Oh no, he knew this place, yet it looked so different in daylight. He remembered those things chasing him, the fall into darkness and their tendrils clustering around the hole above him. He shuddered and looked around. Nothing moved in the heat, but perhaps they hid during the day.

With more care than last time, he slithered off the rubble and began to amble forward. He planned to explore the city in the daylight and perhaps find the house with that newspaper. If he travelled to the city again, he would need a safe place to hole up. As he walked along, he picked out relics of the past. A broken teapot uncovered by the shifting sand. A child's toy weathered by time; the colours faded into pale shades. The grand facades of houses now open to the elements. Their paint peeled, their windows broken and their doors filled with rot. Yet the desert preserved as much as it decayed. In Central America, a vehicle would rust to nothing inside twenty years but would remain recognisable for one hundred in Arizona. Next, he considered the architecture; although this looked like a typical American city, he could see differences. The buildings had an unusual style, reminding him more of northern Europe. As far as he knew, there weren't any European cities surrounded by mountains and desert.

The city centre layout felt oddly familiar as well. Great skyscrapers cluttered the skyline along with what had probably been a mall. Once a civilisation not unlike those he knew stood here. People had lived and worked in these very streets, but now they were gone. How had it ended? Curious to see more, he moved closer to the mall and stared in through the broken windows. It looked wrecked and someone had cleared out anything of value. Cody wondered if anyone had been here to rummage through the remains, even with those 'things' around. They would need armour to keep *those* barbs at bay, although in the heat they would cook to death. He gave a grim smile. Cody could think of better ways to go than simmering gradually in his own skin.

As Cody went from shop to shop, he found one building with a sign above the door. The lettering appeared so worn that he found it difficult to read, but in any case, the letters appeared unfamiliar. No point in going back for that newspaper then, he wouldn't be able to read it.

Cody became conscious that he hadn't seen any living creatures. He would have expected something, even the chirp of an insect but not this complete and now that he thought about it, somewhat eerie silence. The wind wasn't blowing so nothing rattled or tumbled. He remained thankful for that last part, although after last night he realised that the creatures didn't rely on wind. They used another method of propulsion. He wasn't sure how but perhaps those razor-sharp barbs flexed like claws digging into the dirt as they rattled along.

The sun had climbed quite high since his arrival, and Cody had become thirsty. He took refuge in the shade of a wall. His thirst made him consider those creatures. Cody didn't really think of them as plants although technically they might be. Maybe they had something in common with Venus flytraps. With mountains acting as a rain shadow, the desert would have limited supplies of food and water. He wondered if the creatures had evolved to find them both from a single source, blood.

The absurdity of it all made him laugh. Here he sat in a dream wondering about the evolution of species. Perhaps he should think outside the box and follow his grandfather's advice. A dreamer needed a spirit guide, and right now, Cody would consider any help from any quarter. That left the problem of how to attract the appropriate spirit.

If he already existed within a dream, none of the usual rituals would apply so maybe if he concentrated hard, help would come. Perhaps he could even enter a dream within a dream.

Cody sat with his back against a wall and thought of his ancestors in general and his grandfather in particular. After a while, he began to doze in the afternoon heat. As his thoughts muddled, a bird screech echoed in the distance. Cody opened his eyes and looked up. There on the horizon, he could see a black dot circling over a thermal. The first and only living thing he'd seen today. With a quick prayer of thanks, Cody stood and walked in that direction, following the bird as it circled. He had gone a few blocks when a strange metallic squeal caused him to flinch. Heart racing, he ran towards the noise, then stopped and stared down a great flight of concrete stairs. There at the bottom stood a short blond man obviously as surprised as Cody to see someone else. Another much larger man with his back turned lifted metal struts onto a strangely constructed cart.

Cody yelled and waved, overjoyed to see other people. "Hey! Hey there!"

He hurried forward and began jumping down several steps at a time. When Cody reached the bottom, he thought he had merely stumbled. He looked down and saw the ground start to crumble beneath his feet. With a sickening feeling of Deja-vu, Cody dropped into a newly formed hole.

Chapter 31

Adam

The phone rang insistently and then cut to the answering machine only to start again thirty seconds later. Apparently, whoever called didn't want to leave a message. Adam groaned, and clutching his hurting head, finally rolled off the couch. He picked up the phone.

"Hello!" Adam sounded irritated.

"Adam Turner?"

"Yes?"

"Where are you?"

The staccato question raised his hackles, and his reply descended into sarcasm. "This is my home number, so I am probably at home. Who's this?"

The person paused as if trying to hold their temper. "The personal assistant to Mr Hall."

Adam winced. "I'm sorry, no offence meant."

"Mr Hall asked me to ring you to inquire if you planned to attend work anytime today."

This confused Adam. He hadn't arranged an early meeting, so why were they ringing him at home.

He glanced at the time and had a shock. "I'm late!"

"Yes."

"Please tell Mr Hall that I apologise and that I will be there ASAP!"

"Certainly, fortunately for you Mr Knox and his delegation have been delayed and Mr Hall would like to inform you, that should you wish to keep your job, you had better get here at light speed."

The phone went dead. Mr Knox had a reputation for being difficult, and Adam didn't want to give the Lomax Corporation any excuse to turn down the contract.

He hastily dressed and then with big leaps and bounds, dived down the stairs to the front door, where he waved down a taxi. Adam gave him an incentive to be there extra fast. The driver grinned and said he knew a few short cuts. True to his word, he made the trip in an ultra-fast time. Adam thanked him, handed over a hefty tip, and then strolled into Redfern & Brewster, knowing he would keep his job.

He nodded to the reception staff. "Morning Ladies."

"Morning Adam, Mr Hall is looking for you."

Adam nodded. He expected this. He quickly ran up the stairs and dumped his possessions on his desk. A glance around informed him that most people appeared busy or possibly just intended to ignore him. Never mind their loss. Adam wanted to make sure that they had prepared the presentation room, so he poked his nose around the door. What he saw left him pleasantly surprised and he smiled relieved, one less thing to worry about.

Adam turned and saw his friend John who worked in accounting, probably the only person at Redfern & Brewster that he genuinely liked.

"Hey," he said.

John grinned. "Heard you got an early morning wake up call."

"Yeah." Adam grimaced and stood with his hands in his pockets, aware that the office gossip had done the rounds.

"You know the boss is looking for you?"

"Yeah, I know." Adam didn't sound enthusiastic.

"Trouble?"

After this morning, he wouldn't expect to win the employee of the month award. "I hope not."

"Well, good luck."

"Thanks"

Adam's stomach rumbled again as John walked away. He could do without the embarrassment during the meeting, so Adam took a detour past the canteen to pick up a coffee and a ham roll, before heading back to his desk. He had just sat down and started to read his notes when a stern voice called out across the office.

"Mr Turner? In my office now."

Adam groaned inwardly. Mr Hall liked to either praise or admonish his staff members in public, which Adam considered a control thing.

The praise he didn't mind, but today he could really do without the other side of the coin. As he rose and walked towards Mr Hall, he could see people smirk over their desk dividers. They planned to enjoy his reprimand. Even if the boss took him aside, he never closed the office door. He might as well rebuke Adam out in the open, either way, everyone would hear what went on. Still, he would have to try not to look sullen and irritated, so instead, he smiled and walked in. Mr Hall leaned forward, hands folded on the desk, his eyes penetrating and troubled.

"Adam, what are you trying to pull?" he said.

"Sir?"

Mr Hall shook his head. "You know how much effort I have *personally* put into getting Lomax on board?"

Adam nodded.

"What the hell is going on with you?"

Adam looked him squarely in the eye, intending to sound confident and direct. His boss took anything else as a sign of weakness.

"Sorry, Sir. I simply overslept. I can assure you it won't happen again."

"I'm counting on you, and you promised you wouldn't let me down."

"I won't, Sir."

Mr Hall snorted in disbelief and sat back in his chair. "Well, this time, you got lucky."

Adam looked surprised. "In what way lucky?"

"Their flight has been delayed, and they won't be able to attend until this afternoon. It will give you a bit of extra time to sew up any loose ends."

Adam nodded. It gave him a reprieve, but on the other hand, he didn't like hanging around.

Mr Hall inclined his head towards the door. "Well, that's it, off you go."

Adam hated the way his boss dismissed him like a naughty child. Mr Hall didn't suffer from tact unless forced to by circumstances. Outside, the office remained deathly quiet. Everyone had heard the whole exchange. As he walked back to his desk, he overheard each whisper as they talked behind his back. Adam, feeling vindictive, decided to make them pay.

He picked up his notes then raised his voice, "Everyone working on the Lomax contract, proceed to meeting room one now. We are going to check the whole presentation starting with."

He glanced around and spied a likely target. "Your work, Jack."

"My work?" squeaked Jack.

"Yes."

A horrified look briefly passed over Jacks' face, fuelling Adam with some satisfaction. He turned with a malicious smile as the furore swelled behind him. This would be fun. An hour and a half later, he allowed the rattled team members to go to lunch early.

Chapter 32

Karen

Karen ran across the square. Damn that dream. The breath-taking lights had changed into a death-defying fall. What a shame about the terrible ending. She woke, wet with sweat not realising that she had overslept and now she literally ran late.

When she got to her desk, she found Evan waiting patiently, a smile on his freckled face. "Morning."

"Morning, Evan, what can I do for you?" she said, plonking her case down.

"Are you ready for tonight?"

He received a blank look.

"The project, you remember we spoke about it yesterday," he prompted.

The memory flooded back leaving Karen feeling foolish. How could she have forgotten? That conversation seemed like a week ago, not just yesterday.

"Sorry, Evan it slipped my mind but don't worry. I'm happy to stay on."

"Are you sure? I can ask someone else if you can't."

"No that's ok; it would be too short notice for most people. Don't worry as long as I get plenty of coffee and something to eat. I'll be fine."

"No problem, the foods on me, the lads have already decided that if they are going to stay after hours, then I'm feeding them." He smiled. "We will start the database migration today after everyone has gone home. It should take around two to three hours and then we'll test the data."

"That's ok. I'll get on with my own work on my laptop."

Evan smiled and left. Karen got herself settled and then logged into the system. Amongst the myriad of emails, she found one from Rebecca. Karen had met her a few years ago when she had first attended the conference. Friends from the first, they got on famously although they were very different. She described Rebecca as a fiery redhead with a candid sense of humour, unlike Karen, who came across as the logical and careful type. Yet somehow, they had gelled, and Karen thought guiltily, they had spent at least half the conference drinking and laughing in the bar. Rebecca could be so naughty, twisting men easily around her finger. With just a smile and a flash of those lashes, she could get them to do anything. She used charm and seduction, where Karen employed logical arguments and business strategy. The results may have been the same, but Rebecca's way happened to be more fun, a lot quicker and involved significantly less disagreement. Only one thing lurked at the back of Karen's traitorous mind. Rebecca's way would not last forever. Looks unlike brains would fade and then what would she do?

She answered the message, letting her friend know her travel arrangements but Rebecca had other ideas. Karen agreed to her plans with some reservation. A night out with Rebecca would be something to remember, if she survived.

The day passed quickly, and at 5pm, she shut down her computer then began working on her laptop. True to Evan's word, the system came up just after 8pm, and she printed out the test sheets.

The night had set in. Karen stretched, kicked off her shoes, and stifled a yawn. She found it difficult to concentrate. Another round of coffee wouldn't keep her awake, so she gathered up the test sheets and went to look for Evan. After covering all the floors, Karen stood hands on hips and sighed, wondering where he had gone. He wouldn't have just gone home and left everyone to get on with the work. That didn't sound like Evan. He loved IT; to him, it was more than just a job, it had become an extension of his hobby. Karen could think of one place she hadn't looked, the server room, so she made her way downstairs towards the basement. Before she got there, a bright flash in the sky and a deep rumble made her jump. Out of the window, Karen could see the crackles of lightning as they leapt from cloud to cloud, illuminating the city brighter than the day. Once her eyes had readjusted, she opened the server room door, and at first, the room appeared to be empty.

"Anyone here?" she called out.

A small yelp confirmed her suspicions. Karen couldn't help but smile as she peered around the door. A scrawny man looked nervously out from behind a server rack.

"Hey sorry for startling you but do you know where Evan is?"

After a pause that almost bordered on discomfort, he replied, "Uh yeah, uh, he nipped out for food."

"Do you know if he will be long?"

"Err not long; the take away is just around the corner."

"Ok, do you know what I should do with these test sheets?"

He shook his head, obviously uncomfortable in her presence. Poor thing thought Karen as she closed the door. Probably the most protracted conversation he'd experienced with a woman in a very long time, if ever.

As she walked away, she realised that if Evan had bought food, he might be in the staff room. A couple of floors up and Karen could already hear the laughter as it echoed across the open plan space. Once at the door, she knocked politely and opened it, which stopped the laughter in a microsecond, leaving a deafening void.

"It's just me," she squeaked.

One of the guys grinned. "Yep, we can see that."

Karen blushed, feeling foolish. Instead of waiting, she plunged on. "Evan's gone for food?"

"Yep, he left a few minutes ago."

"Oh ok, I'm pretty tired, so I'm going home, but I needed to know where to put these test sheets?" she said, waving the offending items.

He shrugged. "Err put them on his desk. That should be ok."

Karen nodded, feeling glad to get away. Why hadn't she thought of that before? When she got to his desk, Karen understood why it had slipped her mind. Strewn with tools, computer parts, and cable ties, it appeared to be a total mess. After looking around, she finally noticed a box tucked under the desk marked 'Test.' Karen bent down to place the papers into the box when an almighty flash and bang made her jerk backwards. As the lights went out, Karen hit her head hard on the underside of the desk and slumped unceremoniously to the ground.

A microsecond later, the emergency lighting came on. Evan had been outside, as the lightning had struck. For one moment, the searing bright flash had eclipsed his vision, leaving white spots before his eyes, as the light faded. It must have hit something significant because the whole area had descended into darkness. Here and there, he could see just a few dim lights. Some businesses had battery-backup. Not that everyone had bothered to invest so there would be a few red faces in the morning.

As Evan entered the building, he noted that the emergency lighting had come on, but the lifts were out. He hoped the computers would be ok. The UPS and battery backups should have kept them safe and allow any computers to shut down gently. With any luck, nothing had fried. Evan panted heavily as he rushed upstairs' pizza, fries, and burgers clutched in his arms. He dumped the food quickly in the staff room and staggered off towards the basement. God, he needed to get more exercise. When the lifts didn't work, he was in trouble. His feet pounded down the stairs, and he almost bumped into Mick in the gloom of the stairwell.

"Everything ok?" he asked in one heart-stopping moment.

"So far, so good."

He nodded then went to check with the others. Overall, the prognosis remained upbeat.

"It looks as if all the UPS held out. Nothing appears to be damaged as far as we can tell," Evan told them as they assembled once again in the staff room. "Ok, you guys eat up before the food gets completely cold. I'm going to ring the Utility Company and see when the power will be back on."

A few minutes later, Evan returned with worrying news. The lightning had blown a substation, and the power would remain off for some time. The battery backup lasted around four hours if all the equipment on the emergency circuit drew power.

"I'll ring the CEO, and the heads of each department to let them know what's happened. We'll have to shut down the servers."

After Evan made the call, he went back to the staff room, thinking that he'd forgotten something. The feeling continued to nag as he ate until he realised that he had missed something, or rather someone.

"Hey! Have you seen Karen?"

"Yeah, she put the test results on your desk when you were out getting food," said Mick.

"That's odd I didn't see her leave. Has anyone checked the building?"

They looked blankly at him.

"I'll take that as a no then. Keep an eye out for her as we shut everything down."

With a sigh, Evan sauntered off and made his way to his desk. Along with the usual mess, he found his chair overturned. Evan picked it up and looked around, then spotted some paper scattered on the floor. In the dim light, he noticed Karen's name written at the top.

Chapter 33

Adam

The water tumbled and swirled around him. It dragged him under as he tried to surface. Adam flailed around, completely disorientated, running out of breath. The current slammed him off a rock, bruising his ribs. If he didn't drown, the rocks would batter him to death. Fear lent him strength, and he tried to swim in his waterlogged clothes, only to glance off another boulder. Pain shot through his arm. For a moment, Adam surfaced, gasped for breath, and glimpsed what lay ahead. The river poured into a lake surrounded by verdant woodland behind which, a mist enveloped mountain loomed in the distance. He ignored this beauty in favour of something far more important, the end of the rapids. If he could survive the next few minutes, he would be out and free.

The current pounded him unmercifully in the churning torrent before finally shooting him out into calmer waters. It took all his remaining strength to get to shore, where he draped himself across a large boulder. There he lay, battered, and bruised, feeling lucky not to have drowned. That feeling didn't last. Uncomfortable in his wet clothes, Adam turned over and began to peel off his shirt. As he stretched, he winced. His ribs hurt like blazes. On top of this, his shoulder ached, and his head pounded like a drummer in a Heavy Metal band. Adam winced continuously as he stripped before laying his clothes on an adjacent rock to dry. They almost steamed in the heat as he settled down to soak up the midday warmth. The bright light gleamed red through his closed eyelids as he listened to the river running past.

After a while, he became aware that he could hear something. Almost imperceptibly, it danced on the edge of his senses. Yet when he concentrated, it grew clearer before fading away. A moment later, he became conscious that he stood naked on the edge of the woodland. Adam returned to his clothes, and as he dressed, the sound resurfaced, slowly increasing in intensity to become a song. It pulled him forward, and although he had no real reason to move, he felt drawn by its power. It tugged at the corners of his mind, calling him to hurry. Adam began to run along the bank, tripping and stumbling over the rocky surface until the river opened up, revealing a lake, and in the distance, a tree covered island.

In horror, he realised he knew this place. The island belonged to the were-witch Ceola. Faxon had warned about her song, and even though Adam didn't believe in magic, he did feel something real. He tried to turn and walk away but found that he couldn't. His feet didn't want to shift. They seemed anchored firmly to the ground. Adam struggled to close his mind against the song, then attempted to take a step back, but discovered to his dismay that his legs wouldn't obey. Instead, they tried to force him towards the lake. He felt trapped inside his own body, which had a mind of its own, and it wasn't his.

Adam clenched his fists straining against the music, which filled his ears and mind. What had Faxon said? He'd given advice on how to avoid the witch, but Adam's thoughts became cloudy and vague. What had it been? Think Adam think, he almost yelled to himself! He clenched his fists, his nails drawing blood. The pain bought him a moment of clarity. Apart from a bit about nose plugs and not looking her in the eye, Faxon had told him to keep his mind off her voice. He must keep it on something important. It would act as an anchor and drive her out. After that, he said either attack or run away.

What did he find important? Adam searched his memories, reliving his past and saw nothing that mattered. Not his family, his relationships, or surprisingly his work but surely, he could find something that truly counted. Adam had focused on promotion, but it shocked him how little he actually cared. In many ways, the company bored him. He wanted more out of life. Well, he was getting that now, but not in the way, he planned.

Adam shook his head and tried to concentrate on his friends. He could count on John from work, but most people he knew were little more than drinking buddies. He had real friends at university, but they'd moved on with their lives, so he didn't see them much anymore.

Adam felt a twinge of nostalgia. Perhaps this could be an anchor? He struggled to focus his mind, picturing each friend in turn. It helped a little, and with effort, he managed to turn. More memories surfaced. He pictured his friends at high school, then those at university and the times they had enjoyed. What was that song they used to sing? Adam started to hum then began to repeat the lyrics through his clenched teeth as he stumbled forwards through the woodland undergrowth.

"Is this reality? Or nothing but fantasy?" Actually, a good question, what was real and what wasn't.

"The choice is up to you."

Adam ducked under a broken branch and scraped his head on the knotted bark. The pain distracted him further from her song.

"But you're torn in two." That felt true.

"So, if you open your mind."

He fixed his eyes firmly on the woodland ahead, determined to escape her clutches. She wouldn't have him.

"A path you will find."

As he moved, the pressure gradually began to fade away. His legs came back to life, so he broke into a jog, jumping over fallen logs and pushing through the undergrowth. The pain in his ribs ached like fire, but again this seemed to weaken her call.

"You will be set free." If only!

"To be what you want to be."

He could feel her song wavering in and out as if it followed a search pattern.

"But life is easy come and easy go."

Without warning, her music shifted in his direction. Adam felt utterly exposed under the spotlight of her mind. She had found him. He sensed her triumph as her power cut through his memories like a scalpel, almost destroying his self-control. He would come to her, be one with her, belong to her; he could not resist. Adam began drowning in her desires, desperate to hang onto his identity; he tried to hold on to his song.

"Change comes fast and then goes slow," Adam cried out.

The strain on his mind became almost unbearable. The witch piled on the pressure, determined not to let him go. He staggered, as she broke through his last line of defence.

"What the future brings you'll never know."

"But it doesn't matter what you do."

"Time ends all things, including you."

The final words came out in a whisper as he took one last faltering step. It didn't matter. He had come to the end of his strength. She would win, and he would die. In utter despair, he crumpled and sank to his knees as darkness engulfed his mind.

Chapter 34

Lars and Stefan

Lars found himself standing on a small rise amongst the sagebrush. Night had descended. The moonlight illuminated the desert in shades of grey and etched the tall crumbling towers in silver. Lars realised with heart-stopping fear that he couldn't see the cart. He froze his pulse racing as he listened for that characteristic rustle. Every tiny sound seemed magnified by his mounting anxiety. The whispering wind ruffled his hair blurring each creak, click, and chirp before it settled back down. He strained to hear something, not knowing if he should stand still or run.

When nothing attacked, Lars let out an involuntary sigh but didn't relax knowing his luck might not hold. He had to get back to the cart before they found him.

The towers presented a distinct landmark. The men had stared at them as they ate dinner last evening, but now Lars looked at them from a different perspective. It took him a few minutes to guess the probable location of the cart. He should find it if he went diagonally to his right, over the next small ridge and then down into the valley.

Lars started to walk, his footsteps sounding painfully loud on the stony ground. It took determination to quell his desire to run, to get to the safety of the crate right now. If he ran, he might attract attention. As he crested the ridge, Lars saw the cart parked next to the burnt-out campfire. The clearing remained empty. Lars felt a surge of relief and throwing caution to the wind; he rushed down the slope. Once there he rattled the shutters in the hope that the bolts would come free, but as he feared, they remained firmly shut. Even over the noise, he could hear Stefan's distinct snores. Lars knocked gently on the side of the cart.

"Stefan, wake up you lazy lump," he whispered as loudly as he dared.

He needn't have bothered because Stefan continued to snore without pause. Lars sighed in frustration and knocked on the side again, this time louder.

"Stefan!" he growled. "Wake up!"

Yet again, he got no response.

"Let me in!"

Lars kicked the side of the cart and tried to rock it, but Stefan just kept on snoring. What did it take to wake his friend? A mountain could fall down around his ears, and he wouldn't wake up! Lars yelled in frustration, beating on the cart, his anger, and fear bubbling to the surface. Oh, shit! If they came before first light, he would just have to run for it and hope; then an idea dawned on him. Perhaps like any creature, they feared fire. In a desert, fire proved dangerous. The scrub looked as dry as a bone, but at least the vegetation grew sparsely around the campsite. The wind had died back so it wouldn't fan the flames towards the cart. Still, smoke could be a problem. He would have to wake Stefan if of course, he could.

Lars found the flint on the back of the cart, then took a piece of kindling and tied dried tinder around one end. This should light with a single spark.

To one side, an odd noise alerted his heightened senses to danger. He just had time to throw some wood between the scrubby plants surrounding the camp before he heard something else. Another rustle, then another, this time closer and with heart-stopping dread, Lars realised that they were coming from all directions. He quickly knelt and struck the flint several times before a spark leapt igniting the tinder. As the flame sprang to life, Lars stood waving the burning brand in front of him; then he saw it, curled as if to strike, but Lars attacked first. He lunged forward, yelling as he thrust the branch into the scrub, igniting it immediately. The flames spread, brightening the sky, and in the flickering light, Lars could see more movement around the camp. He stared, horrified by their numbers. As he looked frantically around, he saw one hunched over the cart. It pounced.

Lars had laughed when the traders told him about their speed. In disbelief, he had almost mocked the Riverman, but now he witnessed it first-hand. The burning branch saved him. As the tumbler leapt, Lars automatically thrust the brand out for protection, but it snagged in the creatures outstretched tendrils, ripping it from his grasp. He ducked and rolled as it tumbled over-head, only to see the brand caught fast between its limbs, the flames already licking at its woody exoskeleton. It turned and spun this way and that as if trying to dislodge the brand. Instead, the fire, fanned by the movement, caught hold of everything it touched. Soon flames engulfed the glade as the creature burned and died. Lars watched coughing as the tumbler slowed, then stopped. The fire must have kept the others away because they didn't attack, and by the time it reduced the creature to little more than a smouldering ball, none remained.

This could be his one chance to satisfy his curiosity. He bent over to take a closer look. The Riverman said that tumblers would swarm at the scent of blood. Lars couldn't see how. It didn't have a nose; it didn't have any eyes; it didn't even have a mouth, just hollow thorns. He shuddered and pulled back.

In the predawn light, the scrub around him continued to smoulder, but it didn't look as if a major fire would break out. He tried to wake Stefan by giving the cart a hefty kick and yelling. This didn't work because he could still hear snoring echoing from inside the protective crate. How could anyone sleep through this? Lars tried to open the shutters again. In fact, his loud swearing must have woken Stefan in the end, for the snoring spluttered and eventually stopped.

"Get up you deaf lump."

Lars had survived on his own, no thanks to his friend.

After a rattling noise, the bolts slid back, and Stefan crawled out from under the cart. He coughed and looked around at the blackened glade. "What the hell's happened here? Why didn't you wake me?"

Lars rolled his eyes and sighed through gritted teeth, his patience wearing thin. "I swear you're harder to wake than a bear in winter. They attacked me, and you just snored! I had to set the scrub alight to keep them away!"

Stefan looked contrite for all of a second before grinning. "Hey, what are you complaining about, you're alive, aren't you?"

Lars glowered at his friend, about to explode, but instead, he countered with his own argument. "Make those shutters open from the outside! I got locked out!"

Stefan considered this for a moment. "Yeah, I could do that. I'd have to modify the mechanism somehow." He yawned. "What's for breakfast?"

Lars couldn't take any more, so he kicked the blackened tumbler towards Stefan, before stalking off. "This, at least its self-cooked!"

Stefan looked at the burnt offering with disgust. He could still see the sharp thorns on the wiry frame. He reached out, and as he prodded it with his foot, it crumbled scattering the thorns on to the ground.

Lars didn't go far before Stefan caught up.

"Look I'm sorry about last night, but it's not my fault. I can't help sleeping well," said Stefan.

Lars turned to his friend. "Sleeping well is an understatement." He glared and then relented. "Let's move the cart then grab a quick breakfast before we get started. I want to get as much metal as we can today, who knows when we will be back."

Stefan nodded, and they went back to the cart. Once they packed and hitched up, they moved as far into the city as they could. Only a large set of broken stairs stopped them. After a breakfast of cold sausage and water, they split up to see what they could find. As it turned out, Lars hit the jackpot reasonably early on. He had seen a large opening across a wide paved area. Perhaps it had been a meeting place. Once in the middle, he noticed the copper statue. Lars grinned. What a find, but how would he get it down? It only took a few minutes to retrace his steps and call for Stefan. While his friend hammered away at the base of the statue, Lars made his way across the plaza to the opening on the other side.

Shards of broken glass around its edges, indicated that this had once been a window, although who would want windows this huge and expensive? He clambered over the ragged edge and stepped inside into an enormous room. Row upon row of broken shelves lined the walls, and in the middle, square or oblong raised sections. Some had become little more than piles of broken material, but Lars noticed that most contained metal of some sort. The shelves it turned out, just crumbled beneath his touch, but the metal brackets appeared easy to remove. He collected as many as he could carry in his backpack before slipping outside through the broken window. Stefan had made short work of the hollow statue, and now it rested on its side. Far too cumbersome to pick up they decided to roll it across the square. Stefan levered, and Lars pushed until it bounced down the broken steps and rolled towards the cart. Lars unloaded his backpack and then between them, swearing a lot, they bundled the statue onto the cart. It took up most of the space, but there remained room inside for more. In the end, Stefan collected the rest of the metal because Lars, curious to the last, couldn't help but take one last look around before they left.

He stood, staring at the city, contemplating this great metropolis' decay, when he noticed a footprint. At first, he thought it could be his or Stefan's, but when he took a closer look, he realised that it wasn't. Lars had thought they were alone, that they were the only scavengers in this region. No one else could be stupid enough to come up here. Lars glanced around. If someone else had staked a claim, all hell could break loose. He'd heard lurid tales of mayhem and slaughter. The Rivermen had taken great pleasure in describing the gory details, but they had also assured him that few ventured this far north. In the past, it had been better and more profitable to pick sites closer to home. Nevertheless, Lars hurried back to the cart, only to find Stefan loading the last of the metal.

"I don't think we can pull any more than this. It's going to be hard going as it is," said Stefan.

Lars, however, did not listen to his friend. At the top of the stairs, he could see another man. At first, he thought the man another scavenger but Lars dismissed this almost immediately. His clothes looked strange but familiar. Was this man real or just a ghost? He had seen this type of clothing before in the other world, if it was another world and not the past.

"Stefan" he whispered urgently. "Look!"

"What?"

The man had seen him, yelled in delight, and waved before running down the stairs towards them. When he reached the bottom step, without warning, he stumbled and disappeared.

Stefan looked up. "What was that?"

"I saw someone."

Stefan looked dubious. "Now you're seeing things."

Lars glared at Stefan. "He's real I swear," he said.

To prove it, he stalked over to where he had last seen the man. As he came closer, he realised that the man hadn't actually vanished, but fallen down a hole. Lars grimaced, feeling shocked. They had walked over that very spot just a few moments ago. Now a massive hole had opened up reaching into the deep dark depths. He didn't want to get too close to the edge. It might collapse taking him with it. If the fall didn't kill him, then who knew what lived down there.

With some care, he leaned forward and yelled into the darkness. "Anyone down there?"

His voice echoed, but no one replied.

"Are you hurt?"

Stefan started to come over, but Lars stopped him.

"Stay back, ox. You don't want the whole road falling in around you! Get the storm lantern. I want to see if anyone is down there."

Stefan brought back the lit lamp and a piece of rope. Lars carefully lowered the light down, but at this angle, he could hardly see a thing.

"Stefan, can you hold the rope?" said Lars waving towards the hole. "I'm going to tie it around my waist and see if I can get a bit closer."

Stefan nodded and braced himself in case the ground gave way. The edge crumbled slightly as Lars got towards the hole, but after he lay down and spread his weight a bit, it held. Stefan pulled the rope taut as Lars leaned out over the hole. The lamp below illuminated the chasm, casting its rays out towards the bottom, but Lars could not see a body.

"Anyone down there?"

His voice echoed into emptiness. Whether something had already taken the body or less likely, that the man had walked away unharmed, he didn't know.

"Haul me back Stefan."

His friend pulled on the rope, and Lars stood upright once more, before moving gently back from the edge. He had just reached Stefan when they felt a shudder under their feet. Without a word, they both dived out of the way only to see the sinkhole open further, engulfing the area where they had stood moments before. On the end of the rope, the unbroken lamp dangled over the newly expanded chasm. Lars took hold of it and pulled until the storm lantern rattled over the broken ground around the hole. "We got lucky."

"Yeah, the lamps not broken. They're expensive to replace."

Lars rolled his eyes at Stefan. "You know what I mean."

To which his friend just grinned and thumbed at the hole. "Let's get going before that gets even bigger."

Once hitched up, they made their way out of the city. It was a hard slog in the afternoon sun, and both of them had to rest before long. Stefan wiped the sweat out of his eyes and drank from their dwindling water supply.

"Do you think we overdid it?"

Lars looked at the cart and considered his friend's comment. "Perhaps. We'll take too long to get back if we go this slowly."

"Perhaps we can push it down those hills?"

Lars grinned. "Yeah sounds fun, can I ride on top?"

"Not a chance."

In the end, they pulled the cart until almost nightfall. Neither felt much like eating in the heat, but both men managed to chew a few bits of cured meat before settling down for the night. Both felt the need for a good bath, but neither planned to waste any water, so they took a quick scrub with sand. Once under the cart, they heard the tumblers arrive. Lars shook his head, amazed that the fire hadn't deterred them. Instead, it seemed as if there were more than ever. Stefan assured him that his minor changes to the bolt would hold, and true to his word, it did. Even with the constant scraping and scrabbling noise, both men eventually fell asleep.

Chapter 35

Thomas

Ok, so Aeglas had told him to get comfortable, which at first, he found easy. The elf then told Thomas to relax, close his eyes, and let his worries flow out. That's where the problem started. He could relax, but how did you make your worries float away? In fact, he'd have said he didn't have any, but now Thomas thought about it, he started to twitch. His mum and dad must be as mad as hell with him, and he hadn't been to school. Ok, he wasn't so bothered with Billy out of the picture, but his teachers didn't like kids missing classes. He would be in trouble. That made him tense up. He'd tried to relax again but he couldn't, and according to Aeglas, this was the easy part of meditation. Aeglas had told him that once he'd cleared his mind, he should focus on healing his body even if there weren't any apparent injuries. Thomas didn't quite understand this until Aeglas clarified that healing didn't just include fixing cuts and bruises. It helped the body repair in general, like growing new hair or nails. He also explained that the body degraded over time and everything needed patching.

"So, you need patching up?" Thomas sniggered. "I don't, I'm still growing."

"Actually, so am I."

"But you said you were like what, a hundred and nine."

"Yes, but let me put it like this. At what age are you considered an adult?"

"Eighteen."

"Do your people still grow after eighteen?"

Thomas tilted his head and thought about it. "Yes, they fill out."

"Well then, we are adults at eighty, but we still grow after that."

"Grow fat?"

Aeglas moved so fast that Thomas didn't have time to react. He tumbled the boy over on the ground and tickled him until Thomas giggling, squeaked for him to stop.

"Are you going to show me some respect?"

Thomas managed to squirm free and yell, "No!"

"Really? Then I might have to tickle you to death."

Thomas tried to retaliate. He tickled Aeglas but found that the elf didn't respond.

"You're not ticklish; that's cheating!"

Aeglas sighed, let go and rolled onto his back. "I know you're trying to avoid meditating and I haven't even explained what you need to do next."

Thomas rolled his eyes and waited patiently for Aeglas to continue. After healing apparently, he needed to concentrate on individual events throughout the day and let them sink into his mind. This enabled the brain to sort and manage everything from emotional difficulties to new experiences. Once complete, the subconscious could then tick over in the background, which became the equivalent of deep sleep. Thomas found it astonishing that the brain did this naturally all the time.

Aeglas told him to sit down, and Thomas had tried to follow the instructions. It turned out to be more difficult than he thought. Thomas suppressed a yawn then tried to cover it by coughing.

"I hope I'm not boring you," Aeglas commented dryly without opening his eyes.

Thomas scowled at him.

"And don't glare at me."

The boy gawped; how did he know? Aeglas didn't even open his eyes.

"You're scowling very noisily."

"What are you? Bloody psychic?"

"No, I'm an elf."

"So that amounts to the same thing?"

Aeglas shrugged noncommittally. "And be mindful of your attitude. I'm only trying to teach you."

"Sorry, Aeglas," Thomas replied grumpily.

He'd been sitting cross-legged in this little stone circle for ages. This far, he'd only learnt one thing; that sitting like this for a long time made his backside numb.

"I'm not getting anywhere."

"Practice makes perfect and requires quiet contemplation."

"I'm not perfect."

"You're not quiet either."

Thomas groaned and rolled onto his stomach. "This is difficult."

"Yes, as I said, it takes years to achieve, and I must admit I am not the best teacher you could have."

"You seem, ok."

"Have you tried another teacher?"

"No." Thomas had to admit the elf had a good point. "Can we try this again another time?"

"Sure, what would you like to do instead?" Aeglas saw Thomas' face light up. "Or is that a stupid question."

Raphael had exhausted his books and scrolls. He considered the mechanics of how Thomas arrived and departed, less of a problem than, who and why might be responsible. He paced his library and considered each possibility in turn.

The biggest question he faced remained who had sent the boy. It could be their ancient enemy, an old political adversary, the Dark Delvers, Goblins, Troll or Orc Tribes, or a new unknown threat. Raphael considered orcs an unlikely option. They showed cunning in their own limited way, but he deemed this plan too subtle for their ilk. He could include goblins for the same reason. The ancient enemy often used them as tools, but goblins like orcs generally tried to keep out of the way of elves. Many had fled their Drow masters during the Upheaval, only to run into the elves and die. Caught between the two enemies, orcs, trolls, and goblins tended to scatter to the dark regions of this world. Of course, the enemy might not give them an option but left without a magical tether, any goblin or orc would do his best to flee.

Another option could be Dark Delvers. They had no reason to love elves, but mostly they ignored them. They traded with the elven enemy as they both lived in the realm of darkness, but they did not make friends with either light or dark. Raphael thought them unsubtle but honest in their own way. A plan like this would not be in keeping with their character unless coerced.

Instead, it could be one of his opponents, but why now after all this time. These days he presented no threat to the decisions made at the capital, and he could hardly do any high-level research in this backwater town. Perhaps they had discovered that he still practised crystal magic, a skill almost lost in time and they would want to keep it that way. While many people had seen him use a gem for focus, they would not understand the significance. He made it appear to be nothing more than a common albeit beautiful focus item. Anything could enhance focus depending on the spell, a gift from a dear friend, a feather, or even a bowl of water. Each object had a use. A crystal behaved differently, although few knew this fact. Beyond that, a crystal exhibited numerous additional properties when compared with a gem, unless of course, that gem also happened to be a crystal.

Raphael stopped pacing, sighed, and sat down. Even if they knew, why confront him in such an odd manner? Perhaps they could not afford to be direct. In their view, the past should stay buried, and direct confrontation would bring it to the surface. Maybe they wanted to draw him out, but he could think of better ways to do that. He felt a stab of concern. If they were not responsible for the boy's appearance, what would happen if they discovered his presence? It would not matter if Thomas were innocent. He would still suffer at their hands.

Raphael sat thinking over old injustices and injuries; until he finally roused himself from his contemplation and turned his mind to the various probabilities.

Their ancient enemy the Drow remained the most likely option. Yet he could not consider this method in keeping with their character. Oh, they would undoubtedly use magic and force but a small boy? When he considered Thomas, the boy became an unlikely tool. Perhaps that was the plan, to use someone so unbelievable that no one would suspect. The boy may have told him the truth as he saw it and some details concerning where he came from, but he could not explain how he got here. He seemed entirely innocent, unaware of any agenda. That begged the question, had they tampered with the boy's mind? If someone had altered the boy's memory, he would implicitly believe the lies he told. They could have modified his mind, giving him false memories to misdirect and misinform. That made 'Truth Saying' difficult because the boy would display a false positive. Raphael should also consider that simply casting this spell could trigger a reaction. Their ancient enemies regarded an implanted response as a commonplace spell.

Raphael stood and began pacing again. This didn't make any sense. Why had they sent a boy and not an adult? What did they expect to achieve? They could use him to plant an item of power, a disruptor, which could disable Elven magic but surely, any elf would sense that type of power well before it got to the town, let alone anywhere important. Raphael could not help but wonder why they had chosen this town and not somewhere else? A settlement located on the outer edges of the Elven Empire. It remained a backwater of little significance apart from its proximity to a Drow archway. No one of any great importance dwelled here, well no one but him. He snorted at his own arrogance. Once distinguished, now rejected by society, he had become a mere footnote in history.

That left one option. Some new unknown force had entered the fray. Yet if it led to an invasion of sorts why send a single person? Could the boy be a vanguard? What would they send once they determined his people were not a violent race? That left Raphael with only one choice. To observe what happened next but he disliked this option. After he discovered a plan and acted, it might prove too little and too late.

Most likely, the boy presented a threat in some way that he couldn't yet understand. He needed to watch and study him. It would be useful to observe the transfer mechanism first hand to be sure. Yet it would be difficult to spend time with him without drawing some attention to his actions. An elf as young as Aeglas could run around after the child but he could not, but perhaps a way would present itself if he remained patient.

****

The senior police officer in charge stood on the wall and yelled for silence. It took a few moments before the large crowd stopped milling around and turned their attention towards her.

"Gather round. Can everyone hear?"

There were a few murmurs, and people moved closer.

"First, I want everyone to divide into groups of ten."

After a lot of shuffling, people divided into groups. Some wanted to be with neighbours and friends, so this took a little time. She noted that a few people lingered on their own, but these would still prove useful.

"Everyone got a group?" she yelled above the chatter.

Most people nodded and listened to her next set of instructions.

"Right, you are to stick with your group at all times. I want you to walk slowly and remain within arm's length of the person next to you. Please stay at the same pace we don't want everyone spreading out because we might miss something. If you come across anything suspicious, tag the location with a piece of coloured tape but don't touch it."

She indicated the tape that another officer handed out.

"Once the location is tagged, call for a police officer. One of the runners." She indicated the remaining people who didn't have a group. "Will help if none are nearby. I repeat, please do not touch anything that you find. We do not want the evidence contaminated."

She looked over the crowd as if to emphasise this point.

"Right we will start here at the north-west part of the park and head south. We should complete the first sweep before lunch. After the break, we will gather, here again, move to the east, and head south this afternoon. This should cover the whole park. Everyone get into position, and we will start on my mark."

She jumped down off the wall only to find herself intercepted by a member of the press.

"Can you tell us why you released the father?"

She brushed him aside. "No comment, we are about to begin a search, and you are in the way."

This didn't put off the man. "Why arrest him if he wasn't a suspect?"

"No comment."

The reporter blocked her as she tried to move around him.

"Get him out of here," She yelled to the junior officer but the reporter, sensing he wasn't going to get a quote moved anyway.

The senior officer took her place behind the middle of the line and yelled, "On my mark, start."

The line moved slowly forwards. The park was large and grubby, with old shelters, play areas, a small pond, dips, and hollows filled with shrubs. This would take a while.

The reporter stood back and began his piece.

"Here today the police begin the official search of Oldam Park for the missing schoolboy Thomas Harvey. As you can see, this tight-knit community has come out in droves to help. Friends, neighbours, and concerned citizens, it seems as if everyone is here. The police inform me that they plan to cover the park today in two strips, north to south, in the hope that they might find some clues as to the whereabouts of Thomas."

The camera panned around to show the line of people moving slowly forward.

"I spoke with the officer responsible for the search, but she failed to comment as to why the police arrested the father and then released him without charge. So far, there have been no reported sightings of the boy since he went missing on Friday and police seem baffled as to his whereabouts. With no suspect in custody and no new leads, it seems as if the longer we wait, the less likely there will be a happy outcome to this case. This has been Terry Blass reporting to you live from the search for Thomas, back to Sabrina in the studio for more breaking news."

"Thank you, Terry. We have just learnt some disturbing facts concerning the school that Thomas attends. On the day he went missing, the boy failed to report to his afternoon class; however, his teacher didn't notice. A source close to the teacher in question reported that instead of marking him present or missing, the registration form remained blank. After police questioned the Headmaster concerning this disturbing oversight, he insisted that the gates had remained locked so no one could have got in or out of the school. However, our source also informed us because of massive class sizes, a small boy of quiet temperament could go unmissed. This worrying development calls into question the management of Hollis School and even government policy. It highlights the need for parents to remain vigilant at all times."

Chapter 36

Adam

The world shook violently. Adam found himself lying on his back, overturned chairs scattered around him. A memory of darkness and before that, rapids, filled his mind. He sat up and checked his ribs. They were fine. Nothing made sense. What was going on?

Behind him, footsteps approached. He twisted around to see John walking over, looking concerned but amused. "Hey, man, did you fall over?"

"Must have."

Adam couldn't remember falling just darkness and despair.

John laughed. "Are you alright? You must be harder to wake than a bear in hibernation if you stayed asleep on the floor!"

John grabbed his arm and helped him stand before picking up the overturned chairs. Adam rubbed his eyes, yawned, and plonked himself back down on a seat.

John peered at Adam. "You look a mess, what the hell happened to you?"

Adam looked down. His shirt and trousers were creased and dirty, unlike his pristine jacket slung over a nearby chair. He felt confused and more than a little puzzled by this anomaly. "Any idea how long I was out for?"

"It's well past lunchtime, but don't worry Knox isn't here yet. Hey, what's up with you falling asleep at work? You started to snore like an express train during lunch. Everyone laughed at the noise when they left the canteen."

"I snored?"

"Yeah, although Melanie said it sounded more like growling."

"How come you didn't wake me?"

John looked perplexed. "Well, you left or at least I thought you had. You weren't here when I went back upstairs so I thought I must have missed you, but when I didn't see you at your desk, I looked around. The boss was about, so I had to keep him out of the way until I could find you. Didn't think to find you back here though."

Adam smiled weakly. "Thanks, man, I appreciate it. I owe you one."

John grinned. "That reminds me. We're having a party on Friday. Lucy's been insisting that I invite you, but I keep forgetting to ask, would you like to come?"

"Sure," replied Adam, feeling grateful that John had covered for him.

John hesitated. "That girl will be there."

"What girl?"

"That friend of Lucy's."

Adam realised that John withheld something important.

"Spit it out."

John sighed and looked penitent. "That girl, the one you met on holiday last year."

Adam thumped his head back down on the table and groaned. John meant the little redhead that talked so much.

"Her names Gemma, Lucy told me to remind you."

"Yeah, I know." His voice became muffled and downcast, as his head lay on the table. Adam wasn't likely to forget that girl. Ok, so she looked super pretty but oh my god could she talk. If they gave a gold medal for yapping, she would be world champion, but now he owed John, so he looked up and attempted to change the subject.

"So what time is it now?"

"Just past 2pm almost time for a round of riveting presentations with our master of marketing."

Adam sighed. His famous lack of humour made Mr Knox a problematic client. He had a habit of nitpicking at every detail, going through the strategy with a fine-tooth comb until his consultant's mind turned to mush.

"You'd better smarten yourself up," said John.

Adam pondered the option of a superficial clean but quickly dismissed that possibility. He didn't want to look tatty. The shirt had taken the worst beating, rumpled, and stained; now it looked more like a rag. Something else caught his attention. A long rip ran down his sleeve. He shivered, that dream had felt so real, but then his logic kicked in. It had ripped when he had fallen off his chair, but that explanation sounded strangely hollow.

John noticed the odd look on Adams' face. "Someone walk over your grave?"

Adam quickly recovered and changed the subject.

"Yeah, just thinking about stuff. I'm going to grab a new suit from Taylors. Can you intercept Mr Knox? Create some sort of diversion?"

John shrugged. "Sure thing, I'll try but don't bank on it working."

"Thanks, I owe you one."

As Adam hurried away, John called out grinning, "Hey, that's another you owe me. Soon I'll own your sorry ass."

His luck held. Adam made the trip to and from Taylors quickly. John, good to his word intercepted Mr Knox and laid on the gushing admiration. Well enough, it turned out, to lighten the client's mood, which pleased Adam's boss.

Later that afternoon, Adam concluded the presentation. "As you can see, in summary, we can precisely define and contrast market segmentation, product differentiation, and with the demand modification strategy we suggest, your customers will be greatly influenced to purchase your product over that of your competitors. Rigorous market testing will fully determine customer expectations and the most effective promotion methods providing a guarantee that your product will achieve maximum revenue."

A moment's uneasy silence broke with the clients nodding approval. They seemed happy with the presentation, and therefore, his boss felt the same. Even Mr Knox did his best to go from Poe faced undead to a recently deceased corpse.

Mr Hall took his cue and clapped Adam on the back. "Excellent presentation!" he said.

The members of Adams marketing team smiled, looking pleased with the praise because at least some of it applied to them. There might even be a bonus.

Mr Hall raised his voice and called out, "Now would you gentlemen and of course, ladies, like to join us for refreshment and some informal discussion in the corporate lounge?"

Everyone smiled glad to stretch his or her legs after a lengthy presentation. As the room emptied, Mr Hall gave Adam a sideways glance. Adam ducked away from his gaze, hoping that he could join the others and bask in their glow of adoration, but as he attempted to leave the meeting room, Mr Hall leaned towards him.

"I'd like a word with you," his boss muttered in a low voice.

Adam dreaded this moment, but he didn't resist. Once Mr Hall knew they were out of hearing range, he looked at Adam with a soul-piercing gaze.

"You let me down earlier today," he said.

Adam nodded. "Yes, Mr Hall."

"I've been singing your praises. A good man for promotion I said, and then this morning you pull that damned stunt. Could have cost us a bomb but you got lucky, the client ran late."

Adam felt he should at least appear apologetic even though nothing had gone wrong in the end. "Sorry, Mr Hall. It won't happen again."

"You made up for it a bit with that presentation, but I get the impression that you are a cocky little shit who thinks just because you can be a bit of a genius, that entitles you to do what the hell you like. That somehow the rules don't apply to you only to everyone else!"

Adam felt his irritation rise. He had apologised, something he didn't often do. For a second that thought must have shown because his boss sighed and shook his head in disbelief.

"Well it's your future if you muck it up, it's no skin off my nose, there's always another young hotshot to take your place."

He walked away, leaving Adam feeling reprimanded but more annoyed than penitent. John strolled towards him, looking sympathetic. "Tore you off a strip?"

Adam shrugged nonchalantly as if nothing mattered.

"Don't worry about it. Worry about Friday instead." John grinned gleefully.

Adam sighed, no chance of getting out of the party. He would have to face that girl.

John clapped Adam on the shoulder. "Hey, how bad could it be?"

Adam looked sideways at him. "You want me to answer that?"

"You'll thank me later. You never know, this time you might like Gemma."

"You think so?"

John laughed, shook his head, and walked away.

Adam joined the others in the corporate lounge, where he made all the right noises and laughed at jokes that might have been funny in another century. It didn't matter though because at the end of the 'social' session, the clients looked happy and said that they would recommend Redfern & Brewster as their new marketing representative.

After bidding them goodbye, Adam sauntered over to his desk and gathered his case. He wanted to get home. After a beer and some TV, he could relax and unwind over a pizza.

The trip back on the train made his mood worse. He stood sandwiched between a man with rancid body odour, a couple of lads playing not very private music and a gaggle of chatting shoppers. When he finally got home, he threw his case on a soft chair, went into the kitchen, and cracked open a beer. A few minutes later, he slumped comfortably on the sofa, his jacket and shoes off, tie loosened, flicking through the various channels while he waited for his pizza to arrive. The news hadn't changed since the morning. They still harped on about that missing boy. In all likelihood, the little brat had just run away. The endless media coverage, along with speculation and crying relatives, made him sick.

Chapter 37

Glen and Cody

Cody pitched forward, landing face down in the dirt. He lay there groaning before he rolled over on to his back. His face felt hot and tender, so he guessed that he had been sleeping in the late afternoon sun. Cody found it strange that a few moments ago, that dream had seemed so real. Most dreams felt like a dim memory swiftly lost, but this one remained embedded in his mind, a troubling reminder that he would like to forget.

"You alright?" Glen stood over him and peered down, looking bemused. He grinned. "Taking a dirt nap?"

"Ha, Ha."

Cody found it less than funny, and Glen's attitude did not help.

"What the hell were you doing on the floor?" Glen said, hauling his friend to his feet.

Cody just shrugged and brushed the dirt off his jeans. What could he say? Oh, I dreamt of a city probably brought on by some sort of mind control experiment. Instead, he just supplied the minimum of information. "I fell asleep in the sun and rolled off the couch."

Glen snorted, rolled his eyes, shook his head and walked away, leaving Cody thinking about his travels. One thing he'd learnt, dreaming during the day wasn't as bad as the night. Perhaps safer too, if he disregarded holes that opened up beneath his feet. Tonight, he would stay awake no matter what. In the meantime, research and coffee remained the key to success. He brewed a pot of fresh extra strong Columbian Robusta coffee and sat down at his computer. Cody hoped that the effect justified the advert, 'When a sledgehammer is not enough.'

Later that evening, he noticed Glen watching him out of the corner of his eye. "More coffee?"

Glen watched incredulously as Cody poured what must have been his tenth cup. He would need to scrape him off the ceiling at this rate.

"Yes, what's wrong with more coffee?"

"Surely you've had enough to keep the entire English army awake during the hundred years' war."

"Can't have." Cody took another sip looking bad-tempered. "Coffee wasn't invented then."

Glen rolled his eyes and tried to put light into the situation. "Wow, who's lost his sense of humour buff? Want me to recast?" he said, referring to an online role-playing game they played, but not even this slightly geeky reference could lift Cody from his sullen mood. "Well I'm going to fix a sandwich did you want one?"

"Sure, peanut and jelly."

Glen could not adapt to this combination. Peanut fine, jelly or in his mind jam, fine but both together, Yuk! Still, he wandered off to the kitchen to make this meagre dinner.

Cody sighed. He didn't mean to be in a mood but found it difficult to share his thoughts with his sceptical friend. While compiling some odd stories from around the world, he had noticed that 'relevant dream events' circled the net. Obviously, something had triggered more vivid dreams. The theories ran through everything from aliens, additives in the water to government or corporate experiments. Cody thought aliens unlikely and he dismissed additives because he had his own water supply. One theme that kept reoccurring concerned dream control. Just envisage corporate marketing influencing what people bought while they slept. Imagine adverts around the clock, no rest twenty-four seven. Alternatively, governments could change people's behaviour during times of unrest or change minds to accept unpopular policy decisions. It could eliminate its rivals or those that didn't conform. Some even suggested that they could hack the brain. All manner of deaths could then appear natural and remain unlinked to the government. This final thought scared him the most although it came up against some stiff competition.

Either way, he was onto something. Maybe due to his various activities, he had become a person of interest, and now 'they' saw him as a threat. The time had come to test their new device and eliminate him. Perhaps they had designed these dreams to push him to his limits.

They wanted him to die of fright, bring on a stroke or heart attack, or worse make him contemplate suicide.

That thought brought him to Mr Johnson. Had he died of fright? How did the marks on the body fit the pattern? Could they be psychosomatic, as Glen suggested? He shivered, either way, they weren't going to get him. For now, he would keep these thoughts to himself until he had more proof, then he would go public. Afterwards, they would undoubtedly try to kill him in real life and anyone associated. Glen and Sarah would be at risk. He had to find a way to protect everyone. Cody began to search for data concerning insomnia and dreamless sleep. That might be a way forward.

He hardly noticed the sandwich that Glen placed beside his computer although he did actually eat it. Later, he heard Glen say goodnight, but Cody could not risk sleeping. He had to stay awake until morning.

Cody clambered to his feet, feeling disorientated. Above him, the gentle golden glow of false dawn filtered through the crumbling hole. He sighed disheartened. His plan hadn't quite worked. The haunting memories of last time filled him with a desire to leave before something else swallowed him up, or worse the tumbleweed creatures found him. As he had never seen them outside during the day, they must shelter from the heat. This dark hole seemed a suitable place. Cody listened intently and then peered into the darkness. If anything lived down here, he couldn't hear it move, but that didn't mean that something didn't wait in ambush. Intent on finding a weapon, Cody picked through the rubble, choosing one piece of pipe then began to tap his way nervously into the darkness. Each step, each tap, echoed loudly until in the distance, he saw a slight glow. It came from the ceiling illuminating the outline of stairs and something else, which Cody recognised. They looked like ticket barriers similar to those in the Boston subway. He stood in an underground station. His amazement ended when a sound echoed behind him. Cody went from zero to sixty in a matter of seconds. He jumped over the barriers, up the stairs and out into the open, in the blink of an eye. Cody didn't stop there either. He kept on running until he reached the end of the broken road where he stopped to rest, his heart pounding. As Cody bent over panting, he noticed a set of tracks and footprints in the dust. Proof that the people he had seen were real, for a given value of real.

Their tracks led onto the road, which stretched into the desert. He hadn't noticed a mule or horse so the men couldn't travel fast. Cody began to jog. He calculated that if time passed here at the same rate as at home or at least relatively close, then theoretically, he should be able to catch up. Over this terrain, they couldn't cover many miles in an hour. He assumed that they would travel in daylight but where did they go at night. When they slept, did they return home or were these enemy combatants in an artificial reality? If they were like him, would they trust him or view him as dangerous? How could he tell if they were real or fake? The argument raged inside his head, first one way, and then the other as he ran through the desert.

After a while, Cody let out a ragged breath and slowed to a walk as he climbed another small rise. Odd, how his illusionary lungs burned with effort. Yet a tiny lingering doubt coiled around his mind. If this wasn't real, then 'they' were damned good at generating nightmares. As Cody crested the rise, his eyes widened because just off the track, he saw something strange. An undulating lump sat by the side of the road. As he stared, it dawned on him. Under that writhing mass, two men lay trapped buried alive in a coffin of their own making. A safe haven only the word safe had a new meaning.

As Cody stood staring in revulsion, the frantic efforts died down, and an eerie silence descended over the desert. He felt the hairs on his arms begin to rise as the creatures turned in unison towards him. A finger of cold dread spread down his spine as Cody realised his mistake. He had become their target, an easy meal before the heat of the day made hunting impossible. With blind panic, he stared, as the creatures poured off the cart, heading in his direction.

His mind froze, but his body responded. Cody turned and ran back towards the city, only to find the way blocked by more tumbleweed. They must have followed him and just now caught up. In full flight mode, he turned again and dived through the sagebrush. Cody ran until he couldn't breathe anymore. As his heart threatened to burst through his chest, all the strength left his legs, and he collapsed into a heap.

Chapter 38

Karen

The floor felt like polished marble, cold, hard, and uncomfortable. Karen winced and opened her eyes. After hitting her head, she knew she lay on her back but with the lights still out, she had no point of reference. She found it strange that the lightning hadn't triggered the emergency power. Perhaps that's why no one had seen her, but then another thought niggled. Carpet covered the office floor. Only the foyer had stone tiles.

As Karen sat up, pondering this anomaly, she realised that she couldn't see any light coming through the glass doors. Intense darkness stretched out in all directions with one exception. A dim pinpoint of red light pulsed on the floor. Karen relaxed, thank goodness a floor socket, the electricity wasn't completely dead. The IT team would soon have the power working.

It took her a few seconds to remember that the foyer only had wall sockets but dismissed that concern. The darkness must have changed her perspective. The wall just looked like the floor.

She waited cross-legged in the dark, gradually getting annoyed, and growing ever colder and more uncomfortable. Karen began to wonder if she would have to wait until daylight to move. By now, she had reached the point where even sitting with her back to a wall would feel an improvement.

As she uncrossed her stiff legs, she groaned loudly but then froze as the sound rumbled and multiplied filling not the foyer but some dark cavernous space. Cold fear prickled her skin as her imagination ran riot conjuring horrors that lurked just out of reach. Heart racing, the sound of her rapid breathing echoed across the distance as her mind flew through wild possibilities. She could be lost in a cave or arrested and then thrown into a dungeon or kidnapped and locked away. Any of these dreadful options intensified when combined with memory loss brought on by a concussion.

Karen sat, senses on edge, waiting for something to happen, or worse something to arrive. Minutes passed, muscles cramped, but when nothing jumped out of the darkness, she gritted her teeth and forced herself to relax. As her breathing returned to normal, the echoes faded, leaving her space to think. It left her with a gut feeling that this wasn't a building. Yet the way sound travelled, it reminded her of an opera house. Someone had adapted a natural space to intensify the smallest sound. That left just more puzzles. Who had designed it? Why add the red light?

The more she stared at it, the more it attracted her. It acted not only as a focal point but also as a guide in the darkness. Yet a thought popped into her head. This might not be as beautiful as the city starlight, but it still had an enticing although eerie quality. Even though that had only been a dream, she'd almost walked off the cliff towards those lights. She should consider that possibility now.

Karen went from sitting to kneeling. Hands outstretched, placed on the floor, she felt for an edge. Yet her fingers touched nothing more than flat even stone. It gave her confidence to inch forwards, her hands searching for any potential dangers, but nothing presented itself. The floor remained unchanged. Smooth, cold, and Karen noted remarkably easy to slide across. As she slipped gently across the marble, one thing soon became jarringly obvious, the magnitude of the structure. The small red light grew only slightly in size as she progressed across the vast room. Karen paused to brush an annoying strand of hair off her face. The lack of reference points made it difficult to determine her distance from the light, but even so, now it looked less like a socket. Perhaps more like a recessed circular LED with its light shining upwards towards the ceiling. She looked up. Not that she could see a ceiling, walls, or anything else but now that she thought about it, she could hear something. A faint scratching sound echoed in the distance. As Karen listened, the noise petered out but then began again. It sounded almost like the scrape of bristles on a bass broom, except for one impossible thing. It came, from above.

Karen immediately rejected the idea. The cavern just reflected sound, making it seem this way, but then another slightly deeper version began to reverberate. This time she knew it wasn't just an echo.

Not wanting to meet its maker, she slid off into the darkness. The red light grew steadily, and Karen realised that it came from a hole in the floor. A strange sensation began to roll through her mind. Both repulsed and attracted at the same time; her instincts screamed to run away. Behind and above, bristles rattled over a dark ceiling, limiting her options. Either slide off into the darkness, into the unknown or go down into the light. This close the red glow had expanded, illuminating the edge like some great mouth that planned to swallow her whole. She ignored her fear and lay down on her stomach to peer over the edge. Below about fifteen feet or so down a shaft lay a massive oval dish gleaming in the blood red light. At least eight feet across and made of burnished copper, it held at its centre a huge faceted ruby pulsing with an eerie glow. With it came an unpleasant insight into its real purpose. Even so, Karen swung her legs over the rim of the shaft. Feet on both sides, arms draped over the edge, she lowered her body into the hole. From above, a repulsive suction noise followed by a squelch made her look around. In the dim red light, she could see a vague outline, which hinted of something hunched and unpleasant. As she stared, a squat elongated shape emerged from the darkness. Karen screamed and almost fell. It looked like an experiment gone wrong, something twisted and ugly with a hint of spider, squid, and even prey mantis. Dark grey bristles sprouted from its body, with fangs poised, as it kept its many red eyes fixed on her. In a desperate panic, Karen slithered down the hole, and a second later, the creature swiped its claws just above her head. With a shriek, she lost her tenuous grip and fell into the dish. As Karen landed awkwardly on her wrist, a great reverberating boom rattled through her bones. The sound hurt and frightened her, in ways she didn't understand, but the modulating hiss coming from above, made her slither onto the floor and look for an escape route.

Apart from the dais, the circular room remained almost empty. Around the central area, banners adorned gracefully carved archways. Through the furthest, Karen thought that she could see a doorway of sorts. As she stepped forward, a hooded figure emerged from the shadows. "Lu'oh kuuv dos sultha nindol k'lar!"

Karen jumped at the female voice. "I'm sorry, but I don't understand you," she stammered.

"Natha waela rivvil, lu'oh xunus dos inbau ghil!"

Karen felt something strange tingle inside her mind.

The figure stepped out, her dark robe rippling vermillion and amethyst in the light. "I said how *dare* you enter this holy place?"

Karen's jaw dropped, amazed that she could understand, even so, she tried to apologise, "I'm sorry I had…"

This excuse only seemed to anger the individual further. "Silence! How dare you speak in my presence?" She drew a dark hand from the depths of the robe and pointed towards Karen. "This is sacrilege. You will pay dearly for your impudence."

Karen backed away as the woman began muttering some strange words. The glow in the room intensified and just as it reached its peak, lightning arced from the figure, hitting Karen squarely in the chest. The force knocked her back onto the dish. A brilliant red shock wave exploded from the gem flinging the woman across the room but oddly pinning Karen to the jewel. She could hear her assailant's screams and the shrieks from the creatures above. Unable to breathe and filled with terrible energy that coursed through her veins, Karen wondered if she would die. As luck would have it, she passed out in agony before a raging inferno engulfed the room.

Chapter 39

Lars

A boot prodded Lars on the leg. "Hey wakey, wakey."

"Let me sleep," Lars grumbled. The backbreaking haul across the desert had taken its toll. He ached all over.

The prodding stopped, but Lars had no chance to settle back down on his pile of cardboard.

"Hey Lars it's me, Ted, you're going to miss out on a treat."

This roused Lars from his sleep. "Treat, what treat?"

"I've got some mon-ey, lots of mon-ey," Ted sang off key.

"Money? What for?"

Ted heaved an exasperated sigh. "For spending what else?"

Lars yawned and attempted to stand. His legs felt weak and as wobbly as jelly. "I'm thirsty; can we get a drink first?"

"Sure, the shelter is open."

As they wandered out of the alleyway towards the shelter, Lars became aware that passers-by avoided him more than usual. They wrinkled their noses and gave him a wide berth.

"Is there something wrong?" he asked Ted.

"Well, I can't really comment," said Ted reluctantly at first, but then he burst out. "But man, you stink! And I'm used to that, but phew there are limits even for me."

"Oh." Lars felt downcast and embarrassed but noted that Ted looked much neater than usual.

"Look, don't worry about it, get a wash at the shelter, and see if they have any spare clothes."

"Ok, thanks." Lars gave a weak smile feeling relieved.

Once they got to the shelter, even the usually nose dead inhabitants gave him extra room. After he had drunk some juice, he asked a volunteer about a wash and some clean clothes. Instead of a small bowl, the man handed Lars a towel, some soap and pointed him towards a white room.

"Chuck your clothes in this bag when you are done, and I'll leave a spare set on the stool outside the cubicle."

"Ok," said Lars as he stepped inside and closed the door.

He looked around mystified. The room contained a large opening with a small step, which dropped down into a square white tray. On one side dangled a curtain and behind that a white box. Pipes ran up the wall to a round thing in the ceiling. After some examination, he decided that he should stand inside the tray, but when he did, nothing happened. He looked at the white box. It had buttons like the car. Lars wrinkled his brow in thought and then began randomly pressing the controls. After a while, he heard an odd gurgling sound and the pipes started to rattle. Cold water drenched his head. He pushed a few more buttons trying to stop the torrent, but the cold water turned into a scolding hot downpour. Lars yelped and flattened himself against the wall before stabbing at the controls with an outstretched finger. The water stopped. In the tray, a muddy trail of water curled around and vanished down a grated hole.

Now that he had the hang of things, Lars decided to strip. He threw his sodden clothes into the bag and closed the curtain. After another false start, he managed to get the water flowing at a nice warm temperature. It felt wonderful. As he relaxed in the heat, he marvelled at this world. Yet another miracle, hot water within seconds. Lars couldn't help but wish his mothers' house had one of these contraptions. He'd just finished washing when he heard the door open and close. The volunteer had left some new clothes, so Lars pressed the button, and sure enough, the water ceased. He grinned at this accomplishment, feeling a strange sense of pride.

The towel felt beautiful and luxurious by his standards, but the clothes seemed odd. The underpants didn't lace up but stayed up on their own, as did the socks. It took him a while to understand the tooth like thing on the breaches. Lars finally found that if he pulled on the little flap, it knitted together. The shoes he rejected. They didn't look up to the desert, so he asked the volunteer if he could have his own footwear back. The man returned them in a remarkable transparent bag, which Lars examined carefully. Ted stared at him, slightly bemused. He had met some crazy people in his life, but this guy Lars appeared to be out of this world.

"You finished?" said Ted.

"Ah yes sorry I was just looking at this unique material, so light and yet so strong. What do you call it?"

"Plastic, it's useful but it never really rots."

"Isn't that a good thing?" Almost everything Lars knew fell apart eventually.

"Yeah but it stays whether you want it to or not."

Lars still didn't understand. This sounded perfect, imagine something that didn't rot, that he never had to replace. Strange how Ted didn't agree so apparently he'd missed something.

"So, you want this treat or not?" asked Ted.

"Sure, where are we going?"

"You'll find out. It's not a long walk."

Lars found the fresh night breeze a pleasant change from the desert. They wound their way around the city through various side streets, all lit with lamps, their strange golden glow illuminating the pavement as they walked. Ted chatted about his day, most of which made no sense to Lars. He did comprehend, however, that some wellborn lady had given Ted a substantial gift of money. Ted now planned to spend some of this in a wonderful place called a Mall before taking him to a mythical place, the Food Hall. Anything to do with food happened to be a good thing. Lars winced as his stomach made a loud distressing noise much to Ted's amusement.

As they rounded the next corner, Lars glimpsed a massive gleaming building made of metal and glass. For a moment, he stood astounded not only by its immense size but also by its astonishing beauty. Towers lit with coloured lights rose on each side of the building and in the middle stood an enormous archway. He marvelled that from this distance, people looked tiny as they moved in and out of the building, via a strange door. It took several minutes to make their way across the vast black area covered in white lines and thousands of cars. Lars couldn't believe how many people visited this place, so he decided that it must be somewhere important. Once there, Ted guided him through the revolving doors into what Lars could only think of as a magical palace. He stood open-mouthed, entirely overwhelmed.

Ted spread his arms out wide and exclaimed, "Ta-da!"
In silent amazement, Lars looked around dumbfounded.
"Well, what do you think?" asked Ted.
Lars could only stutter before he finally managed to make enough sense to reply. "It's incredible!" he said.

He couldn't decide what he liked best. The high glass ceiling covered in twinkling lights, the peculiar moving staircases, or the massive windows containing all sorts of items. In the middle next to a crescent bench, grew a complete tree surrounded by a fountain. What wealth these people possessed, almost beyond his comprehension.

"Hey, you're causing a scene," said Ted grinning. "Come on, let's get some ice cream."

"Ice cream?"

Lars followed Ted as he went up one of the moving staircases. The odd motion jerked beneath his feet, and he jumped back alarmed as it vanished underneath the floor. Would it drag him under as it flattened out? He watched Ted nonchalantly step off the stairs, so Lars did the same and then turned to stare.

"Where does that go?" he asked.

"Back around." Ted shrugged as if it was the most normal thing in the world.

On the second floor, they walked past window after window as Lars stared wondering what half the items were for until they came to a set of seats. Here Ted ushered Lars into a room and stood next to a glass counter. The girl standing opposite looked expectantly at both men. A tiny frown marred her perfect complexion as she waited.

Lars who had been staring burst out. "You're beautiful!"

The girl smiled, causing Lars to blush bright red. He had never seen a person with such perfect skin. She had long dark eyelashes, lips a shiny shade of ruby red and above her bright green eyes, glittered flecks of silver and green. Ted just shook his head and sighed as the girl giggled at Lars, who wished that the earth would open up and swallow him whole. Yet in the back of his mind, a perfidious memory whispered. He recalled a preacher crying out in the village square, 'Beware beauty lest it becomes vice and vanity.' He covered this unwelcome thought by lowering his eyes and examining the various tubs behind a glass screen.

"What can I do for you?" the girl asked in a sultry voice aimed at the blushing and now uncomfortable Lars.

Ted slapped a piece of paper on the counter. "Two mixed hot fudge sundaes with extra topping please," he said.

She looked him up and down, her expression sour as she noted his mismatched clothes. After examining the piece of paper with some misgivings, she collected two glasses and began to fill them with various coloured items. When it looked full to overflowing, the girl poured over a brown mixture and then sprinkled it with brightly coloured beads. She handed them to Ted and Lars along with two of the longest spoons he had ever seen.

Ted nodded towards the paper. "Keep the change," he said which seemed to improve the young woman's mood.

Ted guided Lars towards a table and chair. Once seated, he pointed at the glass and told Lars to 'tuck in.' Even though the colours gleamed unnaturally bright, Ted seemed to relish the food, so Lars took a spoonful, only to feel astounded by the taste and texture. Soft, creamy, sweet, both hot and cold with chewy, crunchy bits, he decided that nothing could be better. Could this be a little taste of heaven? Ted seemed to wolf it down as if it was his last meal, but Lars didn't intend to spoil it. Instead, he savoured every ecstatic mouthful. When he finished, Lars looked mournfully at the empty glass even though he felt full.

He sat back and looked at Ted. "Thank you. I've never eaten anything so delicious in all my life." With his usual candour, Lars admitted, "It's nice not to have to hunt down dinner and kill it before it kills you."

Ted grinned and shook his head. He decided that Lars might be a nice bloke but what a nutter. "Well if you liked that you'll love what I've planned next."

"There's more?"

"Sure, you gotta see the Food Hall."

Ted beckoned Lars to follow. Again, he took him past window after window and Lars began to realise the extent of the Mall. It seemed even bigger on the inside than on the outside.

The Hall compounded that impression. Food of every variety lay arranged in such quantities that Lars almost panicked and ran. Row upon row, shelf upon shelf, it ran in all directions as far as the eye could see. He felt overwhelmed by more choice than he had ever experienced in life. Never had he seen such perfect fruit and vegetables, all uniform without a single blemish. Like that girl almost too good to be true.

It made him wonder why anyone starved in this world. People in the shelter had so little yet here lay unshared abundance beyond understanding. He felt a stab of momentary annoyance as another preacher proverb popped into his head. 'Greed incites ignorance and leads to destruction.'

For the first time, he wondered if they had a point. Yet the people he'd met didn't deserve punishment. Why should the innocent suffer along with the guilty? In his own world, the Overlords held most of the wealth and power. Yet they always remained unsatisfied and grasped for more. The preachers said that this behaviour had destroyed the world. Would it lead to another levelling? The world laid to waste again by their greed. Wasn't there a better way of doing things? These thoughts depressed him. He stood staring at the food, now bizarrely repulsed by its perfection.

In the end, his strange antics drew the attention of the security guard who wandered over, looking suspicious. Ted shooed him away, pointing out that they were paying customers, and if they wanted to take their time, they could. The guard reluctantly moved away but still kept an eye on them.

Ted realised that the whole experience had nearly been too much for Lars, which he found perplexing. As they wandered back to the shelter, Lars asked some odd questions. Where did the food come from, how did they farm so much, and why did anyone starve? Ted felt confused. It was almost as if Lars had never seen this sort of thing before. Once back in familiar territory Lars seemed to calm down. Ted could not decide if his friend had suffered from a sugar high or had mental health issues. Either way, he acted so strangely at times. Lars reinforced this view when he insisted that he stayed awake until dawn to avoid another attack. Ted didn't wait. He felt tired enough for both of them. When he woke later that morning, Lars had gone.

Chapter 40

Adam and Ceola

Adam groaned in pain and shifted position, rolling off something hard that stuck into his back. As he moved, a bright light shone on his face. Eyes watering, he scrabbled around and slipped on a heap of grass and earth, mixed with rock. It triggered a memory, of a song and a fall into darkness. He rolled again and sprung onto his feet, ready to defend himself. As his eyes adjusted to the lower light levels, Adam looked at his surroundings. Beyond the bright spotlight, he could see dark shadowed passages that extended off in several directions. Probably some sort of cave system. Adam had no idea how far it went, and he wasn't inclined to find out. He felt a pressing need to return to the surface and get the hell away from that were-bitch. He didn't want a repeat performance of their last encounter.

Adam looked up and saw the edge of the tree root-fringed hole. He estimated that it was about another six feet above his head. At just over six foot, Adam thought that might be ok, assuming that the plants would support his weight. There wasn't much room, but he backed up a little, took a running jump, and grabbed a root, which promptly broke off in his hand. He tried several times without success, each time either missing his handhold or dangling briefly before the root broke. Before long, Adam ran out of available roots. After that, he tried jumping and grabbing at the turf, but each time the edge crumbled, showering him with dirt as he fell to the floor. Adam stood panting and wondered if a bit of cave exploration, however dangerous, might be necessary.

"You *can* get out." A deep voice tinged with condescension echoed down the hole.

"Faxon?" Adam queried.

"No, but I know him."

Adam became wary. "Know him, as in a friend or more like an enemy?"

After a pause, the voice replied, "Neither, we have fought from time to time. I would describe Faxon more as a respected rival."

Adam considered that reply. It could be worse. "You said I could get out of here, was that with or without your help?"

The reply annoyed him.

"You feel that you *need* my help?"

Adam didn't like to admit it, but yes, he could have done with a helping hand. With a sigh, he replied, "Yes, but don't rub it in."

Seconds later, he got a cryptic reply. "Well then dig deep and summon the power."

Adam clenched his fists, becoming angry. "I was thinking of something more practical."

The voice outside merely chuckled, which faded as the sound moved away.

"Hey!" shouted Adam. "Hey, are you going to leave me down here?" He waited for a moment. "Hey! Come back!"

When the man didn't reply, Adam swore and began to pace, growing more annoyed by the second. He felt mocked, slighted, and worse ignored. He became determined to give whoever owned that voice a piece of his mind, or more likely, his fist.

"Just you fuckin' wait I'll come up there and beat that sorry face of yours into a bloody pulp!" he screamed.

In the distance, he heard deep mocking laughter. It filled Adam with such rage that he threw himself forward towards the light. With one enormous leap, he sailed past the roots and landed on the surface. This unexpected success made his anger drain away, leaving him feeling oddly unsettled but mostly pleased.

To one side, he heard a small chuckle. When he turned, he saw the owner of the voice. The biggest most muscular man Adam had ever seen lounged against a fallen tree. No wonder the man had laughed at the idea that Adam would beat him to a pulp. He would just hurt his fist on that square bony jaw. Another two feet taller than Adam and built like a tank; his sculpted brown muscles shone and bulged. The dark-haired man eyed Adam critically and then with a slight sneer quickly dismissed him. Like an officer scrutinising a private and writing them off as nothing more than a raw recruit. It left Adam feeling naked and ill at ease, which he considered ironic in his condition. The man unfolded his arms and looked at Adam critically.

"So, you're one of hers then?"

Adam sighed. He should expect this, every time simply categorised as hers. "I'm trying not to be," he said.

The man nodded as if accepting his statement. "The witch came this way earlier so we'd better move out soon. It won't be long before she's back."

Another man broke into the glade and Adam tensed, but the leader stayed relaxed as he turned towards the new arrival. "Report."

"There are signs Hal but no new sightings."

The leader nodded then turned to Adam and looked critically at his naked body. Hal snorted and tilted his head towards the other man. "Give him your bandana."

The other man looked startled. "What?"

The leader gave his subordinate a cold stare. "Are you questioning me?"

The man hesitated about to object then just sagged. "No pack leader."

Adam noticed the word 'pack' straight away and didn't like it.

The man untied the piece of cloth, glowered at Adam, and threw the fabric at his feet.

"Put it on. It will make running easier," said Hal indicating his own loincloth. When Adam just stared at it, not knowing what to do, the pack leader sighed. "Wrap it around and under, and then tuck it in."

Hal rolled his eyes and shook his head in disgust as Adam fumbled around trying to secure the cloth. Not waiting for him to finish, the pack leader stood and moved down an animal track. As Adam did up the final knot, the man who gave him the bandana poked him in the back and indicated that he should follow Hal. Adam resisted, but the man gave him another hard jab. It seemed like they weren't giving him a choice.

The evening sun glinted just above the tree line as he travelled down the narrow path. Hal stopped and waited for Adam to catch up. When they began to move again, unlike Faxon, they didn't jog so fast that Adam couldn't keep up. They hadn't gone far when they arrived at an intersection between two paths. Here the leader slowed, and then he did something strange. He tilted his head back and howled. An eerie almost inhuman sound emanated from his throat making Adam uneasy, but the man just grinned as if this was completely normal. After a few seconds, another person appeared on the converging path. He greeted the leader with deference, but when he saw Adam, he sneered, who returned the look. With a mop of unruly ginger hair, the man had penetrating wild eyes that gave Adam the impression of an unhinged disposition.

"Report."

"Nothing to report Hal, all's quiet."

The newcomer inclined his head towards Adam. "Bait?" he asked.

Hal shrugged a reply.

"What the fuck!" Adam exploded. "What makes you think I'd agree to be bait?"

The man sniggered. "Who said we needed your agreement?"

"I do." Adam snarled.

Around the same size, both men squared face to face, looking for a fight.

The leader sighed and placed his hand on the newcomer's shoulder. "Peace Edric."

Edric stepped back but kept an eye on Adam. "Your will, Hal."

Hal turned towards Adam. "We know she has been searching for someone and now you are here; obviously it's you she wants. You have admitted that much to me."

Adam eyed the man warily. "So, what did you want me to do?"

"Come with us to our village until you make the change, she will want you more after that, so we can lay a trap."

Edric spoke up, "With respect, she won't come near the village."

Hal turned with a cold stare. "Do you think I am an idiot?"

Edric dropped his eyes. "No pack leader."

"Then trust in my judgement."

Adam interrupted. "Is there a reason why we're standing around?"

"Yes, we are waiting for the others."

As they stood in silence, Edric glared at Adam as if trying to intimidate him, but without much success. Adam stared insolently back. After a few minutes, several men arrived.

"Report," demanded Hal.

"Not much to report Hal. There's been some movement on the eastern border, but it smells like one of the other clans. There's been neither sight nor scent of her though."

"Same for us too Hal, I couldn't see any new tracks that led out onto the planes."

Hal nodded. "Well, I know how she's been avoiding our patrols."

The men looked surprised.

Hal nodded towards Adam. "We found him hiding in a collapsed tunnel."

"I wasn't hiding, I just fell."

Adam suddenly felt uncomfortable when faced with six penetrating stares.

"He's hers?" queried one of the men, which annoyed Adam.

"Yes," said Hal

"What are we going to do with him?"

"Tie him up and leave him as bait," suggested Edric.

"No way." Adam clenched his fists as the men laughed.

Edric stepped forward grinning in malicious pleasure. "Don't worry, you'd enjoy it. First, she'd drain your life force and then eat your flesh."

Adam shivered and remembered last time. With his mind enslaved, maybe he would enjoy it, albeit briefly.

Edric's suggestion sparked an argument between the men, but Hal quietly stood there with a long-suffering expression.

"That would be stupid. The witch would be strong and filled with magic."

"Better to catch her before she does that."

"You got a plan for that? The last one worked out so well didn't it?"

"How are you going to resist her spell?"

"I say we kill her."

"What about poison?"

Hal interrupted their bickering. "Enough!"

The men quietened down.

"We will take him back to the village and hold him until the change, and then he will be of more use to us and of more interest to her. It will also increase his chance of survival."

"Increase my chance of survival?" Adam glared incredulously. "Why should I get involved in any of this?"

He quickly realised this wasn't the wisest thing to say. He had just provoked six stony-faced men who didn't plan to give him a choice.

Hal looked at Adam without a trace of pity. "This is too good a chance for us to pass up. We have been looking for a way to lure her to a time and place of our choosing. You present the perfect opportunity." He nodded at his men. "Bring him."

The six men quickly surrounded Adam. He tensed ready for a fight, but instead of knocking him out, they grabbed his arms firmly and bundled him forward. One man stood on each side, while two guarded the rear, scanning the shadows for any unusual movement in the twilight forest. The other two kept an eye on each flank. In the lead, Hal strode through the woods. Adam resisted, but he might as well try to attack a couple of iron bars. Their tight grip kept him in order without entirely cutting off the circulation. He realised that even if he managed to get free from one, the other would take him down. As brute force obviously wasn't going to work, if he wanted to escape, he would have to use his brains. A traitorous thought lurked at the back of his mind. Good luck with that. So far, he hadn't exactly thought things through.

The terrain started to slope upwards with the ground getting rougher and more uneven as they travelled along. At some points, there were sudden dips or rugged rock-strewn holes in the path.

"Ease up a bit," he said as they almost dragged him off his feet.

They ignored him.

"Hey, I get the picture! Resistance is futile."

"Quiet," grumbled one of his captors.

"Look I don't like her either. She did this to me. It's not like I had a choice in the matter."

"I told you to keep quiet!" a giant hand crushed his arm.

Adam winced but decided that he would try to distract them anyway. The light had faded to a dull glow, and he guessed that he didn't have much time to escape before darkness descended.

"So how far is this village?"

They didn't reply, but when they reached the top of the ridge, Adam caught a glimpse of firelight below. Just as they began the descent, something odd caught his eye.

He tried to turn. "What's that?" he asked.

"Don't think we will fall for that old trick," scoffed Edric.

"No honestly, I mean it, I thought I saw something."

Adam struggled. He could feel that strange sensation again. It felt like the witch. Why didn't they sense her?

Hal called out. "Halt! Quiet!"

They came to a stop. Adam could sense the pack's nervous energy. They sniffed the air as they held him tightly. Adam's body shook as he stared off into the night. He knew they weren't alone.

One of the men whispered. "We should be able to smell her even if we can't see her."

Adam just shook his head, unable to speak. He wanted to shout out, to warn them that she hid, shrouded in darkness. His senses screamed at him to run, to escape, but his feet wouldn't move. The fear must have shown on his face because Hal suddenly made a decision.

"Form up! Whether we believe it or not he does. As they are linked, he might sense her when we can't."

"We could run for it," suggested one of the men.

Hal shook his head. "The village is close, but we might not make it if she decides to strike now. Besides, how would the cubs fare against her magic? We must stand our ground here!" He swore. "Along with the tunnels, the witch must have a new way to mask her scent. No wonder she slipped past us so many times. Now we know what she can do, it will not be so easy for her next time." Hal braced himself. "Now ready yourselves."

Each man stood in silence, muscles tensed, their eyes searching for the first sign of movement. Through the misty haze of longing and fear, Adam noticed in a detached way that they were somehow different. His mind felt a long way off, but he found with some effort that he could still think. They were becoming more hunched, hairy, their features gross. He didn't know what this meant, but he felt that he should remember.

"Give him to me," a whisper light as a spring breeze, broke the stillness.

When they did not reply, it came again.

"He is mine; give him to me."

The men shifted uneasily looking for the source of the voice, but with no success.

"If you do not give him to me, I will take him." She gave a silvery laugh, which sent a shiver down Adams' spine. "And some of you with him."

"You shall not have him witch!" growled Hal. As he changed form, he raised his head high and let forth an immense howl.

Adam could hear howls answer from the village. Hal had called for reinforcements.

She replied in a low, venomous hiss, "So be it wolf."

Without further warning, a vast orb of energy burst through the trees. A white flaming comet trailing fire in its wake slammed into Hal's chest catapulting him backwards and scattering his pack in all directions. Adam, thrown forcefully to the floor, lay stunned by the shockwave and blinded by the light. In the background, he could hear screams and shouts, which morphed into snarls. More light flashed, thunder boomed, shrieks of pain and anger followed. The fire blazed and exploded, bursting over the forest. They answered her attack with baying and snapping jaws. Adam kept his head down, but as he lay there, he felt his mind clear as her focus transferred to his captors. He could hear shouts and howls coming from below the ridge, and he knew that the reinforcements had arrived. Light burst above him, scattering his guards. Now Adam had a chance. He turned and started to crawl away from the fight. When the undergrowth grew too thick, he stood and glanced back. Adam saw another bright flash and heard the howls of pain as he turned to run.

The bolt that hit Hal also threw Edric down the bank, but he quickly recovered. He scrambled swiftly up the hill to kneel at his leader's side. Hal lay on the ground in human form, his chest a mass of burnt flesh cauterised by the fire. Edric bent over the body and sighed in relief. Hals' heart beat slowly. He would heal. Hal stirred and moved his lips. Edric bent closer to listen.

"Get him, bring him back, don't let him escape; he must be worth a lot for her to risk this fight." With a sigh, Hal passed out, still breathing.

The howls and shouts from just below the ridge confirmed that reinforcements had arrived. He left his injured leader and ran over to where Adam had fallen in the mud and sniffed the air. The trail wasn't difficult to follow, broken bracken, scuffed branches along with an overpowering scent of fear. The witch's slave might as well have painted a signpost.

The noise of battle faded into the background as Adam ran along the ridge, but it wasn't long before he could hear something behind him. Not that he planned to stop and check. As the noise grew closer, Adam broke into a sprint, jumping over fallen trees and through bracken, keeping marginally ahead. As he ran, he became aware that he could see lights to his left. To his dismay, Adam realised that the ridge followed a tightening arc. Instead of heading away from the village, he had run around it. He tried to change direction, to plough through the undergrowth but something knocked him sideways off the ridge. Adam tumbled down the steep slope, bouncing through branches to lay hurt and winded at the bottom. High above, silhouetted by moonlight, the creature roared in delight. With one giant leap, it landed on its wounded and vulnerable prey. Adam froze in horror as a fanged hairy monstrosity bent over him. It grinned like an evil maniac as it changed through each sickening phase into something more human.

"Now your mine," snarled Edric.

Adam saw a huge fist speeding towards his face before everything went dark.

Chapter 41

Xenis

The intense heat prevented the women from entering the inner sanctum. Thalra of House Velkyn'Zhaunil could only stand and wait, while Larenil paced back and forth beside her. Neither Drow knew what to expect. Tall, her gaunt framed covered by the long black priestess robe, Thalra twisted the end of her waist-length white ponytail impatiently. Next to Thalra, small and curvaceous, her pale hair tight in a short plait, Larenil stamped her thigh booted foot, aggravated by the delay. In response, her warrior like garb rippled with dark light as it reflected her mood.

Both Drow wanted to send runners, but neither could do so until they had something to say, something more than the terrible news that a firestorm raged within the temple. Details would be required, questions asked, answers demanded. Only that knowledge could save them both now.

Larenil continued to pace, her stomach screwed in a tight knot, her mind awhirl. Valene had left her in charge of the temple's day-to-day business, while she met with her mother, the Matriarch. This had happened on her watch. She would be lucky to last the day unless she could find a scapegoat.

As the light above began to dim, Thalra interrupted the pacing. "The firestorm is dying. I will cast a spell which should protect us from the heat so that we might investigate."

Larenil hesitated and then nodded. In normal circumstances, she would never trust another priestess. It would be so easy for the spell to *accidentally* malfunction and cause her death, but this time she sensed this priestess merely wanted the truth.

Thalra began to cast the 'Shield' spell, using the ritual words to focus her mind but strangely, found this more difficult than usual. The incantation first waivered then faltered before finally holding. Now assured of their safety, they slowly walked together up the flame-charred corridor towards the antechamber. The door had vanished, burned to ashes by the heat but when they entered the room, both Drow gasped. The remains of the altar stood in the middle of a black and charred room. The bronze dish, still plinking as it cooled, had flowed like a waterfall onto the ground. The gem in the middle lay undamaged though there remained one significant problem. It no longer pulsed vivid red but flickered dimly. Both priestesses stood silent and horrified as they absorbed the ramifications. They would report this catastrophe to the Five, but they must keep it secret from broader society, at all costs.

Thalra stirred from her shock. She needed to know who could be responsible for this desecration. Yet she found it difficult to maintain the shield and cast another spell at the same time, so instead, she relied on her natural magical abilities. Thalra reached out her mind and sensed the room. She encountered nothing until she touched the gem. Thalra sensed something, so slowly she began to lower the shield.

Larenil felt the change and looked sharply at Thalra. "What are you doing?"

"I mean no harm."

"We will see."

"I sense something strange, but I cannot investigate further while maintaining the shield."

Larenil tensed. The Five had ordained her as a priestess, but because she did not have full mage training, she could not cast a reliable shield. All women received magical tuition, especially royalty, but unless they retained a genuine spark of magic in their soul, none attended further education in the school of sorcery. It remained a cause of disagreement in a society where even males could attend the school if they showed sufficient talent. Those selected underwent the rigorous indoctrination deemed necessary to preserve the Matriarchal system and guard against dissent.

Usually, Larenil would not countenance accommodating a priestess from another house. Under the circumstances, unpleasant though it might be, working together had become a necessity. A sideways glance signalled her capitulation and Thalra continued to lower the shield.

When it dropped completely, both Drow coughed and spluttered in fumes. Larenil managed to cast a light shield that protected them from the smoke, although the heat still penetrated its defences, leaving them both barely able to breathe. Thalra, struggling to concentrate, began to cast an 'Identification' spell. Like the 'Shield' spell, it waivered for a moment before flaring into life. She scanned the room before finally settling on the gem. A strong and powerful female presence hovered over the jewel, yet it had a strange quality. Thalra hadn't encountered anything quite like it before. The rapidly decaying signature felt Drow, but then she touched on something else, something unidentifiable and alien. She found, however, no physical remains. Either the female had survived, or the firestorm had completely incinerated the skeleton. Thalra pushed her mind further, gritting her teeth with the effort. She couldn't be sure, but the ashes didn't belong to a living being. Yet how could anyone survive, it should be quite impossible. Thalra could only conclude that the intruder must have escaped just before the firestorm took hold. If so, then where had she gone? Thalra mused on this idea for a moment then decided to keep this speculation to herself.

"Well?" demanded Larenil impatiently.

Thalra opted for a simplified version of the truth. "There's something, but I can't be certain what it is."

"Why not?"

"Obviously the firestorm obliterated the evidence." This would soon be conveniently true.

Larenil didn't believe her one bit. What was her game? To hide the truth obviously but to what end? Yet she could do nothing to force the hand of this powerful mage priestess. Instead, she would have to rely on Valene. Larenil shuddered as she stared at the blackened floor, soon she would have to send for her sister and inform her mother of this disaster.

"I cannot delay this news any longer. I must send runners to the council and my house." She looked up. "You must stay silent until they are informed."

Thalra shrugged. "As you wish."

Larenil became suspicious at her compliant capitulation.

Both women turned and taking care to maintain the shield, left the room. Once at the interconnecting corridors below the inner sanctum, Larenil summoned the female house runners and gave them identical messages to deliver. Each messenger had their mind encrypted, an unpleasant process, but it ensured that no one else could intercept the information. Larenil should have sent the first runner to Mith'Barra, but she couldn't bring herself to do that. Instead, she directed the message to her mother. On hearing the news, the Matriarch would erupt into incandescent anger. Larenil could almost feel sorry for her sisters Valene and Irae if they remained in her mother's presence.

Thalra surreptitiously turned to leave as Larenil concentrated on the encryption process. She didn't go far, that would be suspicious, but she did enter a nearby room filled with books. When Thalra confirmed that no one else could observe her actions, she concentrated and with two fingers pressed against her forehead, cast an 'Inner Voice' spell. It touched a bound location in her mind.

"This had better be important," whispered a reply.

"Mother, the temple has been defiled. A firestorm broke out and destroyed the inner sanctum. The altar gem is dim."

A shocked silence echoed in her mind. The spell made it impossible to lie using this method of communication so the facts could not be in any doubt. Rather the enormity of the situation kept the Matriarch silent. Less than an hour ago, something had disturbed the equilibrium. She had felt a worrying change in the magical undercurrents that encompassed the city. Now she knew the cause.

Thalra kept silent while her mother processed the information, but the strain of keeping the link open began to tell.

"Mother there is more. There remained a presence over the gem. I identified the signature as female, powerful and Drow but also alien. I could not find any physical remains so she must have escaped."

"Does anyone else know?"

"Larenil from House Zik'Keeshe but I kept the whole truth from her."

"What did you say?"

"That I felt something but that I couldn't identify the assailant."

"Good, we can use that to our advantage, has she informed the council yet?"

"As we speak, she is sending runners."

"Stay close to her. Now, go."

"Yes, Matriarch."

Thalra, shaking with effort, broke the link and sank to the floor. Now that her mother knew the situation, she could only listen and wait for further instructions.

The hooded figure spoke, "They can never know the truth."

The others nodded. They knew the ramifications. If anyone learned what had happened, all the houses would band together and turn against them. They would be unlikely to survive, and even if they did, they would never be in power again. At best, they would be pariahs for all eternity.

"What should we do? The gem has failed, soon every priestess will know. They may feel the change in power even now," one voice asked.

"We will call an assembly. Inform them of the desecration and its implications. After which it will be in their best interests to keep quiet."

The others nodded, aware that they would need to omit some vital details.

"How will we keep this secret from the males?" asked another voice.

"By never speaking of it again, not even a hint."

The speaker pressed the issue. "But what if they found out?"

"They must not!"

The silence stretched out as each female considered this additional complication.

Another spoke up, "Can we lay blame on House Zik'Keeshe? After all, they are ultimately responsible. The desecration has occurred during their tenure as guardians of the temple."

The hooded figure considered that suggestion. "That is one possible option."

A voice cut through that comment, "No, that would be too obvious. We need to take a more subtle and indirect approach. First, we should voice our dissatisfaction and demand a full investigation."

There were murmurs of approval.

"And after that?"

"We could implicate another house and let Zik'Keeshe deal with the fallout. One house could eliminate the other."

"Which house would you choose?"

"House Faerl'Zotreth, everyone would believe it possible after the temple transfer. Then we could ask a neutral third party such as Vlos'Killian to watch both houses. They would be more than willing to believe anything we implied."

"But House Vlos'Killian could hardly be described as neutral," a voice said dryly.

"They don't have any current alliances, so technically within the law they are neutral."

The voice changed tack. "What of the intruder?"

"We are not certain; however, it is possible that she survived."

An air of surprise stirred through the group.

"How can that be? The chamber lies in ruins."

"Officially the senior priestess from Velkyn'Zhaunil stepped into the antechamber first followed by the youngest from House Zik'Keeshe. I have been informed by the Matriarch of Velkyn'Zhaunil that her daughter found magical evidence of a female intruder; however, no visible residue remained."

A voice snorted. "And we believe them?"

"For the moment we have no choice, the signature has decayed beyond recognition."

All present wondered how much Velkyn'Zhaunil already knew. This house had shown no interest, well no outward interest, in ruling for a long time; however, as they all knew, times change.

"If she survived, then we must find her."

A flurry of voices echoed around the chamber.

"Do we know who she is?"

"Where is she from?"

"Who sent her?"

"What does she want?"

"Where is she hiding?"

The silence that followed indicated that there wasn't an answer to those questions.

"No, we have not been able to find her yet. House Velkyn'Zhaunil will aid us in the search."

"And what do they want for this service?"

"A seat on the council when a vacancy arises."

The others nodded accepting this condition, but the hooded figure remained concerned. How much would Velkyn'Zhaunil learn? Would they discover the whole truth? What of House Zik'Keeshe? One of their males had an annoying talent for investigation. It might become necessary in time to eliminate him, discreetly of course.

"Do you think the intruder triggered the sentinels a few days ago?"

"It is quite possible."

"Then we must find her first."

"But if anyone else does?"

"They must not."

From his viewpoint, overlooking the gates, Xenis could see a female runner dashing towards the house. Not a good sign, female runners delivered the most important news. Society taught that males could not withstand the encryption process. It would break their minds although privately he didn't believe it. As a male, he would not be privy to this news until much later. Possibly too late to take advantage of the situation or indeed do anything about it. He needed information now, and although magic bound the message to the recipient, Xenis knew he could get an inkling if he intercepted the female.

She approached quickly, so he took the direct route down, dropping swiftly from the battlements only slowing before he hit the ground. Oddly enough, that required more effort than usual. Anyone else would have dismissed this as unimportant but not Xenis. He filed it away for later.

He landed just as the gates opened to admit the runner. Xenis strode forward and broke protocol. "What happened?"

The look on her face almost betrayed the information contained within her mind. Wide-eyed, she shook her head and then raced towards the throne room. Xenis had rarely seen such fear. It could only mean one thing, disaster for House Zik'Keeshe.

"Quickly," Xenis yelled to the guards. "To me."

They assembled around him swiftly, and he picked one. "Kasen increase the guard, get everyone off duty."

The guard nodded and rushed away.

"The rest of you with me, we march to the temple quick speed."

Even though Xenis knew that each house would be watching with interest, he took the most direct route. Time was of the essence. He guessed that Larenil had sent the runner home before informing anyone else, so the council didn't know the news yet. He wanted to know what had happened before anyone else. It would give him time to plan.

As they reached the temple gates, Xenis turned and gave orders. He stationed extra guards outside while he ordered others to head inside to strategic points. The defence planned; he quickly ran towards the inner sanctum. Xenis couldn't go inside, but he knew that Larenil would be somewhere close.

He found her below the temple at the intersection near the reading rooms. She appeared to be alone.

"Brother what are you doing here?"

Xenis looked around, and then bending close to Larenil, he whispered, "Is there anyone else here?"

Larenil breathed, "Yes Thalra from House Velkyn'Zhaunil. She arrived just as I made the discovery. She is waiting in the reading rooms."

"Can she hear us now?"

Larenil shook her head.

Xenis announced loudly, "The Matriarch sent me here directly to await instruction."

Larenil nodded. "Double the guards make sure no one enters the temple without my permission until Valene arrives. Then report back."

"Your will."

Xenis left but quickly returned with two guards who went to stand outside the reading rooms. If Thalra tried to leave, their polite questions would slow her down. This should give him a chance to speak with Larenil.

He returned to his sister, who waited a little further down the corridor. Never had he seen her so worried. "Tell me all."

She hesitated; after all, he was but a male.

"I'm on your side and if I can help you, I will." He reassured her.

Larenil's voice broke, "The inner sanctum, Valene left me in charge, now it's gone."

"Gone?"

"What will they do to me?"

Xenis held his sisters shaking shoulders. "Nothing if I can help it. Now tell me what do you mean, gone."

She hung her head and told him everything. Well everything apart from the gem, after all, there are some things you don't share even with your brother. Once she finished, Xenis stepped back in shock. He could barely comprehend a disaster of this magnitude.

"Where were you when this happened?"

Larenil looked up sharply.

He held up a conciliatory hand. "I'm not accusing, only asking as others will ask and somewhat less gently."

Her shoulders sagged as she admitted, "I began to explore the temple. I've never been unaccompanied before."

Xenis sighed. Their society did not consider curiosity a virtue. "Say that you were familiarising yourself with the temple as you regarded this as part of your duty. Did you check the guards when you *investigated*?"

Larenil nodded.

"Good, then it's true. If anyone tries to force your mind, you can say this quite honestly but let them pressure you until you can stand it no longer. Then they will feel that you are not holding back." He smiled. "And remember this, it's all in the way you say it."

Larenil got the distinct feeling that Xenis had learned this trick from experience. It also meant that she could not trust anything he said, even under pressure. Would she tell her mother? Possibly, but only if it suited her; she would however never tell Valene. Then a thought occurred to her. Xenis never slipped. He would not have shared this information unless he had something to use against her if she spoke out.

Xenis looked around. "When Thalra arrived, what direction did she come from?"

Larenil pointed. "The opposite direction from me."

"And when you both saw the devastation she seemed as shocked as you?"

"Yes, unless she feigned it well enough to deceive me." Then Larenil frowned. "When we entered the temple, Thalra did something odd. I sensed not exactly a spell but something magical. She dropped the shield to cast an 'Identification' spell, and I took over. She found something but couldn't identify who or what it was."

Xenis showed surprise that they would work together. Usually, a priestess would rather slit her own throat or preferably, someone else's, rather than collaborate with one another.

"And you believe her?"

Larenil snorted. "Do I look that stupid? Of course not, she's hiding something."

"When you both arrived did either of you see anyone apart from guards?"

Larenil shrugged, she didn't know. She had never thought to ask Thalra if she had seen anyone running away, after all, who could survive that heat.

Xenis, on the other hand, assumed nothing. Death remained the most probable outcome, but until they could identify any physical remains, he would presume that the intruder escaped either by another path or through the sacrificial hole. Xenis thought the latter unlikely. Spells shielded the entrance and above on the marble auditorium, guardians patrolled. Their venomous sting could be deadly in seconds. They could also administer a lesser toxin, which simply drugged an intruder leaving them helpless. This allowed the priestesses to question their captive extensively before disposal. No one would be mad enough to risk that drawn-out, agonising death. So, assuming for the moment that they lived, the explosion could have thrown the intruder out of the inner sanctum, clear of the firestorm, before they escaped. Thalra could have seen someone running from the scene and hid that information. Xenis considered this suspicious besides what would she have to gain? A great deal if she could blackmail the guilty house, assuming of course that this was an inside job. Another city could be responsible or even an outsider, but they would be hard pressed to overcome the warding spells that surrounded the temple, and even more so the inner sanctum. He let those thoughts hang, they would need investigation, but he could hardly press Thalra the first daughter of House Velkyn'Zhaunil for further information. Valene would do that once she arrived.

The runner entered the throne room and threw herself flat on the floor in front of the Matriarch. The interruption angered the ruler, but this sign of submission indicated the importance of the message.
"Stand."
The runner complied as the Matriarch rose from her throne and descended the stairs. As she clutched the messengers head in her hands, she whispered the words of decryption before reading her mind. At first, she could hardly believe the news, so she probed deeply causing great pain, but the truth remained. The Matriarch let go, and the runner slumped unconscious to the ground.

Valene and her younger sister Irae could only stare in growing disquiet at the look of shock on the Matriarchs face. Valene unwisely opened her mouth to ask what had happened, but before she spoke, she faced a mental slap that knocked her across the room. The Matriarchs incandescent rage shimmered in the air. Irae could barely stop herself from cowering as Valene stayed on the floor in humble submission, something she had never done before. When the Matriarch finally pulled herself together, she told them both to probe the runner's mind for themselves. They quickly complied and then understood the horror of the situation. The information left them stunned. This could spell the end of House Zik'Keeshe.

"Daughters go to the temple, leave no stone unturned, find out what happened, and use any methods at your disposal. I will remain here. Soon the council will summon me to the chamber. We will see if our house can survive this disaster."

Valene and Irae bowed and hurried away, passing a runner wearing Mith'Barra colours as they left the house. If the next few hours went badly, they would soon have to fight for their lives.

Chapter 42

Thomas

The cleaner shuddered at the scrabbling noise. It made her think of rats. She'd seen a sizeable healthy-looking specimen running across the alleyway last night when she'd put out the rubbish. A second noise made her stop and listen. That didn't sound like rats. Rats didn't knock over rubbish bins. Everyone had gone home, well everyone except for the other cleaner.

"Maureen, is that you?"

When no one replied, Betty listened again. Something moved in the next room. With her concentration focused on the sound, she reached slowly for the broom and then shuffled forward, holding it out like a talisman. "Maureen?" her voice trembled with fear.

She moved a shaking hand towards the door and slowly turned the handle. Click, the door opened. The sound ceased. Betty froze.

Thomas woke in a darkened room. For a moment, he lay there disorientated before he sat up and looked around. Outside, Thomas heard the noise of traffic and cursed. He sat head in his hands, feeling glum. Back here yet again and he didn't remember going to sleep, but even if he learnt to meditate, he would still have to sleep sometime. He couldn't avoid that. Thomas wanted to stop going back and forth; he wanted to stay there and forget here. Yet he couldn't control that either.

Thomas kicked out in frustration knocking over a nearby rubbish bin. He watched it roll across the floor, emptying its contents in a steady, satisfying stream. Someone must have heard the crash because a woman's voice called out. Thomas scrambled quickly to his feet. He didn't want anyone to find him. He was in enough trouble without adding breaking and entering to the list. Thomas ran to the door, but then a dark outline moved across in front of the marbled glass that separated this room from the corridor. The figure stopped, and Thomas heard the sound of the doorknob turning. His heart raced, he glanced around, frantically looking for a place to hide but the swivel chairs, and wooden desks provided little cover. A few short filing cabinets lined the wall, but he would be easy to spot crouched down beside them. Thomas couldn't run, and he had no place to hide. He dived across the room into the shadows and concentrated.

Betty thought she'd seen a flicker of movement, but perhaps it had been her imagination. The shadowed room revealed nothing. She didn't want to turn the light on just in case something lurked in the corners. The truth may well be worse than her imagination. Betty screwed up her face in thought. Perhaps she had those two the wrong way around. Her imagination could generate nightmares far worse than the truth.

As she peered around the room, hoping not to see anything, something shuffled up behind her. Betty screamed and spun around, holding the broom out for defence.

Maureen screamed and jumped back out of reach, clutching at her chest. "What's wrong?" she panted.

"Oh my god, you scared the life out of me."

"I didn't mean to!"

"Well, don't creep up behind me then."

"But I thought I heard you calling my name."

"Well, I did."

Both women looked confused then broke into laughter.

"Sorry Hun, I just heard an odd noise and thought it might be a burglar."

"That's strange. I heard something too."

They looked a little apprehensive, but then Maureen leaned into the room and switched on the light. No burglars jumped out. No rats scuttled between their feet. The room looked normal apart from a bin with its contents strewn across the floor.

"Honestly they leave this place in such a mess." She turned to Betty. "I'll clean this up if you want to finish off the vacuuming?"

Betty nodded and trotted off.

As Maureen bent over to pick up the rubbish, she could have sworn something darted past her, but when she looked up, she saw nothing.

Thomas could hardly believe his luck. They hadn't seen him. They must be blind. He'd even managed to get past the old woman as she bent down to pick up the rubbish. Now the sound of the vacuum cleaner covered his footsteps as he jogged down the corridor. Shame that the sound came directly from in front of him, but after his lucky escape, he felt reasonably sure he could pull it off again. Thomas slowed at the next corner and then peered around it. The old woman bent down, switched off the machine, and after coiling up the cable trundled off to the next location. Thomas waited for a moment for the sound to start up again and then skittered past the room and turned another corner. He came to the door at the end of the corridor, but when he tested the door handle, he found it locked. That meant he had to go back the way he'd come, but it didn't worry him. The vacuum easily covered his footsteps. He just had to make sure they didn't see him. The first woman proved simple to avoid. She had her back to him. The second, however, stepped out of a room just as he turned the corner.

Thomas darted quickly backwards and then waited, but she turned and walked the other way, which proved a blessing. He quietly followed her to the end of the corridor, where she put down the rubbish bag, produced a key, and opened the door. Thomas' heart leapt; he could see a way out! He ran swiftly forward and peered out of the gap. The woman trundled across the vast open warehouse towards some double doors, her footsteps echoing loudly in the enclosed space. Thomas followed, hoping that she wouldn't turn around. She stopped. Thomas froze. She dropped the bag, opened a smaller side door, and stepped outside. Thomas took a chance. He raced through the door and vanished off into the night.

Maureen dropped the bag into the dumpster and turned around to see someone flee across the courtyard. She gasped, so there had been an intruder, but it was just some kid. As she stared, something odd struck her about the boy. He wore weird clothes, almost like some sort of fancy dress.

Thomas ran out of the alleyway behind the industrial building and stopped. He recognised this junction. It went under the motorway and up to his house. If he ran across the next two sets of traffic lights and took the first left turning, he would come out at the bottom of his road. Thomas faltered, caught between two conflicting sets of emotions. He didn't know whether to be happy or sad, worried, or excited? If he went home, what would happen? Had they worried about him, or would they be angry or worse indifferent?

Thomas crossed over both sets of traffic lights, then just as he began to climb the rise that led to his house; he noticed a large crowd of people. Thomas hung back for a moment and then hid up against a wall. The crowd milled around, some talking, others waving goodbye, while a few began to break off and walk away. It wasn't a party, everyone looked far too serious, but then he saw his father walking downhill. Hands in pockets, head down, he appeared dejected, but as Thomas stared, his mum ran out from the crowd. They met and hugged so tightly that Thomas felt a lump in his throat. As they embraced, his father reached out and began to stroke her hair. Click, click, the media swooped in. They snapped photo after photo of the poignant moment getting closer until they jostled the couple. Thomas felt his anger flare. How dare they do this to his parents but then cold misery replaced that feeling. He'd done this. It was his fault and his responsibility to fix.

A policewoman ushered the persistent reporters out of the way and led his parents towards their house. Thomas panicked at the police involvement. This meant real trouble, but his parent's sorrow hurt him so badly that he just wanted to run home. If he could only get to them without the press or police knowing, he could tell them everything, and it would be ok. Thomas waited as the media gathered and dug in outside his house. He had no chance now, perhaps later, when darkness fell, he could get in without anyone knowing, but he could hardly stay here. Thomas looked around. A block of flats on the other side of the roundabout offered a good vantage point. From the top, he reckoned he could see pretty much everything, so he jogged across towards the front door. On the wall, he found a panel with dozens of buttons, one for each of the flats, so he just pressed them all at random. When he got halfway down the list, he heard a buzz and then a click.

Thomas grinned. Someone had let him in. He slipped through the door and ran upstairs to the top floor. A service door led onto the roof, and although someone should have locked it, no one had bothered. The latch had a padlock, but it lay open. When he peered on to the roof, he could see why. A battered couch, some tatty chairs, and a crooked coffee table sat in an untidy circle. Someone had decided that this would be a private place to chill out and watch the world go by. It looked like a suitable place to wait.

The grizzled reporter poked his head around the door. "Boss, can I have a word?"

"Sure, come on in Fred."

"I've been digging around the Harvey case, and I've found some interesting stuff."

"Yeah?"

"Well, apparently the missing boy's father has a bit of a temper, so I looked into Chris Harvey's background. Seems like father like son. His dad Malcolm was a bit of a bruiser too. He got himself into all kinds of trouble. The neighbours complained about the noise multiple times, said the wife's screams made them fear for her life. The boy's mum often ended up black and blue, but she never pressed charges. Eventually, she left him, left the boy too, the old man didn't take kindly to that, and when Malcolm Harvey finally went to prison, Chris Harvey ended up living with his aunt who didn't really want him. Better that than dead though hey. Anyway, these things usually come around, so I've been talking to some of the neighbours. Most of them won't talk, but a few admitted hearing rows from time to time?"

"Think he beats her too?"

"Perhaps."

"And the missing boy?"

"Well, this is where it gets interesting, according to my source; apparently, the boy did turn up at home."

"What? I thought he'd gone missing at school."

Fred grimaced. "Well he did, but here's the thing, he went missing at school, but later he went home. Apparently, they overheard the dad threatening to beat him, but the boy ran off and didn't come back."

"Do you think he's telling the truth?"

"Pfft, who knows, he could have killed the boy in a fit of rage, buried him in the garden, and the wife's covering for him out of fear."

Both men grinned. The paper's circulation would go through the roof.

"We'll run a headline on it tomorrow."

"What? Grieving parents' guilty sort of thing."

"Yeah, that should do it."

Chapter 43

Glen, Sarah, and Cody

Cody came around and went from sleepy to irritated, in just one second. He sat up and slammed his fists in the dirt.

"Shit, shit, shit!"

As he gathered his knees to his chest, he mentally cursed himself. He must have fallen asleep after those things chased him into the desert. Now, this messed up his plan.

Cody growled in frustration, stood up, and brushed the dirt from his jeans before looking around. One good bit of news, though. In the middle distance, he saw his trailer. He relaxed and sighed. His mind ticked over as he began to walk down the slope towards his home.

Well at least this followed a pattern. The 'abductees' or 'dreamers' depending on the conspiracy theory, returned near to where they had left, give, or take a bit. On the plus side, he could use this as another piece of evidence towards his growing hypothesis.

His stomach took that moment to interrupt his thoughts. It rumbled loudly like a blocked drain. With visions of an egg and bacon muffin, he jogged to the trailer but found it still locked. Glen hadn't woken up yet, and due to his security conscious nature, Cody didn't have a spare key hidden anywhere outside. He went around to the back of the trailer and banged on the window.

After a while, he heard movement, and then a grumpy sounding voice slurred a reply. "Who is it? What do you want?"

"It's me, Cody. Let me in."

"Cody? Pull the other one."

"No seriously it's me." He heard a yawn then silence. Cody banged on the side of the trailer. "Let me in you dozy klutz."

He heard a groan and then the trailer rattled a little as someone moved towards the door. It opened a crack.

Glen peered blearily at Cody. "Oh, it is you."
"Who'd you think it was? Attila the Hun?"
"Government agents perhaps?"
Cody reconsidered this comment as he climbed inside. "Ok point taken."
Glen put the coffee on while Cody fried up bacon and eggs. After two toasted muffins and four cups, they both felt more alert.
"What happened to your keys?" asked Glen.
Cody didn't know how to explain or even if he felt ready to do so. Besides, his friend did not believe in alternative theories or ideas. "Dunno I must have been sleepwalking or something. The door closed behind me."
Glen nodded but later on, something occurred to him. The trailer door didn't shut and lock automatically. Another thing troubled him. The keys still hung in their usual place. For some reason, Cody hadn't told the truth.

Later that morning Sarah banged on the trailer door. She waited impatiently, tapping her foot. She didn't have all day. Some people actually had work to do. Just as she began to walk away, Glen peered around the corner, wiping his hands on a cloth.
"Hey, I thought I heard something."
Sarah yelped in surprise and spun around to face him.
Glen grinned and shrugged an apology. "Sorry, didn't mean to make you start. I was just at the back of the trailer trying to fix a leaking pipe. I didn't have anything planned this morning, but if I had, it wouldn't have been this."
Sarah nodded and wrinkled her nose. A metallic smell, tinged with something slightly chemical, wafted through the air. Not revolting, but not particularly pleasant either.
Glen stood, wiping his oily hands on a rag. "I noticed an odd smell this morning. While I'm not much use with tools, Cody assured me that I just had to run some gunk around the pipes and tighten them a bit. Seems to have worked for now although I suspect it won't last long."
Sarah frowned and looked around. "Where's Cody?"
"He's probably still dozing on the couch the lazy toad."

Glen smiled sheepishly, not wanting to invite Sarah inside the trailer, well not without a damned good clean. She'd take one look and classify it as a man cave with a man's mess.

Glen banged on the side of the trailer and shouted, "Hey Cody, we have a visitor."

After a groan then a thump like someone rolling off a settee, Cody emerged bleary-eyed squinting in the bright light. "Ok, don't yell. I'm awake."

He yawned and shaded his eyes, then disappeared inside. A few seconds later, he stumbled out of the trailer wearing his sunglasses and flopped down onto the battered couch, before opening a large bag of chips with a pop.

Sarah frowned. Neither of them had offered her a place to sit. Mind you, looking around at the cluttered outdoor furniture, she didn't have a good choice. The 'yard' had dusty plastic chairs, an old battered couch, a small wooden stool, and a table, all of which had seen better days.

Glen realised his bad manners and grabbed a plastic chair. After brushing off the dirt, he motioned for Sarah to sit. He cleaned another for himself and pulled it up next to the couch where Cody lounged.

Sarah settled herself down and then leaned forward as if she had a tale to tell. "I have some news. I did try to phone, but I couldn't get a signal. I planned to monitor squirrel population densities in the mountains, so I thought I'd take a detour and drop by. I hope you don't mind?"

"No, that's fine. We don't mind visitors."

Glen half-expected Cody to start spouting off about 'visitors' of another sort, but today he stayed silent.

"First thing this morning I went and had a chat with the deputy." Even as she spoke, she shifted uneasily in her chair. "Hank told me something the sheriff missed out. They didn't find any footprints apart from mine at the scene."

Glen's face betrayed a flicker of concern.

She noticed and smiled. "Don't worry, everything's ok. I'm not in any trouble because my alibi checks out. In fact, the deputy gave me more information than expected. I think he wants to make up for his mistake. He confirmed they've performed a full autopsy at the morgue in Phoenix. The coroner's office has become more involved in this unusual death. The body had lost a lot of blood. It should have been everywhere, and it wasn't so they are considering the possibility that someone may have moved the body. Hank also said that they think Mr Johnson died of a heart attack, although they don't know how the wounds fit into that scenario. So, it's a bit of a mystery." She grinned. "Isn't that exciting?"

Glen nodded, surprised that Cody hadn't jumped in with a wild theory; instead, he sat listening, looking thoughtful as he chewed.

"By the way, I had a look at those tumbleweed samples. The cells seem perfectly normal. I'm afraid the cluster, although creepy, is just a coincidence."

Cody wasn't so sure of that, but he couldn't say anything without sounding mad. It wasn't something that generally bothered him. People often thought him a little crazy. He often spouted off about government conspiracies but not this time. If he said his dreams were real, he might as well order a nice white jacket and a comfy padded cell because their reaction would amount to the same thing.

They all sat in thoughtful silence for a while before Glen frowned and asked, "Did you see the depth of those marks?"

Sarah shrugged. "Well a bit but the windows were very dirty."

Without looking up, Cody stated in a flat voice. "About the depth of a large rose thorn."

His comment startled them, but Sarah eventually replied, "I would say shallower. Anyway, how would you know? You never saw the body."

"Just an educated guess."

His Gran had loved her roses. As a boy, Cody had played near the well-established flowerbeds and had on occasion encountered their thorns to his dismay. They were as sharp as they looked and his clothes had not survived the experience.

Sarah and Glen glanced at each other with a meaningful look. Cody sat obviously deep in contemplation.

Glen turned to Sarah. "Do we have any idea what caused them or how they are linked to the death?"

"No, as far as I know, they don't fit the pattern of any insect or arachnid bite. The wounds are too deep. It can't be a scorpion. They are mostly solitary creatures. The same goes for any spider unless they just hatched. Anyway, that would have left one bite mark not dozens. Insect bites are out too. They are much too small. Even considering an allergic reaction, the result would have been swelling, not puncture wounds. So, I'm at a loss." Sarah waited for a reply, but when she got none, she made to leave. "Anyway, that's all my news really. I'll keep in touch. If I find out more when the autopsy report comes out, I'll let you know. The deputy has promised on his honour to keep me informed. Anyway, I'm working nearby, so it's easy enough to drop in."

"Thanks for keeping us in the loop." Glen looked pointedly at Cody and nudged him.

"Yeah, thanks."

Sarah stood, brushed herself down, and left. Glen waved as she drove away. He felt embarrassed by Cody's lack of enthusiasm. This wasn't his friend's normal behaviour. He might be a bit lacking in social graces, but he wasn't intentionally rude, and never came across as uninterested.

Chapter 44

Karen

As the first people to enter the building, the cleaning staff noticed immediately that something had gone wrong.
One puzzled cleaner flicked the light switch on and off. "I don't believe it! The electricity is out, and no one thought to tell us?"
"Don't look at me. I didn't get a phone call."
"Typical, no one bothers with us. As long as this place is clean, we're invisible," grumbled another.
The four of them stood in the foyer at a loss of what to do next.
"It's not like we can vacuum, and the lights won't come on, so cleaning any bathroom is going to be impossible in the dark."
The other three members of staff nodded and regarded their team leader.
"Look, we can either go home." Stella paused while the others appeared hopeful. "Or we can dust the desks, empty the bins, and clean the computer screens. There's enough lighting to do that in most places. We'll just have extra work tomorrow."
With a resigned expression, they gathered their cleaning equipment and each picked a floor.

Evan hurried to the front door through the pouring rain. He knew that the electricity wouldn't be on yet. After the grumpy reply from the CEO, who didn't like to be bothered at home, Evan resolved to come in early. His boss had acted as if he held Evan responsible for the outage. Evan felt if he could conjure a massive electrical storm, he'd have a job as a superhero, famous and loved by all, *especially* women. With a sigh, he shelved that thought, well, he could dream. Evan unlocked the main door and then tucking his laptop under his arm, he walked upstairs. By the time he got to his floor, Evan had to pause for breath. As he rested a moment, he heard a small shriek, then footsteps pounding towards him. Someone flung the door open almost bashing him in the face. When he recovered, he saw a distraught woman.

Eyes wild, she grabbed his arm and stammered, "There's, there's a body, a body of a woman lying on the floor. She's been murdered!"

"Murdered?" Evan could only stare in horror. No, it couldn't be true. "Where?"

In place of a reply, she grabbed his arm and dragged him towards the scene of the crime. Without looking, the cleaner sobbed into an overflowing tissue as she gestured wildly in the right direction. There on the floor, Evan could see a set of female legs poking out from behind his desk. They looked familiar. He turned towards the cleaner.

"But this is my desk," he said. "What would she be doing here?"

A look of horror and alarm quickly passed across the cleaner's face. Perhaps Evan had committed the murder. To make matters worse, Evan reached out trying to reassure the cleaner. Eyes wide with fear, the woman backed away and opened her mouth to scream. A small groan of pain made them both jump.

"She's alive!" shrieked the cleaner.

At, which point, all the lights came on before flickering out with almost perfect timing. Evan looked around. The utility company had made good time repairing the damage.

Beneath the table, a very grumpy and irritated voice commented, "Well I'm not dead, but my head feels as if it's going to split in two. For god's sake, someone help me up!"

Evan grinned at the irony. Like something out of a monster movie, the woman had come alive with a pulse of electricity. An odd thought struck him. Why hadn't they found her last night when they checked the building?

"Are you sure you should stand up?" he asked as he bent over offering her his hand.

Karen groaned, bleary-eyed and tried to stand but even this small movement made her head spin.

"No! No put me back down I think I'm going to throw up!" she said and curled up into a ball, her teeth clenched in an effort not to be sick.

Evan waited for her to settle down before asking, "What happened?"

"I was putting away the test sheets when the lightning struck. The flash made me jump, and I banged my head hard on the underside of your desk. I think I knocked myself out."

Evan felt confused and guilty. How could he have missed her?

"I'm calling for an ambulance and no don't object," he said firmly as he noted her drawing breath to stop him. "You probably have a concussion and should see a doctor."

After a quick phone call, Evan confirmed that the ambulance would arrive soon. He informed them that the lifts were out of order, so they knew to bring a stair chair. Somewhat red-faced and embarrassed by her overreaction to the 'murder' situation, the cleaner decided to take the opportunity to escape. She mumbled an apology, grabbed her equipment, and left muttering something about letting the medics into the building. Evan shook his head and sighed, waiting patiently until they arrived. Little more than fifteen minutes later two men bundled into the office and Evan waived them over.

"She's here."

One bent down and examined Karen's eyes while the other got the chair ready.

"Any double vision?" asked the medic.

She shook her head, but that made her vision spin.

"Where did you hit yourself?"

"At the back of my head."

He looked and felt a good-sized lump, but there wasn't' any liquid leaking out of her ears.

"Any dizziness?"

She nodded and then regretted it immediately.

"Numbness or tingling?"

"No"

Well evidently, she hadn't gone deaf or lost the ability to speak which reassured him.

"Ok, I'm going to test your memory. Do you know where we are?"

"I'm at work."

She knew her location, but then another memory surfaced. A dark cavern, an odd red light followed by searing pain flashed before her eyes. Unsure whether that had been real or just a dream, Karen decided to keep it to herself.

"Can you tell me what you were doing before you got knocked out?"

"I was filing some papers."

"Can you count the months backwards from the current one?"

Karen managed that with ease. He examined her further, noting a red bruise on her wrist, probably a result of the fall.

He nodded and smiled. "Ok that rules out most issues, but we will take you in and run some tests just to be sure."

They lifted her carefully into the stair chair and made their descent to the foyer. Even though she felt sea sick with each movement, Karen marvelled at how easily they descended. A chair designed for stairs, how neat.

Half an hour later as she settled into a ward off A&E, the nurse told her that a consultant would be around in a few hours. While she waited, the nurse also provided some forms for her to fill out. With a sigh, she added Alison as her point of contact, typical she couldn't escape paperwork even when injured. After that, she dozed until the consultant arrived. He carried out much the same tests as the medic but noticed some odd discolouration between her breasts.

"There was no mention of this bruising before, does this hurt?"

He gently ran his fingers over the mark and noted that she didn't flinch when he touched the location with a little more pressure.

"No, it feels fine."

"You fell and hurt your wrist is that correct?"

Karen nodded, so he checked the injury, but it seemed perfectly healed. Strange, the medic had mentioned the wrist but missed this discolouration. It could be blood under the skin, but it looked too dark for that, like a week-old bruise. On closer examination, he decided that it appeared less black and more like blue. From her medical records, she didn't take blood thinners or any other medication. He would need to order more tests.

"I'd like to do a CT scan to see if there is any damage and keep you in for twenty-four hours under observation. Do you have anyone that could bring you nightclothes?"

"Yes."

"Ok, well you'll be called for a scan a little later. A porter will wheel you there."

He nodded to the nurses and left Karen to arrange an overnight stay. It took a while for Alison to calm down. Karen reassured her that she wasn't in danger of dying. An hour later, her friend came bustling in with a set of clean clothes, determined to hear all the details. While Karen changed into her pyjamas, Alison subjected her to a dozen questions. Head spinning, Karen tried to answer them all until finally, the porter interrupted the interrogation and wheeled her gratefully away. Her friend might be a wonderful mum, but she tended to mother everyone, possibly to death if given enough time.

"Ring me, I'll pick you up tomorrow," Alison called out.

Karen hadn't been looking forward to the scan, but fortunately, it wasn't one of those tunnel contraptions. Instead, she laid on her back, and the X-ray tube rotated around her head for about ten minutes. As Karen waited, she thought back to last night. She must have been out for a while. It just didn't seem that long although dreams always seemed longer than the time they actually took. It had felt so clear and real, everything from the creatures, the dark figure to the red flash of light. Why had so much time elapsed? Had she passed out and then slept on the floor? Karen didn't feel rested, but the bump on the head could account for that.

After the scan, the nurse told her that, most likely, she would be able to go home tomorrow, but only after the consultant assessed the results. Until then she had nothing much to do but watch hospital TV and doze.

Chapter 45

Lars and Stefan

From the top of a small rise, Lars marvelled at the clear dawn sky, sea green and blue, shot with streaks of burnt umber and gold. Nothing would attack him at this time of day. He only had to contend with the usual dangers of any wilderness, but he felt tired, dead tired. The food last night sustained him, in fact, better than expected but it didn't make up for his lack of sleep. He felt envious of Stefan. He always went to sleep quickly. Lars had even seen him doze off part way through a sentence. To top it all, he slept like the dead and was more difficult to wake than a bear in winter.

A trickling sound accompanied by a long drawn out sigh interrupted his thoughts. Stefan had woken early.

Lars couldn't resist. "Behind you!" he yelled as he bounded down the hill.

Stefan turned in panic. "What! Where?"

Lars slowed, laughing at his friend's angry face and the wet patch on his boots. "My mistake its nothing."

"Bastard!" Stefan did up his breeches and scowled as he kicked sand over the wet leather.

Lars just grinned and walked down to the cart. "Breakfast?"

Stefan followed and shook his head. "There's not much left, no oats just a little dried meat and worse, not much water."

Lars had eaten well the night before so magnanimously he left the remaining supplies to Stefan. "You need it more than me."

Stefan looked surprised, but then he tilted his head and squinted at Lars. "What the hell are you wearing?"

Lars looked down and then ran his hands over the strange material, feeling something inside the pocket. He pulled out the transparent bag and stared at it, undeniable evidence of his nightly travel. Stefan waited patiently, while Lars spluttered.

He finally burst out, "I have no idea where to start!"

His friend just shrugged. "Well, you can tell me while we pull the cart. I'll chew, you talk, how's that for a deal?"

The sun already felt hot on their backs as they pulled the cart along the broken road. Lars told Stefan everything from start to finish, leaving out no details, although he did jump around a bit if he remembered something part way through. His friend listened and chewed, but once Lars had finished talking, he merely looked at him.

"No, wonder you are so clean," Stefan remarked.

Lars tried to twist around in the harness. "Is that all you can say?"

Stefan thought about it a bit more. "I'm not surprised you didn't eat breakfast."

Lars snarled incredulously. After everything, he had been through, but then he heard a stifled snigger. He could almost hear Stefan grinning and knew his friend thought it payback for the wet boots prank. Well, he had told him everything, now for the crunch.

"Do you believe me?"

Stefan mulled over his answer. "Well," he said in a long, drawn out way.

"Seriously!"

"You want me to be serious?"

"There's a time for everything."

"What everything?"

Lars glowered out into the desert, feeling wound up. "Well if you weren't such a deep sleeping deaf lump, you'd have realised something was wrong before now!"

Stefan paused for thought. "Well, I did think something was off."

"What? Why didn't you say anything?"

He could feel Stefan shrug behind him. "Dunno really, I thought if you wanted to tell me, you would."

Lars sighed heavily. He could almost hear his mother shake her head and mutter a comment about stupid boys.

Stefan interrupted, "I don't know what you're pissed off about. You're telling me now. Aren't you?"

"Yeah, but I could have told you earlier."

"Not my fault you didn't."

For God's sake, we sound like a bickering old couple thought Lars. Not for the first time, he wondered if they needed a break from each other's company, at least for a while.

He changed tack. "What do you think I should do?"

"About what?"

"What I've been talking about!" Lars felt quite frustrated.

"What can you do about it?"

His comment made Lars think. What could he do? Who would understand? Lars needed help, but considering the subject matter, he could not talk to just anyone for fear of reprisal. Ever vigilant, the preachers would soon cut out his tongue if they considered his comments blasphemy.

The two men trudged for a while in thoughtful silence until Stefan finally suggested. "Have you ever heard of the Keepers?"

"What?"

"I remember the boatmen talking about it once."

A memory surfaced. Mura had once talked of a place located far away. A place where people treasured knowledge and didn't welcome preachers. Even if he managed to find them, could they stop him from travelling? Would he want to stop? He found the other place so amazing. Besides, it was the one thing that made Lars feel special. Perhaps he could learn a lot, but it could limit his opportunities in this world.

Once they made it downriver, the two friends could sell the metal. Lars would have money for a while, but what would he do when it ran out? They had planned to come back to the plateau, but now Lars didn't see this as an option. His nightly travels made the journey so dangerous. Stefan, on the other hand, would be all right. He could set up his own carpentry but not in Holmfast. With no reference from his previous employer, Stefan and his family would need to go far away.

Lars shelved those thoughts and changed tack. "What's the first thing you want to do with your half of the money?"

"We gotta sell it first."

Lars frowned. "Well, that shouldn't be a problem."

"You think?" Stefan sounded oddly dubious.

"Don't you?"

"What's to say the Overlord won't confiscate it when we get back?"

That hadn't even occurred to Lars. "You think he would?"

Stefan shrugged. "Generally, I've found where there's a lot of money involved; people will do just about anything."

Lars frowned. Where had his friend acquired such wisdom? He thought about the carpenter and his wife. The new apprentice had lied about Stefan. Now he and he alone would inherit the shop.

"Well, we will just have to sell it to the boatmen before we let anyone know we're back."

"Especially your mother."

Lars blurted the automatic response. "What about my mother?"

Stefan wasn't one to disrespect his elders, but in this case, he felt tempted.

"Do you trust her?"

Lars started to respond 'of course!' because that's what you did with family, you trusted them, but then he paused. "Perhaps not," he said.

Lars hated to admit the truth. She had taken the quick and easy route. Instead of finding an apprenticeship for her only son, she had 'sold' him into drudgery. What would stop her doing something like that again, especially with this much money at stake?

Stefan had clearly put some thought into his response. "I don't think we should tell anyone we're back. I mean no one, not your family, or mine," he said.

Lars knew how difficult Stefan would find that. He got on well with his family.

"Why not your family?"

"I think we should find out what's going on first. After all, I left quite suddenly, and we don't know what happened after that."

"Good point." Lars knew that his friend still worried about the Overlords judgement. What had happened to his grandparents after they left?

"Ok, so how are we going to do that without being noticed?"

"We can camp upriver, scout the area avoiding any patrols, and keep an eye out for the trader's boat."

"Sounds good as long as no one sees us."

They had a plan now. Lars didn't mention the trip back. With his nightly travels, he could conceivably end up in the river and drown. He would have to decide what to do when they got down the cliff.

They stopped for a rest. By now, the sun had passed its zenith, and in the heat of the day, both men felt drained of energy. The carts shade gave them some respite, but after gulping down more water, they hitched up once more in the scorching afternoon sun.

"At least that's getting lighter." Lars pointed at the last of the water supplies tucked away on the cart.

"Not by much."

The water only made up a small percentage of the weight, but if they didn't make it soon, they would run out of drink. Stefan had pointed out, much to Lars disgust that they might have to drink each other's pee. Better that, he insisted than dying of thirst. It might be true, but Lars could not imagine being so desperate, that Stefan's pee would actually seem enticing.

As the day wore on, Lars spotted an odd smudge on the horizon.

"Hey Stef," he said, trying to rouse his friend from his plodding stupor. "What's that?"

Stefan looked up and stopped, bringing the cart to an abrupt halt. "Oh, dear."

"That sounds ominous."

"It is. If I'm right, that's a sand storm, and it's heading right for us."

"A sand storm, is that what it looks like? I heard the traders talking about those; they can be pretty lethal."

"Out here, yes it will get difficult to breathe. I think we'd better camp; we need to make certain everything is secure before it hits."

Lars felt relieved. He couldn't wait to get unhitched and stretch his sore shoulders. It didn't take long to get everything ready although Stefan insisted on a minor change to the shutter lock.

"That should be a little easier for human hands to undo," he said, then grinned. "No good for you then."

Lars aimed a punch at Stefan, but his friend dodged and Lars felt too weary to hit him a second time. Instead, they both slid under the cart and battened down the shutters. It wasn't long before they heard the wind begin to howl around the wheels, shaking the structure as they settled down for the night. One other thing disturbed Lars. He could have sworn that someone got onto the wooden boards above his head, just before the storm hit. He listened intently, but between Stefan's snoring and the sound of the rising gale, he couldn't be sure that the wind hadn't played tricks on him.

Chapter 46

Adam

Adam sighed. Once again, he found himself dirty, naked and sitting in the dark. A dull ache reminded him that his nose should have been a bloody mess plastered across his face. Yet apart from a little drying blood, it appeared to be just fine. He sat mystified, but then he remembered the bite. That too, had healed suspiciously quickly.

Adam stood, stretched, and cautiously reached out. As he began to feel his way around, his hand touched an object. Plastic, square with a long pole, it must be a bucket and mob resting against a wall. As he searched further, his hand brushed against a light switch. He flicked it and after the spots died away, saw to his left a cupboard and some metal shelves. To his right a sink with cleaning fluids. With no windows, it looked like a basement.

His brain finally caught up. "Oh, that's just great."

This might be his own apartment block, but he lived on the sixth floor. It's not like he had keys, and apart from his cleaner, the manager kept the only spare set. The staff at reception could contact her, but she would ask some awkward questions. He could explain that he suffered from sleepwalking. It wasn't a crime, and it had a ring of truth about it.

Adam looked down. The bandana didn't hide much now. The undergrowth had shredded the cloth, so he searched the cupboards for anything useful. Mostly they contained paintbrushes and rollers, but at the bottom, he spied some paint-splattered dustsheets. After giving them a bit of a shake, he wrapped them around his body like a toga. Not his usual designer suit, but it would have to do.

Now looking decent, he went to open the door only to find it locked. He rattled it, then groaned and banged his head on the wood. Nothing was straightforward these days.

Adam hammered on the door and yelled. "Hey, anyone there? Can anyone hear me?"

He continued to bang until his arm got tired. A few minutes later, he heard muffled footsteps approach.

"Who's there?" a suspicious voice asked.

"Adam Turner. I live in apartment 21; it's on the 6th floor."

"Really?" the voice sounded as if the speaker didn't believe a word. "Then why are you in the basement?"

Adam sighed. "I just woke up. I'm not certain, but I think I was sleepwalking."

"Drinking, were you?"

"No!" Adam gritted his teeth, trying to remain polite. "Look, I am getting tired of these questions, please open the door."

A set of keys jangled and the door opened just enough to allow the man responsible for building maintenance, to peer through the crack. His eyes narrowed, as he looked Adam up and down. He recognised him but considered this behaviour well out of order.

"Well, Sir, I will have to report this to the building manager. I can't let this pass. I wouldn't want to get into trouble."

Adam nodded. "That's alright. I need to speak to her."

"Sorry to ask Sir, but why would you want to?"

Adam tried to keep the sarcasm out of his voice. "I didn't remember to pick up my keys when I went sleepwalking."

"Ah yes, certainly Sir, I will contact reception and ask them to speak to the manager."

"Thank you... sorry, what is your name?"

"It's Harold Sir."

Adam gave him his award-winning smile. "Thank you, Harold."

Harold gave a nervous cough. "Err would you kindly wait in reception, please? I can't leave you down here."

This part Adam dreaded. He had hoped to sneak past, but now he would just have to run with it.

"Certainly, lead the way."

Harold locked the door behind them, and then they climbed the stairs out of the basement. Adam followed at a slight distance, in the hope that he could hang around in the corridor, rather than sit on the elegant chairs outside reception. As Harold emerged from the door marked staff only, Adam hesitated. He waited, listening through a crack in the door as Harold asked to speak to the manager and explained why. A muffled snigger followed, and then he heard the receptionist phone the manager.

Harold came over and put his head around the door. "It's alright, Sir. Mrs Peters will be here shortly. Would you like to wait in reception?"

"Thank you, and no I wouldn't want to get those lovely seats covered in paint."

"As you wish Sir."

Adam waited for an uncomfortably long time. He kept to the shadows, almost closing the door as some of the other tenants wandered past chatting merrily. Adam really didn't want to draw any attention to himself. After a while, he glanced out at the reception clock. Now, 6.45am, he realised that the phone call must have woken the manager. When she finally arrived, her face looked like thunder.

"Where is he?" she demanded.

"Over there, Mrs Peters."

One of the receptionists waved towards the door. Mrs Peters stalked over like an interrogator with a cause. After looking around, she stepped inside the doorway and closed the door behind her. In the dim light, she looked Adam up and down, noting his paint-splattered makeshift toga.

"Mr Turner, this is quite unacceptable," she reprimanded in a stone-cold voice. "This is a luxury apartment complex, and such behaviour does not reflect well either upon this establishment or upon yourself. Please explain your actions and appearance?"

Adam had this planned. He put on his best apologetic expression and explained, "I'm sorry for causing trouble, but I think it likely that I have developed a sleepwalking problem. This has never happened before, but work has been stressful, and I have slept badly. I have no idea how I got down to the basement unseen. To be honest, I would have expected the night staff to notice a naked man walking around. Then they could have roused me from my sleep and events wouldn't have gone this far."

Adam shifted some of the blame onto the staff. After all, he found it strange that they hadn't noticed him. Mrs Peters appeared to consider his story. With a sigh, she came to a decision.

She gave him a sympathetic look and said, "Very well, Mr Turner, we will hear no more concerning this, although I will investigate why the staff didn't see you. I will let you into your apartment, but I would ask that you seek help concerning your sleepwalking problem. After all, you don't want this to turn into something dangerous, do you?"

Adam understood the implications; after all, he lived on the sixth floor. Mrs Peters turned and opened the door, ushering him out into the reception. The staff gave him an odd look as he passed by, but he ignored them. He'd made it their problem now, not his. As they waited for the lift, Adam shuffled from foot to foot feeling somewhat self-conscious, wishing it would hurry up. When it did arrive, a couple stepped out and looked at him in shock.

As they left, Adam heard the woman say to her husband, "Well I never! This isn't good enough! What was that, some schoolboy prank?"

To his relief, they reached his apartment without meeting anyone else. When Mrs Peters unlocked the door, Adam thanked her again. Once safely inside, he leaned against the door and sighed. Nothing had changed; his apartment looked just as he left it.

Later as he relaxed in a much-needed shower, his head began to spin. This was going to be a long day. Already dead tired, Adam hung his head and let the water run over his face, wishing that he could pull a sickie.

The rest of the day proved to be just as bad as the start. What with whinging disorganised staff, poorly designed marketing, and missing information, Adam left with a headache that he couldn't shift even when he went to bed.

Chapter 47

Xenis and Valene

Valene strode into the temple, yelling at the top of her voice for Larenil. Irae who possessed a far smaller build could hardly keep up without running. Almost skipping to keep pace with her sister, Irae's plait swung with each semi-jump. The diminutive Drow felt like a servant scurrying at the heels of her master, a feeling she hated to the pit of her stomach. Once again, Irae thought sourly; her mother must have mated with an ogre to produce such a massive, savage offspring. Unlike most female Drow, Valene wore her white hair short, believing it an unnecessary distraction. Her brutish features so unlike Irae's delicate face indicated a different father, not unheard of in Mizoram. Matriarchs mated with whom they pleased when they pleased.

Neither Valene nor the Matriarch had ever intercepted these thoughts. They considered Irae too insignificant to pry. That was the life of a middle sibling. Often overlooked in favour of the older sister and ignored in comparison with the youngest. Today she felt she had one advantage. She wasn't Larenil. So far, Valene had been unsuccessful in locating her youngest sister.

With a snarl of frustration, Valene merely grabbed the nearest guard and lifted him off his feet. "Where is my sister? Get her for me now or suffer the consequences."

She dropped the male who rushed off to comply as she strode on behind him. A few moments later Larenil turned the corner, the guard in tow, who she then dismissed. Xenis, on the other hand, hung back in the shadows and waited for the inevitable explosion.

"I will kill you for this utter failure," hissed Valene. "You will die slowly and painfully."

Larenil hung her head, so she would meet her Goddess in shame.

"Now kneel and beg my forgiveness," commanded Valene. "If you do, then I will spare you the most agonising final moments."

Most likely, a lie, but Larenil did not plan to go out with a whimper. As an ordained priestess of House Zik'Keeshe, she would never beg her lazy, stupid, ignorant sister for anything.

She looked up sharply, her eyes glowing with resolve. "And *our* mother the Matriarch has sanctioned this punishment?"

Xenis smiled inwardly, good point, sister.

Valene raised the Whip of Obedience, typically used on males and never on another priestess.

"You would use that on me?" sneered Larenil. "Your respect is awe-inspiring. I doubt that the Matriarch has given you any such orders and making your own decision at this time could be dangerous. Do you really want to anger her further? That would be unwise in the extreme."

Xenis felt Valene hesitate. He smiled again. Good argument, turn it around.

"Besides, we are not alone," said Larenil.

"I do not care who hears us."

"You should."

"Do not tell me what I should or should not do, you are the youngest, and by that fact, you are subservient to my will."

"I am subservient to the will of the Matriarch only!"

Thalra, who had left the reading room, smiled, clearly amused by the exchange. After dismissing the guards, she stood listening for some time, and now things were getting interesting. She had not been able to hear the conversation between the male sibling and Larenil, but then she dismissed it as unimportant. Probably just giving him orders, as Thalra herself would command her own lesser brothers. Thalra inched a little closer so that she could hear this confrontation in all its glorious technicolour.

"Ah mistress Thalra of House Velkyn'Zhaunil, how pleased we are that you can join us." Xenis emerged out of the shadows and bowed.

Thalra felt both cornered and immensely annoyed that she had not sensed him.

Valene stepped forward and pointed the whip at Thalra. "You! Why are you still here?"

Thalra sneered at Valene. "I am more than happy to leave this little family get together."

From what Larenil said, Xenis knew this female hid vital information.

He turned to Valene and carefully interjected. "Sister, surely the Matriarch and therefore the council will want to know first-hand what happened? Mistress Thalra might be able to provide another perspective concerning events."

Thalra ignored him. "Who is this insubordinate male? How dare he speak?"

For once, Valene could only agree, but Xenis damn him, had made a valid point. The council would question her in depth. Via the runner, Larenil had provided a basic overview, but apart from observing the inner sanctum herself, the priestess from House Velkyn'Zhaunil proved the only other witness. Valene could not afford to lose this opportunity.

She ignored any reference to Xenis and plunged on. "The council will expect a full report. I have heard all Larenil has to say, but what can you add to her account?"

Thalra didn't see why she should answer any questions at all. She disliked the way the male spoke. Valene should have punished him for such disrespect, but instead, she chose to ignore his interruption. Besides, if they found the information she hid, there would be hell to pay. Not that Thalra was worried. Valene may have been powerful, but she had all the subtlety of a charging ogre. All Thalra had to do was dodge the questions.

She gave a non-committal shrug. "Not much, I suspect."

Valene pushed. "Larenil said you cast an 'Identification' spell, what did you find?"

"Nothing I could identify."

"You must have been able to find something."

Thalra narrowed her eyes. "How so?"

Valene gritted her teeth and explained with exaggerated care, "An 'Identification' spell will have yielded something, even if it is only a hint."

"I know that I am a mage as well as a priestess."

"Then, I would have expected a better result."

"It was not possible."
Valene began to lose patience. "Why not?"
"The firestorm obliterated most of the evidence."
"Most but not all?"
"What little remained decayed so fast that I was unable to obtain anything certain."
"How convenient."
Thalra bristled. "I do not like your tone."
Valene ignored her comment. "What did you find? The council will want to know?"
"Then the council can ask my Matriarch. I will inform my mother first of any findings."
"You should inform me! I am the Temple Overseer."
"And what a good job you have done so far," sneered Thalra.

The accurate barb angered Valene so much that she threw her mind out to pressure Thalra, but the priestess resisted her attempt. Evenly matched the two struggled for a moment before Valene broke off the mental assault and tried another approach.

"I could make sure that the council will want to question you personally. They have ways of extracting information that I do not possess."

"Then do so." Thalra knew her mother would protect her from that process. By now, they would have struck a deal, so Valene wasted her breath. With a self-satisfied smile, Thalra turned to go.

Xenis could see the situation sliding further into chaos and the information that might save them, slipping away.

He chanced another interruption. "Surely we should work together to solve this or be destroyed by it."

Thalra sneered before she left. "Listen to your male. You might learn some wisdom."

Valene became too enraged to speak as Thalra walked away. Moments later, possibly while Thalra remained in hearing range, she snarled at Xenis. "Now you have made me look a fool in front of a rival house!"

Xenis felt tempted to point out that she only had herself to blame and barely made any effort to hide that thought. Valene could see the disdainful look on his face and this time untempered by what her mother might say she lashed out with the whip, forcing her brother to the floor. The pain-enhanced barbs stung his flesh as they ripped through his clothing. Only his light leather armour saved him from the worst damage, but the barbs still went through his gloves as he tried to protect his face. As a male, he could not retaliate, not even a male of royal blood could attack a priestess without suffering dire consequences. Xenis could only dodge, roll, and shield himself. Not that he should have done that, convention dictated that he should lie still and accept the punishment.

Larenil stood, watching the spectacle. He might be only her brother, but even so, this display of senseless brutality irked her. If she did nothing, Valene would kill him. On the one hand, he proved an asset to the house and had helped her on more than one occasion. On the other, he knew things about her that she wished he didn't, but in the end, her mother's possible anger swayed her.

"Valene you should stop. He has been punished enough, besides our mother might be displeased if we wasted his life rather than presenting him as a sacrifice."

Valene hardly heard her sister. Only one thing registered. Someone had dared interrupt the thrashing. Out of control and filled with fury, she turned and struck Larenil. She had taken one step too far.

Larenil snapped and screamed, "It was your responsibility, not mine, not Xenis but yours! The council put you in charge, but you left us to do your dirty work!"

Valene stood stunned; a rage so intense that it remained palpable in the air. Larenil shrank from her sister. She had gone too far even though she had only told the truth.

A moment later, a council runner turned the corner, but seeing the expression on Valene's face, threw herself to the floor in submission.

Valene managed with some difficulty to pull herself together before demanding, "Well?"

The runner rose and presented her message. In no mood to be gentle, Valene probed the messenger's mind with brutal force. The runner bit her lip in agony but kept silent before passing out.

Valene merely stepped over the body before speaking in a flat voice, "The council has spoken with my mother, now I am summoned to make an account."

Larenil, still feeling angry, couldn't resist a parting shot. "It's a good thing that you used your time here so wisely. Now you will have much to tell them."

Her accuracy stung Valene, not that she would ever admit to such weakness. Instead, it only further inflamed her hatred. She turned and walked past Xenis who with much effort got to his feet. He stared after her fading form vowing that one day, he would make her pay for this beating.

A few hours later, Valene sat uncomfortably outside the council chamber. The Matriarch waited beside her, fuming impotently. The council had questioned her mother for an hour, not that the Matriarch knew any more than they did. Each member received an identical message from Larenil. They did demand to know why the news had come from the little-known youngest sister and not Valene. The Matriarch explained that they had been in a meeting together. This had not gone down well. Sarnor'Velve wondered loudly why the temple had been such a low priority for House Zik'Keeshe. Were they so sure of their position on the council that they could afford to relax? Could it be that they took their promotion for granted? In any event, this disaster could only have come about through sloppy management bordering on negligence.

The Matriarch goaded into a fury, did consider throwing Valene to the wolves, but she managed to hold her temper. Instead, she commanded Valene to attend the interrogation and explain herself. Valene did better than expected, astonishing how impending death can focus the mind. She didn't go into details concerning the meeting but shifted the blame firmly onto whoever guarded the city. Not that Valene mentioned Zhennu'Z'ress by name. They were temporary allies, but she did mention the possibility that another house had allowed and even helped an intruder enter the temple. The sentinels had sounded the other day. There might be a link, but she would need to investigate.

Apart from that, they might consider questioning Thalra of House Velkyn'Zhaunil. Not only might she have seen the intruder, but she had also entered the inner sanctum shortly after its destruction. The priestess had been unwilling to part with any information, but Valene hoped that the council could extract everything they wished. Valene concluded that whoever had been in charge the same events would have occurred. The council wasn't wholly convinced and Zhennu'Z'ress wasn't very happy with the implications. They sent Valene and her mother outside so they could talk in private and come to a decision. When they finally called the two back to the chamber, the council informed the Matriarch that they had decided to give House Zik'Keeshe one last chance. Find the perpetrators or face the consequences. This included not only the intruder but also all those involved. With a contemptuous wave of her hand, Mith'Barra dismissed both mother and daughter, smiling slightly as they fumed at the indignity.

Once she returned to the house, the Matriarch had thrown a temper tantrum the likes of which many had never seen. She whipped all and sundry present for their incompetence, whether or not they had been at the temple. She even went as far as threatening Valene with dire consequences if she did not find the perpetrators.

Xenis knew all this because a runner arrived to inform Larenil of the situation. On hearing the news, he did think it strange that the Matriarch had not used magic. Perhaps she merely enjoyed the physical sensation of bestowing pain. Fortunately, for Xenis, he had been at the temple with his younger sisters. Once they redoubled the guard, Larenil strictly forbade anyone access to the inner sanctum.

Now Valene had returned from the house in a foul mood. Xenis could hear her shouting once more.

"Where is he? Where is the snivelling wretch, I am unfortunate enough to call my brother?"

What had he done wrong this time? Nothing, but that didn't matter. He was just a whipping boy for her displeasure. Xenis could either accept his unjustified punishment again or remind her of the sharp reality of her exalted position. In the end, the Matriarch would hold her accountable for everything that happened. Ok so that might not stop her from killing him, but at least he would go out fighting.

Valene strode into the room and roared at Xenis. "This is your fault!"

"How so?"

His insolent remark angered her. "How dare you speak to me like that?" She snarled and reminded him of his tenuous position without considering her own. "You were responsible for the temple guard."

"And you were responsible for me."

"I should kill you for that remark!"

She raised the Overseers whip high, but this time rather than taking the pain, Xenis stepped forward and sneered. "Then do so but the Matriarch, *our* mother, will know that you took your frustrations out on me rather than face the facts. The fact is that in the end, the council will hold *you* responsible for the desecration if you do not find out what happened and by inference *our* mother. You might as well kiss goodbye to our house for good. Any chance of power will be gone forever."

Valene knew he was right but barely held her temper in check.

"Let me help," suggested Xenis lowering his voice as he pretended to put aside her previous attack.

"I do not need your help!"

"You know that I often have a different perspective; perhaps this can be turned to your advantage?"

She intensely disliked the thought that he might be right once more, so she rejected that idea immediately. "No, I will investigate. Wait here for your punishment. I will return soon." She motioned for her younger sisters to follow her.

Xenis wasn't about to wait around. After a few moments, he discretely followed. He needed to find out what had happened. He knew that someone had desecrated the temple but he had no idea how or why.

As Xenis approached the corridor that led to the inner sanctum one thing became apparent, this part of the temple looked a mess. Even from this distance, he could see black sooty marks stretching down the corridor. The firestorm must have been intense if there were signs of damage all the way down to the intersection. Xenis, like any other male, could not enter the innermost sanctum. In fact, the 'Safeguard' spell should keep him at bay even at this distance, but today he sensed that something had gone wrong. He inched forwards. By now, the magic should have repelled him, but he felt nothing. It only made him more suspicious. His sisters were investigating inside, so he moved with silent stealth. If they saw him, Valene would brutally lash him as punishment for his curiosity, although he probably faced that prospect already. He should resist the temptation to edge even closer, but their voices sounded unusually troubled. Xenis could hear Larenil comment on the terrible state of the altar. This only encouraged his older sister to rant once more at the injustice. One thing rang true. With the recent promotion to the Council of Five and the Guardianship of the Temple, this couldn't have come at a worse time. If Xenis was suspicious and he was, it seemed almost too good to be true, finally a chance for their enemies to destroy his house.

Valene continued to rant, "Do they think we are stupid that we don't know who is behind this? They think we will just accept our fate, lie down, and die. No, we will retaliate, bring our enemies to their knees, and then grind their faces into the dust. Alliances are shifting. We must have answers and soon. Each house ponders our next move, and if we seem weak, they will attack."

His sisters, Larenil and Irae, remained silent, sensible enough not to interrupt the rant when it erupted into full flow.

"Already our ally Zhennu'Z'ress has withdrawn their allegiance. Now they are busy distancing themselves from us. Will they join with Fashka'D'Yorn who is calling for retribution? Sarnor'Velve has gone even further and suggested that the council should strip our house of power. We could lose the guardianship and the council seat in one swift move. Our mother, the Matriarch, has commanded me to find evidence. I want to confirm my suspicions, that either Faerl'Zotreth or Vlos'Killian are behind this attack."

She paused for breath and Irae took this opportunity to speak, "What would you have us do?"

"Interrogate every guard to see if their minds are missing information. That should indicate if someone has altered their memories."

"That still wouldn't prove who altered them though?"

"You will need to go further. There is always a signature."

"Apologies Valene but I have not been taught the Rite of Velkyn Talinthus."

Xenis winced at this reference, the rite of hidden thought, known to be both excruciatingly painful and invasive. The interrogator peeled away the victim's memory and examined it in detail. If they found inconsistencies, they then probed the mind for a signature. The little bit of magic left behind by a spell. As a male of royal blood, he could possibly avoid this fate, especially as he had not been inside the temple that day. Not that he felt pity for those who suffered, but he felt this line of questioning would prove unreliable. His elder sister really lacked imagination. If *he* had desecrated the temple, he would have planted evidence that implicated someone else. It would be a logical move.

He would look beyond the obvious for answers. The firestorm might have destroyed all magical signatures, but some evidence would exist. If his sisters had found and identified physical remains, they would have denounced the perpetrator loudly. As that had not happened, he could deduce that the intruder had survived, but there remained one major problem. Xenis could hardly imagine any house foolish enough to destroy the altar. What would they have to gain but complete chaos? It could lead to the overthrow of House Mith'Barra. True, this was something that many lower houses would welcome, but it would come at a cost. There also remained the possibility that the intruder might not even have come from this city. How had they neutralised the shield spells surrounding the temple and innermost sanctum? Perhaps they had inside help.

Xenis could hear Valene begin to chant. This time she cast the more powerful 'Major Identification' spell. He should leave now to avoid detection. As quietly as possible, he moved down the tunnel and waited at the intersection. Even then, from this distance, he could feel the spells power waiver and afterwards hear his sisters swearing. Apparently, Valene had found nothing useful.

Yet Xenis began to wonder why so little information remained active? Spells decayed with time, but this seemed accelerated, almost as if someone intended it to be that way. Whomever the culprit, they would need help to erase the evidence. That pointed to Thalra as an accomplice. His spies would have to watch her every move. While he ran through some ideas, a strange train of thought gradually developed. As far as he could see, no one actually benefited from this destruction. It seemed an extreme move just to destroy one house. Everyone in the city and beyond, lost out in one way or another, so why do it? Perhaps their daylight enemies were responsible but if so that would start a war of colossal proportions. They would never be that stupid. That made him consider something impossible. Could this be an accident? If so, no one would ever admit to such incompetence. The whole of Drow society would turn against them. He knew that Valene would never listen to that theory, but he could not reject that idea.

That evening they cleared the temple of all guards leaving only a few females at the entrance with strict orders not to admit anyone else. Never had such a gathering taken place with one single purpose, to hide the truth. Every Matriarch attended, and while the subject matter did not surprise them, the full extent of the problem shocked some. Once they linked hands, and then their minds, the Matriarch of Mith'Barra spoke telepathically and confirmed their worst fears. Something had drained the gem of power. She stressed that if the truth escaped, the Matriarchs should eliminate those involved immediately. In the meantime, they would be vulnerable. They would need many sacrifices for their power to grow once more. At the end of the meeting, Mith'Barra made one final detail perfectly clear, after today, no one should ever speak of this again.

Chapter 48

Thomas

The night stretched to dawn. Chris groaned as he rolled out of bed. He hadn't slept well. Lynn had cried in his arms for hours before falling into a restless sleep. After that, he'd stayed awake, staring at the ceiling, dredging up his past, going over it again and again until he fell into a pit of despair and cold rage.

Now barely awake, he had another long day of work ahead. He turned and saw Lynn sleeping, a strand of hair across her face. As he bent over and brushed it tenderly away, she moved and murmured in her sleep. Chris smiled, she looked so peaceful, what a difference from last night. He suppressed a yawn as he walked towards the bathroom. God, he felt tired; these extra hours were killing him. Half an hour later after little more than a cup of black coffee, he got into his car and drove to work expecting another long day, but when he pulled into the yard, he got a shock. Instead of the usual greeting, the supervisor waved him away. Chris thought it odd, so he ignored it, parked up and wandered over to the shed.

"You can get back in that car again," his supervisor said in a tight voice.

"What?"

"You heard me. Get back in that car. We don't want you around here."

An icy feeling stole over Chris. "What's this about?"

"You know what," the supervisor said slamming the newspaper on the ground in front of Chris.

Chris looked at the upside-down print, but even from here, he could read the headline. He looked around at the other men, from their nasty looks they'd also read the paper.

"What the hell, you believe this rubbish?"

"Wouldn't print it if it weren't true," said one.

The supervisor emboldened by the support snarled, "You heard me you can fuckin well go home, bastard wife beater."

Chris clenched his fists. "Come here and say that."

Another man stepped forward and another, all staring at Chris with disgust and hatred.

"Go on fuck off. We don't want you around here."

Chris turned to go barely holding his temper in check.

"Murderer," someone muttered.

A red haze descended over Chris; he turned and snarled. The nearest man stepped back, fear on his face then it occurred to Chris, they really believed that he could kill. It poured cold water on his anger.

"You think I'm capable of killing my own son?" Chris yelled. His voice cracked, "I may not be a good father, but I love that boy."

Their blank faces showed signs of disbelief.

Chris picked up the paper and threw it at them. "Believe this shit if you want. I know the truth."

The supervisor stared hard at him for a moment, then spoke, "We still don't want you here."

"You're sacking me?"

He didn't reply to that. "Just get out of here."

Chris glowered at him for a second, tempted to beat his face into a bloody pulp but that would only prove him the monster they all thought him to be. A few of the men stepped forward, clustering around the supervisor.

"You've not heard the last of this," yelled Chris and stormed off.

He got into his car, revved the engine, and then roared out of the yard. All the way home he broke the speed limit, not caring if they caught his number plate on camera. Once home, he saw the growing crowd of reporters outside his house. It cooled his anger and left a pool of despair in the pit of his stomach.

Cars and vans, all belonging to someone else packed the road. Chris couldn't stand the thought of pushing through that crowd of vultures, so he parked in another street and approached the house from the park. He hadn't gone far before someone spotted him.

"There he is!" they shouted.

Chris broke into a run, the shouts echoing behind him. He didn't slow as he got to the back gate. Instead, he jumped, vaulted the wall, and rolled over the top onto the ground. Chris gave a cold smile as he heard shouts of disappointment behind him. As he unlocked the kitchen door, he made out the sound of distant talking. Strange, he could hear the TV in the living room. Lynn should be at work by now.

"Lynn, is that you?"

As he approached, he heard quiet sobbing.

"Lynn?" he said softly.

Chris found her crumpled in front of the TV, a picture of their house spread across the screen. He bent down to hug her, but she weakly pushed him away.

"Lynn, honey."

"Don't," she whispered in a broken voice.

He stood there, feeling helpless and worse useless. What could he do to make this right?

"Please," Chris said haltingly. "Tell me what I can do?"

She just shook her head and sobbed as an image of Thomas flashed across the screen. Chris felt his heart almost stop. His boy smiled out from the TV, a happy picture of their time at the beach. They'd played football, laughed when Thomas buried him in the sand and then raced each other down towards the sea, to swim and wash the sand off. He could see it now, a blue-sky day, hot and windless, a perfect family memory.

He bent down and touched her shoulder. "We can get through this."

Lynn turned her tear-streaked face towards him, and he kissed her gently on the lips. She smiled weakly as they huddled together and watched not exactly lies but a twisted form of truth. They watched with growing horror as the reporters spared them nothing. Their lives laid bare to the nation.

Chris Harvey had an abusive father who eventually went to prison. His mother, once beaten and cowed, finally snapped and left him with his father. The young boy then endured the heartbreak and loneliness that followed. Alternatively neglected or threatened. He lived with his single parent who had an alcohol problem and a temper to match. After social services foisted the child on an unwilling aunt, the reporter surmised that Chris Harvey had become a mirror image of his father to survive.

Chris could barely believe what he heard. Yes, his father had beaten him, but that didn't automatically make him abusive too, did it? Dark memories surfaced, his mother screaming as he cowered in the corner crying. He hadn't become like that, had he?

"I never hit you," his voice sounded distant and hoarse to his ears.

"But you did hit him," she replied quietly.

"I didn't want him to be like me."

"He's nothing like you," she snarled, suddenly wild-eyed, face contorted as she slapped him. "You're nothing like him!"

Her sudden onslaught made him flinch, and he turned to look at his wife. Her anger drained away at his expression of dismay, and she lowered her hand.

"He's nothing like you, he's kind and gentle and funny and sweet," she whispered softly. "He loves trees and butterflies and going to the beach."

"He likes football too." He reminded her of the one thing they had in common.

She nodded, repentant and leaned against him as they listened to the reporter. This time she cried so hard that she shook in his arms.

The mother worked too hard, away for long hours, she was never at home to look after her family. Thomas had become a latch key kid, neglected, mistreated and unloved by parents too busy with their own lives to care for their child.

"It's not true." Chris tried to reassure Lynn.

"But there's some truth in it," she replied.

Sick and tired of waiting, Thomas wondered if the reporters would ever leave. He'd stayed up all night. In fact, now that he thought about it, more had turned up. They formed an impenetrable barrier around his house, and there seemed no chance whatsoever of getting anywhere near without someone spotting him. Yet he desperately wanted to see his mum and dad. If he could only explain, it would be ok, but these people just got in the way. Thomas felt half-tempted to try to sleep, go back to the elves, and try again later.

Yet if he slept this high up, he might face a problem. Would he end up in mid-air and not on the ground? He could find himself amongst the branches of the great wood, but he regarded that as a bit of a gamble. Strange how until now he had never considered how this worked.

He peeked again over the little wall that surrounded the top of the building. More vans pulled up, choking the streets around his house, and annoying all the residents. Oh god, he was in so much trouble. Thomas just wanted this to end, but he didn't know what to do. He could ask Raphael who Aeglas regarded as old and wise. Surely, he'd know what to do.

A cold wind whipped over the wall and Thomas pulled the hooded cloak around him. Day after day, he went back and forth without a bath. Tinnueth had finally insisted that he bathe and change his clothes. She had washed the tatty originals and set them out to dry while another elf fitted him with new clothes. Aeglas sat laughing at the long sleeves and leggings that swamped the boy's small frame, especially when the hood fell over his eyes. The oversized boots finished the gangly look. Initially, made for a young female, they flopped around as he walked.

"You'll need to wear an extra pair of socks until you grow into them."

"But my feet will get too hot," whined Thomas.

"Well it's this, or you can go barefoot."

Thomas had almost decided to go with that option, but now sitting on top of this building, he felt glad of the extra warmth.

He peered impatiently over the little wall again. No good, they weren't going to leave. He ducked back down and made a decision. On all fours, Thomas scrambled back towards the sagging couch, drew his cloak around him, and settled down to sleep.

The young man suppressed a yawn, tired after another tedious day at work. TV on, he settled down to eat his pizza. He began to flick through the channels, bored and half-listening, he finally settled on the news. The big story of the day, the one splattered across every tabloid newspaper. How could he forget? Somehow, it had slipped his mind. He'd meant to ring the police. A photo of the father and then another picture of Thomas flashed across the screen. He'd seen that boy sprinting across the park followed closely by a strange man. Now he clearly saw the father; he could see that someone else had chased the boy. The problem came when he'd confronted the greasy man. The boy had somehow vanished.

The young man began to dither, but then the reporter said that Chris Harvey had lost his job over these accusations. That settled it. The man decided to ring the helpline. He tried to get the story right in his head, but when the police answered the phone, it just came tumbling out. Not that it mattered. They reassured him and said not to worry. They would send someone round to take down the details.

Chapter 49

Cody

The sun dropped below the rim of the dried riverbed. Far above, the muted pastel sky signalled dusk. On returning, Cody felt surprised to find himself in this dip and not on the road. The complex transfer mechanism must follow some rule, but the location of exit did not automatically mean the position of return. Where was he this time? That thought made him laugh, at the absurdity. Either he existed in another time, another world or a dream controlled alternative reality. It would take a miracle to work out exactly which one. Still chuckling to himself, he clambered out of the riverbed and looked over the sage scrub. Not too far away, he could see a gap in the vegetation. After a quick jog in that direction, his educated guess proved correct.

To his left and right, the crumbling black road stretched out into the distance, but something else caught his eye. A dark orange smudge extended across the far horizon. It looked like a dust storm and here, out in the open, he had nowhere to hide. He looked up and down the road. If he assumed that the sun rose in the east, he could either run north, towards the city or south away from the storm, towards the cart. He might not make either in time, but the city felt like a retrograde step away from potential answers. After calculating the risk, he turned south and began to run. Still stiff from the other day, he took a while to get into his stride. He had no idea how far the cart had gone but even considering all the variables; it could be significant. Would they travel at more than three miles per hour? Would they rest? Perhaps they had pulled off the road and taken another route. At home, the dust storms travelled between twenty-five to seventy-five miles per hour, but that didn't mean that this one would exhibit the same behaviour.

His thoughts cleared as he ran, long strides, even breathing, eyes focused on the road ahead. Cody ran until his lungs and legs burned, hoping beyond hope that he would see somewhere to hide. In the end, he had to slow and rest. As he panted and shook out his legs, he took a quick look at the storm. Even from this distance, he could see the front wall rising up into the sky. Too close for comfort, he picked up the pace once more. Cody ran along the undulating desert road for miles, but with each hillock, he lost more and more momentum.

On top of everything, the light had begun to fade, blotted out by the impending storm. Behind him, the front edge rose at least five hundred feet into the air, a massive orange wall that engulfed everything. Cody desperately looked around for somewhere to hide, he didn't have a lot of time before it hit, and then suddenly he spied something in the distance, sitting just off the road.

The cart, it looked like the cart! The sight filled him with relief, and he found some extra strength to sprint towards it. When he got there, he could see they had battened down for the night. Rocks braced the wheels, and they'd covered the top with a tarpaulin. He also noted that the cart had shutters, which reached the ground. He marvelled at the secure design. There remained, however, no time to investigate or even talk to the occupants. The storm's edge darkened the road behind him. Cody pulled his shirt over his mouth and frantically pulled at the cords, which held the tarpaulin. He got one free but found limited space underneath. They had filled the cart full of metal shelving and to one side a bent copper statue. He quickly shifted some of the metal, then got onto the vehicle and squeezed down beside the metal figure. The edge of the tarpaulin flapped energetically in the wind, and now that the storm had hit, the visibility dropped to zero. He tried, by touch to attach the cord to the statue. After a few goes, he wound it around something and hitched a knot. Even covered by the tarpaulin, sand blew through every hole. It stung viciously and blasted Cody's skin red raw. Outside, the wind howled, and the cart rocked as the storm's full fury passed overhead. It lasted for a few hours. By the time the worst of it had passed overhead, Cody exhausted by the run, had fallen into a deep sleep.

Chapter 50

Karen and Xenis

The hospital bed felt cold and hard, tucked up in a thick plastic coating like a shrink-wrapped brick, it offered little comfort. Even so, Karen hadn't expected it to be this bad. Her shoulders ached, and she felt chilly. Goosebumps prickled the back of her arms. Karen groped for the sheets only to find her legs uncovered. No wonder she felt cold. The bedding must have fallen onto the floor. Her mind still hazy with sleep; she tried to swing her legs out of bed only to discover that she couldn't. She had been resting on the tiles. No wonder the 'bed' had felt so cold.

Awake now, she stood up. Karen recognised the location. The word 'hospital' didn't spring to mind, not when the word 'temple' jumped around trying to get her attention, but unlike her last visit, only a dim red glow remained. In the weak light, she could see the scorched black walls and hole-pitted archways as if a firestorm had raged through the building. The acrid smell of smoke still lingered in the air. Beautiful, but eerie, the metal dish had become a bronze waterfall, frozen in time as it cascaded down the pedestal. Yet in the middle, the red gem remained intact, untouched by the inferno.

It pulsated with a dim, ghostly light as if signalling danger, but for some reason, Karen knew instinctively that it did not. Almost entranced by its enticing glow, she stood, staring intensely at the gem, becoming aware that an odd sensation had oozed into her mind. Insidious and invasive, it tried to worm its way through her subconscious to the core of her soul. It did not feel like an attack, more like an intimate connection, drawing her inexorably towards the light. Karen found herself pulled forward, her feet moving of their own accord, seduced by the bond that joined them together. They would be one. They would be power incarnate. If she just reached out, everything would be hers. Deep within her soul, beneath the enticing offer that threatened to engulf her mind, Karen screamed for freedom. If she succumbed to this intense desire, her essence, her conscience would fade and die. She would lose her soul now and forever. With an almighty wrench of her will, Karen broke the glamour only to find she stood a hairbreadth from the altar. This close, she sensed that something strange existed within the ruby, something beyond raw power. In some ways, it seemed alive, and that reminded her of the city lights. Karen narrowed her eyes and thought cynically, yeah that had gone really well too. The time had come to learn her lesson and keep well away, starting right now in fact. Karen wanted to put as much distance between herself and that infernal gem as possible. Another unpleasant thought occurred to her. She remained alone for now, but it wouldn't last. She should leave before that dark figure returned. If discovered, there would be hell to pay, probably quite literally.

It took considerable effort to back away, but Karen felt determined to escape and with each step, the power that tempted her, diminished. When she finally left the room, the invisible cord that bound her, snapped, leaving her doubled over, panting, and breathless but free, for now.

The red light illuminated one way out, a single blackened corridor that ran steeply downhill. She took it, her bare feet tiptoeing silently upon the cold stone as she made her way down towards what looked like an intersection. There Karen stopped and listened. No sound, no footsteps but someone could still wait in the darkness beyond so she peered cautiously around the corner. After reassuring herself, she remained alone, Karen encountered another problem; she had no idea which direction to take. The wrong choice could lead to a dead end, guards, or worse some malevolent hooded figure. As she considered each option, something tugged at her mind. It prompted her to take the path ahead, so she stepped forward and started down the corridor, but then suddenly stopped. Could this be another lure? Karen risked a glance back, but she couldn't make out the red light, yet weirdly she could still see in the dark. The illumination had dimmed as she escaped from the gem, but somehow that didn't matter. Her eyes had gradually adjusted to the low light levels. With growing unease, Karen realised the darkness had become very dark indeed. This revelation left her feeling uncertain if she should be pleased or concerned about the newfound skill. Karen stared into the distance. It felt both strange and impossible. She could sense the walls, feel the flow of air, and as she looked down most disturbing of all, see the warm outline of her hands against the cold grey rock. It seemed senseless to panic, nothing terrible had happened, only something odd. Ok, very odd. She should get out of here and worry about it later, as long as there remained a later to worry about.

Karen moved forward again and within a few moments came to yet another intersection. This time she could hear muffled voices and after a few seconds realised that they walked this way. Karen back peddled quickly and hid in the curve of the hallway. After anxiously waiting, she worked out that they had moved across the junction. With nowhere to hide, she'd been lucky for once. Back at the intersection, Karen stood, and this time concentrated. A fresh, crisp sensation feathered her face as if a light spring breeze had sprung up. It came from the left, and when she made her choice, it felt like the right decision.

Under the sanctum ran a maze of tunnels, some barred with doors, others leading off into more darkness. Each time Karen got to a crossroad, she concentrated and tried to sense the correct direction. A large number of guards patrolled but almost miraculously, she managed to avoid them. Each time her desperate wish to remain invisible worked. She had luck on her side, but it could run out so quickly. Almost to prove that point within seconds, Karen narrowly missed a squad as they emerged from a wide corridor. This must be the main thoroughfare, and hopefully the way out. Here the walls became ornate and carved, depicting violent scenes, highlighted in some strange luminescent paint. To Karen's eyes, they almost glowed with heat and life. It left her feeling both revolted and repelled, so she kept to the middle of the corridor.

On edge, she tiptoed nervously down the hallway, only to come up against another obstacle; a closed double metal door surrounded by a massive rune carved archway. Yet oddly, it didn't appear locked. With no bolts, no keyhole, nothing to bar her passage, Karen wondered perhaps she could push it open. Yet when she approached, Karen soon realised why no one considered such security necessary. A strange ethereal light rippled across the metal. Faces formed and flowed into one another, tortured, twisted, and gross; they silently gibbered then stared. The door then exuded such a sense of fear and loathing that Karen almost turned and ran. It took all her will to meet their evil leering expressions. The thought of touching the metal grew from disgusting to nearly impossible. Yet she had no other option. Before she summoned the courage to move, one door shuddered and swung partly open. Karen froze, but nothing happened. No guards came to arrest her. No hooded figures approached casting lightning from their fingertips.

It was now or never, so breathing in, she slid between the doors. A horrible sensation crawled across her skin. A thousand hands pinched and caressed, examining her right to be there. Karen clenched her jaw to avoid screaming as she passed through the narrow gap. No wonder no one bothered to stand guard. Unwelcome intruders could not enter, and she found it as much as she could do to leave. The sensation intensified her desire to get the hell out of this city, but she shelved thoughts of 'where to,' and concentrated for now on the 'away from.'

Once past the doors, Karen felt a sharp sense of relief, but this only lasted seconds. She looked around and realised that she stood out like a sore thumb at the top of a massive set of pillar-lined stairs. Karen quickly dodged behind the nearest pillar and then gradually snuck down to the bottom step, where she hid behind the last column. Here she peered out and realised the stars now glimmered above. Again, they were both beautiful and tantalising but oddly without their gripping allure. After some consideration, Karen decided that they remained the same; however, her perception had changed. Each light shone from the top of a tower, many of which graced every building. From here, she could just make out the fairy tale turrets and crenulations, although she suspected they had a practical use as well as being pretty.

Footsteps in the distance kept her hidden until the sound began to fade and she risked glancing out. The group had passed, but Karen could still see their backs, unmistakably, in uniform and heavily armed, they moved like a group of disciplined soldiers. Like a little mouse in fear of a cat, Karen took a gamble and darted out into the shadow of the building opposite. The darkness offered some comfort but not much protection. She could still see the outline of her hands. If anyone looked in her direction, the shadows would not provide sufficient cover, so she kept moving. As Karen skated around the wall, she noticed how the city had become almost unnaturally quiet. She could hardly imagine groups of laughing children playing in the streets. Instead, she visualised a world of severity and quite possibly, pain.

A loud humming noise from above made her shrink back against the wall. After a moments silence, a group of people emerged from a nearby doorway. In long simple hooded robes unlike those worn by her assailant, they walked smartly across the thoroughfare, towards one of the castles. They reminded Karen of students coming out of university. More sounds echoed as other doors opened, and people left their respective buildings. Did the hum signal the end of the workday? With no natural light, how would people measure the passage of time? This proved the least of her problems because more people meant more chance of discovery. Butterflies fluttered in her stomach as she glanced about.

With no one nearby, Karen ran out from her hiding place and darted across to the next building. As she slid behind a pillar, a group of armed men walked around the corner. Their hoods drawn over their heads, swords attached to their backs, they spoke in hushed tones. Tense and awaiting discovery, Karen held her breath, but oddly, they walked past without a glance. Their lack of reaction surprised her. The pillar didn't provide good cover. They should have seen her. With that thought, Karen felt a strange tingling on the back of her neck. As she peered out from behind the pillar, the sensation increased then changed as something exploded in her mind.

Hit with sudden knowledge, Karen knew that dark and malicious eyes had watched her for some time. She had become the entertainment. Nothing more than a small and insignificant creature that tried to evade certain death. The sensation grew, but instead of terror, Karen began to feel annoyed. In the end, she couldn't stand it anymore. With a flash of anger, she turned around, stamped on the floor, and looked up scowling into the darkness. Someone watched her. She would show them. She clenched her fist and waived it violently towards the nearest castle. A feeling of amusement flowed over her and then vanished, leaving her empty.

Karen fled. Yet as she skittered from building to building, she realised this person had watched her for some time. They had not informed the guards, she thought cynically, only because that wouldn't have been any fun.

Now out of the watchers' sight, she came to the last fortress before the main gates. Not wanting to stand out in the open, Karen tried to sneak up against the castle wall only to have a horrible shock. It throbbed. A strange purple, green mist oozed from the stonework and reached out towards her. The air became greasy and thick as the stench of rotting flesh flowed over her. Both dragged forwards and repelled at the same time, Karen twisted and turned violently struggling to break free. Like the gem and the doors, the mist had some strange quality. It tried to probe her mind for information. Karen snarled, rejecting its attempts, casting it out with a thrust of her will. To her surprise, it let go and oozed back into the wall. Now free of interference, she looked at the main gates. From here, she could see that they remained open and appeared to be unguarded, but then Karen remembered the statues that defended the bridge. Would they act as a warning? Who would come running when the alarm went off? Did it matter as long as she could get away? Well, she could make a run for it but running always got people's attention. Better to keep calm and just walk out.

"Don't see me," she thought.

Like a mantra of protection, Karen repeated it over again, under her breath. Each step felt like wading through treacle. So close, yet so far from escape. Face flushed with stress; she felt sure that even her feet glowed red. Just when she got to the gate, a man stepped out and stood a few feet away.

Frozen in horror, Karen stared at his face, wishing beyond anything that he would not see her. She had no hope of going unnoticed, yet strangely, he didn't move. Heart beating so hard Karen thought it would burst; she stayed motionless, while he just stood there. A puzzled look passed across his face then he tilted his head and sniffed the air. His head turned this way and that as if listening for something.

Karen realised to her horror and elation that he could not see her, but perhaps he could both smell and hear her.

On tiptoes, she moved to one side, wishing all the time that he would not sense her. It took a moment to circle around him and pass through the gate. Not looking back, Karen crept down the bridge. No footsteps followed; no commotion exploded. Intent upon her escape and her mind focused on her newfound skill, Karen forgot about the sentinels. As she passed the sculptured figures, she felt them shudder. Statue still, like them, she looked up. A sensation flowed over her, almost like a scan. Another followed, accompanied by a shudder and a moment's indecision. A wailing broke across the city. Behind her shouts erupted from the gatehouse.

Her cover blown, Karen abandoned her plans and sprinted up the path that wound steeply along the cliff. When she reached the top, she stopped, panting hard. Karen glanced back and saw the outline of soldiers gaining quickly, but something else caught her eye. The soft city starlight illuminated a mass of creatures that writhed along the ceiling towards her. As they grew close, the cavern came alive with the sound of chittering. Her acceleration would have shocked any Olympian as she raced off into the depths of the mountain. With no thought of direction, Karen dived with unnatural speed, twisting, and turning down each passageway, outdistancing those behind her. When the pain in her lungs became too much to bear, Karen slumped to the ground gasping for breath. When she didn't hear the sound of pursuit, she sighed and lent back against the wall only to find that it didn't exist. With a small shriek, she tumbled backwards down a slippery chute, which had laid hidden in the darkness.

Chapter 51

Lars

Lost in the city, Lars tried to ask for directions but found that people ignored him. In the end, a man in a blue uniform helped. By the time he got to the shelter, dusk had turned to night. He found Ted inside drinking hot coffee. Lars always found this amazing. No need for flint and tinder, no need to haul the water before boiling, just fill a kettle and flick the switch.

Ted hailed him and beckoned Lars to sit down. "So, do you fancy a trip into the city?"

Lars frowned and looked confused. "Aren't we there already?"

"Nah, this place is on the outskirts."

Somewhat shocked, Lars asked, "How big is this place?"

"Fairly big I would say, not as big as many cities though, it is home to about three million people."

"Three million?"

"Yeah you know, three with six zeros."

Lars had never heard that number, but it sounded a lot. Once again, Lars wished he could read and write.

"Why do they all come here?"

Ted shrugged. "Work mostly, some visit for shopping or entertainment."

"Entertainment?"

Ted grinned. "You'll see."

They took a bus, and when they arrived, Lars almost burst with amazement. Every colour imaginable lit up the square. Great flat surfaces clung to the walls, which had men and women talking, moving, and dancing around. Yet Ted explained, these 'screens' played artificial pictures. Thirty-foot high people didn't exist.

Lars couldn't help staring as Ted dragged him over the crossing and into the park. Here people chatted and walked past a massive fountain. Lars found the combined din of people and traffic almost unimaginable and quite overwhelming.

"Is this entertainment?" he yelled above the noise.

Ted just laughed. "Not really, people are just passing by. They're on their way to bars, restaurants, cinemas, nightclubs, theatres that sort of place."

Even though Lars didn't understand some of the words, he asked, "And this makes them happy?"

Ted struggled to explain. Life in this city turned out to be hectic and complicated. People had very little time for one another. How could anyone know three million people? Instead, each person lived their lives surrounded by strangers.

To someone like Lars who came from a small village and knew each person, not only their virtues but their faults as well, it seemed a strange and detached way to live. It made him understand that these people weren't unhappy but actually lonely. With that, the wonder he felt turned to sadness and an odd longing.

Ted recognised the look. "So, you miss home? Where are you *really* from?"

Lars slumped on to the edge of the fountain. This time he told the truth. "Another world but even there I am far from home."

Ted wasn't sure about the 'other world' thing. His friend showed some strange behaviour even for the 'care in the community' brigade, but he just kept quiet and let Lars talk.

"I grew up in a small village, but then my mother sold me into serfdom for ten years. Yet as soon as I got home, I left again. Partly for adventure, partly for money, but this place makes me realise what I have been missing and what I might never have again."

"What's that?"

Lars thought of Holmfast and then the Keep. "A place where I belong."

Ted understood, but he found it best not to dwell on the whys and wherefores of how he got into this situation. Pride came before a fall, and he had fallen far.

Lars must have sensed his thoughts. "Do you have a family?" he said.

Ted wanted to avoid this subject. "Not anymore." This remained roughly true if he left out the important bits. "What about you?"

Lars nodded. "A mother and my younger sister Asta are waiting for me back home, at least I hope so."

Ted raised an eyebrow.

Lars felt a guilty twinge. "I've been gone for months so who knows what's happened."

He'd just left them to fend for themselves. Maybe his mother had been right. He was selfish.

"Are you on your own now?"

"No, I have my best friend." He smiled and confided in Ted. "Most of the time he comes across as a dumb ox, but sometimes he can be a sharp as a razor."

To his shame, he had forgotten his friend. He might have eaten, but Stefan had nothing. Lars resolved that when he got back to the shelter, he would cadge some supplies for the next day.

****

"I won't do it," yelled Asta.

Malena glared at her daughter. "You will do as you're told."

"I don't want to. He's old and fat."

Malena didn't bother to deny the obvious, instead, concentrated on the crucial fact. "And rich."

"I don't care."

"You will have lots of pretty things."

"I *don't* care."

Malena sighed. Bribery hadn't worked, so she tried to appeal to her daughter's sense of duty.

"We don't have any money now that your brother has gone."

"He'll be back, he promised."

Malena snorted. "That silly boy is probably dead."

Asta gasped.

Malena realised that she'd gone too far, so she tried to look sad. "He's been gone for months. If he were coming back, he would be here by now."

Asta glowered at her mother. "He will be back."

"Hope is all very well, but you have to be practical. We need the money, and the wool merchant is well off."

"Well, you marry him then."

Malena paused, she remained a good-looking woman, but the merchant only showed interest in young girls.

She patted her daughter's shoulder. "If I were young, I would."

Asta shuddered and tried to shake off her mother. "The way he looks at me. It makes me feel sick."

Malena tried another tactic. This time she went for guilt. "I'm sorry. I'm just worried."

Her daughter nodded, but Malena noticed no contrition only further defiance, but she decided to ignore it. "I will speak to him tomorrow."

Asta pursed her lips and glared. "But I don't want to get married."

"What would you have me do? We don't have enough supplies to make it through the winter."

"I don't care. I'd rather starve than have that old mans hands on me."

Malena lost her temper. "You may be happy to starve, but I'm not."

She grabbed Asta's wrist and twisted it. Her daughter cried out as Malena pulled her around and dragged her outside. The girl kicked out, but her mother avoided the blows as she pushed her daughter into the wood store and locked it behind her.

Without regret, she yelled, "And you'll stay in there until you've come to your senses."

When she turned and walked away, Asta began hammering on the door, pleading for her mother to let her out.

Chapter 52

Adam and Faxon

Adam woke face down in the mud and groaned. Could this get any worse? When he thought back, he decided, yes it could. As he lay there, the woodland noises filtered through his senses. The wind in the trees, a murmuring brook, all sounded natural and reassuring. He tensed, waiting for the punch line. It always came. He knew that now. Nothing good happened when you woke face down in the mud. A growling bellow echoed nearby. Ah yes, life didn't disappoint him. He listened intently and immediately recognised the voice.

"You say you searched all night and found nothing!" Hal snarled, his voice betraying a multitude of emotions. He sounded tense and irritated, frustration and anger bubbling almost to boiling point. Adam sensed that Hal barely restrained himself from unleashing a torrent of violence if he didn't get a satisfactory answer.

Adam slowly raised his head and peered through the undergrowth. He wasn't far from the village. He'd been lying in a muddy puddle, and the mud had blended him nicely with the surrounding woodland. He also realised that it must be masking his scent else they would have captured him long before now. Adam shifted position to get a better view. Through the bracken, he could just make out a group of people, and then he grinned to himself. Edric and his men knelt on the ground; their heads bent in disgrace. In front of them, Hal stood simmering with rage.

"Answer me!" Hal clenched and unclenched his fists as he leant over Edric who cowered away.

"Yes, Pack Master," he replied in a low and respectful voice, and then paused in apparent bewilderment.

"Go on, or do I have to rip the words from your throat?" Hal roared.

Edric looked up and bared his throat, a bold move that surprised the crowd. Adam sensed this subservient gesture conveyed complete and open honesty from the supplicant.

"Pack Master, if I tell you the truth, you will not believe me. I'm not sure that I believe it myself, even though I saw it with my own eyes."

Hal glowered sceptically but nodded for Edric to continue.

"I chased him through the woods along the ridge, and when we came to the scarp, I grabbed the witch's bait. He tripped, then fell and tumbled down the slope."

Witches bait. Adam glared at Edric. He didn't like that label.

"I pounced, caught my prey, and punched him."

Edric hesitated for a second and then looked directly into Hals' eyes.

He spoke softly, "I swear on my life that this is true when I punched him, he vanished."

"Vanished?" Hal looked at him, doubt reflected in his eyes.

"Yes, Pack Master he vanished into thin air as if by magic. For a moment, I didn't believe it. I thought the witch had saved him, but when I searched, I found nothing, no sign, nor scent. Afterwards, I returned to the village to get help, only to find many of our pack injured and some even dead."

"And this is your excuse?"

"No excuse Pack Master only an explanation, we were defeated by magic."

A murmur of agreement swept through the crowd, although the Pack Master remained the strongest, he ruled by consent.

"Magic." Hal spat. "The bane of our lives."

Edric's men relaxed a little at this sign. The Pack Master had accepted their account.

Hal raised his voice, "Today we will hunt the woods for our prey, then tonight we will mourn our losses and plan our revenge."

The crowd roared their approval. Adam didn't like that sound. He backed away on all fours, keeping close to the ground and climbed out of the puddle. At the last moment, his foot slipped in the mud with a squelch. Adam froze, listening intently, but it seemed that no one had heard his mistake. With a barely audible sigh of relief, he moved off, crouching in an attempt to remain camouflaged beneath the uppermost fronds of the undergrowth. When the village became distant, he gave one backward glance and saw small groups gathering. Soon they would hunt. Fear trickled down his spine. Edric, Hal and the villagers would exact revenge for their dead. He turned, and keeping low, started to run up the scarp.

It wasn't long before someone picked up a strange scent. "Over here."

Another sniffed. "Is it the witch or the witch's bait?"

Edric ran towards the group. When he sniffed the ground, he identified the scent. As his eyes glowed red, his smile broadened with malice.

He roared, "It's him!"

Hal jogged over and grinned. "Get him."

The pack bayed in delight. Even at a distance, Adam could hear them bellow as he scrambled up the scarp taking less care with each step. His life now depended on speed. The slope rapidly increased, and the ground, covered in wet rotting leaves became slippery. Adam slithered and fell to his knees. Behind him, he could hear shouts changing into snarls and howls. His blood ran cold. They had changed for the hunt. On all fours, they could easily outdistance him, their paws faster and more secure than his mud-covered feet. Their pelts wouldn't suffer cuts and scrapes, unlike his skin. Yet in myths, were-wolves like wolves while smart remained no match for a human. Perhaps his intelligence gave him an advantage or so he hoped.

As he reached the crest of the scarp, Adam stood breathing hard wondering which way to go. He should head to the river. Maybe he could escape through the water. With a flash of inspiration, Adam remembered Hal's advice. Dig deep and unlock the powers you possess. Eyes closed he concentrated breathing deeply. As he inhaled, he tasted the slight metallic scent of water and knew which way to run. Almost laughing, he grinned at the idea that Hal had provided the very information needed to elude him. Behind Adam, the baying increased wiping off that smile. He could hear them gaining, getting closer by the minute but then he detected a distant roar of water. It would be a close call, judging by the noise, so he redoubled his efforts and raced towards the river.

A sudden snarl came from his left. A red-eyed wolf went straight for him. As the creature launched itself upwards, he could see its jaws open wide, its mouth flecked with drool. He ducked and rolled, instinctively kicking out towards its head. As his foot connected with the eye socket, he heard a satisfying squelch and a yelp of pain. Adam landed on his feet and raced away, leaving the concussed wolf lying on the floor. Adam sensed it was Edric, which left him feeling satisfied. It was payback for that punch. The attack, however, had done its job. That brief connection had slowed him down, the hunt closed, now hot on his heels. Their growls echoed in the woodland and Adam knew that at any moment they could rip him apart. Only one hope remained, above the baying, he could now hear the close roar of water.

The path, however, had a different plan. It began to turn left as if running parallel to the river and to make matters worse; Adam saw wolves running directly towards him. They had trapped him with a pincer movement. With wolves in front and wolves behind, he had nowhere to go. A loud growl erupted from the pack. Adam made his choice. He picked the most direct route towards the roaring water and spurred by fear, wrenched the last bit of strength from his muscles. He leapt through the dense woodland. As he approached the river's edge, the undergrowth became thick and tangled. The dense mass of plants and water debris slowed him further.

Then what seemed like misfortune struck. Adam caught his foot and fell to the ground hitting a hidden tree stump. The impact left him winded, but a split second later, he sensed another attack. He rolled over, narrowly avoiding a wolf as it dived towards his back. It turned swiftly around, latched onto his forearm snarling, and tearing with its jaws. Adam screamed in pain and grabbed the wolf by the neck, hugging it tightly to his chest. The pressure crushed its windpipe, and he could feel its hot breath as it thrashed around becoming weaker as it ran out of air.

Adam only let go when its body became limp, but another wolf bounded towards him. He kicked out viciously catching it in the throat, leaving a second unconscious body at his feet before he jumped through a gap in the trees. Behind him, the next wolf could only snarl and struggle, stuck in the dense undergrowth. Body covered in cuts and bruises, his arm dripping blood, Adam stumbled the last few steps into daylight. The river lay before him in full flood, running white between the rocks as it travelled through the rapids. Behind the trees, another wolf leapt, intent upon its target, but Adam dived forwards, plunging into the frothing waters. The wolf scrabbled on the rocks and howled with frustration as its prey evaded capture.

For Adam, the world morphed into a confusing mass of rolling white water as the river tugged him down. His body, battered by the current bounced from wave to wave. With no focal point, he flailed around, unable to tell where the river ended, and the surface began. He slid by a rock only just missing it by a hairsbreadth. The next time his luck failed. With a crunch, Adam hit the rock. Intense pain shot down his back, turning his flailing arms numb and expelling what little breath remained. His lungs burst into fire, he needed to surface now, but as he savagely kicked out, the river pulled him down once more.

Adam found himself bumping along the bottom; his eyes open as he saw a dark shape loom up in front of him. In desperation, he pushed down on the riverbed and launched himself out of the water onto a large smooth rock that jutted out in the middle of the river. There he lay panting, his arm bleeding freely before he gradually pulled himself out of the water, to lie exhausted on the rock. Adam could still hear the wolves as they travelled down the riverbank, keeping pace with his progress. So much for his higher intelligence, the plan almost got him killed. He just hadn't considered last night's rain. Apart from trying to cross at the rapids, the worst possible point, the river had turned into a raging torrent. With effort, Adam managed to raise his head and look downriver. He could see the water rushing down towards the lake. At least it hadn't swept him *that* far. He shuddered partly from cold and shock but also from the thought of seeing the were-witch again.

A howl of triumph caused Adam to turn his head. He saw the pack gathered, snarling, and baying as they came together in a large group. Some pushed forwards, their paws on the edge of the rocks, snapping in his direction. Others trotted up and down the bank growling, but none followed. Perhaps they couldn't cope with the strong current.

Seconds later, this proved wrong. The pack turned and parted, allowing a massive black wolf through into their midst. It stood glowering on the riverbank, its eyes glowing red as it snarled at Adam with froth lined jaws. The wolves, now silent, watched their leader. Adam already nervous now stared as something utterly horrific happened before his eyes. Its form began to twist and change; the gelatinous muscles shuddered as the body gradually deformed. With a spasm, the wolf hunched over as a sickening squelch reverberated from its body. A sound like ruptured gristle and sinew popping echoed as its muscles began to distort. Its voice rose in pain rasping and gurgling as if it struggled to breathe. Patches of black fur began to disintegrate into scraps, only to be absorbed back into the body, to form skin. Its form changed snapping and shuddering as bone fractured and reformed. The creature changed from four legs to two. From snout to mouth, fur to skin, until a man stood on the bank, his massive brown muscles gleaming in the sunlight.

Adam stared in horror, unable to tear his eyes away as the pack followed, each one completing the same process. The urge to vomit became overwhelming. He turned to one side and began to retch and heave, as he spat the contents into the river. On the bank, the men laughed at his weakness. The revulsion must have shown when he glanced towards them. As he wiped his face, a foul acid taste still lingered in his mouth.

"Something for you to look forward to," One sneered.

Adam could barely get away fast enough. He slid into the river and thrashed through the water with renewed vigour driven by fear and disgust. All the while, the men laughed, and catcalled on the bank, mocking him for his weakness. As Adam came out of the rapids, the river carried him downstream, but he tried to angle himself towards the bank. When he finally reached the shore, he began coughing and spluttering as his heart pounded in his chest. Adam could hear someone shouting above the roar of the river. As he pulled himself out of the water, he turned back to see Edric pacing along the rocks on the opposite bank, screaming insults.

"You cowardly long yellow streak of piss. You're not worthy to lick the shit off my arse." Edric spat into the water and screamed, "I spit on you, you worthless little turd."

The pack howled with laughter, some making rude gestures.

Edric pointed at Adam, jabbing his finger in the air, and shouted, "You! You are the reason for their deaths, you, and no one else!"

The pack screamed its agreement. Hal stood listening in quiet malevolence.

Edric turned slightly towards the men lowering his voice in respect. "They were our friends, our family, and our valued pack members, each worth a thousand times more than the witch's spawn. Warriors and husbands, their loss will be keenly felt by all for many years."

The men nodded their agreement, some looking at Adam with cold hatred. They had changed their plan. Instead of bait, they now wanted him dead. Adam wondered why they blamed him for the deaths and not the witch. Perhaps they feared her and rightly so. In the end, he decided that it all came down to pride. The pack marked him as a scapegoat. It kept their honour intact in the face of this crushing defeat.

Edric turned back towards him and snarled. "But you, you are nothing, nothing but a stinking pile of shit! Don't think that you've escaped. I will do all in my power to catch you one day and then." He laughed high and crazy. "I will find the slowest and most painful way to kill you and all that you care for. I will rend you limb from limb, breaking each bone into little fragments."

He smiled in pleasure, pulling his fists apart as if tearing Adams flesh, then with a cutting gesture. "I will slit you across the belly and laugh as you try to claw your entrails back into your body." He ripped. "I will rip off your cock and make you eat your own balls."

The movement caused Adam to jump, and the pack howled with mocking glee.

Edric gouged. "I will cut out your eyes and feed them to the crows as you slowly bleed to death in despair and agony."

Yet there remained a nagging suspicion at the back of Adams mind, something, apart from the obvious was wrong. If Edric and the pack hated him so much why didn't they follow him across the river? In human form, the water shouldn't put them off. Why stay on the opposite bank?

Edric continued his volley of threats each with an accompanying gesture designed to intimidate Adam, but oddly enough, it no longer worked. He merely felt distant and unaffected by the words. The pack stayed back jeering and laughing, like a bunch of brainless bullies. The pack once together behaved worse than any individual did, egging each other on until they sank to the lowest level. Hardly more than animals, then Adam corrected himself, less than animals and without the decency that some humans could display. He stood up and stared, his calm face clearly upsetting them. He should have felt fear, but he didn't, and that obviously annoyed them as they screamed further insults, snarling at his unruffled demeanour.

Behind him, a distant howl went up from the woods. Adam turned alarmed, waiting for yet another attack. A new howl, closer this time, came from upstream, and the pack opposite started to chuckle. They seemed to know what would happen next.

Edric roared with laughter and punched his fist in the air. "It seems like I won't be disappointed! You will die this day, not by my hand, more the shame, but you will die anyway. They will do my dirty work for me, and the pack will celebrate."

Adam glanced worriedly upstream and then back to the pack. It didn't matter. He would run anyway; he would not lie down and die. They jeered at him as he turned and jogged unsteadily off into the woodland away from the oncoming noise. With effort, Adam galvanised his body, forcing his cold damaged muscles to work as he picked up the pace and started to run. He knew he moved too slowly, partly from the cold but mostly from blood loss. He put these things out of his mind and concentrated on the hunt. Adam did not want to be the prey again, but it seemed that fate was not on his side. Either way, he would make it count; he would run, and when caught, fight to the death.

Adam stumbled through the undergrowth and ventured on to a path. One way led to the lake, the other to the wolves. What choice did he have? Torn to pieces or enchanted into a mindless slave. He didn't like either option, so he crossed over the path and ran parallel to the shore, listening to the gaining pack. Adam could hear the growls and barks coming from several directions. Through the forest canopy, he could see a patch of growing daylight. As Adam broke through the woodland edge, he entered a glade only to find a wolf on his left. He turned quickly and tried to double back, only to see another barring his way. Adam raised his wounded arm in self-defence, but they just herded him further into the glade. As he twisted around, he could see wolves approaching from all directions. This was it then, the end. It would soon be over. They had cornered him. He stood, waiting for them to tear him to pieces. Instead, they formed a ring around him, cutting off his escape.

When he felt unable to bear the suspense any longer, Adam screamed, "What are you waiting for? You're going to kill me anyway!"

A low growl caused him to spin around, and he caught sight of a large dark brown wolf. With that noise, the pack backed off to the woodland's edge, and there they began to transform. In the dim forest light, watching this pack change didn't seem so bad. Now, as men, they stood tense and ready to leap should he show any signs of trying to escape. Unlike Hals pack, they radiated restrained strength rather than barely contained violence.

Last of all, the large brown wolf shifted, but in contrast with Hal, he didn't twist and jerk. He transformed rapidly in one complete fluid movement as if both forms were merely an extension of the other. The man became immediately recognisable. Adam sighed with relief. Faxon would not allow his men to attack without good reason.

"You have some explaining to do," observed Faxon dryly. "Starting with who you really are and why you vanished the other night, at the river crossing. Then you can finish with why Hal's pack is hunting you."

Adam hesitated not sure where to start. His name at least didn't present a problem. Faxon waited, his men alert but not threatening.

With a shrug, Adam started. "As I said, my name is Adam but explaining what happened the other night that's more difficult. I'm not sure, I mean I know I fell into the river, bashed my head under water and then I wasn't here." Adam frowned. How could he explain what he didn't understand? "At first I thought I dreamt this whole thing, but this seems too real." He sighed and shrugged. "And sometimes I wonder if I am going mad."

He looked around at the men standing at the woodland edge and noted their expressions. "I come from another place quite unlike this one. It's full of cities, and there are millions of people. For the most part, it's a civilised society with health care, education, and rules. It's reasonably safe too, well for most people anyhow. Oh, and there's metal cars that run fast on roads and planes that fly in the sky."

The pack looked at each other, some dubious, others intrigued.

"I'm sorry I'm not giving you a good picture."

Faxon laughed. "I hope the rest of it will make more sense. Are you usually this bad?"

The pack chuckled more relaxed now as Adam gave a rueful smile.

"In answer to my other question, why does Hals pack hunt you?" Faxon asked.

Adams shoulders sunk. "Huh that one's easy. I fell down a hole and found myself stuck in a cave."

Faxon grinned. "Falling seems to be one of your skills."

Adam smiled sheepishly acknowledging the truth before continuing. "The cave ran off in several directions. I think it forms some sort of maze. Either way, I didn't fancy finding my way in the dark. I'd only fall down another hole and die like a rat caught in a trap. That's why I tried jumping out, but then Hal came along. He didn't offer any help, but he did suggest that I use my powers to get out. His attitude pissed me off. I wanted to leap out and strangle him."

That got a slight laugh. Adam looked no match for Hal.

Faxon smiled and shook his head. "Well, I don't doubt your bravery only question your foolish ambitions."

"One thing though, when I told Hal about the caves, he became really interested. He said that she, meaning the witch, didn't travel above ground but underground. I guess she uses the tunnels to get around their patrols. Who knows how many other entrances she has scattered around the woodland and in lands beyond them? The caves could run for miles."

Faxon and his men looked at each other interested in this choice piece of intelligence. This could be useful.

"Anyway, Hal knew she'd bitten me and decided to use me as bait. After that, the pack started to bicker about the best plan to trap her. He stopped them and said that I should stay in the village until I transformed. Then they could use me. At any rate, they dragged me off, but before we got to the village, the witch attacked. She must have sensed my return and come for me."

Adam raised his hands in supplication as the pack muttered. "Not that I wanted to go with her and still don't. She demanded my release, but when Hal refused, she blasted him with a great white ball of lightning. I thought she had killed him, but obviously, he's even tougher than he looks."

Faxon nodded, acknowledging Hal as a formidable opponent.

Adam continued, "Then all hell broke loose, thunder, lightning, fire, and screams coming from all directions. I lay stunned, and when I came to, I decided to make a break for it. In the background, I could hear the pack fighting the witch as I fled, but I had no idea that Edric had followed. He chased me through the woodland, but I stumbled and fell down a slope, again."

Adam looked resigned to his fate as Faxon chuckled.

"When I rolled to the bottom of the scarp Edric leapt on me." Adam shuddered at the memory of that huge fist accelerating towards his face. "Then he knocked me out. I don't remember anything after that except waking up at home. Later, I found myself back here again near the village with Hal berating Edric for losing me. Edric swore blind that as he hit me, I vanished. He wondered if the witch had helped, but after everything, I've been through, I doubt it. Something else is going on here."

"Any idea what?" said Faxon.

"A curse?" suggested one of the men.

Adam shook his head. "I don't know, but I need to find out. Anyway, after that, I tried to leave, but they caught my scent and hunted me down. I barely escaped by diving into the river and almost drowning for my pains. The rest you know."

Adam stood in silence, waiting for their reaction. He hoped Faxon would believe him.

Faxon appeared to be in contemplation and eventually, he nodded. "That one," he said, meaning Hal. "Has always had more brawn than brains and that goes for the rest of his pack too. I could have told him if he had bothered to listen that the witch and her powers are not to be taken lightly."

The pack relaxed fully and grinned. Adam smiled, relieved that Faxon accepted his explanation but then frowned.

"One thing though, when I dived into the river, why didn't they follow?" he asked. "Edric could have caught and killed me himself, but he didn't."

Faxon inclined his head. "They would need to enter another packs territory. Without permission, it is an act of war. Even if they were to ask, they would not attack until they had my agreement. In that time, you could have escaped; however, they could ask us to capture and return you to them."

Adam tensed at that statement, but Faxon stepped forward and patted him on the shoulder.

"Don't worry, my friend, that won't happen. You are safe with us and free to come and go as you wish. That being said, the witch is still out there although she will be nursing her wounds. I doubt she will pose any threat for a while, but you should think of moving on before she recovers. She might decide to pursue you just because you have escaped, for there is nothing worse than a thwarted woman."

Adam could only agree from experience. Never cross a woman intent on revenge.

"You are tired and have lost blood," said Faxon as he looked at Adam's forearm. "Why not join us at our camp. You will be safe, and there is food and drink available. A fire will warm your bones, and if you wish, our medic can look at your wound. Don't worry, it will heal quickly. Wounds that would kill a human will not kill us."

Adam instinctively shied away from that comment. He didn't like to think that this applied to him. Yet he would have to face it eventually so he might as well ask now. "What will it be like?"

Faxon tilted his head. "What did you want to know?"

"The transformation, will it hurt?"

Faxon understood it remained a common worry with the newly made. "It isn't pleasant, but sometimes it's easier than others."

"Why?"

"In the heat of battle or during a hunt, when the adrenalin flows, you hardly feel a thing. Yet if it's done in the warm light of day then it can hurt like hell, but it won't kill you."

"I can choose to transform during the day?"

"With training and practice yes but not to begin with. Instead, anger and the full moon will trap you. But enough of this. What is it to be? Will you come with us?"

Adam paused, but his stomach gurgled as if prompting him to decide.

Faxon laughed at the sound. "Well your body has made up your mind, come join us."

The night had drawn in making the path awkward to distinguish from the surrounding woodland. The trip, however, took less than thirty minutes. Adam felt relieved. The day had taken its toll. Ahead he could see a glow and smell the tantalising aroma of roasting meat. As they ushered him into a glade, he saw logs around a fire and makeshift canopies, built above bracken beds.

Faxon smiled. "A home away from home, come let's get that arm seen to and then we will eat."

A man came over to look at Adams' arm and pronounced it a nasty bite. After washing it out, he produced a pot containing some sticky green paste. The medic liberally smeared it inside and around the wound, although it smelt musty and unpleasant, he assured Adam that it would work wonders. Afterwards, he took a leaf, stripped off the outer layer, and laid it lengthways over the bite. It stuck tight as he pulled it across, closing the wound. Adam considered it remarkably effective for a leaf and tried to thank him.

As he stumbled over the words, the man smiled. "My name is Nash, and although I don't need it, I will accept your thanks."

Adam now thoroughly starving joined the men at the campfire. They handed him a large wooden plate heaped with meat, which he wolfed down. After Adam had eaten, they passed around a leather skin filled with beer. Once satisfied with food and drink, he relaxed in the company of men who laughed and joked with each other. As he watched their antics, he started to feel very tired. Faxon noticed his sleepy state and nodded towards one of the bracken piles. Adam stood, wished everyone good night, and stumbled over to the bed. He lay down, closed his eyes and within seconds, he fell asleep.

Chapter 53

Thomas

The officer knocked on the door. "Got a moment, Sir?"
"Yes, detective."
"It's an update on the Harvey case. We have a description of the assailant from the park witness. After we sat him down with a sketch artist, I ran the picture through the database."
"Any luck?"
"Yes Sir, the description was spot on, but it's not good news."
The captain raised his eyebrow.
"Dylan Ellis. The man's a known felon, convicted for child kidnapping, the problem is we don't have a current address."
"Why not?"
"He's on parole, and when I contacted his parole officer, it seems that the offender failed to show last week. The officer reported it and then visited the address we have in our system. Unfortunately, the landlord told us that the man had moved."
"Any forwarding address?"
"I checked with the post office, and it's a PO Box."
"So, he's just vanished?"
"Afraid so, Sir. I have some of the lads out canvassing the area around the Harvey house to see if anyone has seen him. If he's moved in recently, someone will know."
"Thank you, detective, keep me updated. We will have to move quickly, once we find where he lives."

The constable knocked on the door and waited. At this time of day, most people were on their way home from work, so he'd had little success with the photograph. He knocked again but then noticed the twitch of net curtains in the bay window.

He waved the photo and spoke loudly, "Could I have a moment of your time, please?"

A rattle of chains echoed behind the front door before it opened an inch.

The constable couldn't see inside so he picked a gender, "Could I have a moment of your time, Sir?"

"That's Mrs Sedgemoor to you, young man!"

"Sorry, Ma'am."

"Well don't stand there like a wet hen, what do you want?"

"Have you seen this man?"

The constable slid the picture through the crack in the door. A gnarled old hand grasped the photo and yanked it inside. The door closed. Oh great, now he'd lost his only copy. He stood for a moment, waiting patiently then as he turned to go, the door rattled again. It opened, and the hand thrust the picture through the gap.

"Nasty piece of work."

"Beg your pardon?"

"Clean your ears out, I said, he's a nasty piece of work."

The constable's heart leapt. "You've seen him?"

"Yes, he moved in next door last week, and since then there's been nothing but trouble. Noisy, inconsiderate, and messy, we don't want his sort around here."

The door opened a little wider. The constable saw a shrewd and calculating eye peer at him through the gap. "You going to take him away?"

"Sorry Ma'am I can't comment on current investigations."

She took that as a yes. "Good. I hope you string him up by the knackers."

The door slammed. The constable knocked again.

"What do you want!" she yelled in a muffled voice.

"You said next door, can you tell me which side please?"

The door opened. "Didn't you listen to a word I said? I said, next door." The gnarled hand jabbed to the right.

"Thank you, ma'am."

She snorted and slammed the door again.

The constable walked down the steps to the pavement and then up the path to the next house. It contained four flats, the top three had names against them, but the bottom didn't.

Hidden in the shadows across the street, a greasy man watched and cursed softly as the constable walked away.

Thomas had given up trying to sleep on the old couch. He felt cold, and the cloth smelled of wee. The media weren't going to move. They just hung around his house, cluttering the streets, and littering the pavement. Thomas stood up and jumped around, flapping his arms, trying to get some warmth into his frozen extremities. When they began to thaw, he felt a little better, albeit hungry. The elven food had sustained him for a while, but now his stomach rumbled every few minutes. It distracted him and made it difficult to relax, another reason why sleep remained elusive. Thomas sighed this hadn't worked. He'd have to find some other way of getting into the house. Perhaps he could go to a friend's place, and get his parents to meet him there. Kev lived close by, and he could probably keep a secret. Shame about his parents, they would just ring the police, so he'd have to sneak in. That shouldn't cause a problem; they never locked the back gate either.

Thomas grinned, pleased with his idea. He bounded downstairs, pushed open the front door and peered across the roundabout. It looked as if the worlds press and his dog camped outside. To avoid them, Thomas went two streets to the east; then he hid behind a parked car to escape a copper. In the glow of the lamplight, he could see the street name, Brecon Hill Road. An old road filled with terraced houses. Once grand, they each had four floors and a large bay window now crumbling with age and disrepair. He'd gone halfway up the road when someone wearing a trench coat stepped out in front of him.

Thomas looked up into a face he recognised.

Dylan recognised him too. "You!"

The man lunged forward and tried to grab Thomas, but the boy dodged and twisted out of the way. He ran out between the parked cars without looking. A squeal of breaks echoed down the road. A motorbike swerved violently, trying desperately to avoid a collision. With incredible agility, Thomas rolled and slid past the bike. The rider came to a skidding halt on his side, narrowly missing a parked van and lay there cursing as the boy pelted off into the night. The greasy man in the trench coat stood amazed for a second then followed the boy. Dylan bumped into the swearing motorcyclist and knocked him over as the man tried to get to his feet. The biker snarled and lashed out; catching the coat, but Dylan kicked him off and started to run.

Thomas lengthened his stride, no longer a fearful little boy. He felt he could outrun this old man. He crested the top of the hill, turned the corner, sprinted across the interconnecting road, and through an alleyway. This connected to a small avenue of shops, mostly takeaways, betting shops and off licences. People would notice a man chasing a boy, but then Thomas wondered; would anyone care? Would anyone help? He quickly ran down the road and slipped into another alleyway behind a burger bar. It appeared empty apart from a few plastic crates and a large lidded dumpster. He opened it. Full of rubbish bags, it smelled horrible but looked an unlikely place for the man to search. Thomas jumped in and buried himself at the bottom.

Dylan slowed and bent over, wheezing. That little brat ran fast, much faster than last time. He looked around and swore at the brightly lit street filled with people queueing for their takeout food. There were too many places for a kid to hide, even if he hadn't run off. The man peered cautiously into each shop, getting funny looks, but after a few minutes, he gave up. He should get home and pack, time to move on. After all, that copper sure hadn't come around to wish him a happy birthday.

The judge quickly issued the search warrant, a child's life was at stake, and now the police prepared for the raid.

"Right, when we get there you lot can take the back of the house. We want to make sure that if he runs for it, we don't lose him. The rest of us will go around the front. If he doesn't answer the door, we knock it down. We don't know if he's armed, but from previous convictions, we know he has a history of violence. Shoot only if necessary and remember that the boy could still be in the house. We don't want this turning into a hostage situation."

The men nodded, ready for action.

A short while later, the vans squealed to a halt, the armed police officers jumped out and ran up the steps. They took up their positions. Some stood at the sides as back up, while two officers readied themselves with the battering ram.

The lead officer knocked on the door hard and yelled, "Mr Ellis, open up, it's the police. We have a warrant to search this house. If you don't open up, we will knock down the door."

They waited. There were no sounds of footsteps or breaking glass, so the officer stood back and nodded to the others. They brought up the battering ram and slammed the door hard. First, it left a dent and then the wood began to splinter before it finally gave way. The police ran into the house, knocked down the inner door, and entered his flat. Dark and silent as the grave, the house appeared unoccupied, but they never made assumptions. They raced through the rooms, weapons drawn, covering each other, prepared for anything.

One went through the lounge. "Clear."

"Clear," yelled one as he examined the bedroom.

"Clear," another called from the kitchen.

An officer carefully opened the bathroom door, still nothing. "Clear."

They relaxed, disappointed by the empty house.

One of them reported to his superior. "All clear Sir, there's no one here. It looks as if he's scarpered."

The detective sighed. The officer was correct. The place looked a mess, but as he scanned the room, he could see signs of hurried packing.

"Right, get forensics and see if they can find anything. We need to know if the suspect held the boy here."

The detective wandered out, disappointed by their lack of success. Lost in thought, he didn't see the man waiting by the police van.

"Did you get him?"

The detective looked up. "And who are you?"

"I live at the end of the road. Did you get that bastard?"

The detective carefully arranged his face to give nothing away. "Get who?"

"The man running after the boy."

"When did you see this?"

The man thought. "Less than an hour ago."

"Describe him."

"About 5 foot 8, thick-set, dark greasy hair, going a bit bald and he wore a trench coat."

It sounded like their man. "What happened?"

The biker told him about the incident, how the man had kicked him and run after the boy. In less than an hour, the man couldn't have gone far.

The detective called for an officer. "Take this gentleman down to the station and get a statement from him."

He called the rest of his men. "We have a lead. A witness saw the suspect here less than an hour ago. Get the station to contact the other forces and distribute the felon's picture. In the meantime, check the train and bus station. We might still be able to get him before he leaves."

Chapter 54

Glen, Sarah, and Cody

His hands should have been red and raw, but they looked perfectly normal. This puzzled Cody. In a dream, this made sense, but not in reality. He shook his head and began to speculate about transfer mechanisms or enhanced abilities as he walked downhill. It didn't take long before he stepped onto the mountain road and turned east. Deep in thought, he hardly noticed when a jeep pulled up beside him. It honked, and a woman wound down the window.

"Hey, I was just coming to see you guys."

"Sarah?"

"The one and only."

Cody considered the illogical nature of that comment. There must be millions of other Sarah's but remembering Glen's remarks on social etiquette, he kept quiet.

"You want a lift?"

"Sure, thanks."

He hopped into the truck, and they drove off.

"Are you jogging out here?"

He gave a terse reply, "Yep."

Cody could hardly tell her the truth, well not yet, not until he knew her better.

Sarah gave him an odd sideways glance. "I called in at the sheriff's office today, and the deputy gave me the latest info." This got Cody's full attention, but Sarah grinned, a glint in her eye. "But I think I should wait until we can talk to your friend Glen as well," she said.

Cody rolled his eyes. "Oh, ok."

After all, they were almost there now, so he guessed he could wait. His stomach grumbled again.

"Missed breakfast?"

"You could say that."

They pulled up in front of the trailer and Glen poked his head out of the door. He looked surprised by their arrival and asked, "Hey, you two want coffee?"

They both nodded then Glen stared at Cody. His clothes looked battered, and orange dust covered him from head to toe.

"Did you sleep outside all night?"

Cody scowled. Glen sometimes behaved like his mother.

"I might have."

"Well, no wonder you are covered in sand."

Sarah tittered at this typically British comment. Desert did not always equal sand.

Instead, Cody ignored this comment, grinned, and said, "Well, the old couch is pretty comfortable, and you were snoring loud enough to wake the dead."

Glen replied with a snort of disbelief. Sarah waited outside while Cody fixed himself a sandwich and Glen brought out the coffee.

Once seated, she leaned forward and shared recent developments. "I asked the deputy today for any news, but he seemed reticent to tell me anything."

Cody and Glen looked mystified.

"Why?" asked Glen.

"Well, it was kinda funny. Hank stared at his boots and mumbled before bursting out, 'don't think I'm crazy.' I assured him that I would keep an open mind and he replied, 'it's like the X-files'."

She had Cody's rapt attention, but Glen looked more sceptical.

"The autopsy actually raised more questions than it answered. Mr Johnson didn't die from anaphylactic shock. They confirmed that he died of a heart attack, probably brought on by blood loss and shock. But and this is the big thing, those marks I thought were bites, are actually semi-healed puncture wounds. Originally, about an inch deep, they had partly healed so they couldn't have caused the blood loss, but also they couldn't find any other wounds."

Sarah turned to Cody and said, "Looks like your educated guess about rose thorns wasn't too far off."

Cody almost blurted his secret, but part of his mind urged caution.

"In the end, although they knew the cause of death, they didn't know the reasons behind it. The deputy said Sheriff Miller didn't know what to make of it. He couldn't decide whether to categorise it as death by natural causes or murder. The evidence is contradictory. Mr Johnson suffered massive blood loss, but there are no signs of it on the floor. Ok so someone could have moved the body, but there is no evidence to that effect. Then the wounds are a mystery, and if that wasn't enough, they can't find any motive for murder. For the moment they have labelled it as unknown, and unless they get any new leads, it will go into an unsolved file somewhere."

Sarah paused to let them take in this information.

"Then just before I left, the deputy joked nervously and said that unless blood-sucking monsters roamed the desert, they had no suspects."

Glen laughed. "That's not likely."

Cody, on the other hand, looked as if he considered that an option. Glen stared at Cody. "You can't seriously think that's possible."

Cody shrugged. "It's not if you don't have an open mind and let's face it, no matter what *you* think, something is odd about this case. The facts don't add up."

"Well that much is true, I suppose. What do you think, Sarah?"

Sarah let out a sigh and sat back in her chair. "I've been wracking my brains, and I can't come up with anything probable or even possible, but you can see why I didn't speculate in my blog or on Twitter. I don't want to get a rep for being a mad scientist."

"Besides, you could get into trouble. It's not as if you are supposed to know all this," said Glen.

They all sat in silence, drinking their coffee, and thinking while Cody munched his sandwich.

Before long, Sarah made a move to go. "Well, I can't sit around here all day. I've work to do."

"Thanks for bringing us the information."

"Yeah, keep in touch and thanks for the lift."

Sarah smiled. "No problem. If you get any ideas, give me a call and feel free to visit me anytime."

Cody remained deep in thought as Glen waved Sarah off. If he slept now, he could get back there and find some answers. Safe from those creatures in daylight, the men would move, but they couldn't have gone far. Besides, if he stayed inside on the couch, Glen should see him vanish. It would finally be the proof Cody needed, then his friend could not dismiss him or think his ideas crazy. One problem, the caffeine would keep him awake.

After cleaning himself up, Cody tried to sleep without success. He couldn't seem to get comfortable. His muscles ached every time he moved, but if he didn't move, they cramped up. Cody didn't dare go onto the computer. Glen always vanished off to read or do something else, so instead, Cody sat bored in front of the TV. In a way, it turned out to be a good thing. His mind felt like Swiss cheese. When the adverts came on, Glen got up to make another drink and nipped to the restroom. Cody hardly noticed his departure as he dozed lightly on the couch, barely listening to the jingles. As Glen washed his hands, he heard an odd noise, and at the same time, the trailer shook ever so slightly.

"Cody? Did you hear that?" Glen walked into the kitchen. "Cody?"

He looked around, calling out but got no reply. Glen couldn't find Cody either inside or outside the trailer.

Chapter 55

Karen

The senior nurse did her usual rounds, checking the patient's condition. So far, apart from some rather massive nasal snores, everything appeared ship shape. The overnight ward off A&E would be her last port of call. Once complete, she looked forward to a well-earned cup of tea.

As the nurse popped her head around the door, she noticed an empty bed. The rumpled sheets tossed to one side, indicated a missing occupant. She walked over and scanned the notes at the end of the bed. After a head injury, the paramedic admitted Karen McGommery for overnight observation. Further tests might be required concerning her concussion.

The nurse frowned. Perhaps the patient had gone to the toilet. A sudden dizzy spell could cause complications. A cursory check of the nearest bathroom yielded no result. An additional foray into the day room and other rooms nearby also proved fruitless. She grew alarmed. Perhaps the patient had started to sleepwalk. It often occurred while under stress in unfamiliar surroundings. With that in mind, the senior nurse co-opted some help and began to search further afield.

Karen slid gently along the slick, cold floor and stopped, with her head resting against the wall. Somewhat surprised, she sat up, rubbed her forehead, and looked around vaguely puzzled by her method of arrival. In the muted light, she could see tiles chequered in black and white, some slightly tattered lounge chairs, and a pile of worn magazines. Against the wall on the opposite side of the room, an antiquated radiator gave off a reassuring glow. Karen crawled over and snuggled up against the heat, trying to warm her icy extremities.

As she rubbed her numb feet, she heard footsteps echo down the corridor.

"Hello!"

A nurse let out a small squeak of surprise as she passed the dayroom. "Hello, who's there?"

"I'm Karen." Aware that this did not give sufficient information she added, "Karen McGommery, I've been in the A&E ward overnight."

The nursed sounded relieved and smiled, shaking her head. "Oh, Ms McGommery, you scared me, why are you sitting here in the dark?"

To Karen, this room hardly seemed dark. In fact, she could have read a magazine.

The nurse flicked the switch, and the fluorescent lights sprung into life. Karen squawked in pain, utterly blinded by the sudden brightness.

"Oh sorry, Ms McGommery I forgot that your eyes would adjust to the dark."

Karen blinked as tears streamed down her face. Beyond all expectation, she felt blinded as if staring at the sun. Even covering her face hardly helped. "Could you switch it off?" she asked, gesturing wildly.

The nurse nodded, much to Karen's great relief but not before turning on the hallway light. The sunspots continued to prickle her eyes as the nurse guided her back towards her bed. Once settled, the nurse enquired why she had been huddled in the dayroom.

Karen merely shrugged and replied, "That's where I woke up."

Fortunately, she didn't need to explain further as the senior nurse bustled into the ward.

"Ah, I see you have found our patient! Ms McGommery you really shouldn't wander around in the dark. Please ring for assistance next time."

"I think she was sleepwalking. I found her huddled in the day room."

The senior nurse nodded sagely. She wasn't surprised.

"Any chance of a cup of tea please?" Karen asked and tried to look rather pathetic in the hope that this might work.

Both nurses smiled, and one replied, "It's some time till breakfast, but I will see what I can do for you."

Now, settled rather more comfortably than before, Karen's eyes gradually adapted to the light. Her condition improved further when the nurse arrived clutching a hot drink for which Karen quietly but effusively thanked her. As she drank, she considered that peculiar dream. Again, the bizarre three-dimensional reality felt overwhelming. The sights, sounds and even the smell seemed completely real. Once back, here though, it began to fade and take on an almost hallucinogenic quality. In fact, she felt just plain daft to consider it anything more than a bad dream, but that didn't stop her mind from drifting back. What had happened? No one had spotted her darting through the city. Somehow, her desire to remain invisible had succeeded. Except on him, and she'd never seen him only 'sensed' what he felt towards her. How had she done that? Like her newfound ability to see in the dark, it just happened. That brought her on to the whole episode with the guard. He had the outline of a stereotypical good-looking, muscular man. Somewhat less heavyset perhaps but she also 'perceived' other information.

Karen grimaced at the next crazy thought. For want of a better description, she could see his life force. She knew that he, oh my god; she was going to think it, that he wasn't quite human. Karen squirmed uncomfortably. After that, the statues' reaction had mystified her. For a moment, they shivered with indecision as if trying to determine whether she presented a threat. No, she had sensed something else. It felt more like whether she belonged or not. The answer had obviously been no. The siren had gone off, but along with the vibrations, she heard the wail. Another mystery and that didn't even include the way she ran. Perhaps her desperation and adrenaline could account for the speed. If only she could do that here, she would be world champion. That final thought stopped her in her tracks. Even in the privacy of her own mind, she felt crazy. Let's face it; she didn't have special skills. She couldn't run faster than a horse. She remained Karen just normal old Karen. Ok, a bit less of the old but hey.

Deep in thought, she continued to ponder the situation as the hospital began to wake, although it never really slept. It behaved like a cat dozing in the sunshine, one ear open for a small-feathered snack incautious enough to stray too close. Cups clattered, trolleys rattled, orderlies and nurses bustled as the ward sprung to life. Karen found breakfast a welcome distraction and once over, the nurse told her to wait until the consultant appeared. After a few tedious hours, the nurse explained that an emergency had pulled him away. Not wanting to keep her and the other patients waiting, she relayed his diagnosis. Apparently, he deemed Karen well enough to return home, only saying that she should take a few days off, and make a follow-up appointment with her doctor. Eager to leave, Karen rang Alison promptly and began to pack.

The journey home consisted of the obligatory interrogation. Yes, she felt all right. Yes, she planned to take some time off. No, she didn't need any further tests. Yes, she had to make a follow-up appointment with the doctor, and finally no, they hadn't found anything particularly wrong as far as she knew.

Karen sighed irritated by her friend's clucking. "Stop worrying! I'm fine."

"Oh alright," Alison replied, most reluctantly. "But you must tell me if they find anything wrong."

She settled into silence, but Karen could tell that this wouldn't last and sure enough a few seconds later, her friend piped up. "It's the mothering instincts. I just can't help them. What sort of friend would I be if I didn't worry?"

Karen chuckled. Alison had become an inveterate worrier.

"A lot happier, less stressed, perhaps?"

"Well, possibly although Michael says if I had nothing to worry about, I would worry about that."

Once home, much to Karen's relief, Alison didn't hang around. With unusual insight, she merely waved goodbye and made Karen promise to ring if anything should go amiss.

Weary, Karen trudged upstairs then dumped her overnight kit on a chair. She changed into another set of pyjamas and a fluffy dressing gown. The bruises on her chest had spread. Yet with all the knocks and bumps she had taken recently, either real or imagined, she didn't feel worried. As she tied up her hair, she noticed another on her neck. Like the others, it had gone a dusky blue-black. Yet when she touched it, the patch didn't feel sore. It felt normal.

Chapter 56

Lars and Stefan

"Oh shit!"

After the bright city lights, his homesick mood made him forget the danger. Lars cursed again as he looked around in the pre-dawn light. He'd gone to sleep too soon and woken in the desert. How could he be so stupid?

The sagebrush grew too high to see the cart, but Lars spotted a nearby rock. Bread and water swinging in the plastic bag, he scrambled up the flaking surface. From this vantage point, Lars saw a dark outline and felt relief. As he jumped down a sharp thorn scratched his arm. It stung like mad, and he felt a warm trickle of blood dribble down his skin.

Lars ignored it and ran towards the cart. When he got there, he noticed sand piled up against the wheels. Its pristine state indicated that the tumblers had not attacked during the night. Hope soared; he would be all right, as long as sand didn't jam the shutter mechanism. After dropping the bag, he clambered quickly on to the cart and then searched for the punch and mallet in the tool bag. Lars jumped back down and turned towards the shutter. The first hit knocked bolt number one open, and then he moved over to the other side. Just as he struck the second bolt, he heard a sound behind him. Lars froze and cursed silently. He slowly glanced to one side and then gradually turned his head. At first, he couldn't see anything, but he knew that tumblers could blend effortlessly into the surrounding countryside. Only a slight shaking motion alerted him to its location. Lars stood motionless almost transfixed. What was it waiting for?

Behind him, the shutter rattled. Lars divided his focus between the two noises. Part of him remained mesmerised by the tumbler. The other part hoped like hell Stefan would hurry up. In one swift motion, the shutter opened. A hand grabbed Lars leg and hauled him inside. Whatever kept the tumbler inert ended. It pounced with blinding speed swiping its claws towards Lars' head, missing only by a narrow margin as he slid beneath the cart. Stefan slammed the shutter down but too late. A tendril shot under its edge and grasped his arm. It sunk one barb deep into his flesh and began to feast. Stefan yelled with pain but refused to let go of the shutter. He jammed it into the ground pinning the writhing tentacle, preventing more from entering. As the other arms scrabbled ineffectually outside, Lars yanked at the tendril trying to pull it free but without success.

Stefan gritted his teeth. "Get my knife!" he yelled.

"Where is it?"

"At the end shutter, inside my boot."

Lars turned around and slid headfirst down towards the other end. He fumbled inside Stefan's boot and pulled out the small hunting knife. He found wriggling backwards wasn't as easy, and he almost kicked Stefan in the head.

"Watch out, mind your feet and hurry up this bloody thing's killing me!"

Lars managed to worm his way out of the crate and twisted to face the writhing tentacle. With some satisfaction, he attacked it with the knife, cutting the woody exoskeleton with the saw-like part of the blade.

Stefan yelped in pain. "It's digging itself in deeper!" but Lars didn't stop

The blade cut into softer tissue and blood spurted into Lars' face, but he kept on sawing until the tentacle released. It slashed at Lars, spraying blood as it flapped around. When he finally hacked it in two, Stefan jammed the shutter into the ground, and Lars reached across to lock it. With disgust, he flicked the severed tentacle away as outside the disfigured tumbler scrabbled at the wood.

In all the confusion, Lars had dropped his bag, but fortunately, the water bottle had rolled inside up against a wheel. Lars opened it and cleaned out their wounds. This was all his fault. He should be more careful. Lars felt glad of the dim light because he could hardly look his friend in the eye. When both men finally got comfortable, they listened to the frantic scrabbling outside.

After a while, Stefan spoke up. "Did you go to that other place again?"

"Yes," replied Lars quietly. "Look I'm really sorry about all this. I never meant for it to happen."

Stefan just snorted. "Of course, you didn't." He paused. "But I think it would be a good idea if we have a plan for next time."

"Sounds good, what do you suggest?"

The cart rocked interrupting Lars. "Shit it's true then, there must be dozens of them up there. The blood must have drawn them from miles around. Good thing it's going to be daylight soon."

"Do you think they will leave?"

Lars grimaced at that nasty thought. "Yeah, yeah I'm sure they will." Then something else dawned on him. "I knew something was missing. I didn't hear you snoring!"

Stefan laughed. "Yeah, I lay awake thinking about the metal. We need to sell it to the traders without anyone seeing us. That's when I heard you digging around the cart. I knew it had to be you because you weren't here when I woke up."

"Good thing you were awake!"

"Yeah," said Stefan then winced as he moved. "We should set you up with some armour."

"But you saw how tough those things are, I don't think that leather would keep them out, and metal is hot and too heavy. I don't want to baste inside my own skin."

"Good point," mused Stefan. "I'll have to give it some thought."

The scrabbling had begun to die down. "I think the sun must be coming up."

"Yeah let's wait a bit longer though."

Once the silence stretched into the sounds of dawn, Stefan opened the shutter. They both got out and looked around. Great tracks led off in all directions. Lars counted them and whistled, more than thirty. He also found the bread battered and looking worse for wear, but Stefan munched it along with some water. It was going to be another long day, and neither of them felt at their best.

Once hitched, it proved slow going. Lars' arm itched unpleasantly but worse than that, Stefan had fallen completely silent. As the day wore on, Lars noticed that Stefan began to flag. Even after several rests and some food, his friend didn't look his usual self. In the end, Lars made him stop. He gave Stefan the last of the water and vowed that he would bring back more. Even though he hadn't really slept, Lars had gone through a second wind, but he knew that soon his body would exact revenge. It would just shut down and nothing but nothing would wake him. He put those worries to the back of his mind and began looking for the marker. Now, if his calculations were correct, it should be somewhere close. That is if the sandstorm hadn't covered it up. After a few hundred yards, he saw a small cairn poking up from under a pile of sand. Lars grinned, feeling relieved. Tomorrow if their luck held, they would make it to the top of the cliff. Perhaps they could camp at the old site in relative safety and bring the metal down another day. After this infernal heat, he longed for the fresh river air. Lars jogged back and let Stefan know that they were close to the cairn.

Later, when they settled down to sleep, Stefan asked, "Is there any way to stop this?"

"Not that I know of."

"Have you tried?"

"Tried what? Not sleeping? Not getting knocked out?"

"I dunno. Try not doing whatever makes you do this?"

"Well I don't know what makes me do this, so I can't stop, can I?"

"Ok, ok don't get tetchy, I was just asking. Just don't come back before sunrise, ok? I don't want a repeat of last night."

Lars smiled ruefully in the dim light of the crate. "I'll do my best."

"Humph!"

A few seconds later, his friend began to snore.

Chapter 57

Adam

The buzzing noise came from far away. Adam lay in a warm stupor unwilling to move. The persistent sound gradually grew louder until finally, he couldn't stand it anymore. Adam groaned and threw his arm out of bed, knocking the alarm clock to the floor, where it lay still beeping. Adam sighed. He hadn't meant to do that. He could either put up with the infernal noise or get up and switch it off. It took a few minutes before he sat up, swung his legs out of bed, and finally silenced it. Adam sighed again, half-asleep and rolled back into bed. He really didn't feel like going into work today.

A groan echoed from the other side of the bed. The shock woke Adam. He didn't remember going to bed with anyone; then he realised this wasn't his bed. He sat up abruptly and looked around. In fact, this wasn't his apartment not unless he had redecorated it in pastel shades last night. Adam leaned to one side and gently pulled back the duvet. A mass of tousled dyed blond hair blocked his view until the woman snorted and turned over. An attractive woman of perhaps fifty plus peered at him through sleep laden long false lashes.

Adam froze. Oh, Shit. What had he done? He gently lowered the duvet, slid out of bed, and tiptoed around the room, looking for his clothes but without any luck. In desperation, he picked up the only item of clothing he could find, a pink bathrobe.

Behind him, a slurred voice spoke from beneath the rumpled covers. "Hey, gorgeous, where are you going? Come back to bed and give momma some of your sugar."

Adam ran for it, darting through the apartment. He grabbed the door handle and twisted but to his horror found it locked. As the woman called out again, demanding more attention, Adam spied a bunch of keys. Without responding, he quickly opened the door and dived towards freedom. Once well away, Adam slowed and rested against a wall near the elevator on floor three. When it arrived, he dashed in without thinking and pressed the button for floor six, but instead of going up, it went down. Oh shit, he would be at reception again, but for once, he got lucky. When he arrived on the ground floor, his cleaner entered the elevator. She gave him an odd look but didn't say anything.

"Erm," said Adam sheepishly. "When we get to my apartment is there any chance you could let me in?"

"Sure." She looked him up and down. Her expression said it all.

Adam felt as if he had to explain further but couldn't finish. "I locked myself out, when I was, erm, you know."

She just grinned as if to say 'you've been a naughty boy, haven't you?'

Once they got to the sixth floor, she let him in, and he sighed. "Mind if I head for the shower while you work?"

"It's your apartment." She shrugged. "You do as you like."

As he relaxed in the shower, Adam remembered last night. His arm looked as good as new. That disgusting paste had worked wonders, or perhaps he just healed fast? He stopped thinking and shook his head. It wasn't real; it was just his imagination. He frowned troubled not only by his arm but by the way, he ached today. It felt odd, more like the build-up to a yawn or sneeze. An all over body sneeze, he chuckled and then stopped. It wasn't funny; it felt just plain weird and perhaps a bit creepy. Just like his nightly dreams.

Later as he passed reception, he suddenly had an idea.

"Would you ladies do me a favour?"

The receptionists smiled as he moved closer and leaned over the desk as if conspiring with them.

"Can you keep a secret?"

This piqued their interest, and they moved closer.

"I keep sleepwalking and locking myself out. If I give you a spare key, would you put it somewhere safe? I could bring you a little reward for your help?"

Both women smiled, but one asked, "What sort of reward?"

Adam gave his best dreamy smile. "What would you like?"

The woman blushed. He knew what she wanted. "What does every woman want?" she replied in a sultry voice.

"Oh chocolates!" replied the other woman who received a sour glance from her work colleague. Chocolate had not been on her mind.

Glad at such an easy bribe, he slipped his spare key into her hand and gave her a conspiratorial smile.

"Our little secret," he whispered in a voice like a lover's caress. The woman gave a shy smile and slid the key into a lockable drawer.

Once Adam left the building, he switched off his charm. He didn't notice the crowds as they flowed around him, avoiding his growing personal space. The train journey didn't improve matters. No one sat next to him, and he found himself glaring at anyone who dared glance in his direction. Their reaction irritated him. They went pale and ducked their heads as if frightened. When he finally strode into the office, he bumped into John and almost growled at him.

"What's got into you today? You're like a bear with a bad head."

Adam shook his head and shrugged, trying to throw off the feeling.

John waited for an answer that never came. "Ok then, I'll see you later." He turned and walked away.

"Later," Adam grunted at the retreating form.

Adam flopped into his chair and sat there, trying to gather the energy to move, but he could hardly be bothered. He made do with looking busy, grunting one-word answers to anyone that approached. Despite the constant interruptions, he did manage to knuckle down and read all the reports but found it slow going. Later that day, when his patience had worn thin, Adam growled at one unfortunate member of staff. After that, everyone shied away, some even leaving work early. Only John showed up, just in time to see Adam give a giant yawn.

"Get a good night's rest, tomorrows the party, and we expect you at your best."

Adam groaned. He had forgotten about his promise.

John chuckled at his response. "Don't worry; it won't be as bad as you fear."

The journey home passed quickly. Adam remained locked away in his own little world. If he had been more aware of his surroundings, he would have noticed that everyone in the crowded train gave him a wide berth. No one sat next to him. No one stood near him. Instead, they all watched from a distance, oddly disturbed by his presence although most couldn't put their finger on why they felt this way, except for one young man. After some thought, he realised why. He likened it to watching an escaped tiger. It sat lounging on the seat, deceptively calm. That view suddenly changed. He had visions of a blood-splattered carriage filled with screams. He gasped when he understood. It hadn't happened only because the tiger didn't feel hungry… yet.

Chapter 58

Thomas

All night they endured the emotional bombardment. Lynn hadn't moved from in front of the TV, but Chris could barely watch it any more. He wondered why she sat there, eyes red with grief, torturing herself. She was just another working mother, no more at fault than any other and certainly better than he was. Yet the press portrayed her as a monster. She'd stayed glued to the newscasts all night, sleeping only fitfully in a rumpled dressing gown. Not that he could sleep, the noise outside kept them both awake. Now that a new day dawned, the media churned out the story once more. No rest for the wicked Chris thought though he wasn't sure if that meant them or him. He got up and went to the toilet, on the way back he put the kettle on and called out to his wife.

"Lynn, do you want anything to eat?"

She didn't reply.

Chris came over to check if she remained awake, only to find Lynn biting her nails to the quick.

"Lynn, honey, you have to eat."

She shook her head. He didn't want to pressure her.

"Coffee then?"

She nodded.

They sat together, listening to the news, and wondered if they would ever see their son again.

Dylan Ellis struggled with his bags. He'd paid for his ticket with cash. Cash was always good, difficult to trace, difficult to link to a specific person. The coach would leave soon, bound north of the border. Dylan had a friend of sorts there, although he doubted the man would be pleased to see him. They'd met in the clink, both convicted

337

of abduction and grievous bodily harm. They got along well enough in the same cell, but when they released his mate early, he had a new boy. Young, stupid, and ripe for exploitation, the lad hadn't lasted long. The screws couldn't pin anything on him, Dylan hadn't participated in the young man's misuse, but he'd enjoyed watching. After that, he'd had an older man in the bunk bed above until his parole hearing. Since getting out, he'd learned that his old mate had inherited a rundown house from some elderly aunt and that's where he planned to go now.

Dylan sat down next to an old lady who took one look at him and promptly moved. He couldn't help but smile, that stare always worked. Part psycho, part leer, it never failed to make people around him feel uncomfortable. If he used it again, he would get a double seat on the coach.

The armed response unit had split up into two groups, one covering the train station, the other the bus. Each had a plain-clothes officer who radioed back to their supervisor.

"Alpha one, waiting outside the bus station."
"Confirmed."
"Alpha two, waiting outside the platform."
"Confirmed."
"Move in, ARU's wait for confirmation of sighting."

With the order to proceed, the plain-clothes officers moved into their respective stations, while the two ARU's waited outside in the vans.

Detective Sergeant Phillips waited briefly in the queue before speaking to the ticket clerk. He discreetly slid his ID, and a picture of Dylan Ellis over the counter then asked in a low voice, "Have you seen this man?"

The clerk looked at the picture, considered it for a moment, and then nodded.

"When?"
"Not long, five minutes or so."
"Do you remember what bus he intended to catch?"

The clerk looked back through his records. "I think it's this one. The coach should be leaving from bay twenty-one in about ten minutes."

"Can you give me a blank ticket?"

The clerk looked a little confused then handed over an unprinted template.

The officer nodded his thanks and moved off to one side behind a pillar.

"Alpha one, possible sighting of the suspect at the bus station. Checking it out will update."

He moved casually towards bay twenty-one, glancing around as if a little lost. Blend in, don't alarm anyone, he checked his phoney ticket as if looking for information. As he scanned countless faces, he spotted the one he wanted. The man sat on a bench, with, as luck would have it, no one nearby. The detective found that hardly surprising considering the suspect's unsavoury aspect.

"Got you," he whispered under his breath and turned away as if looking for another bus. Once out of view he spoke, "Alpha one confirmed sighting in the bus station at bay 21. I repeat confirmed sighting in the bus station at bay 21."

"Understand Alpha one ARU move in to make an arrest."

The armed response unit jumped out of the van and led by Phillips, spread out to cover all angles and escape routes. Once in position, they nodded, ready to go. They drew their weapons and went in yelling.

"Everyone down on the floor."

The crowd erupted into screams as people scattered away from the armed police. The suspect froze.

"Don't move. Get down on your knees, hands behind your head."

He didn't move but looked wildly around as they all advanced and surrounded him yelling.

"Get down on your knees. Get down on your knees, hands behind your head."

It looked for a moment as if the man would run, but then he sighed, slumped to his knees, and slowly put his hands behind his head.

"Cuff him."

One officer holstered his gun and approached cautiously from behind. He took one hand, cuffed it, and then took the other. Once they had secured the suspect, the detective came over.

"Dylan Ellis you're under arrest for the kidnap of Thomas Harvey. Now read him his rights."

As the arresting officer dragged Dylan Ellis away to the van, Phillips reassured the public. They could go about their business. "No need to worry folks, everything is in hand."

Their suspect sat glowering in the interview room. He wouldn't speak except to say he wanted a lawyer. It didn't matter how much they yelled at him, demanding to know where he'd stowed the boy. Dylan Ellis wouldn't answer.

Now after speaking to his lawyer, he agreed to an interview.

Phillips and Brent sat down.

"My client, although innocent of the charges, has agreed to speak freely with you concerning Thomas Harvey."

The detectives didn't bother to hide their scepticism.

The lawyer noticed their attitude. "I would like to warn you, however, that my client is innocent until proven guilty. He will not provide you with a confession, but he will tell you the truth."

Phillips regarded the suspect. That will be the day he thought, but he nodded.

The lawyer looked at his client who sighed and then he too nodded.

Dylan shifted in his seat and grudgingly started to speak. "I didn't do it. I have done many things but not this. I did see the boy last week in the park."

"What day?"

"Friday night."

"What were you doing in the park at night?"

The suspect gave a nasty grin. "Taking a breath of fresh air for my constitution."

"And what happened."

"He kinda ran into me, seemed like a bit of good luck at the time." His face turned sour. "Although not so much now."

The detectives gave him a hard stare.

"Couldn't resist it, gave him a bit of a fright that's all."

"What did you do?"

"Just chased him across the park but then this man came over and asked me what I was doing like it was his business. So, I shoved the boy out of the way, but when I turned around the boy had vanished, guess he'd scarpered."

Both detectives glanced at each other. They knew this already; the other witness had said as much. They still lacked one piece of relevant information. The boy had been missing for a week. What had happened to Thomas in the intervening time?

"Then I saw the boy again today, just after I saw that copper at my house. He recognised me too. I was pissed by the media coverage, thought it would come back to bite me in the ass eventually, so I yelled at him. He ran out into the road and almost got himself knocked over by a bike, the stupid brat, but I chased him anyway. Fast little bugger he is, I lost him outside the betting shop in Royal Dale Road. That's the last I saw of him." He saw their looks. "I swear I didn't touch him."

"That's not what we heard."

"Well, apart from pushing him over on the grass, I didn't touch him."

The lawyer bent close to caution him not to say more.

"We have enough to hold you while we investigate."

"I'll get out on bail, and you know it, you only have circumstantial evidence."

"Along with your criminal record, and a parole violation, that's more than enough to convict you."

The lawyer intervened. "I think my client has been helpful enough for today gentlemen."

Dylan Ellis sat back in his chair and mimed zipping his mouth.

That gesture ended the interview. The detectives hadn't learned everything, but it didn't matter, they had plenty to go on.

"What an interesting smell."

The voice woke Thomas.

"Aeglas!"

Thomas smiled, delighted to be back. He ran and hugged the elf who then leaned over and picked some onion peal out of the boy's messy hair. "Where have you been?"

Thomas launched into the story about the creep, the biker, and hiding in the dumpster.

"I can't believe I fell asleep in there," he said, thinking he should have stayed on the rooftop couch. He sniffed his shirt. "Can I have a wash and my old clothes back if they are dry?"

Aeglas grinned. "I thought you'd never ask."

Thomas attempted to thump Aeglas, who dodged with little effort. When he tried to chase Aeglas back to the city, the elf effortlessly kept out of reach.

An hour later, clean and wearing his washed clothes, they sat in the feasting hall. This time he ate a breakfast of roast wild mushrooms, eggs, and some sort of nut cutlet. Thomas preferred meat, but this tasted an unusual and delicious alternative.

"So, what are we going to do today?" he asked once he finished.

"The scouts were planning to practice their archery skills at the range."

"You're a scout?"

"Yes, myself, Tinnueth and others."

"Sounds fun."

Thomas followed Aeglas to the archery range, nestled between the great trees. He'd expected a bunch of stationary targets with the elves shooting from one end but not this. They climbed a high ladder then walked along bridges and platforms above the course.

"It allows us to watch the practice from above, plus it's an excellent way to view our yearly competitions."

Thomas gawped, staggered at the array and scope of the challenge. It looked like a three-dimensional obstacle course and maze combined, rather than any range he'd ever imagined. Ramps, walkways, ditches, tunnels, sheer jumps, twists, and turns. The participant had to complete the course and hit targets along the way, often as they ran or jumped.

Aeglas pointed out some additional features. "Some objects are hidden from view until the competitor approaches."

"Like what?"

"Moving objects, or sudden traps plus they need to be able to identify friend from foe."

"You can't just shoot at any target?"

"No, you have to pick which targets to hit, some you should avoid. Others can have knock-on effects. You have to hit something to open the next section."

"How do beginners learn?"

"We teach them in the nursery."

Thomas made a face. "Baby stuff?"

"Everyone has to start somewhere."

"Can I have a go?"

"Yes, but first, we are going to run through the trials."

That took several hours, but Thomas found it exhilarating to watch. The elves moved with unbelievable speed and agility, but many of the less experienced scouts still failed the course. Tinnueth and Aeglas appeared to flow through it with ease. By the end of the session, Thomas wanted a go, but instead of approaching the course, Tinnueth took him to the beginner's area. She picked a bow, appropriate to his height and showed him how to hold it with the string held between his two forefingers. Next, Tinnueth indicated how to notch an arrow and how to stand. When he had the correct stance, she showed him how to pull it back, keeping his arm straight with the string resting gently against his cheek.

From behind Thomas, she instructed him. "Now carefully without pulling, sight down the arrow, and simply let it go."

He did and amazingly hit the target. Not dead centre but not an embarrassing first shot.

"Good now do that again."

He repeated it several times, improving quickly until he could hit the centre on every occasion.

She smiled. "You have a natural ability."

Thomas blushed. The praise went to his head like honey mead.

"Could I try something harder?"

"Certainly, we have a place for intermediates with moving targets, be warned though it's much more difficult."

Thomas nodded, but he didn't care, he wanted to show off in front of her. Tinnueth showed him the course, and this time Aeglas came to watch. It seemed quite simple. Run to a mossy tree stump, jump up, and then hit a target on a moving string. He found this feat harder than it looked. After a few frustrating attempts, he managed to nick one edge. As he turned jumping and whooping for joy, he slipped on the mossy surface.

Earlier that day, Chris had rung work. The receptionist put him on hold and left him waiting until it became evident that his boss didn't want to speak with him. Lynn remained in too much of a mess to go into work. On the bright side, he thought cynically, at least neither of them felt like eating, so they didn't have to worry about shopping. Which meant one less bill to pay in a mounting pile of final demands. Now darkness had fallen with no new information. They sat listlessly on the couch as Chris flicked through the channels.

A newscaster appeared. "We'd like to interrupt this broadcast with breaking news. Police have made an arrest in connection with the missing boy Thomas Harvey."

Chris and Lynn sat bolt upright, their hearts pounding, fearful of what they might hear.

"Oh, Chris," moaned Lynn. "I can hardly bear to listen."

He held her, hugging her tightly as she rested her head on his chest.

The newsreader continued. "Eyewitnesses report two daring raids, one on the house in Brecon Hill Road, the other in the Rapid National Bus station."

Chris and Lynn looked at each other. "Brecon Hill, but that's only two streets away."

"If some bastard has our boy…" Chris couldn't finish his sentence.

The reporter supplied more information. "Earlier this evening, armed police broke down the door of number 142 in search of this man."

A picture of Dylan Ellis flashed across the screen.

"Dylan Ellis, age 49, previously convicted of child abduction and grievous bodily harm. Now, over to our reporter Terry Blass, who is on the scene."

"Thank you, Sabrina, as you can see, I'm outside number 142." Terry turned and pointed to the house behind him. "Armed police raided this house earlier today after a witness came forward to say that he had seen the suspect running after a boy in Oldam Park last Friday. According to the witness, the youth fitted the description of Thomas, but when confronted, the suspect denied any involvement with the boy."

Chris clenched his fists. If he ever met that man, he would make him suffer.

The reporter continued, "There are also unconfirmed reports that not long before the raid; the suspect was seen chasing a boy up the road after a near miss with a motorbike."

Lynn's heart leapt, was Thomas alive? She hugged Chris tightly and whispered, "Oh my god, I hope it's true."

Terry Blass added, "Unfortunately, the raid did not have a successful conclusion. Police confirm that neighbours saw the suspect leave hurriedly only minutes before they arrived. Now a forensics team are searching the house for any evidence linking Dylan Ellis with the kidnapped boy. Only time will tell if they can find the boy alive and well. This is Terry Blass reporting from Brecon Hill Road, back to Sabrina in the studio."

"Thank you, Terry. Now we will go over live to the Rapid National Bus Station with our correspondent Nathan Jones."

"Thank you, Sabrina, I am reporting from the location of the second raid where passengers witnessed amazing scenes. I'm here now with Mr Lewis a ticket clerk working for Rapid National. Thank you for talking to us."

The clerk smiled nervously.

"Mr Lewis, can you tell the viewers what you saw today?"

"Well, err, yes, a plain-clothes policeman showed me a picture of this man, and I recognised him immediately. He'd purchased a ticket for a coach going north of the border."

"I hear that the coach was about to leave?"

"Yes, they only had a few minutes before departure."

"Then what happened?"

"He spoke to his team on his radio and vanished off towards bay 21. Then after a few minutes, suddenly the bus station was swarming with armed police. I heard them yelling for everyone to get down and sure enough all the passengers hit the deck."

"Thank you, Mr Lewis."

Then Nathan Jones turned towards his second interviewee. "Mrs Brent, I hear you saw the whole arrest?"

"Yes, Nathan." She smiled, happy that she could elaborate on camera. "I nearly sat next to that terrible man, but the look on his face made me think otherwise." She grimaced and then shuddered. "Such a horrible stare, eyes like dead fish."

The reporter leaned in, showing concern.

"Instead, I went and waited to one side, but I kept an eye on him, just in case. Then all of a sudden, the armed police appeared. It was quite a shock. They shouted for everyone to get down, so I threw myself on the ground, but the man didn't move. They surrounded him, yelling for him to get down on his knees. I didn't think he would for a moment, but then he did, and they arrested him. I felt really relieved."

The reporter nodded his agreement. "Thank you for your account, Mrs Brent." He turned back to the camera. "Shortly afterwards the police drove the suspect away for interrogation. They cannot confirm if they have enough evidence to charge Dylan Ellis, but a legal representative has stated that it is possible, with the eyewitness statements and other evidence, to charge Mr Ellis with the abduction of Thomas. Unfortunately, sources close to the investigation confirm that the suspect is refusing to speak. However, unless the suspect co-operates, the current whereabouts of Thomas will remain unknown. This is Nathan Jones reporting live at Rapid National Bus Station now back to Sabrina in the studio."

"Thank you, Nathan. We will bring you more news updates as the story unfolds."

Chris and Lynn listened intently, one moment filled with hope, the next despair. If only that man would talk, the police might find Thomas alive.

Chapter 59

Cody

The cart had moved on without him. Cody swore under his breath. He'd been away too long. He wanted those answers now more than ever. This late in the afternoon, it would take some time to catch them, but the endless running and lack of sleep had taken its toll. He found it hard to concentrate, and his muscles ached as if he had slept on a bed of rocks. His legs felt stiff and sore, but still, he urged them onwards. The journey along the road proved tough and tedious. Cody felt his mind begin to wander. Perhaps he should just lie down and sleep. That would take him back home again, wouldn't it? There remained at least two problems with that solution. Out here in the open, he would be prey for anything that passed, and when he came back, he would be even further behind.

In the end, Cody just kept on running, doing his best to close the distance. He managed better than expected, and as the sun began to sink below the horizon, he saw the cart. Neatly packed away, it looked ready for the night. It seemed that the men had quite a routine and stuck to it. Cody slowed to a walk and then slumped down next to a wheel. He knocked on the side and waited a moment. Sure enough, he could hear someone snoring inside. All he had to do was wake them, so he knocked again, and when they didn't respond, he hammered on the cart. Cody began to get frustrated and more than a little afraid. The night would soon be here and with that, the tumbleweed creatures. Too tired to run, he wouldn't make it more than a few yards before they caught him.

Cody stood up and banged on the side again, but nothing seemed to interrupt the rhythmic snore. These men slept as if they never intended to wake, and at that moment, he felt a pang of jealousy. If only he could sleep like that. Well if the occupants weren't going to wake up, he would have to break in. The carts' design looked quite impressive. It had sturdy shutters around the base. With no visible bolts on the outside, they must be on the inside. As he circled the cart, he noticed one screen had a slightly different design. Unlike the others, it had two small squares cut into the wood. On closer inspection, he realised that this must be some sort of locking mechanism. He pushed one square with his finger, but it didn't budge. It would take some force to move and open it from the outside. If not, he would be in real trouble. After a quick look around, he selected a small, sturdy stick from a pile of firewood and a nearby rock, which he used as a mallet and a spike. To his relief, the peg gradually slid back inside the hideout. He repeated it with the other square, although the stick only lasted a few taps before he needed to replace it. When the peg finally shifted, Cody knelt down and managed to prise open the shutter.

The snoring sounded louder within the confines of the cart. Whatever noise Cody had made had not disturbed the sleeper. As he ducked down, he caught sight of an interior box and marvelled at the design. The shutters eliminated most danger, but small gaps remained around the wheels both above and below. They had built a narrow space between the shutters and the box, but it wouldn't be a hundred per cent safe. Still, beggars couldn't be choosers. Darkness had almost descended, and he knew he had run out of time when a rustle sounded behind him. With one swift motion, he dived feet first into the gap. That left just enough time to grab the shutter and haul it down before something rattled across the clearing. With frantic effort, he managed to slide one bolt partly into place, but he couldn't reach the other side. Well, not without getting too close to the wheels. Perhaps one bolt would hold it closed.

Outside he could hear the creature scrabbling around. In the confined space, he tried hunching up to avoid the flying dirt, but this didn't amount to much. The noises grew louder as others joined the digging. The nearby snores partially covered their efforts, and Cody began to wonder if the sound actually attracted the tumbleweed creatures. He felt like swearing loudly but worried it would only make things worse. Here he lay under attack and the very people he wanted to speak with, slept as he faced death. As he tried to wriggle further down the crate, something managed to hook itself under the shutter by the wheel. Cody began banging on the side of the box and yelling. It didn't help. The sound merely aggravated the creature. It wiggled its tendril through the gap and took a swipe at Cody. He reacted automatically, jumping back as a claw flashed beneath his nose. A sharp pain followed as his head hit something hard. In the darkness, he hadn't seen the fixtures, which protruded from the ceiling.

Chapter 60

Ellen and Brennan

Something disturbed her sleep. Half-awake Ellen frowned then realised that she could see a strange orange glow through her closed eyelids. She sat bolt upright, expecting to see her bedroom on fire but instead of her room, she found herself sitting on a grass hummock staring out towards a village bonfire. Open-mouthed, Ellen gasped and looked around. To the left a waterway snaked into the distance, orange firelight shimmering on the surface. Behind her, the river stretched into a dark forbidding forest. Ellen shuddered. As she turned back to stare at the strange village, a large splash echoed behind her.

Heart pounding, she leapt up and saw a dark shape swimming rapidly towards her through the water. Socks slipping on the grass she turned and ran across the field towards the light. Behind her, the creature splashed out of the river and gave a deep snarl that echoed across the valley. Ellen broke into an all-out sprint. Over her ragged breathing, she imagined she could hear its bounding strides; almost feel its hot breath on her neck. Her muscles burned with desperate fear. She wrung the last bit of speed from her legs and threw herself over the village threshold. A bright flash lit up the sky, followed by a yelp of pain. As she rolled over, she saw a wolf-like creature flung high into the darkness.

Ellen laid on her back, panting hard, relieved to be alive. From around the village, small groups of people hesitantly emerged from each house. As they moved cautiously towards her, she could hear their conversation although initially, she didn't understand a word. Each sentence gradually coalesced into a language she recognised.

One man snorted. "Must have been a new one to not know about the shield."

"An outcast too I bet," another agreed.

"Stupid enough to hunt around here; they mostly keep away now."
"Where are the watchmen? Shouldn't they have been on patrol?"
"Ha! Bet they were sleeping on the job again."

An old man with long grey curly hair and a massive curly grey beard came forward. "Who are you, child?" he asked kindly.

She sat up still panting and looked into his startling blue eyes. "I'm Ellen."

He looked at her and then around at the bemused villagers. The old man turned back and spoke, "Well, while we will always protect one of our own from the wolf, we would ask what tribe do you belong to? We do not recognise any of your markings."

Ellen stared at the old man feeling confused. What did he mean by markings? Did he mean her shoulder length brown hair, her pale complexion or even as she admitted, her roman nose? Tall, thin but athletic, Ellen wasn't under any illusions that she possessed standard beauty. Even her eyes were an ordinary hazel brown.

As the crowd gathered around her, a dark-haired young man dressed in leathers and armed with a spear came forward. He glared at Ellen, a look of distrust on his sallow pinched face.

"Master Brennan, look at her! Does she look like one of the people?" He demanded as he waved his hand expansively. "Her clothes are fine. Surely she is an enemy agent sent to spy on us?"

Some of the crowd murmured their agreement. The old man appeared to consider those words and nodded slightly.

He turned to Ellen and said, "Well child is Nolan correct? Are you an agent of the enemy?"

Nolan snorted in disgust and scowled at Ellen with scepticism. "If she *is* an agent then she's not going to answer *that* truthfully!"

Master Brennan looked at her. "Well, are you child?"

"Err I'm sorry, but I'm not sure who you mean by the enemy, and I'm *not* a child," Ellen replied, disliking her petulant tone.

Master Brennan smiled slightly while Nolan paced around and gestured at Ellen's clothes.

"Ha! See she's one of *those* that exchange their will for comfort and servitude!" Nolan turned and addressed the villagers. "She should be thrown into the pit at the very least. Then she can't report to her masters. Who knows what secrets she could learn and share with the enemy?"

A sound of agreement echoed through the crowd.

"T'is true she could be a danger."

"Perhaps she belongs to them."

"Or she could be a thief."

"Why should they hunt her then?"

"What do you think? To make it look real, of course!"

Master Brennan listened to their comments and then stared with a strange intensity that made Ellen feel uncomfortable.

Another young man broke away from the crowd. His appearance and bearing struck Ellen as utterly different from Nolan. Short with a mop of curly brown hair, he had intelligent green eyes and a kindly face. "Master Brennan, while I sense she believes she's telling the truth should we not be careful? After all, the enemy has a way with the mind. They may have conditioned her to think she has never met them."

The crowd murmured their agreement.

Master Brennan nodded to his apprentice and said, "Aye, you may be right Connery. I sense the same thing. We will hold the young woman until we can determine her underlying intentions. However, let her be treated with some consideration lest she is innocent," he said, eyeing the man determined to imprison her in the pit. "Please take her away Nolan."

As the crowd dispersed, Nolan hauled Ellen to her feet and bundled her roughly into a wooden shack. There wasn't much inside just a wooden bench, a chamber pot in one corner, and a hatch in the ground. This must be the infamous pit. Nolan threw a blanket into the shack and then bolted the door. Ellen retrieved the covering from the floor and wrapped it around her shoulders, closed her eyes and tried to relax. At least that old man seemed to believe her even if the others did not.

****

After a while, the phone began to ring. Unable to ignore it any longer, Ellen struggled to wake. She found herself sitting in her armchair in a darkened room. "God my legs are so stiff," she groaned.

Ellen felt damned cold too. It took all her effort to move as she creaked over to the phone and answered it. "Hello?"

"Wow, you sound rough, are you ok?" said Gemma.

"Yeah." Ellen yawned. "I fell asleep in an armchair and woke up in the dark. Not that it's done me any good," she said, rubbing the back of her neck and stretching. "I feel as if I've run a marathon."

"Grab yourself a hot bath and soak those muscles. You'll soon feel better."

"Oh, that's a great idea." Ellen smiled weakly.

"What are you doing tomorrow night?"

Ellen's mind went blank, unable to think of anything specific. "Err nothing I think, why what did you have in mind?"

Gemma lowered her voice in a conspiratorial manner. "Well Lucy and John are having a party; we're both invited and guess who's been invited too?"

Ellen gave a dubious sigh about the last-minute invite, but she guessed Gemma wanted encouragement and of course an audience. "That guy who works for Redfern & Brewster, the one that you keep talking about? Didn't you meet him on holiday last year?"

"Yes! That's the one." Gemma sighed. "He's so tall and muscular..."

Ellen listened to her friend drone on about her potential date. He's probably an arrogant asshole, she thought. He sounded like the usual guy that treated women either as playthings or as something pretty to impress other men, never as actual people with real feelings. She hoped her friend wouldn't get hurt, although that might be too much to wish for this time. Gemma had a habit of moving from one disastrous relationship to another, always picking the wrong man. Why they went out with her, she didn't know. They always seemed to want something else, the flawless movie star model, taller, thinner, and perfect in every way. Of course, no one looked like that. Not even the movie star. They had their imperfections airbrushed out; how could any real woman compete? Gemma didn't conform to that image. Petite, curvy, with freckles, and long ginger hair, she had a beauty of her own. Ellen could only watch in sadness as her friend's confidence shattered with each failed relationship. That's probably why Gemma overcompensated by talking as much as possible to calm her nerves.

Yet she remained hopeful that Mr Right would come and sweep her off her feet like a knight in shining armour. Ellen wasn't quite sure why so many women seemed to have this unrealistic fairy tale view of relationships. From her experience, reality only brought disappointment.

"Hey, are you listening?" said Gemma.

"Yeah, sorry. I'm still half-asleep. Can you repeat what you just said?"

"I asked if you wanted to come along tomorrow."

Ellen grimaced, oh fun a party.

When she didn't answer straight away, Gemma wheedled and pleaded, "Oh go on, you know you want to go. You wouldn't let me face it on my own, would you?" She sensed Ellen's reluctance and played her trump card. "Pretty please with sugar on top? I'll owe you one," she said.

Ellen relented. "Oh ok, just don't do anything I wouldn't."

Gemma gave a sassy reply, "Huh, that doesn't leave me with a lot of options."

"Hey, are you saying I'm boring?"

Gemma laughed. "Got you going there! Ok, get a taxi to pick you up at 8pm tomorrow. Make sure you wear something sexy. I don't want you to let the side down."

She rang off. Great, thought Ellen now she would have to think of something to wear. She happened to be more of a jeans and T-shirt girl when she wasn't at work. This meant shopping in her lunch hour, another thing Ellen didn't cherish. Some women loved to shop, and that was fine, she didn't fit into that category.

Her stomach rumbled, reminding her that she hadn't eaten yet, so she sauntered into the kitchen, grabbed a coffee before making a quick ham roll. While she nibbled her food, she slumped in front of the TV and switched on the news, to watch the ongoing story about a missing boy. The media were having a field day as usual. The story contained lax parents, a disorganised school, and baffled police. The whole shebang, so they were making the most of it. Like a good old-fashioned witch-hunt, they expounded and examined every part of the story to the nth degree.

Chapter 61

Karen, Xenis, and Valene

Valene glowered when the runner entered the room. She knew what to expect and found no surprises when she read the runners mind. Once more, the council pressurised her for information and yet did not provide assistance. Already angered by her lack of success, she sent the runner away, empty-handed. This further interruption frayed her nerves to breaking point. Valene growled with irritation and then finally called for her younger brother. The goblin servant scurried away, driven by the knowledge that if he didn't find the errant brother quickly, dire punishment would ensue.

Valene contemplated their predicament while pacing up and down, waiting impatiently. Even the 'Major Identification' spell had not yielded any information, and so far, none of the guards had seen anything suspicious. Even though she had pressured them to almost breaking point, not a single mind showed signs of tampering. There remained a few to interrogate, but her hope waned. For now, it seemed as if those responsible had simply vanished.

A day later, someone had triggered the sentinel's alarm again. A person or person's unknown had escaped the city, and although the bridge guards had pursued, they had lost the perpetrator in the Under Dark. In one way, Valene considered it fortunate that house Zhennu'Z'ress retained responsibility for the city's protection. In another way, it presented a problem. They point blank refused to allow Valene to interrogate the guards concerned.

To make matters worse, many of the guards belonged to different houses. It fell to each house to question their males and then pass the information onto Zhennu'Z'ress, who failed quite deliberately to inform her. Valene petitioned the council to intervene, but they declined to help. They claimed this matter remained unconnected to the temple desecration and therefore none of her business. Any fool, however, could see that they merely withheld information out of delighted spite. It left her feeling angry and worse helpless, a rare emotion.

As she paced with her head down, she found herself growing ever more short-tempered. Her brother demonstrated poor punctuality at the best of times, a trait not tolerated in their society. A dark scowl spread across her face, indicating that soon she would take out her frustrations on someone else if he did not arrive.

"I will not be held accountable for his failure," she hissed in frustration.

By the time Valene seriously considered sending another servant or worst still, having to search for her brother herself, the door opened, revealing the retainers worried face.

"He is here, mistress." The goblin bowed with his voice as low and apologetic as his demeanour.

She glared at her ineffectual servant and spat, "Do not think that this delay will go unpunished. I will deal with you later."

The goblin merely lowered his head and nodded, unfortunately, familiar with the ordeal that he would suffer. Valene dismissed him with a wave that sent him scurrying before she turned and glowered at her brother who swaggered insolently through the door.

"Where have you been?"

Xenis simply grinned disarmingly and shrugged. "If I had known my dear sister desired to see me so urgently, I would have made an effort to leave my Tarot game somewhat earlier."

He had begun to play Tarot only after he received a report from one of his spies. Malafice of House Mith'Barra had warmly greeted Thalra of House Velkyn'Zhaunil, a small gesture but a significant one.

Valene fumed at his nonchalant and informal manner. She knew that he attempted to goad her. Yet if she exploded now, he would have won. That knowing look would creep into his eyes. His habit of teasing and taunting at every opportunity got him into trouble. One day soon, with any luck, it would be the death of him. Valene sighed and tried to relax. If only he didn't prove so useful. She wouldn't use the word gifted even in the privacy of her own tightly fortified mind, but she knew that he remained an asset. Her mother had made that abundantly clear. He could think laterally, investigate, and plan in ways considered unusual amongst the city dwellers. In the past, this had given the family an edge over other houses more powerful than themselves. The actual organisation he left to Valene and her younger sisters. His two older brothers while superb warriors were little more than meat shields in her mind, useful in their own limited way but without any far-reaching potential. It remained unfortunate that the family could not do without Xenis. With that thought, she gave a secret smile, well not yet anyway. For now, she would have to remain resigned to her situation, so she stifled her irritation and tried to exert some authority.

"You heard the sentinels wail and did nothing? Did you not think to act?" her voice as icy cold as the streams that ran around the city.

With a sigh and a shrug, he flung himself into the nearest chair and draped one leg across the arm. "And what would you have me do? Jump into action without your permission?"

This disrespectful behaviour irked her. "I would expect you to come to me immediately and await your orders! Yet here I find you once again playing cards and avoiding your responsibilities to this house. You know that we could plunge into complete disfavour. Already we are teetering on the edge. Someone defiled the most sacred altar. Does it not bother you that this occurred during our tenure as guardians?" She almost spat out the next sentence as it left an unpleasant taste in her mouth to admit that he could be useful. "As you pointed out if we do not find the perpetrator soon, the council will hold us responsible for the breach. I need to find answers quickly!"

"So, your investigations yield nothing?"

Valene felt her anger swell. Again, his face, although almost blank, held just the slightest suggestion of a smirk. "Perhaps you feel you would be more suited to the task?"

His smile spread as if she had fallen into his trap. "Dear sister, I would be most happy to help, but you know that I am not allowed into the innermost sanctum. It is reserved for the priesthood only. I am, however, willing to review the evidence in the hope that I can come to a swift conclusion."

He hinted of course, that she lacked the skills to complete this task and that he, only he could find the answers. How he taunted her! She turned her icy gaze towards him. "No, that will not be necessary; instead, I have another task for you."

Xenis raised his eyebrow in feigned interest, but privately he already knew what she intended to say. He found his sister so predictable and only intelligent in the dull way reserved for the truly unimaginative. She followed guidelines with hardly a thought outside the usual confines of their society. Really, he wondered if there was any hope for her. Her actions, her words, her unintended facial expressions remained transparent. They told him everything he needed to know. Amongst other pieces of information, he knew that she desired him dead on a daily basis. It had become another reason why he chose to taunt her more often than he considered strictly necessary. That and the fact that he enjoyed it, seeing Valene quash her rising ire with more and more effort had become a joy to behold. Perhaps he should temper his natural inclinations to see how far he could push her, but that had become difficult, oh so difficult to resist.

Her eyes narrowed as she watched his innocent expression. If only she could find a good excuse to explore his mind although she realised with rare insight, it would do her no good. Apart from the fact that it would anger her mother, she would have to sort through the vast array of irrelevant details. The only benefit would be his pain as she extracted the information. At least she would find that enjoyable. For now, she would have to put such desires on hold, so with a mental sigh, Valene turned from the pleasant daydream to the matter at hand.

She towered over her brother and looked down on him. "I want you to find the reason for the alarm."

Xenis sneered. "Isn't it obvious?"

Valene leaned forward and returned the sneer. "Obvious to everyone even you, but what I want to know is, where did the intruders hide and where have they gone? To hide in this city for two days, without anyone noticing, it can only mean that the perpetrators had help. I want to know the names of the houses involved and if they were complicit in the temple's destruction."

Typical of his sister to miss the point, but never mind he would do as she bid, all the time collecting information for his own use.

Valene stood back and motioned towards the door. "Now go, I want you to report back later today, and remember I will not tolerate any excuses."

With a lazy, mocking smile, Xenis stood, and after a small irreverent bow, he turned and exited the room.

Her temper, which she had only just held in check, cooled a little as she relaxed. Now that she had some time, she had a servant to punish. With a smile that would frighten the most ardent serial killer, Valene left to relieve her tension.

Xenis sighed. As usual, his sister could not think outside the box. For her, the insular political struggle between the houses remained the be all and end all of everything. True it existed as a significant part, but that did not tell the whole story. His spies informed him that rumours had become rife around the city. Some thought rogue political elements responsible. Others thought an assassin from another Drow city while several spies reported that dissenting servants were to blame. Xenis thought it unlikely that orcs or goblins had triggered the sentinel or defiled the temple. He considered another possibility. The Under Dark did not represent the whole world. Beyond lay other creatures, other civilisations and even further in the daylight world, old enemies. For him nothing should go unconsidered, no stone unturned, no theory, however strange rejected without evidence. Her narrow-minded investigation posed a problem for their house, and this would lead to their downfall if he so allowed. He would not, of course, but how he could take advantage of this situation, remained a mystery.

Xenis had another problem. He did not have a habit of sharing information unless it proved strictly necessary. A lesson he had learnt the hard way as a child. If right, they ignored him, and his sisters took the credit. If wrong, they blamed his meddling and mischievous nature. The punishment for his crime of innocence had been more than just starvation and a beating. It had opened his eyes to the way of the world. It had also been, in an odd way, his reward.

This afternoon Xenis had failed to share one piece of valuable information with his dear sister. Unlike the rest of the city, he could guess who might be responsible for the sentinel's wail. He also considered that the figure in white could have some connection with the temple's destruction. Earlier, purely by chance, he had passed a window, when out of the corner of his eye; he had caught the unfamiliar flicker of white cloth. Yet when Xenis turned to look directly at it, he could see nothing at all. Either it had been a mental aberration, or it had vanished. One did not survive long in this city by dismissing anything unusual, so instead, he moved across to the other side of the window and put his back to the wall. As he turned his head slightly, he peered out of the corner of his right eye only to glimpse a slight shimmer in the darkness. Once he knew what to look for, he could follow its progress. Someone was trying to hide and quite successfully too, although due to the unstable nature of the enchantment, he suspected a novice spell caster. A powerful novice he admitted, but if imprudent, quickly discovered. Now that he could study the magic, he could determine a few details. The caster was female not male, not Dark Delver nor any daylight enemy although he perceived something quite strange about her. Yet it remained difficult to identify because the magic appeared oddly out of kilter.

Xenis watched the shimmering figure for some time, amused by its antics, particularly when she skittered between buildings like vermin. He wondered how long it would be before someone caught such an inept magician. As he watched, something unexpected happened. She appeared to become aware of his presence. He saw a flash of white hair and some movement followed by the stamp of a foot. Xenis drew back from the window and laughed silently. To draw attention in such a way seemed foolish in the extreme. Still, it gave him an insight into her weak personality and those that might control her. With that thought, he began the spell to close his mind. Surface images and emotions swirled down into that deep dark secret place. Here they would remain safe from all but the most prying eyes.

Xenis then turned and with his usual grace leapt downstairs to the barracks. Here he knew there would be a Tarot game, if not in progress, then most certainly about to start. It was a common passtime for the guards and although technically a noble, as the youngest son, he did not have that much social standing. Unlike his brothers, who spurned the company of their underlings, Xenis did not. They often proved useful, unwittingly providing information that he could use. Besides, they had become company of a sort, and the men respected him more rather than less. The barracks also offered an excellent place to meet his spies. It was here much later that the hapless goblin found him, but Xenis true to his style made him wait until the round ended.

After the meeting with his sister, he followed her command to investigate, but he had his own ideas on how to start. From the sentinels perch the figure had raced off into the Under Dark, but it would not be there that he would begin his search. Instead, Xenis went to the end pillars of the temple and cast an 'Identification' spell. After the magic waivered, he picked up a small inconsistency, someone who didn't belong.

At this distance from the temple doors, Xenis could feel the 'Repellent' spell, and he wondered at the intruder's strength to pass this close without going mad. Devoid of the 'Acceptance' spell, the doors would trap anyone, or so that remained the accepted wisdom. His sister had not even contemplated the possibility that someone could resist. Yet how was it possible that this female had both entered the temple and then exited the day after its destruction. Where had she been hiding in the meantime? Guards abounded, yet she had slipped by all and sundry with one exception until the sentinels' wail. Either she had incredible luck, or there was more to this than he realised.

Xenis cast a 'Seek and Find' spell then as he began to follow her path, he tried to sense her enchantment. Magic left an imprint that defined the caster no matter how subtle, yet hers proved awkward to capture. The trail shifted and waivered becoming as slippery as an eel in jelly. How could anyone be so inept and yet hide their identity so completely? It just didn't make sense. The mystery continued to haunt him as he made his way across the square, following the path as she skittered this way and that. At one point, she had almost bumped into House Vlos'Killian. The castles magic should have trapped her like an insect in amber, but somehow, she escaped. He would not want to come that close to their defences. He would not be as lucky.

Instead, Xenis noted her direction of travel and quite nonchalantly, passed through the gates. The guards of his house bowed slightly acknowledging his presence. Unless he could find answers soon, one of these hapless males would suffer another agonising interrogation. His sister would enjoy extracting every minute detail from her screaming subjects. He suspected that she would gain very little. The guards would have seen and sensed even less than Xenis.

He sauntered casually across the bridge as if unconcerned and then turned left even though he knew that twelve houses watched his every move. The path ran along the edge of the river and up into the Under Dark. They would send people to follow him, but Xenis knew how to hide better than most. His sister would undoubtedly admonish him for not taking a squad of soldiers, but he worked better on his own. He could hide his magical trail. Twist it, and turn it, so that those following would find themselves back at the beginning, but he could not do that reliably for more than one person. With some effort, Xenis cast a 'Darkness' and 'Confusion' spell before running off into the black tunnels. Instead of following her trail, he started in the wrong place to deceive anyone who followed. Still, he kept in mind that he must regain her trace if he had any hope of finding the powerful novice mage.

It took him some time to get back to the central tunnel and even more to pick up the trail. The glow had become so faint in places that it flickered in and out with significant gaps. He felt as if the caster had abandoned the 'Invisibility' spell and instead invoked one of 'Speed.' No wonder she had moved so far away from the city in such little time.

After losing the trail once again, Xenis paused to rest and recast his spells, which took more effort than usual. He sat chewing on a piece of dried meat, sipping from a waterskin as he considered his options. The female might have turned down one of the previous tunnels. It was easy to miss a turn with such large gaps, but even now, he could not be sure that he followed the correct path. Xenis sighed and wondered what to do next. It was unwise to return home without any useful information. His sister's nerves were already on edge. Any further failures would only destabilise her volatile temperament. Besides this mystery interested him, he would continue the pursuit until he had some answers.

With a slight groan, Xenis stood up, stretched his legs, and resumed the search. Rations aside, he would need to fill up with water, and he could hear the tinkle of a faraway stream. He could use magic to identify its purity. Perhaps it would be better to fill up now when it was available, rather than wait until his supplies ran out.

Karen opened her eyes and immediately recognised the tunnels. Memories flooded back, of the city, the escape, and lastly the fall. It sent a shiver down her spine. Last time she had been lucky, the chute hadn't been vertical. She stood and stretched, trying to get some feeling back into her body. Pins and needles tingled before settling down to leave an ethereal sensation. Her body felt lighter than usual, more agile, and oddly flexible. It must be her imagination, although her ability to see in the dark was not.

Again, her eyes picked up strange details and her senses stretched well beyond her visual range. Small noises registered in the distance along with the drip of nearby water.

Xenis bent to fill up his water skin from the small pool when he heard the echo of gentle footsteps. The person did not appear to be in any hurry, so possibly they remained unaware of his presence. Tense and ready to leap into action, he stood statue still, his spells of 'Darkness' and 'Confusion' wrapped around him.

Karen rounded a corner and bumped into something warm but unyielding. She yelped, and automatically recoiled but then hesitated. It hadn't attacked. Why hadn't she sensed another person? She concentrated and peered into the darkness. A subtle shift in the air occurred. A purple, red smudge gradually grew and coalesced into a figure. It appeared to be male, although his outline wavered slightly as if in a breeze.

Xenis eyed her warily and wrinkled his perfect nose at her unfamiliar clothes. Gauche wide leggings combined with a long fluffy robe. She appeared to be alone and unarmed, but appearances could be deceptive. No one went into the Under Dark without protection, so he had to assume she could defend herself, but there remained another problem. Xenis couldn't see her magical aura. Without that, he couldn't tell if this was his intended target, but he didn't dare cast an 'Identification' spell. She might see that as a personal insult or a precursor to violence. He should proceed with caution.

They stared at each other unmoving, each waiting for the other to react. In the end, Xenis got impatient.

He bowed. "Mistress, I am Xenis of House Zik'Keeshe," he said, breaking his spells of 'Darkness' and 'Confusion.'

Karen jumped when the figure suddenly clicked into place. Somehow, she understood him. His deep, seductive voice hinted of forbidden pleasures, of all the things she wanted but knew she shouldn't have.

When she didn't scream at him demanding his subservience, Xenis grew bolder. "May I ask who you are?"

"Err, Karen."

"Mistress Karen, are you here on your own?"

Karen didn't like that question. It left her feeling vulnerable. "Why do you want to know?"

"This is a dangerous place, even for a female. Do you not have any companions or guards?"

"You're out here on your own," she challenged.

"True, but I know these tunnels. I am armed with both magic and weapons while you appear to have nothing but the clothes on your back."

His attitude worried Karen, but she couldn't appear defenceless. "How dare you presume that?"

He took a more conciliatory approach. "My apologies, Mistress I am only concerned for your safety."

He slipped in her estimation from being gorgeous to a predator. Now Karen wanted to get as far away as possible. "I can look after myself."

He intercepted her. "May I escort you home?"

"Thank you that won't be necessary," Karen said as she tried to walk around him.

"I am heading to Mizoram."

"Where's that?"

Xenis smiled, so she didn't know the name of the capital city. "You don't live there?"

Karen shook her head.

He grinned to himself, good; he could deal with her without any consequences. He decided to push his luck.

In a low, menacing voice, he asked, "So help is a long way from here?"

Xenis heard her indrawn gasp. He could tell that she intended to run. Although it wasn't in a males training to lay hands on a female without orders from his Matriarch, he had found that he could overcome that conditioning. Besides, this close to home, he could argue she presented a threat. Yet part of him baulked. If he handed this female over to Valene, she would torture the truth out of her slowly, oh so slowly. How would that help him? Perhaps he should see what he could learn first. That way if he were careful with his next move, there would be nothing to fear.

Without warning, he gathered his magic and with almost instantaneous acceleration, he lunged. As the 'Stun' spell activated, Karen folded up in a heap and then to his surprise, she vanished.

Chapter 62

Lars

Lars had developed a mental map of the surrounding area, which served him well. Each time he returned to the city, he found himself in a different location and in many ways that helped fill in the gaps. Tonight, even though Lars felt dead tired, he quickly found his way back to the shelter. When he got there, he noticed people filing into the community centre opposite, while Phil stood chatting to someone outside. As Lars approached, he heard Phil say goodbye to the man who left and walked towards the open door.

Phil nodded. "Hey, Lars."

"Hey." Then his curiosity got the better of him. "What's going on over there?"

"They are running a free first aid course."

This didn't mean a lot to Lars, so he just nodded.

Phil peered at Lars. His shirt looked torn and splattered in blood.

"Did you cut yourself?"

"No, I was attacked."

Phil looked shocked. "Are you ok? Who attacked you? Did you report them to the police?"

Lars didn't know what to say. It wasn't likely that they had tumblers in the city so Phil would hardly understand. Instead, he plumped for a version of the truth. "Yes, I am ok, and no, I don't know who they were, so I haven't reported them."

Phil sensed his reticence but didn't question him further. Attacks happened regularly on the streets, particularly to the homeless. It had been just another reason why they had set up the shelter.

"Do you want to head inside and clean up?"

"Sure, that would be great."

"Then I'll get Ian to check those cuts and make sure they don't get infected."

Lars followed Phil into the shelter and went for a shower. Like before, they gave him some replacement clothes, a chequered shirt, and baggy blue britches. This time he insisted on keeping his boots.

Afterwards, Ian checked his wounds, which turned out to be nothing more than a few scratches. Lars thought they had been much worse. It had sure seemed like it at the time. Yet as Lars sat watching him disinfect the damaged skin, the volunteer gave him a lecture on the importance of keeping a wound clean. Lars found it fascinating. Tiny creatures called bacteria, which he could only see under something called a microscope, lived everywhere, especially in the dirt. If dirt got into a wound, they grew and tried to take over. The body had its own defences and attacked the invaders, but if the invaders became too strong, the person would get sick and perhaps die. Before that happened, a doctor would prescribe antibiotics to help the person recover.

It sounded like two opposing armies to Lars with these antibiotics acting as a relieving force. This information overturned everything he had heard before. At home, for the most part, people were on their own. If lucky, they lived, if not they died. Physicians appeared to be a bit of a mixed blessing. They prescribed the oddest thing like a dung poultice and declared that humours were the basis for all illness. Earth, water, fire, and air, when a patient had an imbalance in one of these, they got sick. He told Ian who just laughed and derided those ideas.

"What a load of rubbish! In the past, they had such absurd concepts and worse, they didn't work. The poor patient survived more by luck than judgement."

That sounded familiar to Lars.

"Mind you, we have found that certain things naturally contain antibiotics. Mouldy bread or spiders' webs for instance, and did you know that sphagnum moss was useful for treating wounds?"

Lars didn't know so he shook his head.

"Are you interested in medicine?"

Lars nodded. He found the conversation intriguing and wanted to learn more.

"Well, you can always head over to the community centre. It's only the basics, but if you go now, you won't have missed much."

Medicine remained the preserve of physicians, and they guarded their knowledge with jealous zeal even though Lars now suspected it was not worth the effort.

"You think they will let me?"

Ian shrugged. "Sure."

Lars beamed. "Thanks!"

He ran out of the shelter and across the yard into the community centre, almost bumping into Phil, who along with other people stood watching the demonstration. A strange human rested on the floor with a man kneeling over him.

"What are they doing?" whispered Lars staring at the corpse like figure.

The man kneeling on the floor looked up. "What was that? Does someone have a question?"

Lars blushed and apologised, "Sorry I'm late. Would you mind repeating what you just said?"

The teacher smiled. "No problem, we've only just started. I'm Dan by the way. We are doing CPR, which stands for cardiopulmonary resuscitation. If someone has stopped breathing, say, for instance, if the person drowned or had a heart attack, then this can help. Now I will demonstrate what you need to do. First, if you can't see the chest moving, place your ear next to their mouth or nose to see if they are breathing like so. If they are not breathing, then check their pulse. One thing to remember, if someone has drowned turn their head to the side, allow any water to drain from their mouth and nose before turning their head back to the centre. Does everyone understand?"

The crowd murmured and nodded.

"Ok then, now you place your hands on the centre of the chest like so. Then with the heel of your hand press down like this at a steady rate, around thirty a minute ok? Every thirty compressions give two breaths like this. Tilt their head gently and lift the chin up with two fingers. Pinch the person's nose and then place your mouth over their mouth, then blow steadily and firmly."

Dan demonstrated this technique and then continued his lecture. "If for some reason using the mouth isn't possible, then the same method can be applied to the nose like so, ok? Then you keep doing this until they either start to get better or the emergency services arrive." He looked around. "Does everyone understand?"

There were a few nods.

"Ok then, do I have a volunteer?"

Oddly enough, everyone but Lars suddenly decided to study the floor. Lars, however, still felt confused. The man on the ground hadn't moved, and he sure wasn't getting any better.

He turned to Phil and quietly quizzed him. "So, is he dead?"

Phil almost choked with laughter. "No, he's made of rubber!"

"He's not real?"

"Nah he's just a dummy."

Lars tilted his head and thought of Stefan. "Bit like a friend of mine."

This chat caught the instructor's attention. "You there, would you like to have a go?"

Lars considered this suggestion. "Sure, why not."

It turned out to be more difficult than it looked, and the first time, he forgot to do several things. Dan commented on each mistake, gently correcting Lars. By the third go, he got it right.

"Excellent, well done!"

Lars stood up and beamed, feeling proud of his achievement.

"Now, does anyone else want to have a go?"

This time Dan had plenty of volunteers.

"So, what's next," asked Lars turning to Phil as the rest of the students crowded around the instructor.

"I think that's it for tonight. People need to practice what they have just learnt."

"Aren't you going to have a go?"

Phil looked at the crowd. "Not tonight I should get back to the shelter."

Lars nodded, but he decided to stay. He liked watching people try to revive the dummy. After a chat with the instructor, he discovered that this free session would be available again next month. By the time Lars finished chatting, the community centre had closed. He sauntered over to the shelter. At this late hour, there were no beds available, but he still managed to cadge some hot food and a cup of coffee. The volunteer staff didn't like to chuck anyone out into the night, but when it came to closing time, Phil asked everyone else to leave. People didn't create a ruckus because if they did, they could not come back another night.

Before he left, Lars nodded to Phil as he grabbed some food and drink for Stefan. "Is it possible to have a bandage or something? A friend also got attacked, and he's worse off than me."

"You should take him to a hospital if he's that bad."

Lars paused, it's not as if he could do that, so he replied, "If I would, I could, but he can't go."

Phil nodded and went over to have a chat with Ian. He came back with a bandage, a few plasters, and some sort of bottle. "This is disinfectant. It should help if your friend's wounds are infected."

Lars nodded and thanked him before going outside. With many hours until dawn, he dared not sleep, so he kept walking through the city, avoiding anywhere unlit. Even sitting on a park bench for a while, became a problem. His heavy eyes started to droop, and before Lars knew it, he began to doze. Only a sudden sound to his right jerked him awake, but he didn't need to worry. It came from another person trying to get comfortable under the boughs of a low spreading tree. After many hours of struggle, he saw the light begin to blossom in the sky, and Lars felt safe enough to sleep.

Chapter 63

Adam

Darkness never bothered him, but tonight that changed. Adam felt different, on edge as if he stood on a precipice, waiting for something to happen.

His skin began to crawl, then a gut-wrenching pain shot through him, and he doubled over feeling sick. Waves of nausea followed, and he retched, vomiting onto the forest floor. Bile rose up to fill his mouth and lungs with hot burning acid. Adam began to cough and gasp, finding it difficult to breathe. As he rasped, another pain swept across his body. Adam cried out and fell to the ground. His body jerked and twisted, shocks pulsing through every muscle. Eyes closed, fists clenched, teeth gritted in agony, every muscle strained at the bone as if trying to pull free. He could feel his heart pounding faster than a galloping horse as it attempted to leap from his chest.

Overhead the dark clouds parted. Soft moonlight swathed the forest floor in silver. It struck Adam like lightning. He shrieked; his voice pitched higher than he ever thought possible. His whole body felt pulled apart, but his mind although terrified, remained razor sharp. He seemed to stand back from events, viewing it from afar, detached, and disembodied. Without warning, his bones snapped. Adam almost fainted and wished he could, but something prevented him from blacking out. Instead, he had no choice but to endure the agony. His skin began to change, flowing over his body like hot tar. Hands and feet deformed. Face cramped as jaw muscles rippled, twisting, extending outwards. Adam screamed again this time in abject fear as his mind began to float away. When the pain faded, his soul and centre dwindled into darkness. Only the faint memory of a man lingered in his mind, but the beast quickly dismissed it as unimportant.

Light from the clouded sky dimly illuminated the glade where he crouched. Beyond, the darkness grew more intense, and he could only see vague shadows flickering in the murky woodland, but it didn't matter. The beast breathed deeply, aware that his other senses had intensified. A riot of smells reached his nose, most of which he couldn't identify. Deep green damp and musty, brown, and earthy, grey sharp and metallic, they made no sense to him, but he knew with time they would.

Sounds also echoed in his ears, he could hear everything both near and far. Close sounds of burrowing mammals, claws on branches above in the windy trees and the minute wheeze of sleeping animals as they breathed. In the distance, he could hear the movement of nocturnal creatures as they scavenged beside a deep flowing river. Closer still, he sensed a stream. He could smell its sharp, tinny odour and hear the trickle as it ran between some rocks. Thirst swelled in his throat.

The beast leapt up and ran full tilt, covering the intervening distance in a few minutes. He took pleasure in the run. Something deep and primal stirred and he plunged into the stream, throwing his head beneath the water, drinking deeply. He delighted in the cold sensation as he quenched his parched throat. Once satisfied, the beast raised his head and shook the water off his fur. His thirst might be sated, but his belly rumbled. As he sniffed the night air, he searched for prey. He needed meat, sweet with the taste of fresh running blood.

A sound to the right caused him to stop; fully alert now, he looked around and sampled the air. Something remained close, something he couldn't identify, but it smelt warm and tender. A hunger swelled deep within. The beast felt ravenous. He could eat for a thousand years and never feel satisfied. As he launched himself out of the stream, he heard little creatures scattering in wild panic. Nearby, he picked up hoof beats and charged through the undergrowth, accelerating towards the target. His powerful legs launched him over fallen trees and branches as he raced into the murky depths of the forest. Such a feeling of power, above anything he had ever felt, coursed through his veins. He revelled in the chase, enjoying the laboured panting of his prey, so close now he could see its panic flecked flanks in the dappled moonlight. As he became engrossed in the hunt, he failed to notice the light growing brighter with each step. A second later, his prey twisted and ran along the edge of the woodland. The move surprised him. The beast overshot then stumbled as the forest suddenly thinned and gave way to grassland. He stopped feeling oddly vulnerable in the open space.

Ahead of him lay a wide flowing river and beyond, lit by the glow of a bonfire, stood a village. A scattering of houses, some large, some small arranged in an arc around the fire. Small torches burned at the edge of the settlement, illuminating the buildings with a flickering orange glow. He stared distracted by the light before he became aware that he had lost his prey.

As the clouds parted once more, something else caught his attention. A figure rose somewhat unsteadily from the grass on the opposite bank. He sniffed the air. A sweet scent filled his nostrils, female and young. The smell filled him with hunger, and he lunged into the water. The woman turned and looked at him in shock and disbelief. He looked nothing more than some dark shape surging through the water, but the beast saw realisation dawning in her eyes. She turned and fled across the field towards the village lights. An intense pleasure coursed through his body. She ran fast. It would be an excellent chase. Within moments, he had left the river, and after quickly shaking his wet fur, he growled and leapt forwards towards his prey. With immense acceleration, he covered the distance between them. Yet as he closed, he began to feel a strange sensation flow over his body. A weird metallic, almost sour feeling tickled his senses, unpleasant in its gathering intensity. The beast began to slow as if his body sensed what he did not understand and acted accordingly. His mind started to fill with apprehension, but with his prey so close, he pushed those feelings aside and went for the kill.

She must have sensed his intent because he saw the woman summon every bit of strength she possessed. As she dived towards the village boundary, she rolled over and looked at him just as he accelerated towards her. Eyes locked together, he could not help but see the shock and revulsion as he leapt. Instead of landing on his prey, he hit an invisible barrier. A bright light seared his flesh, and he screamed as some force flung him backwards high into the sky.

Chapter 64

Ellen and Brennan

The sound of shouting gradually roused Ellen from her sleep. She yawned and opened one eye. In front of her, she could see the open door.

"I tell you she's not in there!"

"Search the village she can't have gone far."

"Do you need more proof that she's working for the enemy?"

That comment irked Ellen. She hadn't left the hut and did not work for the enemy, whoever this enemy might be. She coughed slightly and decided to speak up just as a huge face peered around the door. It had a bushy brown beard so massive that it could have stuffed a sofa. Ellen let out a small squeak.

The giant man snorted and turned back towards the other guard. "Boden you are as blind as a bat, she's still in the hut."

"What? She can't be I just checked a short while ago?"

"Check again. I tell you the prisoner is still in there!"

Another man, blond and pale, peered around the door to see if the giant man told the truth. An expression of shock and surprise quickly replaced the scowl, and then it shifted to suspicion.

"She could be doing this to make me look stupid."

The great bearded man laughed heartily, clutching his stomach. "She doesn't need to do that. You do it well enough on your own!"

Boden's mouth clenched into a tight line as his eyes narrowed. "She could still be a spy sent to search the village. After all, she managed to sneak in and out of the hut without me seeing her."

The bearded man looked dubious. "As far as I can see she never left the hut," and then he prodded Boden with a brawny finger. "If she did, whose fault was that, the man who opened the door?"

Boden glared. "It's not my fault! I'm not to blame!"

"Then who raised the alarm and had half the village running around like headless chickens on a wild goose chase?"

Ellen chuckled at the mixed metaphor. Both men looked at her quizzically.

"Chickens don't chase wild geese," she said.

The bearded man grinned. "That they don't, lass."

Boden didn't relax so quickly. "We will see what Nolan has to say."

This threat didn't impress the other man. "Lad, we will see what Brennan has to say," he said. "It's his voice and wisdom that counts."

Boden growled and grumbled under his breath, but he couldn't gainsay that comment. He stomped off determined to find Nolan and any other allies he could muster.

The great man looked at Ellen with a kindly expression. "Don't worry lass. Everyone knows Brennan is a wise and just man. If you are innocent of the charges brought against you by Boden and his ilk, you'll have nothing to fear."

Ellen didn't like the sound of this. From history lessons, she knew that the defendant often started as presumed guilty rather than innocent. Either way, the bearded man didn't move although he did introduce himself.

He said, "I'm Golof warrior of the People from the Tribe of the Bear."

Ellen smiled, thinking that this seemed entirely appropriate. This man's emblem was a bear, and he certainly looked like one. He stood waiting patiently for a while before Ellen realised, he expected her to return the introduction.

She said, "Oh sorry, I'm Ellen Duncan. I'm a Project Analyst."

From his blank expression, it was clear he didn't quite understand her words, so she just smiled.

Golof cleared his throat and said, "Well Ellen Duncan from Analyst welcome to the village of Riversmeet."

His body language indicated that she couldn't leave the hut, but he did allow her to stand by the door. As Ellen peered out, she could see the village in more detail than the night before. The buildings were mostly round with thatched roofs and whitewashed walls although the large elongate hut also had some ornate stonework. Ellen had seen something similar when visiting a reconstructed ancient village. From around a corner, she noticed a gaggle of people heading this way with an old man at the lead. When they arrived, he stopped and looked at her, his expression gentle but with a hint of steel.

He smiled and introduced himself. "I am Master Brennan. We met last night. I'm the village wise man and leader of the elders' council."

Ellen held out her hand, but the old man just looked at it.

"Err, this is what we do to say hello," she said. "We shake hands to show our good intentions, and historically, it came from showing that we didn't hold weapons."

"Oh well, hello then," Master Brennan said, holding her hand, and shaking it. "You said your name was Ellen, Ellen who?"

"Ellen Duncan."

The old man raised an eyebrow as if waiting for more information, while still shaking her hand.

"I'm not from around here," she said.

He smiled. "Well, I can tell that."

The handshake went on for longer than expected, which made Ellen uncomfortable.

"Shaking hands is normally a short event, just a couple of shakes and that's it," she said hinting that he should let go.

"Ah sorry," he said, releasing her hand. "Not a custom of our people."

Ellen smiled cautiously feeling awkward. "Where is this?" she asked.

"The village of Riversmeet."

This enlightened her no further.

"It is a name that sprung from the rivers around us. We also abide close to the edge of the Were Woods, but the people here belong to various tribes. Some come from the Bear, the Eagle, the Boar, or the Pike."

Still, without any comprehension, Ellen just stood and stared at the old man.

Master Brennan tilted his head and looked at her. "Young lady, while I sense no malice, your arrival, and then subsequent temporary disappearance is cause for concern. I would be remiss in my duty were I not to investigate."

Ellen nodded. "I understand," she said. "I'm just not sure how I can help."

"We have our ways."

Ellen looked nervous at that comment.

He noted her expression. "Do not worry; it's nothing terrible, just a little test, although it will be a while before we can perform it. It is something my apprentice and I are working on." He turned and motioned for her to join him. "Walk with me a while."

Ellen ambled by his side as they meandered through the village.

"As long as you stay by me and do not run off, you will be quite safe."

Ellen didn't feel terribly reassured. Some of the villagers had unfriendly expressions while others bordered on hostility, although more than a few looked merely curious.

"This place you come from, is it far away?" Master Brennan asked obviously plugging for information.

Ellen honestly wanted to tell him, but home seemed so alien in comparison with this place that she doubted he would believe her. As for how she travelled here, that remained a complete mystery, so she hedged her bets.

"A very long way," she said.

"How did you get here?"

Again, Ellen didn't know how to reply, so she stuck to the truth. "I woke up on the banks of a river."

Master Brennan frowned. "Do you remember how you got to the river?"

"Before I was at home and then here, that's all I can tell you."

That explanation didn't impress him. Master Brennan raised his hand and wagged a finger as he spoke, "Well for the moment until we can prove that you are not an enemy agent, we will have to keep you securely locked in the hut. We will permanently post a guard so there will be no disappearing this time."

She wanted to say that she would do her best, but somehow, it felt beyond her control. This would be another thing against her. Instead, she nodded and smiled.

Her compliance did not fool the old man. He eyed her with a thoughtful expression. "It is obvious to me that you are withholding some information, maybe out of fear or darker reasons. Perhaps one day you will trust us enough to share."

"Trust works both ways," blurted Ellen.

Master Brennan smiled. "That is true, and it *must* be earned."

That served as a warning to Ellen to be more forthcoming, but she knew she would sound crazy. They would lock up an insane woman as quickly as they locked up a potential spy.

"Now, it is time for me to return you to your captivity. The villagers are wary of the limited freedom I have given you."

He nodded at the bystanders, their eyes rich with suspicion and hostility. The only notable exceptions seemed to be Golof and Master Brennan's young apprentice, Connery.

The old man took Ellen by the arm and guided her gently back towards the hut. "You will stay here now, but food will be brought to you. We are not monsters, unlike those that seek our destruction."

Master Brennan turned and walked away, nodding at Golof, to take over. The great man indicated that she should enter the hut before he closed and bolted the door. This place remained such a mystery. Ellen wanted to ask so many questions but sensed that they would be unwelcome. Who were these people? Why did they live in such primitive conditions? Where did they come from? Even what year was it? Perhaps she had travelled to the past, but if so, then how could she understand their language? The questions poured out, but one reared its ugly head. Who was this enemy? Whatever attacked her didn't seem to fall into that category. The villagers had spoken about it with such derision. If they feared that monster, then they would show a different attitude. An unpleasant thought occurred to her. How many hideous creatures existed here?

A knock on the door grabbed her attention then the bolts drew back. Ellen held her breath, wondering if they had come to a decision. The smell of food wafted into the room. She relaxed, nothing to worry about, just dinnertime. A young boy brought in a bowl with a spoon and a lump of bread. He smiled nervously, put the food on the floor, and then scampered quickly away. So much for gaining the hearts of the villagers, thought Ellen. At least they trusted her enough to connect with their children, albeit chaperoned by the mighty Golof.

Golof nodded at the food before he closed the door. "Eat! It's good. Mmmm spiced goat stew, you are favoured."

Ellen had never tried goat before, but she picked up the food then sat on the floor cross-legged to eat. She tasted the stew. It tingled hot and spicy on her tongue. She dipped the crusty fresh bread in the rich gravy, enjoying every bite. Full and slightly sleepy Ellen moved to the bed and leaned back against the wall of the hut. Now all she could do was wait and hope that they didn't determine innocence by dunking or some other illogical and ancient means.

Chapter 65

Thomas

Chris stood at the door and hesitated as he heard the second knock. He heaved a disheartened sigh, probably just the press again pushing for another interview. He didn't dare hope for more, but his wife waited in ragged anticipation. She needed to know. Chris summoned his courage and opened the door, outside stood two police officers.

"Have you found him yet?" he blurted, heart, beating fast.

"Can we please come in, sir?"

Chris just stood, dazzled by the flashing cameras, and deafened by the reporters.

The police officer leaned in to speak to him above the hubbub. "I recommend that we should speak somewhere more private than on your doorstep."

Chris opened the door wider to let them in and then shut it with a resounding slam. The police officer smiled at him in an understanding way. Chris showed them into the lounge where Lynn stood, her body trembling, whether from fear or anticipation he didn't know.

"Please sit," said the police officer.

Chris feared the worst, and it must have shown on his face because the man smiled reassuringly.

"We haven't found your son yet, but we haven't given up either. We have a witness, who saw a boy fitting the description of Thomas. He was seen yesterday evening running up Brecon Hill Road, less than half a mile from here."

Lynn moved across the room and hugged Chris.

"Oh, please let it be true," she said.

"We don't know why your son hasn't come forward, but we believe he may be hiding having escaped his kidnapper Dylan Ellis. We hope that once he knows that we have apprehended the man, he will either come home or go to the nearest police station. At the moment, we are following up on new leads that he was seen in the local shopping parade."

"Do we know for sure that this Ellis is the kidnapper?" asked Chris. "We heard on the news that he's not talking."

"That's not exactly correct, he has talked just not confessed, but we have plenty of evidence to convict him. Witnesses saw him chasing Thomas on two occasions, one in the park, the other right outside his house. Besides, this isn't the first time he has done something like this."

"Why did they let him out? Why did no one stop him?" Chris snarled.

The police officer took this comment in his stride. "Well, Sir, he served his time, and the parole board let him go. He has since violated the terms of his parole even before this offence. He will go back inside and considering his age and the fact that he obviously hasn't reformed; he probably won't get out again."

The police officer looked sympathetic. "I know that's no great comfort to you and your wife having suffered as you have, but we have got our man, and he will have his day in court."

"What will happen to my poor boy?" Lynn cried.

"He will get help if we can find him," reassured the police officer.

Chris patted his wife and spoke softly, "Don't worry Lynn, they'll find him in the end. If he's smart enough to escape that monster, he's smart enough to hide. No wonder they are having trouble. Do you remember that holiday a few years ago, none of the kids could beat him playing hide and seek? They thought he'd run off, but he'd just picked a perfect hiding place."

Lynn nodded and smiled weakly.

Chris turned towards the police officer. "On that day in court, I want to look him in the eye and see what sort of man took my son."

"I understand Sir, I have a young lad myself, and I'd move heaven and earth to get him back again if anyone did this."

Chris winced, move heaven and earth, he hadn't done that. He'd just cowered in this house, what a great dad, Thomas, deserved better.

****

The two elves did not understand what they had just seen. A human would say, I can't believe my eyes, but elves aren't like that. They did believe their eyes. Unlike other races whose eyes operate in a shutter like fashion every time they blink, elven eyes are more fluid, more analogue than digital. They can distinguish so much more, take in more information than others can even conceive. They can see what humans cannot.

When Thomas stumbled, he slipped, sliding backwards, as if in slow motion. Tinnueth anticipated his fall and threw out a poorly prepared 'Levitation' spell. It hit her intended target but instead of floating, his body twisted. This only softened the blow. When he hit his head on the tree stump, in place of a resounding crack, they heard a dull thud, but then something else happened.

As Thomas slipped into unconsciousness, the air around him began to distort. A rippling translucent orb surrounded him, with the boy at its centre. Thomas' body started to fold in on itself as if sucked down a funnel before compressing into a single dark point, which vanished. The watery distortion sprang back and dissipated, restoring normality. All this happened in a microsecond too fast for human eyes but slow enough for the elves to take in everything that happened. Tinnueth moved gingerly to where Thomas had disappeared and examined the area. She closed her eyes, concentrated, and felt a slight, tingling sensation.

"Magic," she commented. "But not a sort, I recognise. We should speak with Master Raphael immediately."

"Yeah and find out what the hell is going on."

Tinnueth looked disapprovingly at Aeglas. "Do you think it's your place to question a venerable master?"

Aeglas came from a different school of thought than Tinnueth. It's not that he didn't believe in respect; it's just that he didn't think that older people were automatically right. They didn't know everything. The older someone got, the more cautious that person became, and sometimes that distorted their judgement. They could be too conservative, and because of this, they could fail to act when they should. Nevertheless, Tinnueth made it clear she planned to speak with Raphael so he might as well go along.

They ran through the woodland and summoned the rope ladders into the city. Master Raphael wasn't in his library. Instead, they found him watching the sun as it began to set.

"Master Raphael," Tinnueth began to speak, but he silenced her with a wave of his hand.

"I know what you are going to say. I felt the disturbance."

"Why have you not mentioned this before?" asked Aeglas, and then added, "Master," as Tinnueth glared at him. After all, Thomas had appeared and disappeared many times.

Raphael looked at him and sighed. "The magic that surrounds this city is not absolute. It fluctuates with the rhythms of nature, so if a disturbance is small enough, it is easy to overlook. It simply blends in with the ebb and flow. This time, however, I knew what I looked for; in fact, I watched Thomas as it happened."

He opened his hand to reveal a crystal.

"Why were you watching Thomas, Master?" asked Tinnueth.

"I have found it interesting how quickly he learns for a human, too quickly in my estimation."

She frowned, and he noted her expression.

"I know you have grown fond of the boy but remember he is not one of us. We still do not know why he is here. I have spent time researching and speculating, but this particular incident has given me further insight."

"You believe him to be a threat?" asked Aeglas his expression carefully schooled.

Raphael did not miss the tiny incredulous hint in his voice and grew slightly exasperated with their naivety. "Do you believe him innocent? Perhaps you are both right. Perhaps he is just a little boy with something odd happening to him but would you gamble with the lives of our people, based upon this assumption?"

Tinnueth looked upset, but she nodded, understanding that Master Raphael felt responsible for their safety.

The magician sighed. "The boy believes what he tells us and appears at first glance to be a victim of circumstances, but whether he knows it or not, he is a threat to us."

"Master, how can you know that?"

"There are things that I know that you do no, and I cannot explain."

"Cannot Master or will not?" asked Aeglas.
"Will not, at least not yet."

****

Thomas groaned. His head ached horribly for a moment before the pain began to subside. He lay in a dark tunnel. Lights flickered on and off above his head. The roar of cars echoed at each end, their wheels rattling over the concrete slabs as they thundered on by. The underpass reeked of piss and rain; graffiti covered the walls lending it a menacing air.

"Are you alright?"

Thomas flinched. He hadn't heard anyone approach. He scrambled quickly to his feet, preparing to run but the man didn't move, he just stood and stared.

"Hey, you're that missing boy, the one from the TV. They showed your picture yesterday."

"What if I am?"

The man didn't understand. "The police are looking for you." He saw the boy's worried look. "But not in a bad way, I don't think you're in trouble or anything. It's just your parents miss you." He bent his head, concerned that the boy didn't react. "Don't you want to see them?"

Thomas sniffled and nodded.

"Look son whatever happened they will want to see you. Come on now, let me ring the police, they can come and pick you up. My house is just across this road."

Thomas backed off a little, worried that he'd met another creep.

The man held up his hands. "I won't touch you, and you don't even have to come with me, I'll just walk past and go home. You can wait outside my house if you like for the police to arrive."

They eyed each other up and then Thomas cautiously agreed. The man smiled encouragingly, walked past Thomas, keeping to one wall, and went out of the underpass.

Thomas waited a moment and then followed at a distance. True to his word, the man did not look back or do anything suspicious. He went inside a house with a red door, and that was it. Thomas sat on the wall and waited. Five minutes later, a police car roared up, and two police officers got out.

The police officer's com unit crackled. She picked it off her jerkin and spoke, "Bravo one, repeat that?"
"Delta four, we have found the boy."
"Confirm that Delta four, you have found Thomas Harvey?"
"Confirmed."
"Copy that, I'm with the parents now."
"Oh my god, Chris!" Lynn leapt into his arms. They hugged each other tightly, Lynn crying as Chris buried his head in her hair.
The police officer smiled and asked, "Bravo one, can you confirm the location of the boy?"
"Delta four, we are holding him at Langston Police station."
"Copy that, bringing the parents in."

Chapter 66

Glen and Cody

Glen opened the trailer door. Cody stood there looking bedraggled and strangely defeated.
"What happened? You just vanished. I searched everywhere," asked Glen.
His friend shrugged and pushed past.
"What the hell is going on?"
Cody turned. "If I tell you something, don't think I'm nuts ok?"
Glen looked amazed. Why would a conspiracy junkie worry what other people thought?
"Ok," he agreed.
Cody slumped to the floor and stared out into space. Glen sat down and waited. After what seemed like an eternity, his friend began as if admitting to some dark secret.
"My Grandma used to read this to me every night. It's supposed to be some sort of comforting prayer. *Now I lay me down to sleep. I pray the Lord my soul to keep, if I die before I wake, I pray the Lord my soul to take.* I never told her that it scared the shit out of me. I used to lie there after she had gone, clenching the bedclothes under my chin in terror, waiting for the angel of death to appear. He never did, of course. Eventually, I would drift off to sleep, but it wasn't peaceful. I often had nightmares. These are like those except different and worse."
"So, they are similar but different, and how come you keep vanishing, are you sleepwalking or something?"
Cody shook his head. "Yeah, yeah, I know how it sounds, it's a contradiction, but it's just how they are. When I am there, I'm sure they are real, as real as sitting here. In fact, in some ways, it feels as if this life is a dream."

Glen looked around. In his estimation, a tired rundown trailer, cluttered with old furniture and computer parts wasn't exactly the dream of the century.

"Honestly, this life isn't much of a dream." He felt slightly unfair for pointing this out.

"No, you don't get it."

Cody grimaced frustrated at his attempt to explain. He wasn't always good with words. "When I'm here, the dreams seem like a memory, not a dream at all."

"You mean like a memory of a dream?"

"No! A real memory. They make sense. They follow a logical pattern, even if they are weird. Normal dreams are all over the place. Sometimes you suddenly sprout wings or find yourself jumping about from one location to another, or people change becoming other people. That doesn't happen. If I walk down a road when I turn back, the road is still there. I don't suddenly find it's changed into a river or that the mountains behind it have moved."

"I see." Glen looked thoughtfully at his friend. "What makes them worse than your childhood nightmares?"

"This bit kinda freaks me out. I dream of the same place every time."

"Exactly the same place?"

Cody grimaced. "This is going to sound crazy."

Glen wisely kept his mouth shut. This would be worth listening to, but he began to wonder if his friend had suffered a mental breakdown.

"Well not exactly it's more of a continuation from where I left off the previous time, but not quite."

Glen struggled to understand. "Not quite, what's missing?"

"Time and space."

This didn't enlighten Glen any further. "Cody, you'll need to elaborate, what do you mean by time and space?"

"Well, time seems to have passed while I was awake." Now Glen looked even more confused, so Cody jumped in again. "The amount of time from when I woke up to when I fall asleep again has also passed in my dreams. Say, for example, I have been awake for twelve hours then it will be at least twelve hours later on in my dreams."

Glen understood. "That's a bit weird, are you sure? Is the time difference exactly the same?"

Cody shrugged but looked relieved that Glen seemed to be taking him at least a little seriously.

"I can't honestly say there's any definite evidence but if I fall asleep at night then its night where I dream, the same goes for, during the day, my dreams are in daylight. It's difficult to say how much time has elapsed, but there is a distinct pattern of day and night. Then as far as I can see, I have missed whatever has gone on during that time, and I pick up roughly where I left off."

He would have added, I think it's on another planet, but Glen would only doubt him further. As it was, his friend struggled to understand, let alone believe.

After some thought, Glen replied, "There's got to be some reason for this, some rational explanation? Dreams don't normally follow a pattern."

Cody sighed. "Well, at least you don't think I'm crazy."

"Well, no more than usual," his friend grinned. "But seriously you should see a doctor or something it could be medical."

"Oh, so you do think I'm going mad?"

Cody felt relieved he hadn't mentioned the tumbleweed creatures or government dream hacking. It would only make things worse.

Glen tried to reassure him but failed miserably. "No, I'm thinking more along the lines of a brain infection or something like that."

Cody stood up and waved his hands dramatically. "Oh, that's just great, now you think I have a brain tumour?"

"Well, probably not but you should get yourself checked out." Glen always remembered what his mum said. "Health is important if you don't have your health; you don't have anything."

Cody sat back down slightly mollified. "Look I don't want people thinking I'm a nut job ok?"

"Ok."

A thought passed across Glen's mind, this was the USA, not the UK, and in the land of the free, medicine wasn't.

"Err do you have any health insurance?"

Cody nodded and then reluctantly replied, "I make a bit of money from companies who pay me to test their systems, so I've been able to keep my subs up to date."

"Well then there's no excuse," Glen replied in his stern do as your told voice.

The wagging finger didn't exactly help, but it made Cody grin. It also ended the conversation. Glen lay back on the couch, and flicked on the morning news, pleased that his friend planned to seek help. As he and Cody watched the latest storms crossing the mid-west, Cody couldn't help feeling just like the weather, unsettled. Something lurked just around the corner, just out of sight and he had the impression that metaphorical dark clouds hovered on the horizon. Cody glanced across. Glen might be his friend, but he didn't really listen. How could Cody explain this without sounding like a paranoid tin foil hat wearer? Maybe he could find a biological reason for all this, some sort of hallucinogenic compound introduced into his system by a government agency. He had become an unwilling test subject, but he needed evidence. As Cody mulled over that idea, a solution flashed through his mind. He would need Sarah and her lab.

He decided to prepare for the worst. After sending a message to a trusted friend, he shut down his computers and grabbed his jacket. Without a word to Glen who dozed on the couch, he left.

Later as he drove down the highway, he rang Sarah on his mobile. "Hey Sarah," he began, but then the message kicked in.

Cody waited and then left a message. He had to get some help before they got to him, whoever they were.

"Look something's happening to me. I'm not sure quite what although I have some ideas, but it's not safe to talk over the phone. We need to speak face to face. I think you may be able to help me so I'll head over and wait for you to get home."

Chapter 67

Xenis

Xenis paced back and forth, feeling worried. The woman calling herself Karen had vanished right in front of him, just in his moment of triumph. Where did that leave him? Xenis sighed and considered his options. He had nothing but bad choices to make. Apparently, she had exceptional magic, strong enough to conceal her aura. She also used it to escape so instantly, so absolutely, that she could foil any attack both now and in the future. Now, what could he do? If he reported this to Valene, it could go either way.

On the one hand, he would bring back valuable information. On the other hand, he had lost his prisoner. It took little time to decide that either way, his sister would enjoy punishing him for this failure. Xenis would not give Valene that satisfaction.

For now, he should continue his search and say nothing. After all, they could not link Karen's disappearance to him, unless they searched his mind, which didn't seem likely. This, however, didn't address his problem. On the surface, the strange female didn't appear to be a threat. This Karen certainly didn't present herself as a ruthless leader bent on conquest, but that didn't consider her power. Yet she had managed to trick him. In one swift move, she had eluded capture even when she had appeared entirely vulnerable. This ability to conceal and use her magic troubled Xenis. Would she be able to hide an army or move without detection? He couldn't guess the extent of her powers, but he could hardly discuss this with any of his sisters. After losing a captive, they would dismiss that idea or worse mock his fears. In fact, they would do nothing, except punish him. So why bring up the subject? Overall, Xenis felt it best to keep quiet. It would indeed prove the safer option.

His mind finally made up, Xenis ran carefully, quietly and above all swiftly down through the interconnecting tunnels. Before long, he became aware of movement up ahead. To avoid any confrontation, he jumped gracefully up to the left and settled down on a small ledge overlooking the tunnel.

As he waited, the sound of footsteps grew closer. A group of heavily armed soldiers led by an armour-clad female appeared from around the corner. They stopped almost below him and looked around.

Zilva stood, head tilted, listening for a moment, and then motioning with two bound fingers, she cast a 'Seek and Find' spell.

"I know you are there," she whispered. "The spell does not lie."

Xenis shrank back into the alcove as he recognised the female. Damn she belonged to House Zhennu'Z'ress. Up until recently, House Zik'Keeshe had been their ally. With the desecration of the temple, they had broken that alliance and distanced themselves. Not that any of the houses got along that well, but some had more issues than others. A long history of political and sometimes physical struggle did not make good and reliable allies. Everyone was out for themselves. Well, it could have been worse. It could have been Vlos'Killian or Faerl'Zotreth. They would have taken delight in eliminating even a minor noble of House Zik'Keeshe. Here out in the Under Dark, they could give any excuse for his untimely demise, or he could just vanish without a trace. He knew that his departure from this world would not especially trouble his sisters. Their only issue would be the insult to House Zik'Keeshe. It would be that and that alone, which would prompt them to investigate. These thoughts had taken only a minute.

Below, waiting impatiently the female became annoyed. "Come forward," she commanded.

Xenis considered running, with luck he could get away. If he cast an 'Obscure' spell, it would cover his tracks, and they hadn't seen his house colours.

"I can sense your aura. I will know who defied my command," said Zilva.

Xenis relented and jumped down from the ledge. He eyed a perfect female, tall, dark purple eyes, full lips, long white hair tied back in a plat. He liked what he saw, and she could tell. Her eyes narrowed slightly in response, but she did not strike him. Perhaps he could charm his way out of this situation.

"What are you doing here?" demanded Zilva.

Xenis smiled and taking a step back bowed slightly. She seemed unimpressed by this show of courteous deference. In fact, he didn't intend to reveal any information. Instead, he planned to skirt around any delicate issues, and of course, whenever possible, he would lie.

He came up with the usual excuse. "I am on business for my house."

She considered him. "You were sent to this location? What did you find?"

Xenis shrugged apologetically. "Nothing as yet my lady," he replied.

Zilva seemed surprised by his direct response but appeared unwilling to let him go without more information. "What is your task?"

He tried to appear humble and respectful, not something, that came naturally. "Apologies my lady but I cannot divulge my task to you, in the same way, that you would not divulge your task to me."

Zilva appeared irritated by his reply but let it pass, snapping orders, she commanded her guards to scout ahead. "Do not think that I will forget your insolence. I will deal with *you* another time," the priestess threatened as she turned to follow her men.

Left alone in the tunnel, Xenis wondered what she found so urgent that she didn't deal with him now. Most females would have continued to press for further information, but she had not. This roused his suspicions. He needed to know more.

Unable to resist the temptation, he followed at what he hoped was an undetectable distance. It wasn't long before he realised that they closed on the exact spot where he had met that woman. Somewhat concerned, but driven by curiosity, a trait that occasionally caused more trouble than it was worth, Xenis decided to eavesdrop. He turned right and entered an adjacent tunnel, which ascended above the location. He knew a gap existed on one wall, which should allow him, with some effort, to overlook proceedings. It would require him to lie down on the floor and peer over the edge. He would need to be particularly careful. Sounds echoed and magnified down the chute. It would only alert them to his presence.

Xenis could hear the trickle of water in the background as he inched his face over the edge. Once he settled in the right position, he could just see the group. The female performed some sort of magic ritual, most probably an advanced 'Major Identification' spell. When Zilva completed the incantation, the red end of the spectrum flared in a particular pattern confirming his suspicions. Ordinarily, there would be an outline of the object above the floor, something to indicate who or what had been present. In this case, nothing appeared apart from an almost perfect representation of Xenis.

Zilva skirted the magic circle, viewing the figure from all angles. Something remained absent, another person perhaps. The shape appeared to be in a conversation, but the other aura seemed erased. That begged the question, who had obliterated the evidence? She had her suspicions. Zilva passed her hand over the edge casting a small 'Compare' spell, which matched the aura to someone she had seen recently. She began cursing with a foul string of words as she realised that the male she had just met, might hold the key.

"Find him!" snarled Zilva.

The guards obeyed her order immediately. They fanned out searching the nearby tunnels for their prey, but Xenis had gone. He continued to move quickly and silently away. Once out of hearing range, he began to sprint down a tunnel towards a vast narrow cavern formed for the most part by a river, which flowed at the bottom of a ravine. Along one side, a small ledge followed its path, but across the river lay an entrance into a rather unpleasant region. They didn't call it Cress d' Ulnen, the web of lies, for nothing. A set of tunnels some large, some small, carved for millennia by rock worms, arachnids, and the passage of water. Eerie and beautiful in many ways, its tall spires, and glistening rocks distracted the eye, but the path remained deadly underfoot. Holes and cracks covered by detritus could give way without warning. He would need to travel through this area if he wanted to avoid pursuit.

The ravine was relatively narrow at this point, but he knew if he used magic to bridge the gap, they could easily track his aura. Instead, he walked around the corner to lay a false trail and then ran back up the tunnel. Xenis stood at the top of the path, mentally preparing himself before he started to sprint, accelerating rapidly down towards the ravine. At the last moment, he gave a massive leap, landed on the other side, and rolled to his feet, his back against the wall. He smiled. That would slow them down for a while. They would need to come across and cast an 'Identification' spell to know that he had been there.

Xenis didn't gloat for long. Aware of his dangerous surroundings, he drew his swords and quickly disappeared down a small side tunnel into an area of Cress d' Ulnen known as The Warren. Few would travel this region alone. There were too many hidden dangers in the twisting tunnels and dead ends. Massive spiders, insects, and rats were in abundance along with other much more sinister creatures. Goblins, ogres, trolls, or orcs, however, weren't stupid enough to venture into this part of the Under Dark.

Xenis zigzagged through the myriad of tunnels, avoiding the worst areas. He slashed at the webs that hung like ropes from the ceiling, creating a path through the labyrinth. All the time, he listened to the chittering sound from the disturbed inhabitants. The best route took him parallel to the river. In fact, had Zilva known his location, she would have felt annoyed that he had passed so close.

When he finally exited The Warren, Xenis stood to the northeast side of the city. As guards often patrolled these corridors, they remained moderately safe, well safe apart from the presence of his kind. Vigilant, he jogged at a comfortable pace avoiding any patrols as he made it back to the city. At least now, he had something to report, something that didn't include that strange female that vanished. Instead, he could tell his sisters about Zilva from House Zhennu'Z'ress and the ritual she performed. He had searched the area, so that explained his aura. If one of his sisters cast the same spell at the same location, she would find the soldiers, the priestess from House Zhennu'Z'ress along with Xenis himself. That wouldn't look dubious at all. He smiled, pleased that he now had an acceptable solution as he sauntered casually back through the main gates.

Chapter 68

Adam

Adam screamed as he hit the wall. Every nerve burned. Every muscle cramped in agony. He lay panting, seeing spots before his eyes as he waited for the feeling to subside. When his vision cleared, the pain faded to a dull ache. Where was he this time? He looked up and tried to stand, but the world span. A wave of nausea hit him. Almost losing control, he lurched down the alleyway holding on to each wall as he struggled to keep upright. Vision blurred, mind reeling, he caught his foot and stumbled over a drain. The movement jarred his stomach, which gave way to mounting internal pressures. Almost immediately, he felt better, but the bile rose again, and he heaved. It left an unpleasant, acrid taste in his mouth. As he lent against the wall, he fervently wished that everything would go back to normal. How long could this go on? Each night another nightmare, each day another crisis, or like today, he found himself dirty and naked in an alleyway.

"Good thing you didn't barf on my turf!"

Adam jumped and turned with astonishing speed. Eyes peered out from under layers of cardboard and paper. What he had taken for a pile of rags and rubbish appeared to be a tramp. Adam wrinkled his nose and sniffed. Now that his nausea had passed, he could smell the unwashed human stench. He glowered and leaned forwards snarling. A strange sensation rippled across his body as if something attempted to get out.

The tramp took one look at the undulating muscles and shrank back into the pile of rubbish, wishing he could be somewhere else. "I spoke out of order. I meant nothing by that."

The man's voice quavered in fright, but Adam felt no pity, only contempt. "Give me your coat!"

"You want my coat?" The man looked confused, but he parted with the garment, anything to get rid of the nightmare standing in front of him.

Filthy and frayed at the edges, it covered Adam so that he could leave the alley without facing arrest for indecent exposure. In his current mood, he wouldn't have minded a tussle with the law. Yet it would cause more problems, something he didn't need right now.

In the early morning light, few people passed and those that did just ignored him. Along with his demeanour, the coat seemed to act as an effective camouflage device. People didn't want to see him, which felt good until he got to his apartment block. There it became a problem. He banged on the glass door, trying to attract the night security guard. The receptionists wouldn't be in for a few hours, and the guard simply ignored him, until Adam banged so hard on the safety glass that it flexed.

The guard glowered, sauntered over, and tapped gently on the window. "Break this, and you go to prison. Now move along and bother someone else."

He turned to walk away, but Adam wasn't going to put up with that shit. He managed with some effort to hold his temper as he tried to invent a story. An idea flashed into his mind, and he banged on the door.

The guard turned back. "Didn't you hear me? Fuck off before I call the police."

Adam smacked his hand on the window. "Listen to me, you fool!"

The guard stopped, slack-jawed, and stared. He blinked twice. No, it must have been his imagination. He'd seen fingernails and not claws.

"I woke up in an alleyway just now to find that I had been robbed of everything, and I mean everything literally. If that wasn't bad enough, I had to borrow this coat from a tramp, and now *you* are keeping me from my sixth-floor apartment."

The guard looked dubious but worried in case this dirty menacing person told the truth. Besides, he couldn't imagine anyone being brave enough to rob the horror in front of him.

Adam looked almost ready to explode. "Don't you recognise me? I'm Adam Turner!"

The night guard didn't get to see many residents, so he just shook his head apologetically.

Adam banged on the glass with his finger. "Go check the computer then!"

"Ah yes, I will, sorry, Sir."

Good, at least the guard called him Sir now, and that was only one step away from getting inside. Within a minute, the guard came back to unlock the door. "Sorry, Sir didn't realise Sir."

The guard now had a problem. Apparently, Mr Turner didn't have a key. He would have to call the building manager and explain, but how could he? This early in the morning, Mrs Peters would be in an awful mood, and he'd made a mistake. The guard started to tremble with anxiety. He could lose his job over this. Adam sensing his fear leaned closer and gave the man a way out.

"There's no need to call the building manager. The receptionist keeps a spare key at my request. It's in the locked draw below the computer. Give me the key, and I won't tell the building manager."

The guard sagged with relief. "Thank you, Sir, very grateful Sir."

Adam gave a regal nod as he left, which worked even though he looked like a tramp and smelt like a latrine.

Once in his apartment, Adam took a shower almost hot enough to burn his skin. He enjoyed the heat and only reluctantly stepped out knowing that if he didn't hurry, he would be late for work.

Without thinking, he shook himself like a dog. "What the fuck?"

He wondered if he'd lost his mind. Adam had another surprise when he got dressed, nothing fit. He flexed in the mirror. Lean as hell, his muscles not only bulged, they shone. Adam grinned. Never mind, he would have to wear his gym kit and grab a new suit on the way to work.

His stomach rumbled. Adam suddenly wanted meat. The intense feeling mounted as he locked his apartment, then driven by a sense of urgency, he broke into a jog and then into a run. Once at the train station, the crowds forced him to slow down. A train had recently arrived, and people surged from the station. Adam ignored them, pushing his way through the mass. Drawn by the strong smell of cooking, he didn't notice their looks of fear and anxiety. Adam found himself almost salivating at the thought of food. Luckily, when he entered the café, no one stood waiting at the counter. It wouldn't have mattered. He would have pushed them out of the way and jumped the queue. At the bar, a boy stood arranging the cookie stand. As he looked up, he stiffened in fear. A puzzled expression quickly crossed the boy's face as if he didn't understand his fright.

Adam broke the tense silence. "I'd like to order a rare bacon burger."

The boy gave a timid smile and took his order to the kitchen. After paying, Adam sat down and waited, tapping his foot with impatience. When the food arrived, he snatched the burger and gobbled it down in one mouthful. The juices ran down his chin and dripped onto the table as Adam devoured the hot bloody meat. After that, he ordered another and then another, until finally satisfied. Adam belched and wiped the food from his mouth before noticing that he had an audience. While the customers whispered to each other in disgust, the boy stood and stared at Adam in morbid fascination. Adam narrowed his eyes, irritated by the attention. The boy took one look and fled into the safety of the kitchen. In response, Adam stood up and threw down his napkin. As he glared around, suddenly everyone looked elsewhere. They kept their heads down and studiously tried to ignore him. He threw them a contemptuous glance and strode out of the café onto the platform. The information board informed him that the next train to work would be along shortly, so he waited.

As he stood, he noticed that people flowed around him like water around an iceberg. It seemed as if his personal space had expanded well beyond his body. It didn't bother him that they wanted to keep away, although he found their stares baffling. When the train pulled into the station, he jumped aboard and sat down. Adam didn't notice for a moment that everyone picked another carriage. Only when the others were full, they entered his. In the end, the carriage seemed to contain mostly women with a few men tucked at each end. As he looked around, Adam noticed the men kept their heads down, their eyes averted except for one man who looked at him in puzzled anger. The women, on the other hand, behaved oddly. Adam enjoyed a lot of female attention, but this seemed beyond what he would typically expect. Most glanced at him, unable to keep their eyes off his body. Others stared fixedly, trying to catch his eye, as he looked past. He felt distracted by their perfume. An overpowering clash of floral scents, mixed with the acrid aroma of unwashed fear from the angry man. Like a haughty king, Adam fixed his eyes on a single point and decided to ignore them all. When it came time to disembark, no one got in his way, and like a tiger moving through the jungle, everyone gave him a wide birth.

Work turned out to be no different. In his new suit, he sauntered through the main doors as if he owned the place.

The receptionists greeted him in tandem. "Morning, Adam."

"Good morning, ladies."

"Looking good today," called one.

A giggle caused him to turn, and he could see them whispering to each other. Not for the first time, he wondered why everyone acted so weird today. Adam bounded up the stairs and went into the office, where his friend waited for him.

John scowled and said, "Late again. Do I always have to cover for you? Luckily the boss isn't in yet."

Adam looked so shocked. He couldn't remember hearing a cross word from John, who must be one of the most amiable and laid-back people that he knew.

"Err sorry I needed a new suit, and I stopped off for food."

John relaxed, rubbed his face, and shook his head as he looked away. "Nah it's me. I dunno why I'm on edge today; it's not your fault." He sounded oddly weary.

Adam shrugged and let it pass. "It's ok, not to worry."

John smiled. "Come on, let's grab a coffee."

As they walked towards the canteen, they chatted about the new client. Everyone they met along the way acted as if they had bumped into either a celebrity or a serial killer. Mostly the women smiled and hoped to catch his eye, while the men glowered with fear and dislike.

Even John noticed and commented, clapping Adam on the shoulder. "Ah, the joys of fame, has the Lomax contract turned you into a celeb?"

"I don't know what's up with people today, but it's starting to get on my nerves."

When Adam got back to his desk, he sat down to rifle through the paperwork, answer his emails, and read the submissions from his team. He hadn't been working for long when Lilly came over and smiled. She leaned over the desk divider, provocatively and gave him a long, suggestive look, drawing her eyes up and down his body. Adam leaned back in this chair and responded with a lingering stare.

"What can I do for you?"

She blinked slowly then bit her lip and smiled. "Mm well, now let me think."

Adam grinned. "Nothing you shouldn't do?"

Lilly lent forward, revealing a plunging cleavage. "Nothing I wouldn't do," she said in a deep husky whisper.

A loud voice caused them both to jump. "Adam a word with you, and bring any submissions you have."

He could see Mr Hall waiting outside his office. Lilly gave Adam one last suggestive glance before flouncing off, obviously irritated by the interruption. Adam picked up his work and joined Mr Hall in his office. The desk acted as a barrier, which seemed to please Mr Hall. Adam realised that today his boss felt afraid of him, and strangely, he rather enjoyed it. He showed Mr Hall the work that his team produced. After all the arguing, it turned out to be quite good, and he did give credit to everyone.

When the interview ended, Mr Hall looked relieved. "Well done, glad to see you are on top of everything."

Adam couldn't resist looming forwards in an intimidating manner. "No problem Sir, I have everything under control."

Mr Hall's eyes widened slightly, and he gave a sickly grin. "That's good to hear."

As Adam strutted out of the office, he heard a small sigh of relief, which made him smile in malicious satisfaction. It must have been a rather nasty expression because Jack, who had been striding over in grim determination, stopped short.

"Taking all the credit again?" He managed to say.

What was their problem? This attitude had worn thin, so Adam stalked over and poked Jack's chest. "Back off, for your information, I gave credit where credit was due."

Jack looked apprehensive and recoiled as Adam pressed his point. "Now if you are unhappy with this, I can withdraw my goodwill and give you a really '*glowing*' report next time. It will be something that your children, should you have any, will remember, as they lie starving in the gutter. Do you want me to do that?"

Jack managed to squeak, "No."

Adam growled. "Well get lost then."

Jack turned tail and tripped over a waste paper bin as he scampered away, much to the amusement of the office. Adam surveyed his audience. They responded by ducking down behind their desk dividers in an attempt to convince him that they actually worked very hard. He smirked and dismissed them as insignificant, before strutting back to his desk.

Adam had almost completed his work when John sauntered over. He stared at Adam for a moment, looking perplexed as if something bothered him.

"Problem?"

John shook his head and shrugged, something about Adam put his teeth on edge today, but he didn't know what. "Are you ready for lunch?" he said.

"What time is it?" Adam leaned back in his chair, stretched, and yawned.

"Just gone 12.30pm."

"I'll just finish off here if I can stay awake." Adam rubbed his eyes, trying to keep his vision straight.

"Too tired for the party?"

Adam grinned, knowing that he couldn't get out of it, even if he wished to. He blinked and yawned again. "Nah, I'll be ok, but I could really do with a nap or several pots of coffee."

John laughed. "You're getting old, not man enough to take on Gemma?"

"Just you try stopping me."

Chapter 69

Ellen

Ellen woke on the couch. Why had she fallen asleep in front of the TV instead of going to bed? No wonder she'd had a strange dream. Yuk, even her mouth still tasted of the spicy goat. The news continued to revolve around one, or two stories interspersed with celebrity gossip. Today it endlessly covered the story about the missing boy found by a member of the public. Awash with pictures, the media covered every angle. The relieved parents, the overawed boy, the witnesses, repeated every half hour. The police still refused to answer questions as enquiries remained ongoing.

"Oh my god," she stretched and groaned as she wiggled her dead toes.

The pins and needles hurt like hell as the circulation gradually returned. Ellen sighed and glanced at the time. It remained dark outside, and another round of news started at 6.30am. At least she had time for that bath she meant to have earlier. Tonight, she would get a proper night's sleep in her bed and not in a chair. Ellen winced, as she stood up, still wobbly on her legs and wandered off towards the bathroom then suddenly stopped.

"Damn it." The phone conversation with Gemma suddenly resurfaced. How could she have forgotten the party? "No early night for me," she mumbled.

She would have to cat nap else she wouldn't last past 9pm. Ellen ran a bath then soaked in its luxurious warmth, the stiffness flowing out of her muscles. She started to feel almost normal and not like an eighty-year-old who had just hiked up a mountain. When she left at 7.30am, the rush hour had begun. Ellen considered the strange phrase 'rush hour.' In any city these days, it had become two hours or more. As usual, she sat in a long line of slow-moving cars. Ellen found it maddening that an elderly lady with two walking sticks could outdistance her in a few minutes.

People walked by, bikes and cyclists weaved through the traffic on either side of the car. Sometimes it felt like she played dodgems, but with more dire consequences. At times, Ellen hated the city. It seemed grey and dirty, even where the council had tried to brighten up the skyline by painting the high rises with bright, garish colours. Shame, it lacked trees and plants. They broke up straight lines and added a bit of natural colour. Ellen lived in the suburbs, but the drive reminded her of how lucky she was, after all, many people lived in those tenements, constantly surrounded by noise and traffic pollution. Perhaps they liked it, or perhaps they had to put up with it having nowhere else to go. Why did humans create monstrous environments in the pursuit of money? That was an easy one to answer because they didn't have to live there. A squeal of tyres broke Ellen's contemplation. She stamped on the breaks coming to a halt just shy of the car in front.

"Keep your mind on the road, Ellen," she murmured. A crash would really muck up her day.

As a senior member of staff, she had a parking space of her own. To one side sat Garret's large executive saloon. On the other, Alan's four-wheel drive, which looked as if it had more in common with a tank than a civilian form of transport. She could hardly open her door, and if she ever put on weight, she'd never get out.

At lunchtime, Ellen had about half an hour, so she just picked her favourite store. Make or break; she wouldn't go elsewhere. Ellen quickly rifled through the various racks. Her wardrobe already consisted of black and a little more in black with some grey for good measure. An easy colour to match and it went fine with jeans. Today, however, this wasn't going to be the case. The fashion went in for bright colours, but Ellen really couldn't see herself in some pink flowery number, so she picked the least hideous example. Outside the changing room sat the usual line of bored men, husbands, or boyfriends judging by their glazed looks. Their vacant stares or desperate twitches gave the game away.

One woman exited the changing rooms. "Darling?"

No one replied. The woman put her hands on her hips and started to tap her foot.

"Henry!"

One of the men, his eyes glazed over, suddenly jumped, now alert. "Sorry, dear, what did you want?" he said.

She gave a twirl. "How do I look in this?"

He committed *the* cardinal sin. "You look fine."

Ellen winced, *fine*, always the wrong thing to say, and men really didn't understand why. In her opinion, women want men to take an interest in clothes, which she considered a lost cause. From observation, Ellen determined that as long as a woman doesn't need a bag over her head, the average man didn't care. In contrast, after some positive feedback, a woman just wants to know whether she looks fat. All the man wants to do is get out of the shop as quickly as possible and watch football. It wasn't a great combination. Ellen nodded sagely to herself as she tried on a dress, which she decided even without male feedback looked unflattering. In the background, she could hear an age-old argument building.

"You never take an interest in me or anything I wear."

"Well, I like it if you do."

Another bad thing to say, it prolonged the shopping agony. Better to say: "I like that colour on you" or "I prefer the second outfit." Even if the man couldn't remember any outfit from start to finish. This will keep the shopping torture to a minimum, and the man will get home to watch TV.

It sounded as if the couple had developed a fully-fledged argument. Soon the shop assistant would have to intervene to avoid bloodshed. Ellen peeked out of the changing room. The woman flounced by tore off the clothes and got dressed. In the end, she threw the offending garments at the shop assistant, before storming out, the apologetic husband in tow. The shop assistant sighed and began to tidy up.

Ellen dared a quick word. "Err excuse me, do you have anything that isn't floral?"

The girl looked up. "Did you want an outfit for any particular occasion?"

Ellen shrugged. "I want to look sexy. I'm going to a party tonight."

The shop assistant rushed off to gather a selection.

Ellen tipped her head in consideration. "But I want something stylish as well!" she called.

The girl apparently had been out of hearing range. When the assistant came back, Ellen considered the choices and decided that sexy must equal short. Some of the skirts looked so tiny that she couldn't see any point in wearing them. Better to go out in new lingerie because let's face it, her underwear would show anyway. The tops didn't appear any better. They tried to show more cleavage than Ellen actually had. Some of them looked padded and underwired obviously trying to fool men into thinking that breasts existed where none was present. Ellen wondered if this worked *right* up until the time when the top came off. Then there might be a lot of explaining to do unless alcohol suppressed the man's judgement. Perhaps by the time, any man had got that far he didn't care.

Those thoughts must have shown because the shop assistant grimaced.

"I had something more mature in mind," said Ellen but judging from the look on the girl's face she took this as code for frumpy. Ellen sighed. "I mean, I want to look stylish, not cheap."

The girl looked affronted, perhaps like many women; she considered that less equalled more. In fact, Ellen thought it better to leave something to the imagination, the mind being far more inventive than reality.

"Well if you don't mind pink, there is something that might be ok," the shop assistant said.

"Well pink isn't exactly my favourite colour but I'll give it a go."

The shop assistant brought back a dress. Actually, it didn't look as bad as it sounded being more of a peach than a bright pink. It had little tucked sleeves and a slightly flared skirt. It also ended at the knees, which Ellen thought great. She tried it on, and fortunately, it fitted.

"You'll want some shoes to go with that too?" the girl enquired.

Ellen shrugged. "I guess so."

The assistant presented Ellen with a range of options, none of which looked comfortable. She groaned, why did society programme women to believe that sexy meant wearing shoes that had more in common with stilts than footwear? A few hours standing up and her feet would be in agony. She would be in less pain if a torturer slowly pulled out her toenails. In fact, it would probably come as a relief. If she picked the platform heals, by the end of the night, she would be walking barefoot, sexy shoes swinging by their straps as she carried them along with her handbag.

"Is there any chance of finding something without six-inch heels?"

The girls look said it all, ok so you want to look sexy then you must be prepared to suffer.

"Go on, you must have something else in size six."

The assistant just sighed and brought back a pair of flat ballet shoes. Bingo! Ellen tried them on and yes, thank goodness they fitted perfectly. "These look just right," she said then glanced at her phone and sighed, late already. "I'll take the lot. Could you wrap them up while I get dressed then I'll pay?"

The drive back to the office remained mercifully clear. Ellen quickly parked and sneaked in via a rarely used side door. Once in the office, she pretended to be busy. Best to stride along purposefully, carrying something as if on route to a pre-arranged meeting. It always worked.

Chapter 70

Cody

Cody found himself lying in the dirt. He groaned and struggled to sit up. It felt as if he had a stone sticking in his side.

"Oh, no."

This afternoon he sat in his truck outside Sarah's house, now he sat in the desert a world away. It looked as if he had a few hours of daylight left, so for now, he remained safe. With resigned acceptance, he rolled onto his knees, stood up, and brushed the dirt off his jeans. After that, he picked the nearest rock, jumped up and looked out across the inhospitable landscape. From this vantage point, he could see the arid desert stretching away in all directions but no road.

Cody groaned. Last time the cart travelled south. He turned, assuming the sunset in the west then he would need to run with the sun to his right. It would drop behind those mountains in the far distance. After scanning the horizon, he took his bearings then jumped off the rock and began to jog south. It wasn't easy. He had to semi concentrate on running over the rougher terrain and dodging through the sagebrush, but he couldn't stop his mind from ticking over.

Where did they plan to take that metal? They couldn't drag that cart forever, but a horse in this desert would be dead meat quickly and literally. Lack of water and the tumbleweed creatures made that impossible. At a guess, they wouldn't last more than a week in this heat. How long had it been? It took him a moment to realise that it had only been a few days. It seemed more like a month, so, supposing his assumptions were correct, sometime soon, they would leave the desert. They would need another form of transport. A horse and cart or even a boat seemed likely. If they could build trains, they wouldn't use a cart to collect metal. That begged the question, when and where would the men take it? Cody stumbled and caught himself. He just wanted to rest, but he knew that he couldn't do that yet. Salty drops of sweat trickled down his face stinging his eyes, but they made him feel more thirsty than annoyed.

As the sun dipped towards the mountains, the shadows began to lengthen. Cody saw a large weathered boulder not far ahead, so he jogged gently over and climbed to the top. As he rested, peering into the distance, he realised that he could see a swath of dark green. They looked like treetops, and that meant a valley. The men must be heading that way. He felt a surge of hope.

Cody jumped down and stumbled. Legs braced, he slithered down a steep sandy bank that ended in a deeply eroded dry riverbed. After a few minutes of fruitless scrambling, Cody gave up trying to climb the banks. They only crumbled beneath his feet and he slid unceremoniously back down. Cody shrugged; perhaps he should consider this good luck. It would be more straightforward and less prickly than weaving through the sagebrush.

The course ran straight as if carved out by swift running water. In the fading light, Cody made good time. The gently sloping riverbed gave him a limited view of the skyline over the mountains, but he began to see a spattering of dark clouds. That did not bode well, the rainclouds had that nasty bruised look, and he could feel the temperature dropping. The light had faded to a residual glow as the sun finally sank behind the mountains. In the dark trench, it became increasingly difficult to see.

Cody had slowed his pace to a walk when suddenly a sound caused him to stop and listen. Above him and to his right something rustled in the sagebrush. He turned, his heart thumping. A set of yellow almond eyes regarded him with curiosity before vanishing into the undergrowth. It reminded Cody that other creatures survived in this harsh environment. Still, the encounter made him feel vulnerable. His footsteps echoed loudly as the riverbed deepened into a miniature rocky gorge. Above him in the desert, he could hear more noise coming from other animals.

Without warning, the sound ceased, and then something with tentacles dropped onto his back. Cody screamed as it clung to his shoulder. He thrashed around, trying to knock it off, but its grip tightened. As he struggled, he slipped and fell on his side. A loud crack like breaking branches echoed down the gorge, but the creature hung on. Its other tendrils flailing around as it tried to latch onto bare skin. Cody fought. He didn't want to end up like the old man; a corpse sucked dry. He rolled over and grabbed a stone with his left hand. With all his might, he twisted around and hammered the woody exoskeleton flat against the ground. Even under this violent onslaught, it seemed reluctant to let go. When its grip slackened, Cody slipped out of his leather jacket and ran down the valley before more tumbleweed joined the hunt.

Ahead of him, the valley suddenly opened up. The dry riverbed ended in a dry waterfall. Dirt plummeted down the cliff as Cody skidded to a halt. With nowhere else to go, he turned and scrambled up the dusty gorge losing precious time as he fought his way to the top. Once there he ran along the cliff edge. Behind him, the mass movement raised large clouds of dust. On the uneven ground, exhausted and afraid Cody ran then stumbled, falling to his knees. It took every ounce of strength to get up and move. The rattling grew louder. Too late, he couldn't outrun them. As he teetered on the crumbling edge, he saw a distant pinprick of firelight. It must be the men's campsite, so close to answers and yet impossibly far away. He wanted to call out, but they would never hear. Cody turned to see a mass of writhing tendrils coming towards him out of the dust cloud. He looked down at the dark swirling water at the base of the cliff and made up his mind. He jumped.

Chapter 71

Thomas

Lynn could barely contain herself as they pulled into the police station car park. She tried the car door several times, but it didn't open, so Lynn complained loudly in frustration.
"Ma'am could you just wait a moment? I have to unlock it for you."
Lynn stopped and listened. When she heard a click, she threw the door open and ran, diving into the police station.
They stood and waited for her. "Your son is in the family room."
A police officer escorted Lynn and now Chris to the room. There sat Thomas, a little dirty, but well.
"Mum, Dad," Thomas yelled as he jumped up.
Lynn threw herself at her son and hugged him so tightly he could barely breathe. Chris looked at them solemnly then encircled them both in his arms.
They stayed in that embrace until Thomas squawked, "Mum, honestly, I'm alright."
Lynn let him go a little, brushed back his long hair, and kissed him gently.
Thomas looked at them both nervously. "You're not mad at me, are you?"
Both parents quickly denied it. "Why would we be mad at you, honey?"
"Because of all the trouble I've caused."
"You haven't done anything wrong."
Thomas looked at his dad and said in a small voice, "But I ran away."
Chris looked stricken. "No, it's my fault. I should never have been cross with you."

A slight hopeful smile appeared on his sons face. Chris couldn't help himself. He grabbed his son and held him fiercely, his eyes shining suspiciously bright. Lynn had never seen her husband cry before today. She hugged them both again, smiling and crying in relief. When they finally pulled away, both her son and her husband beamed brightly, something she had not seen in a long time.

Chris turned to the police officer and thanked her, and then he asked, "When can we take our son home?"

"We will need to ask him a few questions, and he will need to see the medical examiner before we can discharge him."

Chris nodded and turned back to his family. He stared at them and realised how lucky he was. He would remember this day for the rest of his life.

The policeman took Thomas into an interview room and sat with him while they waited for another officer and a social worker to attend. Thomas seemed a little nonplussed that his mum couldn't be with him, but then the officer explained that he needed to feel free to speak. They didn't want him to hold back for fear of upsetting his parents. He sat, shoulders hunched, his arms crossed, jiggling one foot. They were going to ask him questions, and that could be a problem.

The door opened. Another officer and social worker entered the room. Both women sat down, smiled at Thomas trying to reassure him, but from the look on his face; this didn't work.

"Thomas, we are just going to ask you a few questions about what happened."

Thomas nodded.

"Tell me what happened the day you went missing, starting at the beginning."

Thomas thought back. He ran through the day, the usual journey to school, and then the bullying. He didn't tell them the truth of what happened next; instead, he made up a story. "I hid in the toilets all day until home time."

"And no one noticed?"

Thomas shook his head.

The social worker looked sour. The school would be in trouble once that got out.

"Then, I walked home."

"Your mum didn't pick you up?"

Thomas shook his head.

The policeman nodded. That tied in with the late arrival of the mother.

"I took a long time and dad sounded mad at me for worrying mum."

Thomas stopped and looked anxious. He didn't want to get his dad into trouble. The social worker put her hand on his arm to reassure him, but Thomas pulled it away. For some reason, he didn't like this woman, and he sure didn't trust her. Something about her didn't add up, as if she wasn't particularly interested in what he had to say but had an agenda of her own.

She gave a waxy smile, but what came out of her mouth had the opposite effect. "It's important that you tell the truth, the whole truth and nothing but the truth."

The policewoman managed to stop herself from rolling her eyes. This would not get the boy to speak his mind.

Thomas glowered at the social worker. "Then I ran away because he was angry."

"Did he threaten to beat you?" she asked

"I don't remember," lied Thomas.

"Surely you'd remember something like that," she said sweetly.

Thomas shrugged. "I told you I don't remember." He added. "Some things are pretty foggy."

"Really?"

The policewoman stared pointedly at the social worker whose face turned sour, but she shut up. "Tell us what happened next Thomas."

Thomas told them about the park, about the creep and banging his head.

The police officers glanced at each other. The medical examiner could confirm any injuries. One of them pushed over a picture of Dylan Ellis.

"Is this the man that chased you in the park?"

Thomas nodded.

"What do you remember next?"

"I don't remember anything after that, not for days."

"Can you remember anything, anything at all?"

412

Thomas hazarded a guess. "It was dark."

"What's the next thing you remember?"

Thomas told them about running out into the road away from the creep.

"Was it the same man?"

"Yes."

"Do you remember how you escaped?"

Thomas didn't understand for a moment. Escaped, what did they mean by that, then he realised? They thought the man had kept him captive. He shook his head but asked, "Is he a bad person?"

They didn't reply, but from the looks on their faces, they thought so. Thomas felt better. He wasn't getting an innocent person into trouble.

The policeman thought it an odd question. Surely, the boy would know, but the mind worked in strange ways, perhaps he blotted out what happened.

"What happened next Thomas?"

He told them that a bike nearly hit him as he ran up the road towards the shops. There he hid in a dumpster behind a burger bar.

"I stayed there so long I fell asleep. When I woke up, it was cold and smelly. I wanted to go home, but I was afraid of the reporters outside my house, so I waited in the underpass for them to go. That's when the other man found me and phoned you."

That tallied with much they already knew. Yet something in the boy's expression made the police think Thomas had a secret either that or he suffered from a post-traumatic stress disorder.

"Thank you, Thomas, you've been very brave."

"Can I see my mum again?"

"Yes." They noted he only asked for his mum.

When Thomas had first arrived at the police station, a police officer had given him something else to wear and then taken his old clothes as evidence. Now, the police officer took him into the medical examiner's office.

The nurse smiled reassuringly and asked, "Now Thomas, I need to examine you from head to toe is that ok?"

He nodded warily.

"Could you put your clothes on that table and slip into this gown?"

Thomas sighed but undressed and slipped into an odd gown with a gap at the back. "Is this thing supposed to be like this?" he asked as he twisted around.

The nurse smiled. "Yes, it allows me to examine you while still giving you some privacy."

Thomas looked dubious. "Not much."

She smiled again. "Please lie on your front on the couch. I'll start at the top."

She touched him gently on his head and asked him if it hurt.

"Not much now."

The nurse spoke into a recording device. "Note old contusion on the back of the skull, partially healed, estimate time of blow around one week. Location and extent of the damage indicates a possible concussion."

"Does anywhere else hurt?"

"No, I just ache a bit."

She moved down his body. "Back of body shows no additional signs of trauma. Now don't be alarmed; this will tickle." She prodded his anus.

"Hey, watch it!"

"No signs of forced entry."

Thomas didn't like the sound of that.

The nurse continued with the examination, took a few swabs, and then asked him to turn over. She moved the gown, noting nothing amiss.

"Subject seems to be in fine health, except for the contusion."

"Is that it now?" he asked.

"Just one more thing to do."

She took out a syringe. "I'm going to take a sample of your blood if that's ok?"

He nodded.

"You'll just feel a little prick."

Thomas decided she lied. It hurt.

"Do you want a bit of cotton for the blood?" the nurse asked as she put the sample away, but when she turned back, the pinhole had gone. "Well, you heal quickly."

"Is that it?"

"Yes, you are free to go home once your parents have signed a few forms."

"Great!"

Thomas jumped off the couch and got dressed. They allowed him to wait in the family room for his parents to complete the paperwork.

The medical examiner spoke to both parents. "While your son seems in fine health, I am going to recommend that he sees a child psychologist. He's been through a lot, and it will take time for Thomas to readjust to normal life. There might be issues. He will need to discuss what happened with someone other than his parents."

They nodded and signed the paperwork, agreeing to the interview, the medical examination, and then the follow-up appointment.

Lynn hugged her son as they prepared to leave. Chris smiled and patted Thomas on the shoulder.

"Time to go home, son."

A police officer escorted them through the foyer and reassured them that the investigation would continue. When the officer opened the front door, a light blinded Thomas as a thousand cameras all flashed at once. People yelled and shouted questions, demanding answers as they surged forwards towards the family. Chris grabbed Thomas and Lynn. He held back the hordes of reporters as the trio tried to force their way towards the police car that waited to take them home. The din became unimaginable, unbelievable. A cacophony of sound that deafened Thomas as lights flashed all around. He flinched and ducked under his father's arm, afraid that he would fall as they jostled him unmercifully.

One reporter stood right in their path and jammed a microphone into his father's face. "Mr Harvey, Mr Harvey, do you feel vindicated?"

"No comment."

"Mr Harvey, will you sue the police for wrongful arrest?"

"No comment." Chris tried to push him out of the way, but the man refused to budge.

"How did you feel when they thought you murdered your own son?"

This time Chris couldn't ignore him. "Don't you mean when *you* accused me?"

Thomas looked up horrified.

"Mr Harvey, what do you think of the rumours that you orchestrated this fiasco to get sympathy and a promotion?"

"What the hell are you talking about?"

The reporter grinned; he'd heard about this guy's famous temper. Perhaps he'd get a story out of it.

Thomas couldn't stand his father's look of horror or the reporter's expression of gloating triumph.

"Get away from my dad," he screamed, thumping the reporter hard in the stomach. "He's done nothing wrong!"

The reporter stumbled back from the onslaught. Thomas might only be eleven, but he hit the man with all his might.

Chris grabbed him and hauled the struggling, spitting Thomas back. "You keep away from my family," he snarled at the reporter.

Lynn grabbed Thomas and yelled at the press. "How could you torture my son this way? Hasn't he been through enough?"

The family rushed through the parting crowd towards the police car, while the journalists continued to take pictures and yell. Once the vehicle sped out of sight, most of them relaxed and appeared quite happy. It wasn't the story they'd expected, but it would still look great on the front page.

Chapter 72

Adam

It wasn't particularly painful, just an irritating prodding sting that penetrated his sleep filled muzzy mind.
"It's alive."
"Are you sure?"
Prod.
"Yep it's breathing, can't you see?"
Prod, prod.
"It's not moving." The second speaker sounded unsure.
The first voice paused as if considering something. "It's sure dressed funny."
"Yeah."
After another pause, the first spoke, "I bet it won't move for a while."
"How come?"
The answer took a while to arrive, and when it did, it sounded like a wise sage imparting their deep insight. "I bet this is the one that hit the shield last night."
"Why? It looks human." The second speaker sounded dubious.
"Of course, it looks human now," the incredulous voice replied. "You should know that. Werewolves look human right up until the point when they don't."
Silence except for the slight sound of a foot twisting in the mud.
"What should we do now?"
"Dunno."
Prod.
"Can I have a go?"
A slight snigger followed a giggle from the first voice. This annoyed Adam. He didn't like people laughing at him, and it happened

too often these days. With a massive roar, he leapt to his feet. The two young boys shrieked. White with fear, the elder of the two inexpertly jabbed a spear in his direction, before dropping it and backing away. Adam raised his arms high and roared again. Their eyes widened in horror and with a wail like a foghorn, they turned tail and scurried back towards the village.

Adam stood and grinned, that showed those cheeky little beggars. It occurred to him that the boys would come back with adults. It felt too early to face an angry mob, so with a deep sigh, Adam turned and looked around. He stood close to the woodland edge, which lay just beyond the river. That bloody river, again, he would have to get wet, unless of course, he could jump its span. Behind him, he could already hear shouts coming from the village. The boys must have reached their elders. Adam broke into a run picking up as much speed as possible before he reached the bank. With an enormous leap, he jumped. Adam just missed the opposite bank and without any dignity plunged heavily into the water. Waves erupted out in all directions as he hit the bottom. Water sprayed up his nose and filled his ears, but Adam paid it no heed.

He pushed off, leapt out of the river, and rolled into the long grass on the bank. Across the other side, Adam could see the village guards running this way, but he knew he would be long gone before they arrived. With speed, he turned and thrust his way into the woodland trying to run as Faxon had demonstrated, with silent grace. It proved more difficult than it looked. It required observation, balance, knowledge, and above all, skill. It reminded him of those urban runners that jumped from building to building. Perhaps they were part werewolf. That thought stopped him cold. He stood shivering in the bright daylight remembering the night before. Had it really happened? He sensed that something had changed since meeting the witch. It had all started then, the strange dreams, the desperate lack of sleep and then last night in the full moon. He had become different. He had watched Hal, and his men transform on the shore, then later Faxon and his pack. They morphed from one state to another, but he also remembered Edric in that odd halfway stage. That's what they had meant by newly made, making the change, one of hers. The witch had done this to him. She had turned him, and he could hardly admit this to himself, he had become a werewolf. His mind baulked. He worked at a marketing company. That represented the real world, and yet when he came here, that life seemed like a strange and, to be honest, rather boring dream. Adam looked down as if seeking proof. He wore his regular clothes, albeit wet, so it must be true. Yet when he came here, this seemed like the real world, and home a dream. How did he know which one was real? Adam could only assume that her bite had started the transformation but before that? How and why had he come here in the first place? His mind whirled around in circles. In the end, Adam grew angry with himself. He could speculate forever, but one person might be able to help. By now, Faxon would have seen Adam disappear twice, once when he fell in the river and again when he fell asleep at the camp. That gave him an idea.

The pack must regularly use that campsite or another. If he found one and lit a fire, eventually someone would turn up. Adam closed his eyes and concentrated. Above the background smell of the forest, he caught the distinct smell of charred wood. Adam turned towards it and began to run. After a few minutes, he burst into a woodland glade, but it wasn't the same one as before. Still, it didn't matter because in the middle lay the charred remains of a fire.

As a child, Adam had been a proud member of the Explorers Club. Not that he would admit that to anyone. It just wasn't cool. It did mean, however, that he had some idea on how to start a fire. Some dry wood, tinder, and a spark. The wood, the leaves, and some bird feathers he found easily enough but the spark. What could he use?

At a loss, he began searching through his semi-dry clothes, but they contained nothing more than a ballpoint pen and a set of keys, which considering his plunge into the river, he had been lucky not to lose. Adam pursed his lips as he scanned the glade, but when nothing came to mind, he slumped down and put his arms around his knees.

As Adam sat there thinking, he noticed light glinting off his watch. It had a glass cover and glass equalled a lens. He could use the lens, assuming he could get it off without breaking it. It took him a few minutes to get the back off using the pen as a screwdriver and then prize the workings lose with his nail, before pushing hard on the outer glass. To his relief, it popped out in one piece. After kneeling down, Adam carefully picked up the cover and held it in the air about a foot away from the tinder. He twisted it, so that it acted as a lens, concentrating the sun's rays to form a single small hot spot. A few minutes later, Adam blew gently, and a tiny flame erupted around the feathers. He cupped it in his hands, feeding dry leaves onto the small but growing fire. The smoke rose high into the sky. While he waited, he hung his clothes on a branch to dry.

A little later, as he dressed, he heard a noise. Adam sniffed the air. He hadn't felt that strange sensation, so it wasn't the witch, it smelled like a man.

As the newcomer stepped cautiously out of the woodland, he stared at Adam through a bushy mop of brown hair then said, "Who are you?"

"Adam, who are you?"

"Oswald. Which pack do you belong to?"

"I'm a friend of Faxon's," said Adam.

Oswald sniffed the air. "You don't smell like him." His dark eyes narrowed. "You're not one of Hals pack either."

"That's also true." Adam could guess what would come next.

"Who do you belong to?"

Adam hesitated.

Oswald sniffed again then growled and spat. "You're hers!" He looked around wildly and hissed, "Is this a trick?"

Adam backed away. "No trick! Faxon saved me."

"That's a lie. This is a trap!"

With one quick motion, the man threw himself towards Adam, who dodged just in time. He turned back and grabbed Adam, tackling him to the floor. As they fought, Oswald began to change. His face became more elongate, his teeth transformed into jaws. The half-wolf thing lay snarling and snapping on top of Adam, who kept his arms braced across its throat. It took all his strength to move his knee upwards, underneath the wolf. Once in position, he kicked. The fully transformed werewolf yelped as Adam catapulted it through the air, but his success proved short-lived. The werewolf quickly recovered and jumped towards Adam as he tried to stand. The momentum sent Adam reeling backwards onto the edge of the fire. A lance of searing pain shot through his hand, and he rolled away, trying to stand. The wolf didn't give him a chance. It leapt again, slamming Adam hard against a tree trunk.

Lilly heard an odd noise, almost like a popping sound but backwards, except that she never had time to think about it because of the massive crash. Yelps echoed across the office as people jumped in surprise, but their shock quickly turned into derision. Adam lay on the floor surrounded by a mass of office debris. Some of the women ran over to see if he was all right, but the men reacted differently. Their laughter and ridicule echoed throughout the office.

"Hey did I hear you scream like a little girl?"
"Nah it's just his balls haven't dropped yet."
"Been missing your beauty sleep?"
"That won't do any good; he's well past it."
"You look a mess have you been sleeping in your clothes again?"
"Thanks for your encouragement and support. I see office humour doesn't have to be funny," Adam replied sarcastically, rubbing the back of his head. He wasn't particularly hurt, but their comments injured his pride.

Drawn out of his office by the commotion, the boss yelled, "Come on now, this isn't a circus, we have work to do people."

He nodded towards Adam, "My office now."

Adam slouched after him. Odd, how he didn't remember going to sleep. Usually, he felt so full of energy that other people had trouble keeping up.

For once, his boss closed the door and then sat down. He stared at Adam for a while as he leaned back in his chair. Adam tensed ready for a fight, but Mr Hall quietly sighed.

"Look you're not a fool even though recently you've acted like one. You know it's not right to fall asleep at work. As one of my best employees, you're setting a bad example."

Adam nodded dumbly. He'd expected a rant, and in the old days, Mr Hall would have torn a strip off him. This concern left him feeling deflated.

"I will let it pass this once, but if this happens again, you will receive a written warning. Also, I would personally suggest that if this continues to be a problem that you seek medical advice."

Adam smiled weakly. "Thanks, it won't happen again."

His boss nodded. "I hope not. You've been one of my high flyers, so I don't want to see you crash and burn but in the end that's up to you. There are plenty of people out there who would give their right arm for a chance like this."

He waved Adam away and returned to his work. Adam closed the door to find most of the staff staring at him. He felt annoyed and stared back unblinking, hands in his pockets. This phased most of them but still one or two smirked.

"I'll remember you," he muttered under his breath.

Adam returned to his desk, picked up his chair and slumped onto it, the mess still scattered at his feet. He sat staring at his hands, wondering what to do. Dark dreams of living as a werewolf in another world would get him securely locked away. It wasn't real. It had to be all in his head, but then he noticed something. His watch was missing.

Chapter 73

Ellen and Brennan

A babble of voices woke Ellen from a restless sleep.
"I tell you she's gone!"
"Are you sure?"
"Yes, I checked; she's not in the hut, she's nowhere in the village, just vanished like the spy she is."
There followed murmurs of agreement.
Oh dear, thought Ellen here we go again, more fun accusations even though I'm still here!
"We should have put her down in the pit; she couldn't escape then."
Ellen stood up and pushed the wooden door open. Bright sunlight illuminated the dark interior of the hut. As her eyes adjusted to the light, she could see villagers clustered around Master Brennan. With him stood Nolan who gestured violently towards the building, his spear punctuating each word with a stab.
Ellen stepped out and addressed the crowd. "Sorry is there a problem?"
All eyes turned towards her in stunned silence. The guard stood still, his mouth slightly open, but his expression quickly changed from surprise to irritation.
Master Brennan turned to him. "Missing, is she?"
Many in the crowd just rolled their eyes and shook their heads in feigned disgust.
"Tsk damned guards." One snorted.
"He must be blind, just like Boden," commented another.
"Aye, there's a plague of blind fools spreading through the village."
"Is it catching?"
"Ha! You'll be next."

423

The crowd laughed at the banter, whereas Master Brennan simply shook his head and sighed. "Well, Nolan, as you can see our guest, hasn't run off."

Ellen preferred the term guest to prisoner. It conferred innocence and freedom, a definite improvement, but Nolan scowled unwilling to concede the point.

"Doesn't mean she's not a spy," he said.

"Perhaps or perhaps not."

The old man also seemed unwilling to let Nolan win. He fixed him with a sharp stare before Nolan finally broke and looked away.

"Don't you have jobs to do?" Master Brennan dismissively waved his hands at the crowd.

"Yeah, I have things to do," said Nolan and stomped off.

Master Brennan sighed, shook his head, and watched as the crowd dispersed. "He will not let that drop me thinks," he said.

Ellen shrugged and smiled in a disarming way. "I would sympathise if he didn't want to drop me down the pit."

Master Brennan raised a questioning eyebrow.

"Well, from his point of view, I turned up at the same time as a monster and then keep disappearing," she said.

"Do you keep disappearing?" his sudden piercing gaze made her drop eye contact.

"I'm not quite sure. I do dream when I am asleep and, in those dreams, I'm not here."

He relaxed and laughed. "Well dreaming isn't a crime, and we all do it from time to time. Just before this fiasco, we had a village meeting, and the elders discussed your situation. We have decided to let you out of the hut as long as you have guards."

Ellen nodded glad not to be stuck in the cramped hut that clearly doubled as their jail.

"Golof has offered to guard you although we need another volunteer."

"I offer my services," a voice called out.

They turned to see a man striding towards the small gathering. Master Brennan turned surprised at the offer and said, "Boden?"

"Yes, I wish to make amends for my earlier doubts. If the elders decided to free her, then I will accept their decision." He smiled and gave a small bow to Ellen. "Apologies lady, for my previous behaviour. I hope you can forgive me."

Ellen felt surprised and, in her heart, secretly sceptical, but decided that she should give him the benefit of the doubt. She nodded her acquiescence and gave a timid smile, wondering all the time whether she'd made a wise or foolish decision.

"With your permission Master Brennan, I would like to show our guest around the village and fields where we work."

Boden turned to Ellen. "If you find that agreeable?"

Ellen nodded.

Master Brennan also agreed. "Alright but don't take her too far out of the village confines."

"Agreed." Boden nodded amiably.

Golof gently took Ellen's arm, giving Boden a slight mistrustful glance before looking back at Ellen.

"We could show you the great hall and introduce you to some of the villagers, also something of our everyday life in the fields and waterways of our community."

He guided Ellen around the village with Boden in tow. Each set of people she met nodded and greeted her, although some had apparent reservations. They evidently came from a society where individuals did not easily trust outsiders, but she had some sympathy. After all, she had met the monster as well.

The villager's clothes looked very similar to each other, except that the women wore long tunic tops covering their baggy trousers. They sported patterns with muted colours of brown, green, yellow, and orange. Good colours, Ellen noted for blending into the landscape. Overall, their tasks seemed evenly distributed. Both men and women wove cloth, worked wood and iron, guarded the town, or toiled in the fields. They apprenticed children to each task, although some adolescents looked after the young. Women nursed babies at their breasts while older citizens cooked. Others sat nearby whittling tools and occasionally toys from wood. She commented to Golof about this as they walked along the river's edge.

He smiled. "Apart from babies, we mostly share the tasks according to ability. We find it necessary to work together to forge our lives. If we didn't, the enemy would soon destroy us."

Ellen wondered if she dared ask anything about this enemy and this must have shown on her face.

He stopped and smiled. "I find your lack of knowledge about them interesting, and it is to me an indication that you are innocent. However, if they wiped your mind, you would appear to be as you are, but underneath, somehow, you'd remain their pawn. A single event could cause you to activate and wreak havoc. Nonetheless, your captivity will not be for long. Master Brennan and his apprentice Connery have almost completed their task. A reliable test will soon be available."

He used that word captive again thought Ellen. She wished they would drop that in favour of guest. A young boy interrupted her next question. He ran up and waved at Golof.

"You're wanted in the village."

"Did they say what they wanted Ewell?"

The boy shook his head. "They didn't."

Golof nodded and turned to Boden. "Look after her for a few moments. I won't be long."

As Golof walked away with the boy, Boden suggested that he take Ellen to look at the fishery.

"We eat some of our chickens when they don't lay eggs, and we also hunt, but mostly the village relies upon fish. We have nets set up along the river's edge, which we empty daily. Shall we see if there are any fish today?"

They strolled up to a large bend in the river, its bank high above the water level. Below, at the river's edge, Ellen could see a series of semi-oval nets pegged into the soil. In the middle, a pier jutted out into the river. It had several small boats tied to each post.

Boden looked over the bank. "There's a few fish caught in the nets just beyond the pier. Shall we take them out?"

He must have had better sight than Ellen had because she couldn't see anything, but she walked down towards the nets anyway.

Boden pointed. "I'll grab a basket if you hook them out."

He turned away as if to pick something up. When Ellen bent over the nets to see the fish, someone put a bag over her head and grasped it tightly against her mouth. Ellen struggled violently as he pulled her back across the soft muddy ground. Her left elbow connected with soft flesh. She heard a grunt, and then someone sniggered softly.

"She's a hellcat for sure."

"Well, help me then, I need to tie her up."

Her attacker groaned trying to hold onto her as she gave him a swift kick in the shins. Ellen knew the voice belonged to Boden. So much for trusting him, she should have trusted her instincts instead.

"I'll get the ropes." This voice sounded familiar too.

Fear flashed through her veins. Ellen tried to scream, but he'd pulled the bag too tightly over her head. The lack of oxygen made her feel dizzy. If she blacked out, they could do what they wanted with her. Panic strengthened her resolve. Ellen kicked back hard and twisted. Boden shifted position to catch her, his hand sliding slightly off her mouth. She took that opportunity to bite down hard. He yelped and swore, letting go for a moment. Ellen stumbled forwards trying to tear off the bag and scream, but a heavy weight hit her from behind.

"Quiet you, idiot! Do you want the whole village to know we are here?"

"Sorry, Nolan."

Nolan muttered something under his breath about bloody fools as he held the struggling Ellen down.

"Tie her up while I hold her. Hurry Golof will soon be back," He said and indicated the ropes to Boden.

Boden quickly tied a cord around her hands and feet, then used another piece as a gag over the bag. Ellen almost passed out as they grabbed hold of her shoulders and feet, lifted, and then let go. When she landed heavily on a wooden surface, she realised that they had put her in a boat.

A voice whispered in her ear, "We are just trying to get rid of you. It won't be *our* fault if the rapids claim your life." Then he raised his voice, "Now for one last thing, Boden untie the boat."

Ellen heard a grumble followed by a thump as a body hit the ground.

Someone came over, put their face close to her ear, and whispered, "Oh, and you knocked Boden out when you escaped, how clever of you."

Nolan laughed softly and kicked the boat out into the river. It juddered and spun, picking up pace rapidly as it headed downstream.

Ellen lay trying to focus her muzzy mind as the boat rocked and whirled. Boden had bound her hands behind her back, but fortunately, he hadn't tied them very well. After wiggling around, she loosened the rope but not enough to break free. If she could just get her wrists under her legs and to the front, she would stand a chance. Ellen curled up in a ball and tried to inch her hands gradually down her back. Seconds of agony passed as the rope dug into her skin before it slipped free. Desperate for air, her deadened fingers worked on the gag then finally Ellen hooked off the bag. She lay panting, giddy with relief but then a jolt spun the boat around. She sat up and tackled the knot around her wrists with her teeth. Once free, her aching blotchy hands began to tear at the ropes around her feet.

The boat rocked, and Ellen peered over the side. Ahead, a mass of churning white water foamed against the banks. White with fear, she leaned forward gripping both sides of the boat. With no oars, no way to steer, Ellen felt helpless. She had no option but to hang on tight and hope to survive. Feet braced against the keel, back against the seat, her hands gripped each side as she tried to balance the load. The craft whirled and bucked wildly to one side then suddenly the boat tipped down as it plunged over a ledge. Ellen screamed now certain that the craft would sink, but it bobbed back up. The water raged around her, tipping and spinning the craft so that she travelled backwards down the river. A terrible graunching sound reverberated down the hull. The boat bounced sideways. Ellen whimpered. She could feel the keel scraping and crunching as it grazed against passing rocks. In the bottom of the boat, the pool of water grew deeper. As she hung on with one hand, she grabbed the bag and started to bail. Half the water ended back in the boat, but it worked enough to keep her afloat. She bailed frantically not noticing that the roar began to fade as the current propelled her out into a deep blue lake.

When Ellen finally looked up and saw the rippling surface, she sighed. She had survived, but the elation quickly subsided when she looked back at the rapidly receding shoreline. With arms and legs like jelly, Ellen couldn't swim so she continued to bail, occasionally dipping her hand over one side trying to scull towards land. After a while, she abandoned that in favour of merely keeping the boat afloat but no matter how much she bailed, it looked like a losing battle. Water sloshed around her calves as the boat wallowed in the lake and then without warning, it sank gracelessly to the bottom. It became the most anticlimactic wreck in history. It left her stranded on the shores of an island with the water lapping just above her knees.

Chapter 74

Lars and Stefan

It had been such a long day. Lars had returned not long after sunrise, dressed in yet another strange outfit. Again, he clutched a bag of food and drink. Lars also used his newfound knowledge to treat Stefan's wound. It had begun to fester, so he cleaned it thoroughly with the disinfectant.

Stefan winced and cursed, "Holy shit that hurts, you sure that's going to help?"

"Oh, stop being such a big baby."

Stefan glowered at his friend. "You try some then."

"Sure." Lars put the bottle up to his mouth, pretending to take a swig.

Stefan jolted his friend's hand. "Drink up."

The disinfectant sloshed into Lars' mouth. He coughed, spluttered, and spat it out. "Yuk, that's revolting."

"Now you know how I feel," Stefan said with satisfaction.

They hitched up, turned off the road at the cairn, and travelled over the rough terrain following their old track. Sand had filled in the ruts, but enough remained for them to see where they were going.

The hot, dry air, had taken on a close touch, making it intolerable. The sweat poured off the men as they toiled between the scrubby bushes. Each step became slower than the last until they finally reached a standstill, stuck on a particularly rough piece of ground. Both men felt exhausted and at the end of their tether. Lars went around the front of the cart to pull as Stefan rocked the side, but the wheels remained thoroughly wedged.

"Look we're working at cross purposes; you push when I pull ok?" said Lars.

Stefan ignored him and rocked the cart again. "That won't help."

"Why not?"

"We've got bogged down in the sand. We should shake it free."

Lars ignored him, knelt down, and started to reach under the front right wheel. "No, I think there's also a rock wedged down here."

"Don't listen then."

"I don't see why I always have to do what you say."

Stefan exploded. "You gotta be kidding. This was your idea in the first place."

"Yeah, and it's a good idea."

"So, I'm just the big dumb ox that follows you around."

"Hey, I never said that."

"I've had enough."

Stefan went around to the back of the cart and gave one almighty push just as Lars removed a stone from under the front right wheel. It surged forward narrowly missing his friends head.

Lars yelped. He stood up and almost snarled at Stefan for being so careless, but the look on Stefan's face made him stop. Never had he seen his friend this close to breaking, so with unusual wisdom, he kept his mouth shut.

The two men silently hooked up again and moved off. When they finally cleared a thick patch of scrub and saw treetops on the opposite mountainside, both men heaved a great sigh of relief. They could see the winch not far away but manoeuvring the heavy load into position proved difficult. It had a momentum all of its own. At one-point Lars almost panicked when he thought they would push it over the edge, so he quickly unhitched, and they tried a different tactic. In the end, neither men could be bothered. They were near enough, so they decided to finish unloading tomorrow. It wasn't as if the metal could just walk off by itself, besides they needed their remaining strength for the descent.

Stefan went first. Lars tied the end of the rope to the stake and took the strain. After wedging a rock under each wheel, he also cheekily wrapped the line around the cart. It looked heavy enough to help. Stefan leaned out, rope looped around his waist, his back facing towards the ground and gradually walked down the cliff. The knotting technique seemed to work quite well, so after lowering the necessary supplies. Lars did the same.

As he descended, Lars felt the temperature change. What a difference. The icy river and green vegetation seemed to swallow the desert heat. Now back at base camp, Lars and Stefan could feel the fresh, damp, air as it funnelled down the valley. They stood for a moment; their eyes closed. The refreshing breeze feathered their skin, a truly wonderful sensation after the dust and grime of the plateau. Both men then had the same thought at the same time. On this side of the river, the landslide had created a shallow ledge. They grinned and rushed to the water's edge. After drinking deeply, they stripped off and waded in. The cold shock on their hot flesh, felt like bliss, pure bliss.

After a quick wash, Lars started to shiver, so he waded back to dry land. Stefan, however, chose to stay a while longer. As Lars watched his friend wallow in the water, he decided he wanted fresh clothes, so he slid on his boots and walked over to where they had hidden their stores. The tarpaulin, blankets and warm clothes so needed for the valley, just became an unnecessary encumbrance on the plateau. After some rummaging around, Lars pulled out the spare clothes and got dressed. Stefan however still wallowed in the cold water.

"Hey, are you planning on becoming part fish?"

"Yep." Stefan didn't move. He felt literally chilled out.

"Good, then I can eat you for dinner."

"Dinner!"

Stefan's stomach growled at the mere mention of food. They didn't have any stores, but if he checked the nets, they might have dinner. Stefan waded out galvanised by the thought of a full stomach and donned clean clothes. While he checked the fish traps, Lars lit the fire and unpacked the pots and pans. Before long, a delicious smell of roast trout filled the evening air.

As he tended the dinner, a rumble caused Lars to turn and laugh. "You really are starving!"

Stefan looked up. "That wasn't me. I think I heard thunder, but I didn't see a flash of light."

Lars sighed and looked at the meal. "Let's get the tarp out and the poles ready then as soon as we've eaten, we should set up the tent."

Stefan looked dubious. "Do you think we should leave it that long?"

"You want a burnt dinner?"

"No, but I don't want it soaking wet either."

In the end, Lars just took the fish and put it in bowls before banking down the fire. Better to eat cold fish than soaked fish.

It didn't take long to set up the tent around the campfire. The Hazelwood posts sprung neatly into place in their old holes before they tied them at the highest point. Next, they threw the tarp over the top and staked it to the ground before Lars chucked their supplies inside. They could tidy up after eating.

As it turned out, the fish remained warm enough to enjoy, but as both men sat eating their dinner in front of the fire, they felt the wind increase, battering the sides of the tent. The light had already dimmed to nothing. In the distance, an occasional flash followed a low rumble.

"Sounds like it's coming this way."

Stefan nodded as if distracted. He had been peering out of the tent, off into the distance. "I thought I saw something move on the opposite side of the river."

"Wargs?"

"I don't know."

"Have you set up the barrier yet?"

"Like when did I have a chance?"

"Good point better do it soon though."

They both ate quickly, crunching down the little bones. Afterwards, as they washed their hands and dishes, the first big raindrops began to fall. A flash of lightning followed by a crack of thunder announced the storm's arrival.

Stefan cocked his head. "Did you hear that?"

"Yeah, it's about to piss it down!"

"No, I could have sworn I heard a yell."

Lars looked dubious. "Over that noise?"

"Yeah, can you grab the lantern, I want to check the bridge and set the barrier."

Lars nodded and raced back to the tent. As Stefan stood outside waiting, he peered into the gathering gloom. After all those days in the dry desert, he wasn't going to let a little rain trouble him; in fact, it felt welcome. With one exception, he knew, it wasn't likely to be just a little. They'd set the campsite high above the river, but even so, a massive flood could cause trouble.

Seconds later Lars joined him holding the storm lantern. "Hold it up for me a moment."

Stefan held the lamp, while Lars shuttered it against the wind. As his friend scampered back to the tent, Stefan turned and made his way down to the bridge. A bright flash of light wrecked his night sight, but for an instant, he could have sworn he saw a figure making its way across the trunk.

He called out, "Anyone there?"

After a pause, a trembling female voice replied, its words indistinct against the rising wind and rain.

"Who's there?"

She replied again this time a little louder, but he couldn't understand what she said. He held the lantern high and saw her turn to look at something behind her.

"Come, come," he yelled beckoning. "We have a campfire."

She scrambled across the bridge, stumbling as her pale and ungainly clothes caught on every twig. Stefan started to worry. The storm must be fierce upriver. He could see the water rising rapidly up the riverbank.

"We'll both drown if you don't hurry."

He saw her glance behind again, her red hair glinting in the lamplight. When she turned back, a dark shape emerged from the gloom and leapt. Stefan yelled as the warg hit the woman with a crunch. The tree bridge rocked under the impact. Time stood still. Both woman and warg seemed to hover for a second before they crashed through the supporting branches into the churning water below. In the lamplight, Stefan saw a brief swirl of white and then nothing.

He turned. "Lars!" he yelled, running along the bank. "Lars!"

Lars peered out of the tent. "What?"

"Help me!"

Lars dashed into the night's rain, skidding down the slope towards Stefan's running stumbling outline as he searched the water's edge.

"What's wrong?"

"A warg knocked her into the water."

Lars looked confused. "Her?"

"The movement, it was a girl!"

Lars twigged. "She's in the water?"

"Yes," Stefan's voice rose in frantic desperation. "But we might be able to save her!"

Lars didn't contradict his friend, but he doubted they could do anything now. The fast-flowing river had risen quickly between the banks. It could easily wash both of them away. Besides, they had come to the end of the landslide, and with that, his hope died. Yet as the lightning flashed overhead, he spotted something white.

Lars yelled, "There!"

"Where?"

"Give me the lantern."

Lars raised it high. "There under the tree stump!"

Both men slithered through the mud towards a broken tree trunk. Sure enough, they saw a body pinned beneath the water. Stefan threw caution to the wind and waded into the river. Lars held the lamp high, afraid that he would lose his friend in the strong swirling current.

Stefan grabbed a broken branch. "Help me get her out!"

Lars dumped the lantern on the ground and waded in to help. They struggled in the dim light. Stefan heaved, his muscles bulging as he strained to lift the stump. The tree tilted and began to rise out of the water. Lars reached underneath and tried to pull the body free, but the wet skin slipped in his muddy grip.

"I can't get her out, lift higher," he yelled.

Stefan grabbed both sides of the stump, bent his knees, braced himself, and yelling a war cry, lifted it partly out of the water. Lars ducked under, grabbed some cloth, and pulled. The body sprang free. He staggered backwards, dragging his heavy burden up the ledge, just as Stefan dropped the stump. Seconds later, a wave of water hit the broken tree hurling it downriver. Almost washed away by the powerful surge, both men struggled to stay upright. Lars teetered on the river's edge, holding defiantly onto the body while Stefan held onto his friend's belt. They strained and slipped as Stefan began to haul both Lars and his burden out of the water. When they flopped exhausted onto the muddy bank, Lars stared at him, and then at the body.

Above the wind and the rain, he shouted, "I thought you said it was a girl."

Continued in Book 2
Gather Shadows

Glossary

Drow House Names (phonetic pronunciation, translation) and House Colours

Bel'La'Thalack = Bel La Thar Lack: Holy Battle – Burgundy and brown

Faerl'Zotreth = Fay Al Zot Reth: Magical Strike – Recently demoted from the Council of Five – Yellow and metallic black

Fashka'D'Yorn = Fash Car De Yawn: Force of Will – A member of the Council of Five -White and cyan.

Har'Luth'Jal = Har Looth Jal: Subjugate All - Orange and cream

Mith'Barra = Myth Ba Rah: Grey Shadow – The Ruling House – Silver and pale blue

Renor'Zalisto = Ren Or Zal Ist O: Black as Night –Navy blue and dark grey

Sarnor'Velve = Sar Nor Vel Vay: Swift Blade – A member of the Council of Five – Bright green and silver

Velkyn'Zhaunil = Vel Kin Zaw Nil: Hidden Knowledge – Purple and yellow

Venorik'Sarg = Ven Or Ik Sarg: Silent Valour - Teal green and magenta

Vlos'Killian = V Loss Kill E An: Blood sword – The ancient enemy of House Zik'Keeshe – Red, and gold

Zhennu'Z'ress = Zen Nu Za Ress: Great Power – A member of the Council of Five – Royal blue and pale green

Zik'Keeshe = Zick Key She: Sharp Dagger – House of Xenis - Promoted to the Council of Five. – Deep green and gold